D0422807

Praise for Henry Porter's novels

'A first-rate thriller . . . Porter sustains an elaborate plot skilfully and portrays memorable, multi-faceted characters. *Brandenburg* . . . exhilaratingly testifies to the thriller genre's ability to transcend its primary role as entertainment.'   SUNDAY TIMES

'Another elegant spy thriller . . . not merely a tale of intrigue and deception, betrayal and retribution, but also an examination of the people who live through these experiences.'   GUARDIAN

'A real page-turner . . . a thriller of high ambition.'   DAILY MAIL

'A powerful, propulsive piece of thriller writing . . . Porter has consolidated his reputation for writing some of the best espionage thrillers around.'   OBSERVER

'*Brandenburg* . . . doesn't pester you with its research, nor offer you indigestible chunks of political history. Instead it provides something to bite on and plenty of space to chew it. Porter enjoys himself enough to carry the reader with him. On the way, he continues to breathe new life into spy fiction.'   INDEPENDENT

'A tour-de-force, which is stunning in its execution and masterful in its attention to detail . . . The future of the spy novel is in safe hands. The man writes like a dream. Challenging, ambitious, thoughtful, authoritative, he's a le Carré for this century.'   GLASGOW HERALD

THE DYING LIGHT

Also by Henry Porter

Remembrance Day
A Spy's Life
Empire State
Brandenburg

INNISFIL PUBLIC LIBRARY
P.O. BOX 7049
INNISFIL, ON   L9S 1A8

THE DYING LIGHT

Henry Porter

First published in Great Britain in 2009 by Orion Books,
an imprint of The Orion Publishing Group Ltd
Orion House, 5 Upper Saint Martin's Lane
London WC2H 9EA

An Hachette UK company

1 3 5 7 9 10 8 6 4 2

Copyright © Henry Porter 2009

The moral right of Henry Porter to be identified as the author
of this work has been asserted in accordance with
the Copyright, Designs and Patents Act of 1988.

All rights reserved. No part of this publication may be
reproduced, stored in a retrieval system, or transmitted
in any form or by any means, electronic, mechanical,
photocopying, recording, or otherwise, without the
prior permission of both the copyright owner and the above
publisher of this book.

All the characters in this book are fictitious, and any resemblance to
actual persons living or dead is purely coincidental.

A CIP catalogue record for this book is
available from the British Library.

ISBN (Hardback) 978 0 7528 7484 5
ISBN (Export Trade Paperback) 978 0 7528 7638 2

Typeset at Spartan Press Ltd,
Lymington, Hants

Printed in Great Britain by Clays Ltd, St Ives plc

The Orion Publishing Group's policy is to use papers that are natural,
renewable and recyclable products and made from wood grown in sustainable
forests. The logging and manufacturing processes are expected to
conform to the environmental regulations of the country of origin.

www.orionbooks.co.uk

In memory of Jack Garfitt, who saved my grandfather, Capt Beauchamp Seymour from certain death on the Western Front in October 1914, and for his daughter, Olive Garfitt.

'Two things fill the mind with ever new and increasing awe and admiration, the oftener and more steadily we reflect on them – the starry heavens above and the moral laws within.'

Immanuel Kant

'Common sense tells us that our existence is but a brief crack of light between two eternities of darkness.'

Vladimir Nabokov

'A regime always ultimately seeks to restrict freedom, no matter what reasons it gives for doing so. The total state wants to guide society and educate its citizens. New rules and regulations are constantly being imposed on everyday life . . . The politics of prohibition has long since invaded areas in which the potential damage is either a private matter or at most a matter of opinion.'

Wolfgang Sofksy, Privacy, A Manifesto, *2008*

1

A Death Explained

First was the fall, then came the death, and the death erased all memory of the fall, which was in any case handled in a very British way. The story of how David Eyam was cast from the highest circles of government was no more than a footnote at the inquest, which followed hearings into a teenage road fatality and the electrocution of a tractor driver whose grab snagged overhead power lines.

Yet if there had been a programme that March morning for High Castle's newly refurbished coroner's court, David Eyam's name would have been at the top, as much due to his former positions as acting head of the Joint Intelligence Committee and a succession of unspecified roles in the prime minister's inner circle, as to the tourist's film from Cartagena in Colombia, which contained the record of his very last moments on earth.

The recording was played on three television screens and the sounds of the Colombian evening filled the provincial calm of the court with the heat and exuberance and doom of Central America. The camera jerked from a bell tower, around which white doves circled, to a line of balconies bedecked with flowers, typical of Cartagena's colonial district, then to a street vendor carrying baskets of fruit from a yoke that seemed to be made from part of a bicycle frame. It moved with such speed that the people sitting nearest the screens recoiled as though this would steady the shot for them. Kate Lockhart, seated in the second row, remained still, her eyes watching the clock on the top right-hand corner of the screen – the last minutes and seconds of her friend's life being counted off.

The camera came to rest briefly on the name 'Bolivar Crêperie', written across the length of a red awning under which there was some kind of juice bar with perspex cylinders of fruit and a cashier's desk. Then it swerved to two women and a man – all in shorts – sitting at one of several tables in front of the restaurant. Here, after a wobble, it settled. The party of three produced long-suffering smiles; sunglasses were raised and tall glasses of beer hoisted to the lens. The image froze and the coroner leaned forward and nodded to the clerk.

'This is the important part,' said the coroner's clerk, pointing at the screen in the centre of the court with a remote control. 'Pay attention to the top left-hand corner, where you will see the deceased in a navy-blue shirt and cream jacket, and then to what happens in the background on the far side of the street – over here.' He tapped the screen with the remote.

But Kate could see David Eyam nowhere. She searched the screen frantically again. The pale jacket at the top – no, that wasn't Eyam. Not that jacket, not that lank hair, not that beard, not that emaciated angularity. The man was far too thin. Christ! They'd made a mistake. The fools had got the wrong man. Eyam must be alive. Ever since she'd received the email from the firm of lawyers handling his estate a couple of weeks back, she had felt a kind of incredulity at the idea of Eyam's death. The extinction of one of the foremost intellects of his generation by a blast in some seedy quarter of a tropical port, without the world knowing for an entire month, as if Eyam was some useless hippy or boat bum, was unfeasible . . . unsustainable . . . incredible.

The film was started again: the new shot was in a wider frame. The camera had evidently been placed on a tripod because a second man appeared in front of the lens and adjusted something, during which process his face loomed in grotesque close-up, then sat down with the other three and swivelled his cap so the peak was at the front. Kate's eyes darted to the top of the screen. The man in the pale jacket had not moved. No, that wasn't Eyam: far too untidy. But then he turned to talk to a dark, thickset indvidual with wraparound shades and a black polo shirt on his right, and his face became animated. At a pinch it could be him. The parting was the same, although the hair was a lot longer than she had ever seen it, and the cast of his eyes, his brow and the shape of the nose all did a fair impression of Eyam. Then he handed a book to his neighbour with the sunglasses and he seemed to start talking about it: the court could hear nothing of what was said. The mannerisms of her friend in full flow were unmistakable. He sat back in the chair, caught hold of his right elbow and seemed to draw down the points he was making by opening and bunching his pianist's fingers. When the other man, who was now examining the back cover of the book with his sunglasses propped on his forehead, replied she saw his head go back with his mouth slightly open in anticipation. Even at that distance she could see the eagerness and fun in his expression. This was David Eyam. It couldn't be anyone else.

The cameraman had now taken the role of reporter and, using a small microphone held under his chin, addressed the lens – in what the clerk explained was Swedish. But the noise of the street drowned what he was saying and once or twice he looked round with dismay as a motorbike or truck passed.

The clerk cleared his throat and pointed to Eyam. 'The deceased is talking to a Detective Luis Bautista,' he said glancing at a pad. 'He is an officer with the Cartagena Police. He was meeting his girlfriend at the cafe and was off duty at the time.'

'We shall be hearing from him later,' said the coroner, looking round the courtroom over his glasses with his eyebrows rising and falling independently of any expression. 'Detective Bautista is with the local anti-terrorist force and is coincidentally a specialist in the sort of attack we are about to witness.' His eyes went to the clerk. 'Mr Swift, you may proceed.'

Kate's mind protested. No, she would not sit calmly like the others, now peering at the film with an indecent anticipation, to watch Eyam being atomised. She drew the small shoulder bag towards her and looked for the easiest way out of the crowded courtroom, but then found herself drawn to the sight of her friend helplessly sitting there and she remembered the first time she had set eyes on him in a student common room in Oxford twenty years before: the dark, oblique presence, the swarming intelligence in his eyes, his habit of moving a hand through his hair when asked a question and then leaning forward with his fingers momentarily pressed to his mouth and blocking the inquiry with some diversionary enthusiasm that was so interesting you

3

overlooked the failure to disclose. Two decades ago, Eyam was simply luminous – the smile of reason almost never left his face. She saw him now through the eyes of the people in court: a tourist, good-looking in a dishevelled way, yes, but also a man who seemed washed up and might easily be suffering from some form of mid-life crisis, or addiction.

The dozen or so reporters leaned forward with fascination. 'Any moment now,' said the clerk, 'you will see the white Honda van approach from the right. This vehicle was carrying the device. It parks in the alley, which is bordered by the party headquarters –' he consulted his pad – 'of the People's Party for Unity, which was the target of the attack.'

The van appeared from the right but was held up first by a group of youths crossing the street, then by two men pushing a cart loaded down with bags of nuts and fruit and some kind of cooker. An arm appeared out of the driver's side and waved languidly; a glint of light on the windscreen meant no face was visible as it turned. The van entered the alley and parked but the driver found he couldn't open the door far enough to get out and had to reverse out then park again. Presently a stocky man wearing sunglasses and a cap appeared from the shadows. He paused in a splash of evening sunlight, rubbed his forearms, glanced down the street then sauntered off without the least hurry.

On the near side of the street, the policeman had shifted his chair round to face Eyam, who was gesturing towards the book and nodding. She saw now that he meant the book as a gift. The detective seemed overwhelmed and rose and shook his hand then returned to his seat and began to thumb through what she could see was a slim paperback. Nothing happened for a few seconds, then Eyam slipped a hand inside his jacket, removed a phone and made a call seemingly without dialling. At that moment a wedding party came into view on the other side of the street: the newlyweds – a beautiful mulatto couple – were followed by some children and about twenty guests. A band of five musicians brought up the rear of the procession. They soon moved out of shot. She looked back to Eyam, who had finished his call and was returning the phone to his jacket. He had spoken for no more than thirty seconds. With a start she remembered the call she'd received from him out of the blue one Saturday in January, the first contact since they had fallen out and drifted irrevocably apart. It was at the weekend, and she'd gone to stay with old man Calvert in Connecticut. She returned the call to the unfamiliar number but had got no answer. After trying a dozen or so times over the next week she gave up, assuming he would eventually respond. His message was short – he said he felt like speaking to her – and it was still there. She was sure of that because she was in the habit of methodically erasing all those to do with her work as she dealt with them. But she'd kept this one, out of sentiment and guilt and a hope that the chill between them had ended; also because she meant to copy this new number to her list of contacts.

She watched the film, aware of her short, shallow breaths. The detective's attention was drawn to someone out of shot, and he began to wave. From the right of the screen came a woman dressed in a dark red flared skirt and a white shirt that was knotted at the waist like a fifties pin-up. The detective was saying something about her to Eyam. She paused before reaching the tables, put her index finger to her chin, then raised her hand theatrically and clicked her fingers to suggest she had just remembered something. With a swirl of skirts, she almost pirouetted and walked across the road where she pretended to window shop, bending over and then stretching upwards to examine something at the top of the display, and showing off her figure to maximum effect. She moved out of shot. The detective slapped his thighs with mock exasperation and threw himself back in his chair as though to say he could play it cool too. Eyam nodded sympathetically, then drained his drink and got up.

He took a couple of paces, said something over his shoulder – probably his last words – paused at the kerb for a truck carrying a gang of workers to pass, then crossed over and entered the alley, squeezing past the white van into the dark of the tunnel.

The clerk pressed a button on the remote and the picture froze again, causing kate's eyes to settle on the clerk's head and neck, which rose from his shoulders like a cork in a bottle. 'At this moment,' said the clerk, turning with sudden movement to the court, 'the detective heard the first detonator and realised what was going to happen, which explains his quick reaction. The delay between the first and second detonators, usual in this kind of bomb, was probably intended, but it may have been simply an indication of the amateurishness of the bomb maker.'

'However,' said the coroner, 'the Colombian authorities believe that the delay was designed to allow maximum dispersal of the gas before detonation.' The clerk nodded agreement.

The film was started again. The field of the shot seemed to have changed, as though the camera had been loosened on its stand and the lens had drifted upwards a few degrees. There was an odd moment of stillness when nothing much happened. In the foreground the tourists stared about them without speaking. No vehicles passed. Then the detective sprang out of his chair and sprinted across the street waving frantically for the girl to get down. His shouts were picked up by the camera's microphone. The girl stepped back from the shop window with an appalled and strangely embarrassed expression and began to walk towards him, her arms held outwards interrogatively. The detective reached her, hooked his arm around her waist, lifting her off the ground in one clean movement, then ran three or four paces until they were out of shot. At this moment the cameraman bobbed up to see what was going on and blocked most of the view. A beat later he was surrounded by a halo of flame that expanded fifty yards away from him. Then a shock wave propelled his body to the left and rippled outwards. Even though the clerk had aimed the remote to turn down the volume, the roar that followed filled the courtroom. Astonishingly, the camera remained upright, possibly because its owner had shielded it from the main blast, and the film ran on for a few seconds until the camera was toppled by something falling from above. By this time there was very little to be seen except a ball of fire billowing outwards to touch everything in shot. The street vendors vanished. The people, the buildings, the parked cars, the sunlight and shadows – all were obliterated by the sudden cosmic flare of destruction.

The screens around the court went blank. One or two people murmured their shock but for the most part they were silent. Kate found herself staring vacantly at the courtroom's awful new royal-blue carpeting. There had been no time for Eyam to pass through that tunnel. He would have been killed instantly. It was as if she had just watched his death in real time and had been unable to shout a warning to him. She looked up through the windows. Outside in the March morning some scaffolding was being erected. A man warmed his hand round a cup that steamed in the wind. Eyam had gone. People were oblivious. Life went on.

The coroner glanced down at the lawyer appointed by David Eyam's stepmother. 'Would it suit you, Mr Richards, if we rose now and resumed at – say – two o'clock?'

'By all means, sir,' said the man moving to his feet with his fingers tucked into the back of his waistband. 'May I ask if you think it likely that the remains will be released for burial? My client would like to set the funeral arrangements in train as soon as possible. A provisional date of next Tuesday – the twelfth – has been suggested. There is much to organise.'

'Yes, I think that can be taken as read. Please inform Lady Eyam that she may go ahead.' He paused. 'We will leave evidence of identification and the interview with Detective Bautista until this afternoon.' He turned to reporters who were occupying the benches that would have been used by the jury had the coroner exercised his option to call one. 'A copy of this film will be released after I deliver a verdict, which I expect to be at the end of the afternoon.' With this he rose and left through a door behind the chair.

Outside the court, Kate switched on her phone and worked her way back through the messages from colleagues all expressing disbelief at her sudden departure from the head office of Calvert-Mayne in Manhattan. There was a score of callers wondering why she had left one of the most important jobs in the law firm for an unspecified role in the backwater of the London office. At length she came to Eyam's call on the Saturday of his death. 'Hello there, Sister – it's me. Eyam,' he started. He sounded relaxed. 'I felt like having a chat, but it seems you're busy and I now realise it's not ideal this end either, because I'm sitting outside in a street bar and a bloody wedding party has just appeared so you wouldn't be able to hear much anyway. But, look, I miss you and I'd really love to see you when I get back. Perhaps we should meet in New York. We *will* see each other.' He paused. 'You are in my thoughts, as always, and there's much I want to discuss with you, but now I'll just have to make do with the charming policeman whom I am sitting here with. Speak to you soon – all my love.'

She held the phone to her ear for a few seconds, thinking that if she had answered the call she might have delayed him leaving his table in the bar. The tourists and the policeman escaped with their lives; only the people in the confined space of the alley were killed. She snapped the phone shut, lit a cigarette – one of a ration of five – and then opened it again to search the phone's memory for the time of the call. Five forty-five in the afternoon. She could probably work out exactly what she was doing at that precise moment, but what was the point? Eyam was dead. She just had to get used to the idea.

Part of her wanted to return to the Bailey Hotel rather than go back into the inquest, but then it occurred to her that Eyam needed a friendly face at his inquest. There was no family to speak of. His disabled brother had died while they were at Oxford, his mother succumbed to cancer soon afterwards and she had read that Eyam's father, Sir Colin, a holder of numerous engineering patents, a wily financier and discreet philan-thropist, had died the previous year. So it was as an act of friendship as well as a witness that at one forty-five p.m. she worked her way along the bench to sit behind a flustered middle-aged woman and wait for the coroner to reappear. She wondered about the other people in the public benches, particularly a tall man with large glasses, stiff, wavy, dark hair and an expression of courteous disengagement. She had stood by him when filling in the register required of those attending the court – a new procedure presented as a survey – and read the name Kilmartin but not his address, which was illegible. From his clothes came the particular smell of a bonfire; the pockets of his coat were stuffed with rolled-up catalogues; and he held the *Financial Times* and a journal to his chest.

While they sat waiting in the benches, the woman in front of her turned round and, with her hand rising to pat the flushed skin at the top of her bosom, introduced herself as Diana Kidd. 'Did you know David?' she asked.

Kate nodded, aware of a blousy old-fashioned scent reaching her nostrils.

'Were you an *old* friend?'

'I suppose you could say that. We met at college.' She could see that the woman was trying to work her out: the traces of the East in her appearance – the looks of her father, Sonny Koh – the straight-backed Englishness of her mother, and the American accent which overlaid the voice of a public schoolgirl.

'I began to know David really quite well, considering,' continued the woman.

'Considering what?' said Kate.

The woman ignored the question. 'He threw himself into the local arts scene here. He had one of the most formidable minds I've ever had the privilege to encounter, but you know he was never pushy or domineering.' With each statement her eyes darted about the court. 'He never made people feel ill at ease with that great mind of his. And impeccable manners, of course. Unimpeachable! Kept himself to himself though: an invisible barrier around him, if you know what I mean.'

Kate did, though she wouldn't have put it like that. Eyam was capable of warmth and loyalty but he had no interest in explaining himself and was impatient when others expected him to. The woman asked if she was family, then if she had visited David since he had moved to High Castle. Kate shook her head to both questions and murmured that she hadn't seen him for some time. She did not mention the email from Russell, Spring & Co, a firm of local solicitors, which had been forwarded to her by her old assistant in New York and was how she had learned of his death nearly six weeks after it had occurred.

Once Diana Kidd had decided that Kate had not been a lover and possessed no greater claim on the memory of David Eyam than she did, her interest seemed to wane. However, she told Kate a bit more about Eyam's circumstances. He had bought and restored a black and white A-frame cottage on the edge of the woods overlooking the Dove Valley; he did not seem to have a job; he attended recitals and concerts, and joined the local film society and a reading group, the novelty of which was that books were discussed on rambles through the Marches of Wales.

What utter bloody hell, thought Kate, and not for the first time wondered what had driven Eyam to this provincial limbo on the English-Welsh border. The Eyam she knew was compelled by the centre of things; it was unthinkable that he'd opt for life in the back of beyond nourished only by cultural chats with Diana Kidd.

'Why was he in Colombia?' Kate asked. 'Did he tell you he was going?'

Mrs Kidd shook her head as though this was an extremely stupid question. 'No, he just vanished two or three weeks before Christmas. No one knew where he had gone or for how long. The next thing we heard was about this bomb, but that took several weeks to filter through because no one suspected that he was involved. I mean, how could they?' She hissed this last observation as the coroner entered and the clerk asked them to rise.

A filmed interview of Detective Bautista by a British consular official in Cartagena was shown. Bautista's English was reasonably good but every so often he struggled for a word and looked off-camera to ask for translation. He appeared in front of a white backcloth wearing a neck brace, with a bandage on his forearm and two small strips of plaster above his left eye. Kate put his age at about forty. He had Indian ancestry – an aquiline nose, narrowed eyes and full lips. He talked rapidly, often repeating a question on the in-breath then answering as he breathed out.

The diplomat timed and dated the interview – eleven a.m. Friday February 18th. An oath was taken then Bautista told the camera that he shouldn't have been at that restaurant when the bomb went off. In fact he had arranged to meet his girl, Mira, the night before at the Bolivar Crêperie, but there had been an incident down in the port – a murder. He was unable to keep the date and then he'd forgotten to phone her. She was mad with him. He blew out his cheeks and made a chopping motion with his right hand into his palm to underscore that this was a woman you would not want to anger too often.

So that was how he came to be sitting drinking bourbon outside the restaurant the following day. And of course she had been late just to make her point and he'd fallen into conversation with the man he now knew to be David Eyam and they talked about the book he was reading – *The Story of A Shipwrecked Sailor* by Gabriel García Márquez. It was incredible how much this Englishman knew about the book, about this shameful period in the history of Colombia and how the author had exposed the corruption of the dictator General Pinilla. He seemed to have so much in his head about everything, this Englishman, and the gift of the book now meant a great deal to him. It was the last act of a true gentleman and he didn't mind saying that with the book some kind of good luck had passed from Eyam to him, which resulted in his and Mira's survival. He felt in his pocket, pulled out the book, looked at the cover and held it to the camera.

'What was it that made you run to save your girlfriend, detective?'

'It is the sound of detonator,' he replied, now holding an unlit cigarette. 'You know at the back of my mind I thought there was something wrong about that vehicle. It was there in my head all the time but I was not thinking. Why would anyone park there and block the alley? That was the question in my mind. And then I heard the detonator and I knew what was going to happen. I know this sound well since I study at the Explosives Unit and Bomb Data Center.'

'The Explosive Unit of the FBI – in the United States?' said the official.

'Of the FBI, yes, that is correct, señor. And the Hazards Devices School at Huntsville, Alabama. I study in that place also.'

'You attended training at these institutions last year?'

'That is correct: the programme was six months.' He paused. 'And so, señor, that is why I know the noise of a detonator. It lives in my mind and when I hear it on the street I know that another detonator will follow.'

'Could you explain?'

Bautista put his hands together and began to talk fluently, as though being tested by an examination board. 'This type of bomb need two detonations. The first detonation this blows the valves on the containers of liquefied gas and so the gas is spread. When it has mixed with the air the second explosion comes in a tiny little core of PETN.' He held up a finger and thumb pinched together.

'That is explosive material?'

'Yes, that is pentaerythritol tetranitrate,' he said with a flourish. 'When the second explosion takes place the large volume of oxygenated gas is detonated. In the regular bomb, the energy comes from the tightly packed core and drive outwards like so.' He clasped his hands in a ball then threw them apart. 'But in this devil, señor, in this devil the detonation ignites clouds of gas and there occurs an explosion with a force that becomes greater and greater moving outwards and outwards gaining power all this time.' His hands mimed a billowing motion, then he picked up a glass of water and drank. 'It was this type of bomb used to attack the party headquarters.'

'The regional headquarters backs onto the alley where the van was parked? That was the target?'

'Correct.'

'From your expertise would you say that Mr Eyam had any chance of escaping the explosion?'

He pouted regretfully and shook his head. 'The cloud of gas was too large. We believe there were many containers in that vehicle and there was much gas in the . . .'

'Released into the confined conditions of the alley?'

'Yes.'

The British official spoke his last question.

'From your knowledge of the investigation and your colleagues' work, is there any suspicion that the bomber was not primarily interested in the headquarters?'

The detective seemed surprised. 'Are you saying this bomb was to kill Señor Eyam?'

'No,' said the voice. 'I am asking whether there are any foreign groups who may have perpetrated this crime. And if you are sure that the headquarters was the target.'

'We know who made the attack, señor. This was the activities of a terrorist group here in Colombia.'

'The *actions* of a terrorist group: can you be more specific?'

'We know who these people are. They want to destroy the party headquarters. We know this, señor. We investigate these people.'

The interview ended. Detective Bautista nodded to the camera and struggled up from his chair. Then the screen went blank.

The coroner leaned forward to Eyam's lawyer. 'Mr Richards, I regret that you will not have the chance to question the witness, as I am afraid that the court's budget did not extend to bringing Detective Bautista to England. Are there any observations that you wish to make for the record?'

'Not at this stage, sir,' replied Richards.

'Then we shall proceed with the evidence concerning identification. Is Sergeant Hallam in court?'

A short man in a grey suit and dark shirt nodded and walked to the stand where, after taking an oath, he turned to the coroner.

'Sergeant Hallam, you were responsible for identifying the remains of Mr Eyam. Is that right?'

'In so far as there were remains, sir.'

'What can you tell the court about their condition?'

'The blast created considerable destruction in the area and there was much difficulty in locating and removing the victims from the scene. This was compounded by the collapse of two buildings after the fire, and the heavy plant that was required to shift the rubble.'

'You're saying the bodies were recovered after a lengthy time? How many were there?'

'It is very difficult to know, sir – maybe three.'

'All those killed were in or near that alley? The alley was an inferno. Is that right? There wasn't much left to go on?'

'Yes, sir, a lot was lost in the fire and the operation to clear the area. Some remains were located but the Colombian authorities insisted that DNA tests were carried out locally so as to make certain the right set of remains was sent to Britain.'

'Please tell the court what procedures were followed.'

'Hair samples were collected from Mr Eyam's home in Dove Valley and sent with his dental records to Colombia, where a match was made with some of the remains found in the alley. We received confirmation of this on February fifteenth.'

'Let me be clear on this. Was the readout of Mr Eyam's genetic profile sent to Colombia, or were the samples?'

'Both, sir.'

'And then Colombian authorities did their own test on the remains and found a match?'

The police officer nodded. 'They have a fully operational lab for this kind of forensic work, sir. It is perhaps a . . . er . . . a more sophisticated operation than you would expect in that country.'

The coroner nodded and looked at his papers. 'Thank you. That will be all, sergeant.'

After asking Lady Eyam's lawyer if he had any questions and receiving a shake of the head, the coroner turned to the court. 'We have heard how David Lucas Eyam, formerly a government official who worked in Downing Street, left the United Kingdom for an extended holiday in December last year. Given Mr Eyam's exceptional qualities and outstanding service to this country and to the Prime Minister, it is only right for me to extend the court's sympathy to his family and friends and many colleagues in government at the manner of his untimely death.' Mr Richards bowed his head to accept the words on behalf of his client. 'In the matter of David Lucas Eyam's death,' he said more loudly and formally, 'I find that while holidaying in Central America he visited the Colombian port of Cartagena. On January twelfth this year at approximately five forty-five p.m. he was in the Colonial District of the city when an explosion took place that killed him outright. Accordingly, I record a verdict that Mr Eyam was killed unlawfully by persons unknown.'

The incontrovertible fact of Eyam's death was established. As Kate rose and worked her way along the bench, her resignation was replaced by anger at the waste of the last two years. God knows how things would have been if they had talked on that Saturday – if they had been talking through the two years of his exile in High Castle.

She came to the entrance, where there was a crush of reporters crowding round the clerk who was handing out DVDs of the film of the explosion. She turned to find the tall man – Kilmartin – looking down at her. When the way cleared he gestured for her to go ahead of him and gave a regretful, thin-lipped smile that seemed to solicit something at the same time as suggesting postponement. She recognised that look: the steadiness of the gaze and the tiny pulse of energy in the eyes – the freemason's handshake of the intelligence services – and she wondered about Mr Kilmartin with his smell of bonfires, his academic journals and well-thumbed pamphlets, which she now saw were seed catalogues. What was he doing there? Checking that nothing inconvenient was being alleged in open court? Making sure the government was not being accused of anything low or underhand? The former head of the Joint Intelligence Committee – even if only for a reluctant and brief period – being blown up in a terrorist attack was after all something that must still concern the Secret Intelligence Service. She nodded to him and left the court, dodging the television cameras outside.

2

The Centre of Things

Just three people were working in the Downing Street communications centre when the prime minister, John Temple, slipped in and sat down to watch a TV permanently tuned to a news channel. The lights had been turned off at that end of the room as part of the energy-saving fervour that periodically swept the heart of government and Temple remained in the shadows. He was in evening dress, having recently left a private dinner at the embassy for the American secretary of state, but even after a long day he looked his usual dapper and contained self. One of the garden girls – the secretaries that run the prime minister's office – had pursued him into the communications department with a folder and now hovered about ten feet away wondering if she should disturb him. It was her presence that attracted Philip Cannon, the director of communications, who stirred from his screen, stood up and stretched, then moved slowly towards the prime minister and gave a cough by way of announcement.

Temple looked up. 'Ah, Sarah, what have I forgotten to do?' That was the prime minister all over – blaming himself rather than the people who worked for him. He turned on a desk light and took the folder with a smile that involved squeezing his eyes shut and nodding. She pointed to a passage in the foreign secretary's statement on the Middle East. Temple read it with the warmth still lingering in his expression then handed it to her. She beamed back at him and almost bobbed a curtsy. Temple's manners, his inexhaustible consideration whatever the pressures of office, were such a contrast to his recent predecessors: one addicted to a dangerous informality where no one was sure what decisions had been taken until they read it in the next day's papers;

another given to sulks and rages and epic rudeness, in one famous instance turfing a young woman from her chair so he could use her screen.

Cannon nodded to her as she left and moved to the prime minister's side. 'Is there anything that particularly interests you?' he asked, turning up the volume of the TV a little.

The prime minister shook his head. 'Just thought I'd look in. How's it going, Philip?' Cannon didn't answer because Temple's attention had moved to the bulletin and a reporter who addressed the camera while trying to control her hair in the wind. 'A coroner's court in the picturesque market town of High Castle on the English-Welsh border was this morning shown dramatic footage of the moment a former senior civil servant was killed in an explosion in Cartagena, Colombia.

'David Eyam, once acting head of the Joint Intelligence Committee and confidante of the prime minister, was holidaying in the Colombian port where there has been a long-running campaign by the drug cartels against union power and the political establishment. Mr Eyam, who was forty-three years of age and single, was killed instantly by the blast. After it was discovered that Mr Eyam was a likely victim, the prime minister's spokesman issued a statement saying that all those who worked with Mr Eyam were shocked and saddened by his death. Although he left Downing Street two years ago, he was still remembered fondly by the prime minister's staff for his acuteness and originality of mind. He had made a great contribution to John Temple's administration, particularly, it is understood, at the prime minister's side during international negotiations. The coroner, Roy Clarke, paid tribute to Mr Eyam's exceptional qualities and recorded a verdict of unlawful killing by persons unknown.'

They watched in silence as the film of the explosion was run. When it was over Temple sucked air through his teeth and shook his head. 'Can you get that back for me?'

'What? You want the explosion again?' asked Cannon.

'No, just the report, not the explosion.'

Cannon selected instant replay from a menu on the right of the screen. The woman began her report again. Halfway through Temple jerked forward. 'Stop it now!' The frame froze with the woman's hand reaching up again to her hair. 'No, go back a little.' The prime minister peered at the screen. Cannon did likewise.

'What is it?'

'Peter Kilmartin is there on the court steps! What's he doing at the inquest?'

'I've no idea,' said Cannon. 'You want me to have it copied?'

'No, that's fine,' he replied and leaned over to write on a pad that was on the desk. 'What about the funeral?' He tore the page out and folded it in four.

'It's next week. The home secretary will represent you. He knew Eyam well and I gather he may be asked to give an address – a stepmother is organising things.'

'We should be there.' One of the famous prime ministerial pauses ensued. His index finger rubbed the unusually deep philtrum, the indentation above his lip. 'Seen the early editions?' he said eventually. 'Any adverse coverage on the web?'

'They're taking it at face value. There's no hint of anything sinister, apart from the barbarous act. The film is sensational – it speaks for itself.'

'Good . . . yes . . . that's good . . . we would not want it said that . . .'

'That there was something untoward?' offered Cannon. 'No. There's nothing like that.'

'Yes, well, we're not Russia – the British government doesn't behave like that. We don't have people dispatched.'

'No. Quite. Actually the papers are full of news about some toxic red algae that has appeared in the reservoirs. That looks the most worrying of all the stories.'

'Still, I'm interested in what he was doing in Cartagena.'

'A holiday it seems.'

'In Colombia? It doesn't seem very likely. Eyam was a man for the opera houses of Europe, the great libraries and museums of the world. He failed us, but he did not lose his culture. I mean . . . Colombia?'

'Yet he had a lot of obscure passions,' said Cannon.

'The point, Philip, is that it wasn't *known* he was in Colombia and, given the difficulties surrounding his departure from government, it should have been known. A failure in the system perhaps, or were his plans intentionally obscured? Colombia is after all not a place associated with legitimate activity, is it? And David Eyam was, as I understand it, still regarded as a problem.'

Cannon kept quiet: he had no interest in things that were unlikely to reach the headlines. David Eyam was old news and had long ceased to be of any concern to him. His ejection from government had occurred without publicity and barely any fuss at Number Ten and in the necessary focus of Cannon's professional life the film from Colombia was little more than a brief diversion from the algae problem. The next day a tide of fresh events would need to be finessed, burnished or buried to keep John Temple's government afloat and credible as it moved towards an election. He looked down at his boss – the Everyman of British politics and his best asset in this endeavour – and thought that never was anyone more misconstrued by the public. Seemingly average in all things, formal and infuriatingly prosaic, Temple was one of the most enigmatic personalities that Cannon had ever encountered, a character opaque and inscrutable even, he suspected, unto itself.

Temple rose. 'Yes, I think we will find out what Kilmartin was doing down in High Castle.'

He left the communications centre holding the piece of paper and headed towards his room, where in the evenings he would sit with a whisky, mulling over the day in the worn leather armchair that had moved with him from one ministry to the next as he climbed, un-noticed but inexorably, to the top job. Now he sat at the desk, thought for a few moments while staring at the uncurtained window, then picked up the phone.

3

Night Thoughts

In her dream she was sitting at an outside table in the Bolivar Crêperie. They had made love that afternoon in a hotel overlooking the ocean, with the sound of sea pounding the cliffs below. But then they'd fallen out – she didn't know why – and she was sitting away from Eyam at another table while he spoke on the phone. The little white van stopped in front of the cafe and the bomber got out and waved to her and gestured to Eyam with a grin. She recognised the bomber and she knew what was going to happen. She leapt up from the table and started shouting at Eyam, but he didn't hear. He just kept on talking, talking, talking.

She woke babbling, struggled to find the light switch and threw the tangle of bedclothes back. Her T-shirt was drenched in sweat and her hair was damp and stuck to her neck. She leaned over and rang down to reception to find Karl, the night manager, on the other end. 'The thermostat in my room's still broken,' she said. 'It's like a sauna in here. I thought it was going to be repaired.'

Karl suggested opening windows.

'Right,' she said, catching sight of her naked torso in the mirror and thinking that she should take exercise, maybe return to the swimming regime she'd dropped the year before. 'So when's it going to be fixed?'

'Tomorrow.'

'Can you make sure that happens? Otherwise I'm going to have to move – room or hotel.'

'Of course,' he said. 'Oh, Miss Lockhart,' he said as she was about to hang up. 'You haven't complied with the identity requirements. The form is still here waiting for you.'

'It's three in the morning! I showed my passport when I checked in and you have my credit card details – what the hell else do you need? Hair samples?'

'Tomorrow will be fine. But as a non-UK resident, you must do it. The hotel has a responsibility to file this form with the police. If we don't we get fined.'

'Fix the thermostat and I'll see about your form.'

She replaced the phone and took a shower, letting the water massage the back of her neck while she thought of the dream and then of Eyam leaving the message for her. It was so odd: the silence had lasted over two years, then on the point of death he phones out of the blue and starts chatting aimlessly as though nothing had passed between them – as though they had been in easy and regular touch, as though they were still the intimate friends of university. She stepped out of the shower and dried, again examining herself with detachment in the mirror. She was now fully awake. She turned on the TV and raced through the channels until she reached the BBC's international service and the repeat of a programme analysing the riots that had flared in British cities the year before. She turned the volume down and switched on her phone. Why hadn't she picked up? It was inconceivable because she had been in the office that Saturday, working on the last details of a deal that went through on the following Monday, and they were waiting to hear news of the other side's response. There was no way her phone would have been switched off then. And if she'd been speaking to someone else she would have received the message immediately on hanging up. She tried to remember where she'd listened to the message and what she had been looking at when she heard Eyam's voice, but nothing came to her.

She flung open the windows to a damp and windless night; tiny particles of moisture glinted in the light. Her suite overlooked a wooded valley and she could just hear the murmur of the river below. She went back through the messages and when she reached Eyam's voice placed the phone on the windowsill and pressed the loudspeaker button. 'Hello there, Sister – it's me. Eyam,' he started. 'I felt like having a chat but it seems you're busy.' Eyam was there with her in the room, present and alive. When it was over, she reached for a cigarette, lit up and listened to the message again, straining to hear every sound and inflection in the message. This she did three or four times, staring out into the dark. Then, shaking her head, she swore to the night and viciously stubbed the cigarette out on the stone window ledge. She stepped back into the room, pierced by a shaft of grief, and sank onto the bed. Eyam was dead and it was doing her no good to keep listening to him.

After a few minutes she reached for her small laptop, opened it and logged onto Calvert-Mayne's web mail, using a succession of security passwords, which she kept in her wallet. She began to read the dozen or so emails between them, which she had stored on the site. Up until the final exchange, the emails were rushed but always affectionate. The break came after an exchange that followed dinner in a restaurant on the Upper East Side. Eyam was passing through New York on the way back to London from Washington. The fatigue showed in his eyes and his conversation was harsher than she had ever known it. She remembered returning to their table and finding him lost in thought. When she spoke he looked up, disorientated and in that moment she knew she could have loved him – no, that she did love him in the most unexpressed way possible. She wanted to take his head in her hands and hold his face to hers. He saw what she was thinking and they talked of becoming lovers that night, in his case with scathing and rather hurtful objectivity. She reminded him that once, for a brief period when they were undoubtedly too young, they had been lovers.

'We didn't just go to bed, we made love for an entire week,' she'd said. But he ignored it and then to protect herself she'd matched his flippancy and his cruelty, and very soon it was impossible to return to the point before love and sex were so coolly dismissed. Eyam had a way of moving a conversation along, recasting history, skirting any subject he wished to avoid, and when you challenged him he would turn his mild Socratic genius on you and elicit so many unwilling affirmatives that you ended up agreeing with him.

And on that night he made his usual diversions, but then started criticising her life in New York, which he claimed was 'unmoored' and lacked moral principle. Sitting back with his wine, he told her that although she was successful, rich and sought after she had put down no roots in New York. She was like a beech tree – the tree with the shallowest root system. He called her his big, beautiful beech. She didn't laugh at the pun.

Then a few days later she fired off an email to him late at night.

From: Kate Lockhart <KateLockhart@Calvert-Mayne.com>
To: David Eyam <DEyam@no10.gsi.gov.uk>
You've got a bloody nerve criticising my life here when your career is hardly the sum of all you hoped for. Yes, you go to DC with the prime minister and you have dinner with the president in the White House but, Jesus, Eyam, you seem so damned unhappy and strung out.

I'm doing what I do best and I am doing it very well. You don't have the right to judge the decisions I've made, just as I have no right to question yours – and I never have.

You deny yourself nothing except the truth about yourself; and while that may make it easier to see the faults in others it doesn't necessarily make what you say true or welcome. By the way, you need a holiday.

And you might have thanked me for dinner.

Kate X

To: Kate Lockhart <KateLockhart@Calvert-Mayne.com>
From: David Eyam <DEyam@no10.gsi.gov.uk>
As ever, lovely to hear from you, Sister, though I thought your email was rather sharp. I don't want us to fall out over this but I do not resile from the view that you are made for better things.

When I said you were in danger of becoming a prisoner of your gift I simply meant that your job at Calverts, impressive though it is in many ways, is beneath your actual talent; also your humanity. This could have been expressed with more sensitivity and I apologise for being crass. Your remark that I denied myself everything but the truth was unscrupulous because you attacked me for what you suspect to be your own weakness. For the record, neither of us is that stupid. Thanks for dinner.

Eyam X

It was typical of him to write an apology that had the last word. The email remained in her inbox without being answered and was quickly buried as scores of new emails piled on top. But it stayed in her mind and she now recalled that she did write a long defence of her life at Calverts telling Eyam what she actually did; that for years after the crash her work was saving jobs and technology as huge sovereign funds took over struggling American companies, sacked thousands to make the numbers work and exploited or suppressed the innovations of those smaller companies. She said it was just dumb and narrow-minded of him not to see that this was important legal work, which was as much concerned with injustice as money.

She never sent it. Then somehow it became too late to reply and a silence settled on their friendship that would turn out to be terminal, although at the back of her mind she'd always thought they'd make it up, and when he called that Saturday she had been really pleased, actually relieved.

From the pocket in her purse she took out a slender wallet, which she flipped open to the two photographs. On the left was her husband Charlie Lockhart, dead from cancer, on the right her father, Sonny Koh, dead from suicide. She didn't look at them often but she always kept the dead men in her life with her. They were always there. The little red diptych would now have to become a triptych of remembrance, as long as she could lay her hands on that picture of her and Eyam at Oxford, the only photograph she possessed of him.

She stood the open frame on the bedside table and slid down into the bed to watch the footage of the riots that had been violently put down the year before. Suddenly it occurred to her that she was guilty of ignoring Eyam's less attractive side – in particular his love of exercise of power. For some time before that dinner in New York she'd noticed him becoming colder, more removed and, she had to admit, objectionably pleased with his own opinions. Doubt made almost every personality acceptable to Kate. But as he rose higher and higher, Eyam had lost the ability to express the slightest worry about himself or his decisions. She had to confess that he had become a little boring. 'You were a little bit of a prig,' she said to the room.

Eventually she slept. The following day she stayed in bed late watching the rooks plummet into the trees on the other side of the rocky spur, on which High Castle – complete with Norman fortress, square and church – stands like an Italian hill town. It was a fine and private place to do her grieving for David Eyam.

4

The Prime Minister's Spy

Peter Kilmartin was certainly surprised. He arrived at Number Ten at nine forty-five p.m. on Monday evening, having been summoned five hours before, and was shown into the Cabinet Room by a brisk young woman who introduced herself as Jean. Temple was sitting at the prime minister's place on the curved table in front of the fireplace, reading with his hand clutching his forehead. The cabinet secretary, Gus Herbert, stood back holding a red leather folder to his chest, while his free hand toyed with a signet ring. Temple looked up and removed the glasses that were so rarely seen in public. 'Ah, Peter, good of you to come so quickly. I'll be with you in a second.'

Kilmartin and Herbert exchanged nods then both looked out through the two uncurtained windows at the end of the room. The dense drizzle of the last few days seemed to hang in the glare of the security lights. Some way off in the building there was a muffled whine of drilling, which Jean had explained to Kilmartin was caused by cabling work that could only been done at night.

He looked down at Temple and not for the first time wondered at his extraordinary rise. They'd met a dozen years before when Temple was a junior minister in the foreign office, at a time in his career when he was patronised by officials and had the reputation as a lightweight – a shameless flatterer and seeker of advice. They hit it off because Temple possessed that rare ability in government to listen properly. For his part Kilmartin, who was by no means a natural politician, found that he could influence policy decisions without using his elbows. The combination of his knowledge of foreign affairs and the Secret Intelligence Service and Temple's patience proved very successful for a while and, as each Cabinet reshuffle came along and Temple kept climbing through the ranks, eventually to head two of the great ministries of state, they kept in touch with Christmas cards and the occasional lunch. Temple's manner and his eerie calm never changed and to anyone who listened he would confess his astonishment that he and his worn armchair had travelled so far. Not many did listen. His colleagues still saw him as a quaint and amiable nobody, a bit of an oddball. No threat. But when he was invited to form a government he displayed a rare political savagery, sacking several allies and bringing about an iron discipline in the ranks of his party. He was likened to President Harry Truman. One commentator reminded her readers that the haberdasher from Lamar, Missouri, had dropped two atomic bombs just five months into his presidency. After Temple's narrow win at the polls, a victory fraught with allegations of ballot rigging, recounts and general dismay with the performance of a new electronic voting system, that same writer suggested that the only doubtful part of the phrase 'elected dictatorship' was the word elected. But Temple stammered his apologies and produced a famous display of nervous blinking when the matter was raised in a TV interview, and somehow people forgave him, or at any rate forgot. In the long slump there were other things to worry about.

Temple pushed his chair back with a little cough, handed the file to the cabinet secretary and said, 'Yes, that should do the trick.' Herbert picked up the file and left the room with an opaque Mandarin nod in Kilmartin's direction.

'How good of you to come up from the country, Peter. How are you and the boys coping – Jay and Ralph, isn't it?'

It was a year and half since Helen's death and the boys, though grown up and with jobs, had suffered dreadfully. They were just about over the worst.

'Thanks, they're doing fine, prime minister. I'm amazed you remember their names.'

'One of my very few gifts. And the famous Kilmartin vegetable garden, which I notice now takes precedence over the problems of Central Asia?'

Kilmartin smiled but didn't rise to the bait.

'I hear the new garden is beautiful. You've moved in with your sister, haven't you?'

'That's right – though in fact it is the other way. She came to live with me.'

'Good, good,' he said absently and let out a sigh. 'I expect you've read we've got a real problem with this blessed toxic red algae in the reservoirs. Our scientists have no idea where it came from or how it's spreading. People talk about bio-terrorism, migrating waterfowl, global warming. Nobody knows. It's the sort of thing that can turn an election. Events!' he said with exasperation and the smile lines moved into perfect parentheses. 'But that's not why I asked you to see me.' He coughed and took a step to the fireplace and rested his hand on the mantelpiece. Temple was over six foot tall but managed to appear much shorter to the public. Kilmartin glanced up at the portrait of William Pitt the Younger above him. He'd read somewhere that on Temple's order Pitt had replaced the painting of Robert Walpole, the first man to occupy Number Ten as prime minister and the longest-serving prime minister in British history, because he somehow felt closer to Pitt than any other of his predecessors.

'I heard you were down at High Castle for David Eyam's inquest.'

Kilmartin couldn't have been more surprised. He'd come with a dozen excuses not to go to the Caucasus as special envoy or back to Kazakhstan. 'My word, you've got good sources, prime minister.'

'Well, one hears things. I wondered if you had any special reason for attending.'

'He was a friend and I happened to be in the town – the house I bought is not far from High Castle – so I thought I'd pop in.'

'Tragic business; there's not a day that goes by without my missing him.' Temple paused and rubbed his upper lip. 'He really had such a grasp of the issues – and a most agile mind. That kind of clarity is unique in my experience.' He looked at the portrait above him. 'You know what Pitt's tutor used to say about him? "He seemed never to learn but merely to recollect." That was Eyam. I valued his advice, just as I do yours, Peter.'

'That's very kind of you, prime minister. Is this what you wanted to see me for?'

'As a matter of fact, yes. As you know, I was very fond of David but there were difficulties at the end of his time here.' He paused. 'You know what I'm referring to?'

'I'm afraid not. I was away abroad at the time – Turkey – and then looking after Helen.'

'Well, it doesn't matter: all water under the bridge. But I wonder if you could keep an eye on all this for me.'

'What? I mean how?'

'I'm anxious that neither the violent circumstances of his death nor the facts of his departure from government become a matter of speculation. There will be a great temptation to cause mischief by linking it all to the death of poor Christopher Holmes, who was head of the JIC before David Eyam, as you know. We do not want any *mischief* at this stage.' Mischief was a word the prime minister used to describe everything from anti-social behaviour to terrorism.

'I haven't seen a word to that effect in the newspapers,' said Kilmartin.

'Of course we could have held the Eyam inquest in camera,' continued Temple, 'but I took the view, and the home secretary agreed with me, that it would give rise to speculation.'

'I didn't know you had that kind of discretion in the proceedings of a coroner's court, prime minister, but let me say I think you took the right decision.'

'Did you see Eyam a lot? Were you a close friend?'

'Very little over the past few years, but I liked him.'

'Did you know he was in Colombia?'

Kilmartin shook his head.

'Nor did we, and that bothers me, Peter.'

'Well, he can't trouble anyone now.'

'Of course you're right. But, look, I want you to keep your ear to the ground on this. Let me know if there is going to be any silliness. It would be bad for the country to be distracted by a lot of daft conspiracy theories in the run up to an election. People must feel able to trust government, not just my government but any British government: the procedures, the checks and balances, the good intentions of those who hold power, their fundamental respect for the constitution. People must know that we are trustworthy.'

'Quite. Do you want me to actively pursue this, or simply tell you anything I hear?'

'Yes, tell me, or tell Christine Shoemaker, the deputy director of the Security Service: you know her?' Kilmartin nodded, remembering the blonde northerner with a down-turned mouth, who had all but sidelined the director of MI5, Charles Foster-King, because of her relationships with Temple and the home secretary, Derek Glenny. 'Good. Contact her if I am unavailable; otherwise telephone my private secretary and come in for a chat. Do a bit of digging around. Put your ear to the ground. Find out what's being said. Would that be all right, Peter? Do say if it isn't.'

'Of course, prime minister: I'm happy to help if I can, though I'm pretty sure that there is nothing much to discover.'

'Still, I would be grateful.'

Kilmartin nodded. Unless he was very much mistaken he had just been appointed the prime minister's personal intelligence officer.

The bells were being rung open rather than half-muffled, as is usual for the dead. And when the peal fell suddenly into the cold, bright Tuesday morning the people in High Castle's Market Square glanced towards the church, eyes freshening, as though spring was being announced, or someone had decided that life itself should be celebrated. Kate paused. Above her, a camera in a black hemisphere fixed to the side of a building watched everything in the square yet, like the woman who had followed her on the short walk from the hotel, it almost certainly missed the striking beauty of the moment.

She was certain about this watcher, a slim woman in her mid-thirties wearing a tan trouser suit. She plainly had more training than practice in surveillance. There was no substitute for experience, as she had always been told by McBride, nominally second secretary (economic) at the embassy in Jakarta, but in reality MI6's head of station. That was a lifetime ago, when she was married and living in a flat near the embassy, but Kate hadn't lost the ability to read a street and spot the false moves of a bad actor. And this girl, as McBride would have said, wouldn't cut the mustard in the Scunthorpe Repertory Theatre.

Kate walked on to the stalls at the centre of Market Square. A police helicopter came noiselessly from the south then hovered high over the square sending a rhythmic thud around the walls of the castle. Twice it repositioned itself by falling away down the valley then nosing into the sharp westerly wind blowing across the Marches. Three civilian helicopters followed at a much lower altitude and landed on a piece of open ground beneath the escarpment of red sandstone, where their rotor blades turned and bounced in the wind. Then the official cars began to arrive, two accompanied by unmarked protection vehicles that sat just to the right of the rear bumper of the saloons and stuck to them like pilot fish. The cars swept into the square in a way that made heads turn, then followed Sheep Street to the Bailey Hotel, where their occupants were decanted into a room, which Kate learned had been laid on by Eyam's stepmother for the mourners making the trip from London.

She stopped at a stall selling wraps, shawls and scented candles to get a better look at her pursuer. The woman moved behind a stand of jams and pickles, then retreated to the line of market stalls at the top of the square. Why the hell was she being followed?

Kate picked up a black and mauve scarf.

'It's Nepalese – silk and cashmere,' said the stallholder, placing a rolled cigarette on a battered tobacco tin. 'They call that colour *damson*. A pal of mine imports them from the village in Nepal where they're made. But I got to admit they're dear.'

The scarf went well with the short dark grey herringbone jacket and black trousers she'd chosen for the funeral. She put it on and looked at herself in a smudged mirror that hung from the front of the stall, angling it slightly to see over her shoulder. The watcher had moved behind her and glanced twice in her direction. 'Screw this,' she said softly and turned and eyeballed the woman, who looked away.

'The scarf?' said the stallholder.

'I'll take it,' Kate said with a smile.

'Looks terrific on you: just right for your dark colouring, if you don't mind me saying.'

'I don't,' she said and removed five twenties from her purse.

'What's going on?' he asked, wrapping the money carefully onto a fold of notes. 'The place is crawling with filth.'

'Filth?' she said, smiling. 'The police are here for the funeral.'

'Who's that for then?'

'A friend of mine: he lived near here.'

'I'm sorry.' He paused. 'Old, was he?'

'Early forties.'

'Life is short: art is long. Well known, was he?'

'Not really, but he had many admirers. He was killed while abroad.'

The man slapped his forehead. 'I know, it's the fellow that got blown up – the prime minister's man. He was on TV.'

She smiled a full stop to the exchange and turned away.

'Would you credit that?' he said to her back. 'Look at the way they're treating that woman. I told you they was filth.'

Beyond the stalls on the north side of the square four uniformed police were crowding round a middle-aged woman. One had taken hold of her upper arm. She wore a large black hat that made her seem top heavy. Her voice rose and the words, 'I will not stand here' then, 'I won't be treated . . .' carried on the wind across the square. The woman wrenched her arm down, causing her handbag to fall to the ground and spew its contents. A policeman bent down to help but she brushed his hand away and swept everything back into the bag herself. It was at that moment that her hat fell off and rolled between the policemen's feet. She made an undignified lunge and seized it, stood up and hit the chest of one of the officers with it.

'That's done it now,' said the stallholder with a smirk. 'Assault with a hat. I know that woman. She's got something to do with the Assembly Rooms – arranges the programme and that. You can't park there on market days. There's a sign.'

Kate recognised Diana Kidd from the inquest. Over the weekend she had toyed with the idea of calling the only Diana Kidd listed in the phone book to talk to her about Eyam, which was why she now returned her purse to the black shoulder bag, walked the thirty yards over to where Mrs Kidd was being questioned, and with a smile asked if there was anything she could do. When none of the officers replied she said, 'Are you all right, Mrs Kidd? Perhaps these officers don't know that you are attending David Eyam's funeral.' Then she turned to the policeman who had been hit with the hat. 'I can vouch for Mrs Kidd.'

'And you are . . . ?' said a plainclothes officer in his thirties with razor burns on his neck.

She gave her name.

'Local?'

'No, I'm from London. I'm staying at the Bailey Hotel for a few days. But I do know Mrs Kidd.'

'Well, I am afraid she's in some trouble.'

'In what way? Surely she simply failed to observe the parking restrictions, an understandable error given she's attending the funeral of a close friend?'

'She struck a police officer. She failed to account for her intentions in a designated area and refused to let us search her bag.'

'I'm sure she didn't mean it, did you, Mrs Kidd?' She touched her lightly on the arm. Diana Kidd shook her head and revolved the hat in her hand trying to compose herself. Kate suddenly had a sense of the universe of uncertainty in the woman.

'If she agrees to park her car somewhere else, can you overlook the matter? You can see that she's very upset.'

Mrs Kidd stared at the ground and nodded pathetically.

There was an older man in a short, grey coat, standing a little distance away – hands shoved into diagonal pockets below his ribcage, a gaze that contemplated the castle's battlements and a manner that radiated contempt. Without looking at her he said, 'Sergeant, you can let Mrs Kidd go.'

The police moved back, allowing Mrs Kidd to pass to her car.

Kate thanked him. 'A designated area?' she said incredulously. 'Designated as what? By whom?'

'I'm not at liberty to say,' said the officer. 'We're just here to ensure that everything passes without incident.'

His eyes moved to her and scanned her face, trying to place her in the same way that Mrs Kidd had done during the inquest. 'Got your ID?' he asked.

'My passport's back at the hotel: will an American driver's licence do?' She did not move to open her bag.

'Are you a UK resident?'

'I am a British citizen. I have just come back from a long period in America.'

'You will have to sort out an ID card to live here. Immigration should have notified you when you landed.'

'I read the note,' she said in a manner that gave no ground.

He studied her hard and then waved a hand in front of him as though fanning smoke from his face.

'Now, please move on, madam; we've got a job to do here.'

'There was something else, which is why I came over.' She turned and scanned the stalls. 'You see that woman over there – the one in the trousers – I believe she was trying to steal from one of the market stalls.'

He nodded and said to a uniformed officer, 'Have a look into it, Mike.'

Kate thanked him again, swept the circle of officers with one of her client smiles, turned and took a few paces. Then the wind came and tore the blossom from a line of almond trees along the top of the square and tossed it in the air like confetti, adding to the indecent surge of spirit in old provincial England.

Later she perched on the arm of a bench on some open ground beside a churchyard smoking a cigarette and watching Eyam's remains being transferred from a hearse through the side entrance into St Luke's Parish Church. At first she turned away from the open door, as though there was something private about the operation, but then she forced herself to look on. Four pallbearers lowered the coffin, placed wreaths on top and at each end, straightened the velvet drape covering the trestle, bowed and retreated. The earthly remains of David Eyam – the mere fragments of a man – had come home and were at last being accorded respect. Shipped from Colombia in a battered aluminium box to Heathrow, there to be tested for cocaine, they had mistakenly been forwarded to the coroner's office where the casket – if that was the word – remained like a container left behind by a catering company.

She had learned all this from the coroner's clerk the night before when she'd taken refuge from the hotel in a pub called The Mercer's Arms. Rather to her surprise he lumbered over from a table, saying he'd recognised her from the inquest, then introduced himself as Tony Swift. He seemed intelligent and pleasant enough and although she wondered whether he fancied his chances with her she let him buy her a drink.

Between deliberated sips from a pint of Old Speckled Hen, he told her that it had taken over two weeks for anyone to realise that Eyam had been killed in the explosion. They might never have known for certain if the hotel room key hadn't been found by construction workers near the spot where Eyam had fallen and matched with the room he'd occupied at the Hotel Atlantic until the day of the blast.

'What about the hotel bill?' said Kate. 'Surely the hotel reported him missing?'

'Why? To whom? There was no need. They had his credit card details and authorisation for payment. I checked with one of the managers. There was a small amount of luggage in his room and after a few days they just put it in store, thinking he would collect it: they assumed he'd gone on a boat trip up the coast.'

A big man with a slow, amiable manner, Swift consumed a pie and chips while they talked, looking over his glasses to consider her questions. Why had he come to High Castle? What was he doing in Colombia? And how the hell had someone as smart and dedicated and charming as Eyam lost his job in government? The inquest had established the facts of Eyam's death but the fall, the calamity that pitched him into Mrs Kidd's exciting local arts scene was a mystery. Swift smiled at this but said he couldn't help her on any of these things.

The peal of bells was now abruptly replaced by the toll of a single bell. She stubbed the cigarette out, carried the butt to one of the waste-baskets, and walked to the main door where two policemen stood with weapons undisguised. A woman police officer searched her bag and patted her down and she was handed an order of service with Eyam's photograph and dates on the cover. She took a place halfway up the aisle. About two dozen people had already found places: Diana Kidd was at the front, fanning herself with the order of service. Kate read the short appreciation on the inside cover, recording Eyam's time at Oxford with all its honours and awards, his work in think tanks and the civil service – the Home Office, the Research and Analysis Department at the Foreign Office, Number Ten and finally the Joint Intelligence Committee. It possessed no more feeling than an entry in *Who's Who*.

No mention of his two years in High Castle. No salutes to his intellectual distinction, the range of his interests, his flair, his largely hidden physical prowess. No colour, no observation, no humour. David Eyam was being sent on his way without love.

Just before noon there was a respectful rush of mourners and by the time the bell fell silent well over a hundred people filled the pews around her. The clearing of throats and murmurs ceased; people stopped nodding to each other as the presence of the coffin – of death – imposed an awkward hush on the congregation. In the front row was the actress Ingrid Eyam, David's stepmother and next of kin, who Kate concluded would inherit the entire fortune left by David's father a few months before. She had gone the whole distance with a fitted black two-piece suit and pillbox hat with a springy black mesh veil, from which peeked a dubious tragic beauty. Behind her the mourners fell into three distinct groups: the people from the centre of government, who included two permanent secretaries, the home secretary Derek Glenny, a large man in his fifties with male-pattern baldness and narrow eyes, and one or two political faces she recognised from reading the English newspapers; Eyam's friends from Oxford, most of whom Kate knew; and about thirty locals who, with unconscious respect for hierarchy, placed themselves in the pews at the rear. Mrs Kidd disrupted the pattern and was now looking anxiously about her, wondering if she was in a reserved seat.

The vicar moved from consulting some musicians in front of the altar to the centre of the aisle, and began to address the mourners. 'This is not to be a sad occasion,' he said with a distinct whistle in his voice. 'David's instructions were clear – we are to rejoice in life and the living of it. The music and readings are all his choice, apart from the passage from *Cymbeline*, which will be read by Ingrid Eyam, David's stepmother.'

She thought it odd that someone in his forties and in perfect health would think of planning their own funeral. Eyam was an atheist, incurious about his own death, and as far as she knew had no reason to expect his life was about to end. But he was also more organised than anyone she had ever known and she could easily imagine him sitting down one Sunday night to put his wishes on paper. He had chosen well. A very good countertenor sang from Monteverdi's *The Legend of Orpheus*, there were readings from Byron and Milton, and Ingrid Eyam read from Shakespeare – 'Golden lads and lasses must/ as chimney sweepers, come to dust.' It was all perfectly pleasant but none of it was moving, and no one got near Eyam. When the tributes followed from a professor of eonomics at Oxford and the home secretary Derek Glenny, they seemed to her to be going through the motions. Glenny puffed himself out, fiddled with his glasses, gazed with satisfaction around the church and told them as much about himself as Eyam. He ended with, 'David had that essential gift for a government servant: he understood power and he knew how to use it. This was a rare and good man. He will be missed greatly.'

Kate glanced at her watch and was just wishing the whole farce over when there was a commotion in the middle of the pew behind her as someone pushed past several pairs of knees without apology. A slender Indian man wearing a grey, chalk-stripe suit, red woollen gloves and a tightly knotted red scarf appeared in the aisle, stared about him with a wild, almost insane look, and made his way to the front, where he laid his hands on the top of the coffin. He stood for a full minute with his head bowed. Kate moved so she could see him better.

'Darsh,' she murmured under her breath. She hadn't thought of Darsh Darshan for at least a decade. The first time she had seen him was in a church, a scrawny mathematics prodigy who arrived at Oxford on a scholarship and whom she found one dark winter evening sitting in New College chapel in an almost catatonic state. David took him under his wing and saw he was all right.

Without turning, he spoke. 'In my culture we draw near to death. We hold the dead close and we comfort them on their journey.' He let his hands drop, looked over his shoulder then turned very slowly. His head was curiously oblong and his hair brushed forward so it curled above a domed, almost bulbous brow. His eyes burned with fierce self-possession that was new to Kate.

'We are forgetting David,' he said. 'Don't you see that? This is David, lying here! Can any of us doubt our guilt in that fact?'

The congregation looked at each other embarrassed, shrinking in their seats with the English terror of someone making a scene.

'Even if we shy from death this is no time to forget who David was and what he stood for,' continued Darsh. 'David was murdered. No one has used that word but that is the reality of his death. We still don't know who murdered him, and that is an important fact to remember today.'

The vicar stepped forward, looking flustered. 'Thank you, thank you,' he said. 'But if you *would* return to your place now.'

'I haven't finished,' Darsh said quietly, then rubbed his gloved hands. 'My name is Darsh Darshan and I was a friend of David's for twenty years. There was no one like him, but more than this simple declaration of his individuality and of my love for him I attest to his courage, his loyalty to high principle and the cause of decency. David played the long game and he was good at it. He was patient and he respected detail. Yet he was no machine. He took his bearings early and stayed true to his course: he knew who he was, where he was at any given moment and where he was heading. He was imperturbable, inspired, unbending, brilliant and funny. You could wish for no greater friend. His mind was truly clear. So often the answer came before your question was out because he had already asked it of himself, and on the rare occasions when he hadn't thought of the problem, he seized it with a delight that was a pleasure to behold. His brain was remarkable but his character was a glory. Such a man makes you think God is possible.'

He paused and swept the faces in front of him. Although the majority of the congregation were convinced that Darsh was out of his mind, one or two heads were now nodding encouragement in the curious aquarium light that spilled from the stained-glass windows on the south. He placed a hand on the lid of the coffin again and patted it possessively, throwing a smile of recognition up the aisle as though David Eyam's ghost had stumbled late into the church. Then his eyes drifted to Glenny. 'And when our friend the minister here says that David understood power . . . Well, yes, sir, you are right. He did. But his purpose was not to have it for himself but to control it, to place obstacles in its way and to set up boundaries to restrain it.' Kate was not sure that was absolutely true but she nodded. Darsh stopped and walked to within a few feet of the end of the home secretary's pew and stood in a shaft of light, apparently unaware of the bodyguards who had moved from somewhere behind the altar. He looked drawn and his skin was grey. A shiver passed across his shoulders.

'You see, David found all that repulsive and wrong. He resisted and then he lost. He came up against an enemy and was beaten, not because of the superiority of mission or of mind, but because of the sheer, overwhelming, implacable weight of his foe. David tripped up. He was shamed . . . mortified. And he was forced – I mean forced – out of government. For that mistake he paid with his life. Responsibility for his death lies with the people here, in this church.'

The priest was having no more. 'I think you've made your point. Now, please go back to your seat and we can continue with the service. You don't want to spoil this occasion for others here, who I am sure you will understand grieve as much as you do.'

Darsh moved a step closer to the home secretary, who was now looking extremely uncomfortable. 'This man and all of them sitting here with him know what I am talking about. We don't have the details yet but they put an end to David's life as surely as if they had set off that bomb.'

Someone behind Glenny leaned forward and spoke in his ear.

Darsh continued, 'It's the truth – and you all know it. David was killed. He was murdered.'

At this point two of the protection officers closed in and, with a nod from the priest, descended on Darsh. He dodged the first officer and managed to aim a blow at the home secretary's head, at which a gasp of horror came from the back pews. Kate saw Diana Kidd's hat rise up like a fishing float and Ingrid Eyam slump back in her pew with a look of social horror. Darsh was seized and thrown to the ground like a rag doll. His face was pressed into the two figures etched into medieval brass a few feet from where Lockhart sat. One officer held him down with a hand placed in the middle of his back while the other searched him for weapons.

A man got up and attempted to interpose himself. 'Is this really necessary? I know him: He means no harm.' But they took no notice. Darsh was picked up with the same contemptuous ease as he had been floored. 'I was going to say a prayer,' he shouted out. 'It's a Christian prayer.' He began speaking in a high, panicky voice. 'Though our outward man perish, yet the inward man is renewed day by day. While we look *not* at the things which are seen but the things which are not seen.'

As he was frogmarched towards the door he yelled out, 'For the things . . . which are seen . . . are temporal; the things which are not seen . . . are ETERNAL.'

A moment later he was propelled from the church. A kind of reverence was restored and the service limped to its conclusion. Then it was time for David Eyam's remains to be borne from the church and taken to a crematorium where the job of incineration would be completed. Bach's Toccata and Fugue in D Minor were played on a clattering, wheezy organ and after a moment of introspection the congregation filed out, led by Ingrid Eyam on Glenny's arm.

Kate waited, looking at the faces that passed her, and became aware of Kilmartin, the man from the inquest, watching her from the other side of the aisle with candid interest. When their eyes met he gave her a little bow of his head then looked away. The crush of people in the aisle meant she could not leave immediately. Her eyes fell to some verses on the back page of the order of service, which she had not noticed before.

The Death of Me

Carry me over floods, sister!
Carry me to the other side!
And I'll wait for you here, sister,
'Til we cross the swelling tide.

I may be gone for now, sister,
For others say I've died.
But I'll wait for you here, sister,
'Til we take the waters wide.

I lost my heart to you, sister;
Then death became my bride.
Carry me over floods, sister;
Carry me from where I hide.

Carry me over floods, sister;
Carry me to the other side.
And I'll wait for you here, *sister,*
My truly beloved guide.

Anon: nineteenth-century
American folk song

She read it twice, smiled, put the booklet into her bag and left the church.

5

Sister

Instead of following the other mourners to the hotel for the wake Kate went to the Green Parrot cafe and bar at the top of the square, where she was eyed without enthusiasm by a teenage waitress with two-tone hair and a stud punched through her lower lip. The place was almost empty. She sat down at a table in the window, ordered a brandy and a black coffee, tipped the first into the second and wondered about taking an earlier train back to London.

She watched the square blankly as though it were a scene between moments of action in a film, then without warning was struck by the scale of her loss. It was the verse at the end of the order of service that did it, the memory of when he called her Sister for the first time. Sometimes he reduced it to Sis, a joke referring to her past in SIS, but mostly he called her Sister, as though to underline the dangers of violation. He must have delighted in finding those verses. They had been put there for her – a final message, perhaps of true love. A tear had made its way down her cheek, which she hurriedly dispatched with one of the paper napkins held in the beak of a green plastic parrot on the table.

Her eyes moved to the window. A man was peering into the cafe, trying to see past the reflection, then a look of recognition lit his face and he mimed that he was coming in to join her.

A trim, eager person entered, flattening a tuft of sandy grey hair and brushing something from the jacket of a slate-blue suit that she had seen bobbing in the exodus from the church. When he reached the table he wiped his brow theatrically with the back of one hand and offered the other to her. 'Miss Lockhart? I'm Hugh Russell of Russell, Spring & Co., David Eyam's lawyer.'

She nodded. 'Actually, it's Mrs, but I have given up making the point. Call me Kate.'

'Oh, you're married – I hadn't realised.'

'Was – my husband has been dead for nearly a decade.'

'Ah, I see.' He looked embarrassed.

She asked him to sit and he began to explain that Russell, Spring & Co. had acted for Eyam since he'd purchased Dove Cottage.

'I am so glad that I've managed to catch you before you left High Castle,' he said, wrinkling his nose in an odd way. 'I found your photo on the internet but then missed you at the funeral. Mrs Kidd said that she had seen you slip in here.'

'Ah, yes, Mrs Kidd.'

'Yes, there's not much that escapes her notice,' he said and cleared his throat. 'You may prefer to do this in my offices at a more convenient time, but if it would be of help I can tell you now the substance of what I have to say.'

Kate opened her hands. 'Please do.'

'I don't know much about your relationship with David Eyam, but I'm assuming you were close.'

'We were, yes, but our jobs were on different continents and we saw little of each other over the last couple of years. Close but apart.'

'You work for Calvert-Mayne in New York. That's a famous outfit – you must be damned good at your job.' His face assumed a professional cast. 'All this must be very distressing for you – I mean the circumstances, Kate – if I may, losing such a close friend in that awful manner.' He paused. 'Now, this is going to be a shock to you. It certainly would be to me.' He stopped again to give her time, and nodded to ask if it was all right to continue.

She revolved her hand and smiled. 'Please go on.'

'I have to tell you that you are the main beneficiary of David Eyam's will. I could have informed you by letter but he wanted me to give you the news personally – he was most insistent on that point.'

She put down her cup. 'Left me everything! Good Lord! You can't be serious.'

'I am. His estate comprises a house – Dove Cottage – a flat in London, which is currently rented out on a short lease, a car and all his shares and savings. He's made one or two big bequests to local charities and so forth, but essentially you are his main heir. The estate is worth well over three and a half million pounds. And I should tell you that the savings and cash will very adequately cover the inheritance tax if you are minded to retain the property.'

She sat back. 'I'm astonished.'

'I can well understand that, but I hope you feel that this news is some consolation in what I know will have been a very sad day for you. I have his will here and a letter addressed to you.' He unzipped a leather document case and took out two envelopes, which he placed between them on the table. 'There are also some larger documents, which are in the safe at my offices. Perhaps you'd care to drop by this afternoon and pick them up and we can begin on the paperwork. There's quite a lot to go through.'

'When did he make this will?' she asked eventually.

'Let me think. September or late August. About six months ago: it was after he had had some . . .' He stopped and frowned.

'What?' she said, leaning forward slightly.

'I believe he received some worrying news about his health, though I am not sure of its precise nature. He intimated that he had been told to get his affairs in order. There was hope but he thought it was best to be on the safe side.'

That explained why Eyam had planned his funeral, but not what he was doing in Colombia. She thought for a moment. 'You think it was cancer – something terminal?'

He shrugged.

'Did he say why he was going away?'

'No, I didn't know he'd left until I heard of his death. He was away about a month and what with Christmas, well . . .'

'Why would he go away when he was ill? Presumably he was being treated in England.'

'I'm afraid I can't say because I don't know.'

'And these documents; do you know what's in them?'

'No. These are his private communication to you. The contents do not concern me.' He smiled sympathetically. 'I know this is going to take some time to sink in. It is after all a rather large legacy to come out of the blue. But the one thing I did want to bring to your attention is the house, which has been unoccupied for over three months. There will be things that require attention: we can talk about all of that when you come to see me. The lease on the flat in London is due to end in a few months' time so you don't have to think about that for the moment.'

Her hand moved to the envelopes. 'May I?' she asked.

'Forgive me. All this is a little irregular, but please do.'

She opened the will first and read that Hugh Arthur Russell and Annabel Spring, wife of Russell's partner Paul Spring, were appointed as Executors and Trustees. She read on:

(i) I bequeath to Kate Grace Koh Lockhart absolutely the property known as Dove Cottage, Dove Valley, Near High Castle, in the county of Shropshire, all the contents therein and my car (Bristol Series 4,1974 Chassis number: 18462 Registration Number N476 RXL) and also the property at 16 Seymour Row, London W1, currently let on a two-year lease to George Harold Keenan, together with its contents.

(ii) I bequeath to Kate Grace Koh Lockhart absolutely the sum of £780,000 and the portfolio of shares and bonds held in my name at the time of my decease.

(iii) I give to High Castle Arts Trust absolutely the sum of £12,000 and to High Castle Film Society the sum of £12,000 to be used in an annual lecture and film screening and to The Marches Bell Ringers Society the sum of £125,000.

There were a few smaller bequests – Amnesty International and a charity called Tree Aid. Attached were a paper detailing the extent of his shareholding as of October 21st the previous year, and the address of his accountant in London.

She let the will drop to the table and picked up the letter addressed to her in Eyam's precise little hand.

At the top was a quote from Immanuel Kant: 'Two things fill the mind with ever new and increasing admiration and awe, the oftener and more steadily we reflect on them – the starry heavens above and the moral laws within.'

For the moment the evening is mine, Sister, but soon it will certainly be yours.

If you are reading this, Hugh Russell must have found you and given you the keys to Dove Cottage, which will come to you after you receive the news of my demise. I am dead. How odd that sounds. Anyway, welcome to my home; welcome to your home. I do wish that we had made the occupation simultaneous, rather than consecutive, but leaving it to you is the nearest I can get to that now.

How did we let this distance between us happen? What did we do not to deserve each other? It was, I am sure, all my fault and I hope I have managed to express this to you in person or on the phone before you read this.

Anyway, that is all regrettably in the past and now I give you my life – less tax, as it were – and with all the problems and strangeness of the last year or so; but also all the hidden delights of Dove Cottage, which I believe you will come to love. Look closely, as I know you can, and you will discover much that is surprising here. All my earthly goods are now yours: my secrets too. Think of nothing as too private for your eyes. I am opening myself to you, Sis, and though it is too late to say it, I send my love – the most tender and heartfelt of my life – and I kiss your clever eyes for good fortune and the happiness that has not been ours.

Some of what I have left you will have been handed to you with this letter, but there is more to find because I could not risk placing all my eggs in one basket. What you have is a primer. The full legacy to you and others will reveal itself in due course. I cannot go into details here.

The evening I speak of at the start of this note is perfect. I write on a patch of gravel garden in front of the cottage resting on an old metal table, which I inherited when I bought the place. I have a glass of Puligny Montrachet at my side; a neighbour's dog is making eyes at a bowl of cheese sticks. It has been a very hot day. The sun has set and the sky is bruising a gentle purple in the west. It is just past eight o'clock, and the cuckoos call from the other side of the valley. There are hawks hunting in the dusk above me. As ever, the Dove is their prey. The birds sing but mostly they listen and watch at this time of the day. You will find it all very much behind the times, but I have been happy here.

If you are reading this it means I'm gone. The evening is yours now with all its grandeur and its flaws: you are more than equal to both. Good luck, and look after my books, my beloved Bristol and my garden – especially my vegetable patch.

With my love, David.

Dove Cottage, August 20th

She read it again while the lawyer looked on.

'Do you want some coffee? Have a drink?' she said absently.

'I won't, thanks.' He cleared his throat again. 'Is there something wrong?'

'The letter: it doesn't sound like him at all. I mean the pretentious stuff at the beginning is very much Eyam, but the rest of it sounds like he's on drugs.'

'Perhaps he was conscious that you would read this after his death. Maybe it was hard for him to write.'

She thought for a moment. 'You're probably right. What time do you want me to come in?'

'Any time up to eight.' He got up and gave her a card. 'These days we country lawyers have to keep our heads down to make ends meet. You can give me your contact details when you come.'

'Of course,' she said, returning the letter and the will to their envelopes. 'I'll see you later then.'

'If it's past six and my secretary has gone home, just ring the bell.'

He left and a few moments later she watched him hurrying across the square, nodding to people as he went, one hand on top of his head as though at risk of losing his hair in the wind. From where she sat she could almost see the whole square, and if Hugh Russell had not gone at quite such a gallop, she would probably not have noticed. But what she saw now was the discreet choreography of a close surveillance operation. The moves were all there: the man swivelling from the market stall and walking ahead of the target; the woman with a plastic bag tracking him in the left field, pausing to window shop and watch the target in the reflection; the builder's labourer folding a tabloid and keeping pace behind him as the main 'eyeball', the ordinary silver saloon containing two men whose heads did not look up from their newspapers as Russell and then their colleagues passed.

Russell reached Mortimer Street, a wide thoroughfare with unbroken terraces of seventeenth- and eighteenth-century merchants' houses that ran down to a medieval gate. He crossed the road with a forearm pressed against his jacket to stop it flying up and entered a large cream-coloured townhouse, which the card on the table told her must be number six, Mortimer Street – the offices of Russell, Spring & Co. At this point the energy of the pursuit suddenly gave out and the men and woman dispersed without acknowledging each other.

Kate realised they must have picked up Russell at the cafe for the first time, otherwise they would have known who he was and followed him less aggressively. This could only mean they'd latched onto the lawyer because he'd been seen with her. So, she was the main target, not merely someone who was being watched as part of the security measures in advance of the funeral, which was what she had assumed.

Well, damn them, she thought: if some milk-faced security bureaucrat thought she was worth watching, good luck to him. She didn't give a damn. She didn't belong to the town, nor did she have any part in the morbid hyper-anxiety that seemed to have gripped the country in her absence. But in the next seconds she reminded herself that she was now indeed part of High Castle, even if only for a few weeks. Eyam's will effectively tied her to the coordinates of his mysterious exile. Perhaps he was forcing her to become involved in whatever it was that had made him leave the centre of things.

6

The Mourners

The wake conformed to the pattern in the church. The locals gathered in three defensive circles near the buffet table, juggling plates and glasses; the people from Eyam's Oxford days staked out the middle of the room for a reunion, while the politicians, civil servants and business people claimed the Old Pineapple House, a conservatory built along the inside of a high garden wall, where they were being conspicuously hosted by Ingrid Eyam with veil raised and a sparkle in her eye.

Kate took a glass of wine from a tray of drinks and almost immediately became aware of someone clutching at her arm. She turned to find Diana Kidd with an ardent look in her eye. 'We're claiming you as ours,' she said and wheeled round to the half dozen people. 'This is the person who saved me from those dreadful police. Lord knows what would have happened if you hadn't stepped in. I'd probably have been charged with assault or something. These fine people are David's closest friends in High Castle. Aren't you?' she said encouragingly.

'Do you know the Indian gentleman?' asked a large man with a stubble beard who looked uneasy in his suit and tie. Then he added, 'Chris Mooney is the name. Mooney Photographic.'

'Yes, from Oxford,' she replied.

'What he said chimed with me,' he said. 'It was as if he knew about our problems.'

'Oh, what are they?' Kate asked.

Mooney looked around the group. 'There's a campaign of harassment and intimidation against anyone who knew David.'

'Really!' said Mrs Kidd. 'She doesn't want to hear about that. And anyway we've got no proof.'

'Why do you think you were stopped this morning?'

'I parked in the wrong place. It was all my silly fault.'

'How do you account for that van in the square?' asked a strikingly pretty woman in her late twenties who introduced herself as Alice Scudamore.

'Security for the minister and all those important people: we live in an age of terrorism and assassination, dear. Look at what happened to David.'

'No, they were filming us,' said Alice Scudamore. 'They weren't protecting anyone! The important people had gone. They were filming us, not from above but *head on* so they could get everyone's face.'

'Well, who's to say?' said Mrs Kidd with an apologetic smile to Kate. 'We mustn't bore her, must we? Hugh Russell says Miss Lockhart is a high-powered lawyer from New York. She doesn't want to hear about our little gripes. Did you like the service? The readings were beautiful, weren't they?'

'And you saw the police drone,' said Mooney aggressively.

'No.'

'You don't notice them because they don't make a sound. We see a lot of them in this town. It was over the square. This one was larger than usual. You know what the police use them for?'

'Surveillance.'

'More than that,' said Mooney. 'They mark targets with smart water – crowds and that sort of thing. It's like being pissed on by a bat. The marker chemical stays on you for weeks. They were marking people in the square, as well as photographing them from the van.'

'You say that's proof?' said Mrs Kidd.

A short man with wiry black hair and intense black eyes leaned into the group conspiratorially and raised a finger from the rim of the wine glass. 'Evan Thomas is the name, Miss Lockhart. When are you going to get the message, Diana? We're being persecuted because we knew David.'

'Can that really be true?' asked Kate evenly. 'Haven't the authorities got better things to do these days?'

'Precisely. That's I exactly what I say,' said Diana Kidd.

The man straightened to her. 'There's too much evidence for it to be a coincidence. I mean, look at us. We're ordinary people and we're being hounded as though we were some kind of terror cell.'

A voice came from behind Kate and a hand was placed on her shoulder. 'Well, the day *is* looking up – Kate Koh!'

She turned to see Oliver Mermagen, a contemporary from Oxford.

'You were ignoring me?' He leaned forward to kiss her on both cheeks.

'I didn't see you,' she said. 'And my name is Lockhart now, Oliver.'

'Yes, of course: is the lucky man here?'

'No,' she said.

'What a pity,' he said and then looked at the group around her. 'I wonder if I can borrow our Kate. I won't keep her long.'

She was steered into the middle of the room. 'I don't remember you being very close to David,' she said.

'Haven't lost your bite, have you? If you want to know, we became friends after Oxford. We used to have dinner quite often together in London. Of course I didn't see him much when he moved down here to the sticks.'

'If you saw David you must know about the illness he had last year; it was quite serious apparently.'

'I heard nothing about that,' said Mermagen.

He went on to tell her that he ran a PR and lobbying business, which seemed a plausible setting for Mermagen's talents. At Oxford he was always panhandling the room for new connections. Eyam gave him the name 'Promises' because of his technique of promising someone what he thought they wanted, whether it was his to give or not. Little seemed to have touched Mermagen. His face had flattened and spread outwards and the eyes had become two feverish dots in an expanse of greyish white flesh. Eyam had always said Mermagen reminded him of a Dover sole.

'You must at least know why David came here,' she said.

His eyes glided across her face. 'My word, you have been out of it. David fell from grace big time. Everyone knows that. Easy enough when you get to the very top.'

'How?'

'I don't know the details.'

51

'You didn't talk to him to find out what happened?'

He shook his head. 'I'm afraid not. What about you?'

'I didn't know anything was wrong. I've been in the States for nearly eight years, working at Calvert-Mayne in New York.'

Mermagen saluted the name with a nod. 'So you weren't in touch at all. You two used to be so close. I mean, I'd have put money on you eventually getting together, but then you went off and found someone else. Who's this Lockhart?'

'Charlie Lockhart: he was in the Foreign Office. He died nearly ten years ago.'

Mermagan did a good impression of recollection followed by regret. Charlie's face flashed in front of her. They were playing tennis with another couple from the embassy. Charlie missed a shot at the net and without warning doubled up in agony. When he straightened, his expression had changed for ever. That pain would last until his death from liver cancer nine months later at his family home on the Black Isle in Scotland.

She looked around the room. Mermagen couldn't tell her anything, or wouldn't. Through the glass of the Pineapple House she could see Darsh Darshan sitting on a garden bench. He was staring ahead with his arms clamped round his chest. Glenny's bodyguards stood at a distance.

'I'm surprised Darsh wasn't arrested,' she said.

'The home secretary was very understanding: he put it down to grief. Darsh was always a rather overwrought character.'

'Surely you didn't know him at Oxford? It was just our crowd at New College that knew Darsh.'

'Of course I did,' he said.

'What did you think of the things he said in church – all that stuff about murder?'

'Well, you know Darsh was virtually in love with David.'

'But what did he mean?'

His eyes moved to the home secretary. 'He was blaming them for David's fall and therefore his being in High Castle and therefore his being in Colombia when a bomb goes off and kills him instead of some bloody union leader or whatever – logic that is surely not worthy of the man who invented the Darshan Curve.'

'What was David doing before he left government service, Oliver?'

'He was head of the Joint Intelligence Committee; before that at COBRA – the Cabinet Office Briefing Room "A", mostly to do with energy, I gather but I don't fly at that altitude so I do not know the details of his jobs. He darted about giving a lot of people the benefit of his laser mind. You did know that he was thought likely to become cabinet secretary one day. All he needed on his CV was a big department to run. There was talk of the Ministry of Defence.'

'Darsh said he was *mortified*. What did he mean by that? It's an odd word to use – mortified.'

Mermagen pouted mystification and touched the handkerchief in his breast pocket. 'Better ask him. By the way, how's your mother?'

'My mother!' she said, astonished. 'My mother's fine, thank you: why do you ask?'

'Still playing golf?'

'Yes, between bridge and running the Faculty of Advocates In Edinburgh.' She remembered her parents' excruciating visit to Oxford, her disruptive father smirking in the wake of his rigid wife. Perversely the only student her mother had taken to was Mermagen, who had ingratiated himself by pretending an interest in women's golf.

'Can I ask *you* something?' Kate said. 'Did anyone have a reason to kill Eyam? It was raised – well, hinted at – during the inquest.'

'Kill David? What on earth for? Really, you've been watching too much American television, Kate. What an absurd idea.' His arm swung out towards a tray of canapés that was just about in range. 'I must say, Ingrid's done David proud with these caterers. Are you coming to the dinner tonight? No, of course not. How could anyone know you'd be here?'

Kate began to look for an escape. 'Who's giving the dinner?'

'Ortelius. You know, Eden White, the head of Ortelius and much else besides.'

'Eden White was a friend of David's? I don't believe it. The information systems creep? That Eden White?'

'The same but be careful, my dear Kate. He's a partner of mine, and he's quite a power in the land – a friend of the prime minister's. Hardwired into the government. Immensely influential.'

'Jesus, what's happened to this country? Eden White best friends with the prime minister.'

'They were always friends. Same with Derek Glenny. They go way back. Pity you're not coming to the dinner for David.' He bent forward to allow his jacket to fall open and lifted a printed card from his inside pocket. He handed it to her. 'Here are the names for the dinner. It's quite a gathering.'

Under the heading *The Ortelius Dinner to Celebrate the life of David Lucas Eyam* were twenty names of politicians, business leaders and permanent secretaries. 'Is it Eyam's life they've come all this way to celebrate,' she said, running down the list, 'or his death?'

'Now that's simply not fair, Kate,' said Mermagen. 'In fact I think it is rather silly and disruptive of you.' His attention had switched to a group around Derek Glenny and before she could say anything more he had moved on, leaving her with the card. She looked to discard it somewhere but then slipped it into her jacket pocket.

The wake had become a party and all thought of David Eyam seemed to have left the Jubilee Rooms. She considered going up to her room but then noticed Hugh Russell take a drink and knock it back in one.

She went over to him. 'I thought you weren't going to come.'

'I wasn't, but I did just want to make sure that you were – eh – dropping in this afternoon.' His upper lip was beaded with sweat and the top of his cheeks flushed.

'Has something happened?'

'No, no. Everything's fine, but I want to get as much done as we can. I wasn't sure that I'd made that clear.'

'Are you sure there's nothing wrong?' He looked down to the ground for a few moments. 'Mr Russell, please tell me what has happened.'

His gaze rose to hers. 'These papers should be in your possession. I perhaps underestimated their value to you earlier, which is the reason I came over. I really feel that you should take them as soon as possible.'

'You read them.'

'No.'

'You glanced at them.'

He lifted his shoulders helplessly. 'No.'

'Well, it doesn't matter. Just give them to me later. I'll come in after this.'

'But you will need somewhere secure for them. I feel certain about that.'

'Fine. I'll be there about five.' She felt they had said all they needed, then something occurred to her. 'Tell me, did anyone know that you were acting for David Eyam?'

'Nobody, apart from my secretary of the time, and she has left to work in Birmingham. Certainly no one knew the substance of his business. It was confidential, and David wanted a very discreet relationship.'

'How many times did he come to your office?'

He thought for a second. 'Never, once he had purchased Dove Cottage. We met at a pub and did business over a bite. He always gave me lunch at the Bugle, a pub about twelve miles from here. It has a rather good restaurant, though no one uses it for lunch. I lent him a laptop so he could write out the instructions for the will, then printed it out.'

'Didn't he have his own computer?'

'He said it was unreliable and kept on losing material.'

'That doesn't sound like him.'

'At any rate that was the arrangement.'

'And was that the same for the bigger document?'

'No, he gave that to me in an envelope and told me to put it in a safe.'

'Was that at the same time?'

'No – much later, in November maybe even December.'

'So there was nothing to connect you with him?'

'I don't think so. Why do you ask?'

'Then you've got little to worry about. Nobody knows about the will. Nobody has troubled you about these documents. Nobody has shown the slightest interest in your professional dealings with David Eyam. If you've read something by accident, well, that's between you and me. I'm a lawyer: I understand how it goes. Look, I'll come to your office now if that helps.'

He gave her a stressed look. 'No, no. That's the point – I won't be there. I forgot that I have something on until about five thirty – a meeting outside the office. Come after that.'

'That's fine. I want to see one or two people here.'

Russell departed and she threaded her way to the Pineapple House in search of Darsh. But he had left his spot in the garden and was nowhere in sight. She was making her way back towards a group of people from Oxford days she hadn't seen for twenty years when she turned slap into the path of Kilmartin.

'Again!' he said with a little ironic smile.

'Yes,' she said. 'It's Mr Kilmartin, isn't it? The inquest.'

'But we've met before.'

'Really? I'm sorry I don't . . .'

'That's the trouble with our trade – our former trade, I should say. To be successful you must be forgettable. Southsea – about a dozen years ago, maybe a touch more, Intelligence Officers' New Entry Course. I was one of the course lecturers, though I wouldn't expect you to remember. I never enjoyed doing them much, which showed, I expect.'

'Emile!'

'Yes, the name made me sound like some leftover from the Free French – it really is my middle name. My mother was French.' He put his hand out. 'Peter Emile Kilmartin.'

'Targeting, recruiting and running agents – was that it?'

'No, communications in the field, though God knows why. I was always rather bad at that.'

'Yes, of course I remember you.'

'And you were from Jakarta, recruited there by McBride, and you did quite a bit of work before you actually came back to the office for indoctrination. Very unusual. And they really wanted you to stay. A big future for you but then . . .'

'My husband died and I took another direction. He was in the Foreign Office.'

'But you enjoyed the work?'

She nodded. 'Christ, yes. It was such a bloody relief to find something to do. An embassy wife is like being a geisha without the money.'

There was a silence, which he didn't seem to mind. He looked around the room, she into the garden.

'Were you trying to find someone?' he asked at length.

'Yes, Darsh – the Indian. I wanted to see he was OK. I guess everyone thought he was completely mad.'

'He seemed fine when I talked to him.'

'You know him?'

'Yes, David introduced us and he helped me with a rather arcane mathematics problem for a paper I was writing.' He paused and looked round. 'Anyway, it's been a good turnout.'

'It's not a village fete,' she said.

Kilmartin did not miss the quiet vehemence. 'You're right. I'm sorry. A stupid thing to say.'

'You know, someone said exactly the same thing at my father's funeral. I suppose there was nothing else to say. He killed himself, you know, and that leaves the average emotionally retarded Brit rather stuck for things to chat about at a funeral.'

'You talk as if you no longer think of yourself as belonging here.' He examined her through his large, round, steel-rimmed glasses. His blue and white spotted tie was a couple of centimetres adrift from the top button and his dark-blue suit was made of a heavy serviceable material, which had become shiny at certain points but was in no danger of wearing out: the all-purpose suit tailored – or rather built – for a life-time. He would probably be buried in that suit wearing that same expression of tight-lipped craftiness.

'I've been away a long time and I came back expecting things to be the same, but having spent nearly a week in this godforsaken backwater, I'm beginning to wonder if I made the right choice. Maybe it's this town, but everyone seems so on edge – suspicious. People seem to be so out of sorts.' She stopped. 'Sorry, I'm being a bit of a bore, aren't I? The funeral made me angry. It all seemed so bloodless and damned *English*. I wondered how many people there actually liked David Eyam.'

'Oh, quite a few I should think. He was an exceptional person.'

She nodded. 'You were carrying seed catalogues at the inquest – that must have put me off the scent, though I did feel there was something familiar about you.'

'Yes, I was. For the first time I have a good-sized garden to play with, plus a very good view, plus a good library and the time to think and . . . well . . . exist.'

'You also had some kind of academic journal – *Middle Eastern Archaeology* or something?'

'Spot on. You were noted by the office for your exceptional powers of observation and recall,' he said. 'But David wasn't nearly so good.'

'Eyam? Eyam wasn't on the New Intake Course.'

'We had a look at him the year before you, but then we decided he was not cut out for the life of an intelligence branch officer abroad, whereas you were a natural. They were very sorry to lose you.'

'Eyam in SIS.' She began shaking her head. 'No, that can't be true.'

'He lasted no more than a matter of months and found the whole thing richly comic. Far too intelligent for the work.'

'What's that make us?' she said quickly, still smarting from the news that Eyam had never told her he'd been recruited. Through the whole of their exchange his lips had barely moved, but now Kilmartin's mouth spread into a sardonic smile and his eyes shone. 'I think you know that I meant he was too cerebral.' He took a sip of water from a tumbler.

'I'll settle for that,' she said. 'Was that time your only contact with him?'

'No – we worked together on some issues, mostly to do with Central Asia: oil and gas, water, that sort of thing.'

'At Downing Street?'

He nodded. 'But we were friendly in other arenas.'

'So you know what happened – why he lost his job?'

'I know very little. I've spent the better part of the last five years either looking after my late wife or abroad pursuing the national interest, or so I was persuaded. No, I have no idea what happened, but I'd like to find out. You were a good friend; you must know a lot more than I.'

'No, I'm afraid not.'

'What did you make of the inquest?'

'I'd like to have heard a lot more about the bomb and who planted it. For a lawyer, it is a surprising process to watch – no real scrutiny of the evidence, no cross-examination of the witnesses, no jury.'

'What do you mean?'

'Well, clearly there are grounds for suspicion that David was the target of that bomb.'

'Would it be insensitive to say that you saw less than you wished of David?'

'Would it be insensitive of me to say that you're getting off the subject? Like you, I was abroad and we did lose touch. But it doesn't seem to have mattered because I was close enough to be his main heir.' She regretted this, but it would become public soon enough.

His face had lost its humour. 'Maybe we should meet.'

'And talk about what?'

'You'll know. Contact me at St Antony's College in Oxford. There is a secretary at the Middle East School who takes messages for me. You don't have to be explicit – simply suggest a time and place and give your maiden name. I seem to remember it's Koh.' He was in deadly earnest. 'We *will* need to speak. I promise you that.'

'Is all this intrigue really necessary?'

'You're not in the cosy world of an American law firm – there have been changes here that are about much more than mood and morale.'

'American law firms aren't cosy,' she said. 'But I agree; there's certainly more surveillance than I thought possible in a free country.'

'Of you?'

'Maybe.'

'Then we *must* talk. We don't want a repetition of the Soeprapto business.'

'Not only do you avoid talking about the one thing that wasn't explored in the inquest but you make it plain that you've been reading my office file – only a very few people knew about the Soeprapto.'

'I knew about the whole case. A classic example of an intelligence officer picking up a scrap of information at a social gathering – at a ladies' tea party, I think, an accountant's wife or some such. Soeprapto's was unmasked, the bank collapsed but not before you ensured British interests were protected; no money was lost.'

'A long time ago,' she said.

'But there was a postscript, wasn't there? Which is why I'm digging this up. Soeprapto put out a contract on you from jail, which was taken up by a member of a Chinese gang, who came looking for you in London.'

'Yeah, just after my husband Charlie's funeral.'

One evening she had noticed the young Chinese get off at her stop on the Underground and a day or two later saw him hanging about Queen's Gate near her flat. She changed her routine and established she was being followed, then informed the police. The assassin was arrested in the lobby of her building with a gun. It was clear she would remain at risk in London and after nine months of being comforted by Eyam, she left SIS and accepted an offer from Sam Calvert, Ricky's father, to join the family law firm in New York. She never told MI6 that she'd tipped off Ricky Calvert about Soeprapto's banking fraud.

'You've lost a lot of men in your life,' he said quietly.

'Yep, but I can't see why anyone would be interested in David now.'

'You're wrong. David's legacy is bound to excite some interest. They will want to know whether it contains anything that's a threat to national security. Shall we say early next week?' He raised his eyebrows interrogatively then glanced at his watch. 'Good. Now I must be getting along. I've got a train to catch.'

He made straight for the door with an unambiguous intention to leave – no goodbyes, no nods to people he'd talked to. And then he was gone.

7

The Cut

The Jubilee Rooms were being cleared so that they could be made ready for the Eyam dinner. She went up to her room, changed into a pair of jeans, sweater and a short leather jacket but kept what she now regarded as Eyam's scarf. She briefly looked up Kilmartin on the web. A dozen entries appeared under his name, mostly in reference to a recently published book, *The Town of Naram-Sin*, a study of ancient Babylonian and Assyrian cities. Further down a brief item from a newspaper archive gave her the information she needed. Since leaving the Foreign Office, Peter Kilmartin had acted intermittently as the prime minister's special envoy to central Asia and the Caucasus, spending much of that time in Kazakhstan and Uzbekistan, during which he had produced a book about Tashkent called *Stone City*. A number of diplomatic posts were listed, including first secretary to the Tehran Embassy and second secretary in Damascus and between them spells at the Foreign Office Research and Analysis Department. She felt reassured. Like McBride, Kilmartin seemed to be from the school of spy adventurers who went back to the days of the great game in Afghanistan. It was noted by newspaper clippings that Kilmartin spoke Farsi, Turkish, Uzbek and Tajik and had some Pashto. He had founded a small school outside Tashkent with private money.

She left the hotel at six fifteen p.m. Instead of going by the square to Mortimer Street she strolled down to a seat overlooking a section of the town's medieval wall and sat for ten minutes in the gathering dusk. She turned round a few times and listened hard but no one came. It was dark by the time she left the bench and entered The Cut, a passageway that ran between a confusion of old red brick buildings that she had happened upon while walking the town over the weekend. About halfway along she waited in the shadows for five minutes. A sodium light flickered at the far end. A dog barked but no one came. She set off again. Fifty yards on, she slipped into the deserted beer garden at the back of a pub called the White Hart, passed through an empty bar, then exited onto Mortimer Street about twenty yards below number six, the lawyers' offices. There she waited again, as though she was meeting someone. The shops were mostly closed; a roar came from across the street as a youth pulled down a metal shutter on a store window. The lights inside a bank flickered, then were extinguished. There was little traffic, and only a few pedestrians were about.

She walked to number six and pressed a bell above a brass plaque, which announced *Russell, Spring & Company Solicitors, Notary Public, Commissioner of Oaths.* No answer came from the reception. She pushed on the door. It opened and she found herself in a panelled hallway that was hung with horse racing scenes. She looked into the office on her left. At the receptionist's desk, a computer screen was switched off and a note lay on the keyboard. A coat and a mackintosh were on the stand on the other side of the room. She returned to the hallway and listened for a second or two. There was no sound except the hum and ticking of the fluorescent tube that lit a passageway beyond the stairs. She called up to the first floor. 'Mr Russell? I'm sorry I'm so late. Shall I come up?'

No answer came. But then she heard the sound of a table being dragged across the floor.

'Hello?' she called out louder and began to climb the stairs.

Another sound reached her – the unmistakable acceleration of the drawer of a metal filing cabinet being rammed shut. She came to a narrow landing where there was a delicate little table and a vase of dried flowers. 'Mr Russell? Hugh?' she said more quietly. 'It's me. I hope I'm not too late. I can come back tomorrow if you'd prefer.'

Somewhere above her a light was on, but most of the floor was in the dark. There was a weight to the silence, an air of calculation in the building, which made her glance down the stairway to the empty hall. It was at that moment two bulky shapes appeared above her, silhouetted against the lights on the landing. In an instant, one leapt down and

62

threw her against the wall with incredible force, aiming punches to her head and chest, but finding only her lower back. She was on the ground. She curled into a ball and held her head, somehow registering that the little table next to her had broken into pieces as she'd gone down. The man kicked her once, then ran down the stairs shouting for his companion to get out of the building. But this one wanted more. He dropped down beside her, straddled her and rained blows on her, striking the hands that were wrapped round the back of her head, and cursing when his fist connected with Charlie's diamond engagement ring. He was frenzied. 'You fucking bitch, you fucking cunt.' She could feel his arousal through her clothes and realised he might very well kill her. She let go of her head and using all her might twisted beneath him. The torque of her body unbalanced him enough for her to scrabble in the dark for something – anything – to hit him with. A fragment of vase was in her hand and then the splintered leg of the little table, which was still attached to part of the table, but she nevertheless rammed it upwards towards the man's face. She couldn't tell where it hit but he cried out. He tried to grab the leg, then her neck with his big greedy hands, and at that point she knew she would be killed. But then she was aware of the first man thundering back up the stairs and bellowing: 'Leave her. Get the fuck out! Now! Get out of the building – we've got what we came for!'

Suddenly the weight of her assailant was gone and she understood that he had been hauled away by the other man. She rolled away from the wall and began to struggle to her feet, knowing she might have to fight for her life again. But they were crashing down the stairs and a second or two later the front door banged and they were gone. She got up. She felt no pain, just terrible sickness and fear swarming in her mind.

No sound came from upstairs. She picked up her bag and took the stairs three at a time. The two men had come from a large office overlooking the street. The lights were still on and papers were strewn across the floor. In a glance she saw a small pale-green safe with its door open and a leg protruding from behind the desk.

Hugh Russell was out cold. She ran her hand over his body, checking for injuries and found a small patch of damp blood at the back of his head. She reached for the phone, then thought better of it and crouched down to the safe. There were a few folders in the bottom, which contained title deeds, one or two share certificates and some letters written in an unsteady, elderly hand that was certainly not Eyam's. The shelf was empty. She got up and looked around, then went over to the filing cabinet. There was nothing under Eyam's name or her own. She returned to the desk and searched the papers on the floor.

Russell began to groan. She moved to his side. He opened his eyes and raised one arm to shade them from the light. He didn't know what – or who – had hit him. She helped him sit and examined the back of his head. 'God that hurts,' he said.

'Yes, you'll need a couple of stitches. We'll call the ambulance. Just take it easy.'

He stared blankly at the safe. 'So they've got everything?'

'That's where you kept David Eyam's documents?'

He nodded groggily. 'Yes, I took them out of the envelope and left them in there ready for you.' She noticed a key in the safe, still attached to a chain. They had torn it from his belt.

'Was there anything in the filing cabinet?'

'No.'

'What was written on the documents in the safe? I mean, who were they addressed to?'

He tried to think. 'No one – I took them out of the marked file to look over them this afternoon and then returned them to the safe when I came over to the hotel. All the other material addressed to you I gave you this morning.'

So he had read the documents and was so alarmed by their contents that he had come to find her.

'I think we'd better call the police and ambulance. I'll dial, but I want you to speak to them. Just give them the address and say you've been attacked during a break-in.'

When he had finished she replaced the phone and reached for a bottle of water lying on the desk, and handed it to him. He put it to his lips: the plastic bottle made a cracking noise as he gulped.

'OK?' she asked, kneading his shoulder gently. 'The cut is not too

64

bad. It's stopped bleeding. Don't tell the police I was here, but say what was stolen. It's important that this all goes on record. Say it was private material left by the late David Eyam. Was there anything else in the safe?'

'About seven hundred pounds in cash.'

'Are you sure it's gone?'

'Well, look for yourself!' he said testily.

She didn't need to. It was possible that this was just an ordinary burglary, but the voice of the man shouting on the stairs didn't sound like a local thug, and anyone committing a burglary would surely have snatched her bag when it fell to the floor. This was a professional job and the money had been taken to disguise the real purpose of the break-in.

A siren was making its way up the street. 'Is there another way out of here?' she asked.

'Go downstairs and to the back of the building. You'll find a door with the key in the lock. You'll need to slide the bolts top and bottom.' He stopped, revolved his head then rubbed the back of his neck. 'Did you see the man who did it?'

'There were two of them, but let's keep that to ourselves for the moment.' She touched him on the shoulder. 'You're going to be fine; just stay there. I'll be in touch.'

Downstairs she worked the bolts and found herself in an overgrown garden. In the half-light she felt her way to a gate and wrenched it open. There was a path, which she followed down an incline into The Cut. She was shocked but clear in her mind. If the men were professionals, why didn't they wait until the offices were empty and they could take all the time they needed to search Russell's files? In an hour or so they could have broken into the rear of the building and had the place to themselves without risk of disturbance. She knew the answer to her own question. They didn't have the luxury of time because Eyam's files were so important that once they suspected they were in Russell's possession they had to move quickly. It didn't matter who was in the building or what violence had to be used. It was also clear to her that only after Russell had found her at the Green Parrot cafe did they understand

65

where Eyam's documents might be. From the moment since she'd showed her face at the inquest and rather naively entered her name in the register at the door they had been waiting to see who would contact her.

8

Civic Watch

When she entered the hotel she saw that the Jubilee Rooms had been cleared and a long table set up and laid for dinner. At the reception she was handed two envelopes with her key. The first was from Darsh Darshan and contained his card with a note scratched in childish writing. 'Please contact me in person soonest.' The second was an invitation from Mermagen to a nightcap in the bar after dinner.

Once in her room, she undressed and bathed the gash on her anklebone, then examined the bruises on her shoulder and by her left kidney. Eyam's scarf had done something to protect her neck, but there was a bump on the back of her head which, like the grazes on her upper arm and shin, wouldn't show. Violence shocked her and when directed at her made her feel a sense of total astonishment. She recalled the breath and the violence of the man who held her down, and his evident excitement, and hoped that he had been injured by the jab with the chair leg. From the minibar she took a whisky miniature and Canada Dry, which she drank looking out into the night. At least they hadn't got the will or Eyam's letter, and according to Russell, there was nothing on the documents to show who they were intended for, although that would be easily deduced once the will was known about. Though surprising, the will was straightforward enough. The letter, on the other hand, struck her as bizarre and strained. She took out the envelope and ran her finger along the words of the last passage.

The evening I speak of at the start of this note is perfect. I write on a patch of gravel garden in front of the cottage resting on an old metal table, which I inherited when I bought the place. I have a glass of Puligny

Montrachet at my side; a neighbour's dog is making eyes at a bowl of cheese sticks. It has been a very hot day. The sun has set and the sky is bruising a gentle purple in the west. It is just past eight o'clock, and the cuckoos call from the other side of the valley. There are hawks hunting in the dusk above me. As ever, the Dove is their prey. The birds sing but mostly they listen and watch at this time of the day. You will find it all very much behind the times, but I have been happy here.

If you are reading this it means I'm gone. The evening is yours now with all its grandeur and its flaws: you are more than equal to both. Good luck, and look after my books, my beloved Bristol and my garden – especially my vegetable patch.

With my love, David.

Dove Cottage, August 20th.

It was as if someone else had written it. Eyam's prose was fluent and stagey: long sentences with plenty of asides placed between dashes that could try the reader's patience. These staccato eruptions of sentiment weren't him at all. And there was much else that jarred. For a start, Eyam hated dogs and white wine, even when it was very good. Montrachet was *her* favourite wine, not his. She remembered one of his rather obsessive monologues talking about the village of Montrachet on the Côte de Beaune, where he had once found himself looking for a restaurant. The village was dead; the houses had been bought as investments by the wine growers and were empty. There were no shops and no one about. It was like an abandoned film set, a place with no content, waiting for lines to be spoken to give it semblance of life. Montrachet was a fraud and so was its wine, he said.

He also loathed descriptions of sunsets, once saying to her that it was impossible even for a genius to evoke a sunset without seeming like a booby. Sunsets were off limits, as were all love poetry, walks in the moonlight and nightingales.

Which brought her to the cuckoo. She didn't know much about British natural history but she did remember a verse her English grandmother had taught her: '*The cuckoo comes in April, Sings her song in May, Changes tune in the middle of June, And then she flies away.*' The letter was dated in August by which time the cuckoo was well on its way back to Africa. Like the neighbour's dog and the Montrachet, the cuckoo was a fraud. The cheese sticks too. Eyam was allergic to dairy products, particularly cheese. He had once keeled over at Oxford after eating cheese on top of a shepherd's pie.

The sentence 'I kiss your clever eyes for good fortune and the happiness that has not been ours' touched her but she had to admit it didn't sound like Eyam. He simply didn't think that way, at least he never said or wrote such things. So the entire point of the letter was to warn her that he had been watched and that things at Dove Cottage were not as they seemed. It didn't make any sense to her, because the letter was oblique in its meaning yet at the same time obviously coded. She rose and walked around the room, working through the events of the day.

The process of fixing the elements of a problem calmed her because she had a faith, acquired in part from Eyam, that no difficulty existed without a solution: optimism was the prerequisite for civilisation, he used to say. Without optimism humanity was ruled by fear and super-stition. She dressed again, went downstairs and asked the man on reception if she could use the phone. Tony Swift, the coroner's clerk, answered from his usual stool in the Mercer's Arms. They met forty minutes later at a Thai restaurant a five-minute walk from the eastern end of the square, which with various diversions and feints took her the full forty minutes.

'I wonder if I can ask you a few more questions about the inquest,' she said when she sat down.

'Are you all right? You look distraught.'

'I fell over,' she said. 'Bruised my ribs and ankle. About the inquest: can you tell me about it?'

'Off the record, sure.'

'Why was the hearing held here?'

'When Lady Eyam decided she'd have the funeral where her stepson lived, it became a matter for the coroner, because he has jurisdiction if a body lies within his district. We were notified that the remains would eventually arrive in High Castle and so the investigation – such as it was – went ahead.'

'Its purpose being to . . . ?'

'Establish the cause of death.'

'Was there any kind of official interest in this case? Pressure from anyone?'

'What are you asking?'

'Did anyone try to stop you investigating what had happened in Cartagena?'

He eyed her thoughtfully. 'You're asking if I think he was assassinated, aren't you?'

'Well, it's a possibility, surely?'

'No, I spoke to Detective Bautista by phone before the formal interview and he was clear which group planted the bomb and why. They wanted to kill as many as possible in that party headquarters and not David Eyam. Besides, there was no motive to kill Mr Eyam.'

'What if you were told that Eyam had offended certain parties in Britain; would that alter your view?'

He shook his head. 'I knew that he'd had to resign from government. He told me. He made no secret of it. Everyone knew.'

'Was there anything that you discovered that was not submitted as evidence to the inquest?'

'What do you have in mind?'

'The money – Eyam's father's money. He was worth between twenty and thirty million. I happen to know that Eyam did not inherit anything like that.'

'Maybe there wasn't time. After all, they died only a couple of months apart.'

'So you looked into that.'

'No, I read about his death in the papers. I put things together.'

'Come on, Tony, you talked to people. You followed your instincts. I can see it in your eyes.'

He lifted the glass of wine to his lips and ruminated. 'I am not an investigator,' he said eventually.

A procession of small dishes began to arrive, which he marshalled and addressed with the kind of relish that made her think food was a substitute for something missing in big, slow-moving Tony's life.

'The Swedes – what happened to them? And the man who shot the film?'

70

'They were treated for minor injuries and shock and went home.'

'Why didn't you interview them? They might have seen something that the camera didn't pick up.'

'We had the detective. That was all that seemed necessary, but I grant you that the Swedes might have had something to say.'

'Have you got their names? Contact numbers?'

'No, I don't believe we do.'

'That's an odd way to conduct an inquiry.'

'We have limited resources. We do our best.'

'But no one questioned what Eyam was doing in Colombia? Why was that? There is probably no country in the world that would have been less appealing to him, and yet no one thought to ask what he was doing there. It doesn't cost any money to ask a question like that.'

Swift shook his head and mumbled something.

'Did you check with the border police? Did you find out the flights he took? His onward journey? The government collects all that information nowadays.'

'Of course.'

'So you know when and where he left the country.'

'Not exactly. There are no records of his departure.'

'What . . . Jesus, and you didn't produce that at the inquest.'

'It was in no way relevant to his death.'

'But it could have been, Tony. It could have been.' She slammed her palm down on her table. Then she thought for a second. 'Maybe he left using another name.'

'Then why would he check into the Hotel Atlantic under his own name? Apart from the film, that's the reason we know he was involved. The room key: remember? And his passport was returned to Britain.'

There was a silence while Swift concentrated on his food. He encouraged her to join him by waving his fork at the dishes but she told him she wasn't hungry. 'Look,' he said at length, 'David Eyam is dead and we will never know what he was doing in Cartagena, or what he planned to do in his life. It's wrong. It's wrong such a talented and wonderful human being is dead, but sometimes injustice is the nature of things.'

'Sheer fatalism,' she said and ordered a whisky. 'I don't believe that injustice or mystery is the natural order of things. That is why I am a lawyer.' She stopped and waited until she felt she had his attention. 'I heard that Eyam was sick.'

'Really?' he replied without raising his eyes. 'He didn't look ill. I saw him in November at a screening of *The Big Sleep*. He'd lost a bit of weight but he looked fine to me. That was the last time we met.'

'Maybe cancer,' she said. 'Why would anyone suffering from cancer go for a long trip to Colombia? He looked like shit in the film. Wasted. You know what a wonderful physique he had. A rower's build. But in that film . . . Maybe he needed treatment.'

'Whether he was ill, or not, has nothing to do with the coroner's court. Our business is to establish the cause of death, not what someone might die from if they're lucky enough to live to eighty.'

'You know, Tony, I think you're full of it. You come over as this self-effacing guy, this bachelor who eats on his own, a little disappointed maybe, down-trodden.'

'I'm divorced, of course I'm bloody well disappointed and down-trodden.'

'But I know you're different than that.'

'In this country educated people still say different *from*, not different *than*.'

'And I know you're smarter *than* you're letting on. In my job I see a lot of men come into the room and throw their weight around. I never pay any mind to them. The ones I've learned to watch are the people like you. I know you, Tony. I know you asked all these questions yourself and you've gotten more answers than you told them because nobody of your intelligence could have failed to ask them.'

He looked up and shook his head. 'You just said all that in near-perfect American idiom. You know, you could pass for an American. Look, I wish I was the man you describe but I'm not.' His eyes flicked to the door. She turned to see a slim black man looking in their direction. Swift gave a tiny shake of his head and the man vanished.

'A friend?' she asked.

'An associate,' he said. 'It can wait.'

'Maybe Eyam's other friends can help me. Was there anyone special in his life?'

'I wouldn't know.'

'What about his interest in the bell ringers? Did he do any kind of work? Diana Kidd says not, so what the hell *did* he do out here for two years?

'Why are you asking all this?'

'No more diversions – just tell me about his friends,' she said and then she realised that along the way she had struck a nerve because Tony Swift's expression had become several degrees more resistant. 'I met some people at the wake today – Chris Mooney, Evan Thomas and Alice Scudamore. Know any others?'

He began to reel off the names. She looked in her bag for some paper, ignored the envelopes containing the will and the letter, and withdrew the list for the Eyam dinner. On the back she wrote the names of Danny Church, picture framer and sometime journalist; Michelle Grey, a divorcee who lived with the town's best restaurateur; Andy Sessions and Rick Jeffreys, partners in a web design business; Penny Whitehead, a former probation officer now a local councillor and Paul Sutton, a retired publisher who with Diana Kidd was involved in the Assembly Rooms. He told her that Chris Mooney was a portrait photographer and Alice Scudamore a writer.

The contrast between the list for Eyam's dinner and the people he mixed with in High Castle couldn't have been starker. On one side of the piece of paper Mermagen had handed to her during the wake were some of the most powerful people in the land, all of whom knew Eyam well enough for them to travel to his funeral and attend a dinner in his memory; on the other side were his new friends, people you'd find in any provincial town in England making their lives in decent, humdrum obscurity.

Finally Swift wiped his mouth with a napkin and gazed at her with his tongue searching some particle of food lodged in his upper gum.

'What is it? What do you want me to ask you?' she said.

'Anything. It's not often that I am out with such a beautiful woman.'

'These people: I know it sounds snobbish but they all seem a bit, well, underpowered for Eyam.'

'They're good people,' he said firmly. 'And nearly every one of them is suffering because they were friends with Eyam.'

Then he told her with a series of coughs and murmurs that since Eyam's disappearance, all of them had fallen foul of the law or of the tax authorities. It had taken a couple of months for them to put it together, but as he understood things from his friend, Danny Church, their troubles intensified just after the New Year. All were under some kind of investigation or had been charged under new laws, which they didn't know existed.

'What are they doing about it?' she asked.

'What can they do? Most of them *have* broken the law. Penny Whitehead made the mistake of repeatedly writing to some company about global warming and has been charged under the harassment laws. Chris Mooney had his accounts seized. So did Danny Church. Both look as though they will be done for tax avoidance. Alice was an easy target because she's an ID card refusenik. Her property has been repeatedly seized in lieu of fines for not having a card. They always go for her computer so she can't write her books and they do a fair amount of poking about among her personal papers. I heard Rick and Andy have had some trouble with their business, and their premises have been searched.'

'Sounds like someone is looking for something,' she said.

'Could be,' he said. 'But don't you go asking about that. Proceed with caution, Miss Lockhart. Some of the larger circle of friends belong to Civic Watch, and be careful how you use that,' he said, pointing to her smart phone on the table. 'They can listen to any call or read any message or email you send.'

'I know. What the hell is Civic Watch?'

'A quasi-secret network of volunteers – mainly public officials and council employees – who each have a code number. They monitor the communities they live in for signs of anything untoward. They call it "community tension". It's all very informal; a way of passing information up to people who may find it significant. It gives the state another pair of eyes – actually hundreds of thousands of pairs of eyes. I am a member of CW, though not a very active one it has to be said.'

'A network of spies and informers. I've never read anything about this. Why would you want to sign up?'

'There's discreet pressure. It's easier to join and forget the thing exists than have to explain your reasons for not doing so.'

This depressing fact was the last useful information she got out of Tony Swift. She pleaded exhaustion, paid the bill and left him flushed after darting a strictly consoling kiss to a plump and unloved cheek.

At the hotel, Karl was on the desk. When she asked for her room key he said, 'I'm sorry, Miss Lockhart, the hotel management must now insist you comply with the identity regulations.'

'I repeat: you have seen my passport and credit card. What else does the *hotel* need?'

'We need for you to complete this form.' He slid the papers over the desk with a camp backwards movement of his fingers. She glanced down the list of some forty items contained in the ID Supplement Form which included mandatory fields on credit card details, phone numbers, email address, movements over the last month, including any visits to countries of special interest (Russia, Pakistan, Iran, etc.) and destinations during the period of stay in Britain (dates, addresses and telephone numbers all required). At the base of the form was a panel where the respondent was invited to lift the clear plastic strip, moisten their right index finger with a generous amount of their own saliva and place it firmly on the spongy material in the panel, thus allowing their DNA and fingerprint to be recorded without 'any further inconvenience'.

'Can't we just forget it? I'm leaving tomorrow.'

'It's an offence not to complete it,' Karl said. He handed her a pen with her key. 'Just leave it here when you've finished.'

She sat down in the lobby with the form. Her answers showed an uncharacteristic lack of precision and in one or two questions she simply gave false information and made up her telephone numbers and credit card details. When she came to *Biometric Window* she lifted the flap but failed to complete the procedure.

By this time her concentration had wandered to the dinner in the Jubilee Rooms, now visible through a glass door from which a curtain had just been drawn. Her eyes met the heavy gaze of a man in his mid-fifties at the centre of the table, who wore a simple grey suit and a dark-blue and white striped shirt open at the neck. The other men were in dinner jackets. Behind him stood a tall blonde man whom she had seen with Glenny at the wake. Mermagen was leaning into the composition, his expression eager and confidential. On his left, Glenny expounded, and in the foreground two heads nodded in silhouette.

Eden White in chiaroscuro. The few photographs she had seen of him during Calvert-Mayne's defence of Raussig Systems Inc. showed an unexceptional-looking man of average height, understated in dress with slightly hooded eyes, a smile lurching to the right.

Old Sam Calvert once leaned over her desk to look at the photograph on her computer then placed his hand on the screen to cover the right side of his face. 'That's the man we're dealing with,' he growled. 'He's not the pathetic jerk-off he looks.' The corporate raptor came into focus: all the power in his face was concentrated in his left eye. The smile on the right side of his mouth became a neat incision on the left. When Sam removed his hand, a mild-looking insurance executive reappeared. 'He's a remorseless, two-faced, vindictive bastard.'

In the flesh, White was even less impressive than his photograph, though it was evident from the body language and glances of those around him that he held all the power in the room. He was very still; his eyes moved slowly around the group then settled on her again. She couldn't tell whether he was appraising her or simply lost in thought, but then he seemed to nod in recognition, perhaps to himself, before his attention moved to Mermagen, who was clinking a glass for silence. A few seconds later the door was closed and the curtain drawn again, but she could still hear the rumble of Oliver Mermagen making the most of his audience.

She got up and placed the identity form on the empty reception desk with a scribbled note saying she would check out in the morning. Instead of going to her room, of which she was heartily sick, she crossed the stone flags of the lobby to the bar and ordered a drink, which she didn't particularly want, and stared at a huge log smouldering in the grate. She was there about twenty minutes when she heard Mermagen's voice in the hall, which caused her to sink into the button-back leather armchair. His face loomed in the door.

'Ah, there you are, Kate: I've brought Mr White to meet you.'

White was in the doorway. Kate rose and nodded to him. 'Hello, she said. 'Did you enjoy the dinner? David would have been touched, I know.'

Mermagen was looking agitated. Clearly something more was required of her.

'I would offer you a drink but—' she started.

'Yes, I think we have a few minutes. Mr White was interested to know that you were on the other side of the Raussig deal.'

'A minor legal role,' she said.

'You do yourself a disservice,' said White quietly. 'My information is that you devised the strategy – the use of the public relations and lobbying firms, the approaches to government.'

'To match the endeavours of your company, yes, we did, but I am on the legal side. I am a simple lawyer.'

'I know that it isn't true,' he said without smiling and moved to place his hands on the back of the chair in front of her. 'Yes, I believe we do have time to converse with Miss Lockhart . . . Would you tell them, Oliver.' Mermagen nodded and vanished.

'I don't want to delay you,' she said. 'I'm going to bed soon: it's been a long day.'

White sat down in the chair opposite. 'You should have been at our event for David: a most interesting evening. We had one or two informal presentations.'

'David would have *loved* that,' she said with such underlined sarcasm that it was surprising White didn't seem to notice.

'A deep dive on the purpose of modern government.'

Mermagen appeared between them looking anxious and pulled a chair over. 'As you know, Kate, Mr White has been putting most of his energies into government through his consultation business and Ortelius, his think tank.'

Kate nodded. 'But you still have a heck of an empire to run.'

'I've got good people: they look after the day-to-day business, leaving me free for my . . .'

'Strategic interests,' said Mermagen.

'Right,' said Kate.

'Oliver tells me you are looking for a new position.'

'I still work for Calverts. I'm going to their London office after a break.'

'You should consider coming over to us. We are doing a lot of work on the governmental side, repurposing technologies developed in our corporate arm and applying them to social intelligence programmes. Ortelius has been concerned to deliver solutions that help business and government simultaneously under our long-running Government of Insight project.'

'That sounds like a Powerpoint presentation,' she said. 'What the hell does it mean?'

'It means that government know what individuals want before they know themselves.'

She snorted a laugh. Mermagen looked nervously at White. 'You see! I'd be no use to you,' she said. 'I can't even understand what you're saying. How can the government know what I want before I know myself?'

'Your behavioural patterns: what people of the same generation, social class, income bracket, beliefs and expenditure want will, ninety-nine point nine per cent of the time, tell us what you want.'

'I doubt it,' she said.

'It is a fact. Government is now learning to read the public in the way corporations like mine have been doing for a long time, and that can only lead to good outcomes, better understanding between the governed and those who govern.' He continued with a ten-minute speech full of gristly little abstractions and jargon that was delivered with an accent that oscillated between a functional American management drone and a South African sports commentator. What the hell had Eyam seen in him?

White had good recall, yes, and a certain chilly mental organisation, but Sweet Jesus the man was such a bore and, despite his hard, rather plain face, he seemed vain too. It was her father who had pointed out to her that people obsessed with Napoleon Bonaparte were often psychologically flawed. In Napoleon's self-aggrandising, unprincipled, bloodletting ambition they recognised their own amorality, though it was disguised as something altogether more noble. She remembered now that during the Raussig defence they discovered almost nothing on his

78

personal life: a wife and family long dispensed with, few friends, no culture, and no interest apart from this obsession with Napoleon. There were no skiing or yachting or hunting pictures in the White album. Just White on a dais and White arriving at Bohemian Grove in California for his annual misanthropic jamboree with the boys or at the Sun Valley Conference with media and banking moguls. White became American and connected to the most powerful men in American business very quickly indeed, but you didn't get the impression that his company was sought after. The research department could not work out whether there was a vast secret to White's life or if he was simply a dismal modern success story.

The bare facts were these. Born in South Africa to an engineer of Russian Jewish extraction and an English mother, White changed his name from Riazanov soon after leaving South Africa and finding work for a Bombay-based trading company in Kenya. He rose quickly to a position of trust, which he used to lease planes on behalf of the company. On the outward or return journey, the plane always carried White's own shipments – anything from arms to rare metals such as indium and tantalum. He made a tidy fortune, particularly as he seemed to be able to tap in to supplies that were not available to other companies. This period came to an abrupt end when one of the planes was discovered with twenty crates of small arms on the way to the Congo. Plane and cargo were impounded. White skipped Nairobi. Aged twenty-four he entered Lausanne Business School using a forged degree certificate and a reference from the Faculty of Commerce at the University of Cape Town, also forged. Two years later he turned up in Las Vegas with an MBA working for Saul Carron, the casino and entertainment magnate. White never stayed long in any job. He learned fast, took what he could and moved on. By thirty he had bought his first business, a supermarket chain in the Midwest, then he moved quickly into systems, after realising the importance of customer databases. At this time he became known as The Grinder for his remorseless and punitive business methods. There were periods when he seemed to be consciously softening his image by following Saul Carron's example and making large charitable donations as well as ingratiating himself with legislators by financing their pet projects. But it didn't work for him on the Raussig deal. Calverts and their attack dogs threw up enough dirt to panic the government into finding another buyer, which even Kate admitted was no better qualified than Eden White.

Perhaps aware that she hadn't been listening, White leaned forward and touched her arm. 'We can work together I believe, Miss Lockhart. I have come to love this country – to see a lot of good and some great people who've got much to contribute. Let's be in touch.' He got up, buttoned his jacket and left with a bleak little grin. This caught Mermagen by surprise. By the time he struggled out of his chair White had left.

'He likes you,' he whispered. 'It's those foxy oriental looks of yours, Kate.'

'Oh that's great news. Do me a favour, Oliver, and tell *Mister* White that I'm a dyke.'

'I'm serious, Kate. Someone with your brains could go a long way with White. He owns so much and he's *the* influential person in the private sector in the UK at the moment. It's just the sort of change you're looking for. I'll keep you posted.'

'Don't, Oliver: I am not interested.' She put down the drink she had resorted to while White spoke and got up. 'I'm going to bed.'

At any other time she might have blamed Ella, the Romanian maid, who cleaned her floor and in the evening was responsible for turning down the bed, switching on the bedside light, placing a scented candle on the dresser and chocolate mints on the pillows. More than once she had contrived to allow a mint to slip between the pillows, and Kate had found it in the morning, warm and compressed in its gold foil. The candle was lit but the mints had been put on the bedside table behind the phone, one on top of the other. Ella might have left them there, but it was also possible that someone had removed them to search the bed and forgotten to return them to the little depressions in the pillows.

Charlie used to say she ordered her possessions to withstand military inspection at any hour of the day, which was almost true, and it was why she now looked around the room, alert to a disturbance that could be described as no more than a change in the barometric pressure. If the room had been searched, it had been done by experts. Except for the mints there was no other sign. She went to the desk and looked down at the small laptop. She knew the battery was still out of juice because she'd failed to leave it on charge. So no one could have found anything on that unless they had plugged it in. She checked the lead in the computer case, but it was bunched and held together by a wire tie that she wound in a particular way. The big red folder containing information on the hotel had been moved, again possibly by Ella, and the usual effects of the drawers in a hotel room – the hair dryer, bible, notepaper and pen – might have been rearranged but she couldn't be sure. She opened the doors of the wardrobe, causing the unused hangers to knock into each other and emit the sound of a wind chime, rifled through the trousers, cardigans and sweater and the three jackets, all of the same chic, utilitarian business cut. There was only one mistake: the herring-bone she'd worn to the funeral was on the left instead of the right of the rail and a little of the dark-grey lining protruded like the tip of a tongue from the right-hand pocket. The room had been searched but nothing important had been found because the will and Eyam's note were in her handbag.

She pulled out her cell phone, switched it on and dialled the hand-written number on Darsh Darshan's card. A female voice asked her to leave a message for Darsh. Without giving her name, she said, 'I'm calling on Tuesday evening in response to your note. You remember where we first met? Can you be there at noon on Thursday *or* Friday? Indicate which by text. Don't call.'

9

Dove Cottage

They left High Castle and followed the river road to the west. The brief panorama across the Marches of Wales with all its fairytale promise was soon lost to them as they plunged into a landscape of modest hills and rounded valleys delineated by ancient hedgerows, coppiced stands of hazel, woods of alder, beech and ash. The mild beauty gave no hint that the land was dotted with sites of unspeakable violence and treachery, pointed out by Hugh Russell, who turned out to be an expert on the Wars of the Roses and went into the bloody detail of a skirmish at a bridge they crossed. He drove sporting a small bandage at the back of his head and a bruise on his cheekbone and once or twice assured her that despite the advice of the hospital he was quite well enough to show off his new silver Audi estate.

She kept an eye on the road behind them but nothing showed in the mirror as they approached Watling Street, the old road that once served the western border posts of the Roman Empire, and took a turning north. This led them to a narrow lane, which was cut through steep wooded banks and rose to a summit where there was a gate that announced Dove Cottage. The way was blocked by a herd of cattle being driven along the track by a young man on a quad bike, who did not acknowledge them.

'Bugger,' said Russell. 'I've been caught behind this lot a few times before. We'll just have to wait.'

She began gently. 'David didn't go straight to Cartagena: did he tell you where he was going before?'

He shook his head.

'But he must have mentioned it to you. I mean, when he was drawing up the will you would surely have seen him?'

'Yes, once or twice, but always for lunch at the pub. This was some time before he left in December. But he said nothing about his plans.'

'Do you know who his doctor was?'

He shook his head vehemently. 'No.'

The car crept fifty yards down the track to the point where the cattle had reached. The sun lit a bank of moss and flowers to their right.

'I haven't seen primroses for years.' She paused and turned to him. 'Hugh, I know you saw some of the material that was taken.'

He stared at the cows for a long time before answering. 'Has it occurred to you that if they wanted it so badly it's a damned good thing they've got it? You shouldn't mess with these people.'

'What would you have done if you hadn't found me? What were your instructions?'

'To send the documents anonymously to the newspapers – a liberal newspaper.'

'And you would have done that?'

'Probably, yes. If . . .'

'If you hadn't seen any of it?'

He shook his head. 'I'm not saying that.'

'Technically those documents are mine and now they've been taken you probably have a duty to tell me what was in them.'

'I can't.'

'There are good reasons for telling me, which you may not appreciate.'

'Maybe, but that's not my judgement.'

'Think about it,' she said.

'I have a duty to legality as well as to my client, and in this case I feel I must favour the first.' Russell had reverted to the stuffy provincial solicitor.

She leaned forward so that she could look him in the eye. 'Was it legal to walk into your offices and bludgeon you to the ground and steal the contents of your safe? That's very serious criminality, Hugh.'

'Yes, but one offence cannot be used to justify another. You see what's happened to the others.'

'The others?'

He was silent.

'You're talking about the group? I heard a few people were having trouble, all of them connected with Eyam in some way. Sounds all a bit hysterical to me.'

He was drumming the steering wheel: he felt trapped. 'Yes. My partner, Paul Spring, acts for three of them. They're all being put through the wringer in one way or another.'

'Which ones?'

'A couple of web designers, Andy Sessions and Rick Jeffreys, and a young woman called Alice Scudamore.'

'Look, Hugh, I need to know what I've inherited along with Dove Cottage. I didn't choose to be David's heir. What am I getting myself into? I must know in order to defend myself.'

'Your best defence is to know nothing,' he snapped. A beat later he smiled regretfully. 'I wish I was in the same position.'

One of the cows had turned and was making for the car. Russell got out and flapped his arms at the animal until it wheeled round to join the rest of the herd.

'You told me you didn't come out here to see David, yet a few minutes ago you said you'd been caught behind these cows several times before. So clearly you did come here.'

'You're right, I did, but after he vanished in the winter. Something was going on. Nock, the man who looks after the place, rang to say that the house had been searched. You'll meet Sean Nock at some stage. I kept him on after David's death to make sure the place was safe.'

'Searched by whom?'

'He didn't know, but there were about six of them. He got the impression it was all official.'

'Do you know the exact date?'

'It was the week beginning January 28th or Feb 4th, I am not sure. But I have a note of it at the office.'

'So, that was after David had been killed. Was anything missing?'

'How were we to know? Everything looked all right to Nock. Nothing obvious seemed to have been disturbed.'

The cows were being coaxed through a gateway to their left. Russell edged past the remaining heifer. The track rose and then plummeted to a short gravel driveway and a house that was almost hidden behind trees. They parked next to a Bristol saloon, which was half-covered by a green tarpaulin.

'May I offer some advice?' he said before getting out. 'David has left you something that was dear to him. It's very special. Enjoy it and forget this other business. It's got nothing to do with you now. David is dead. It can only bring you trouble. Let it go.' His eyes pleaded with her. 'I mean it, Kate.'

She looked up at the end of the long, slender building of dark brick and timber. 'OK. Why don't you show me around?'

'What you're looking at now is the original cottage. The dogtooth pattern of the bricks dates to about 1604 – the year that Shakespeare wrote *Othello*. We have all the documentation on the house since it was built, which is quite rare. Needless to say, David organised it all in a binder, which is somewhere inside.'

He led her round to the front by a gravel path. The cottage was surprisingly large with a run of eight small windows along the front and a two-storey extension, added to the far end during the nineteenth century. She peered inside but couldn't see much. Russell touched her on the elbow and showed her the view over the bowl of the Dove Valley. 'It's one of the most perfect spots in England. I've lived in this area all my life but I never knew of it until David came here.'

She glanced at an old green table and thought of Eyam writing his weird note to her, then walked to the end of the garden and looked across the valley. Dove Farm lay below like a child's drawing. Sounds of geese and sheep were borne to her on the updraft that rattled the bare branches of trees around the garden. To her right at the head of the valley was a large wood that was showing the first pale washes of spring. Before that an orchard of apple and pear trees about the size of a tennis court. Little moved. Apart from the abandoned farm equipment scattered over a remarkably wide area, there were few signs of modern life. No telegraph poles or phone masts. She shivered at the ancient stillness of the place. 'Jesus, what the hell does someone do here alone in winter?'

'It has its charms,' Russell said.

'They're not immediately obvious.'

Inside, the cottage had the familiar feel of all Eyam's homes. She recognised several pieces of furniture – a Queen Anne chest of drawers, a large sofa piled with old tapestry cushions, four original prints by the photographer James Ravilious, a black and white portrait of the pianist Glenn Gould hanging over his collection of Gould's recordings, drawings by Henry Lamb and Paul Nash, a high-backed armchair beside which was a footstool with several books piled on it. His library occupied two walls of the large sitting room and an airy passageway to the kitchen. The run of titles were organised as they had been in his London flat, by subject then alphabetically. Along one end of the sitting room books were stacked neatly in half a dozen piles.

'Books are like shoes and spectacles,' Russell observed quietly. 'They carry something of the person long after their owner has gone.'

'Or make the void more obvious.' She folded her arms against her sadness. 'It's my impression he's got more books than he had before.'

'That's how he spent most of his time during the winter evenings. I never knew anyone who read so widely or retained so much from what he read.'

When they had toured all the upstairs and the kitchen he asked, 'What are you going to do with it all?'

'God knows. I can't possibly live here. I mean, what would I do in the English countryside?' She stopped. 'I guess I'll have to sell it.' Her eyes came to rest on a desk and computer in the sitting room. 'And you say that doesn't work – that he had to use your laptop?'

'Er . . . yes. It kept on losing stuff, apparently.'

She darted a look at him. He ignored her and picked up a ringbinder file that was lying on the desk. 'In this you've got all the details about the man who services the boiler, the heating engineer, the broadband connection, et cetera. The cleaner's wages. It's all here, together with the service and council tax bills. You will need to reimburse me on some of them, and the cleaner's and Nock's money.'

'Yes, the man Nock.'

'Sean Nock. He lives in Nestor, a sort of hippy encampment a mile or so from here. He has a mobile if you need anything. In fact I'll try to get him down here to meet you. He's kept the car battery charged and has given the car what he calls a service, though I don't know what that entails. By the way, you will need to register the transfer of ownership: my secretary can arrange temporary motor insurance for you today.'

He left her and went to make a call from a spot at the end of the garden where he knew his cell phone worked. Remembering one of Eyam's obsessions, she went into the kitchen, searched for and found an unopened bag of Blue Mountain Grade One coffee beans. She shook them into the grinder, in her mind hearing Eyam descant on the difference between Blue Mountain Grade One and Blue Mountain 'Triage' which apparently included three smaller grades of beans. 'It's altogether like drinking bark,' he pronounced.

She made them a cup of black coffee each and sat down at a pine table to wait for Russell. Her eyes travelled around the room imagining Eyam eating alone in the kitchen with a book propped up in front of him. And then she froze and had to stop herself springing up to go through the open door of the utility room, where her subconscious had been registering a particular arrangement for some time, because she heard Russell coming down the passageway.

But it was not Russell. A tall man with blonde hair and stubble, wide cheekbones and grey eyes appeared in the kitchen doorway. He was wearing a checked shirt worn over several others, baggy denims and boots. 'Ah,' he said rather stupidly. 'Mr Russell here?'

'He's making a phone call out in the garden. Are you Sean Nock?'

'Yes, Nock from Nestor.' He came across the flagstones leaving wet imprints of his boots and offered her a hand, which he then withdrew and wiped on his jeans because it was covered in oil.

'Nock of Nestor – that sounds like something out of the medieval England that Mr Russell talked about on the way here.'

'Did he tell you about the battle in the valley?'

'No.'

'It was down at the brook. A whole lot of soldiers were slaughtered here before they could join up with the House of York forces at High Castle. The man at Dove Farm still digs up bits of equipment, most of it rusted.'

'So you've been looking after things here. Thank you.'

'And now it's yours. Mr Russell told me you'd be over. It's a sweet place to have as your own.'

'Despite the association with bloodshed and death,' she said, still smiling.

'You'll soon be able to smell the blossom from the orchard and there's nowhere quieter.'

'Yes,' she said, her eyes travelling back to the arrangement in the utility room. 'Did you work for David full time?'

'On and off. We installed the turbine on the stream above the house together and we were working on wind generation. I'm an engineer by training. Well, sort of.' He looked out of the window.

'Coffee? It's just made.'

'No, better be going. Got an appointment. When you need me to go over everything, my number's on the board.'

Hugh Russell came in wearing his default expression of fretful distraction, and after more of the routine English awkwardness – the muttering, unfinished sentences and hesitant body language that Kate had become so aware of on her return from the United States, Nock loped off leaving Russell standing there patting down his hair.

'What would you say if I stayed here tonight?' she asked brightly.

Russell looked in the direction of Nock's departure as if to ask whether it was Nock who'd changed her mind.

'I've got all my luggage with me. Are you OK to drive back to High Castle without me?'

'Sure. That's a very good idea indeed. It would be wrong to give The Dove up without really getting the feel of the place. And tomorrow you can always phone for a taxi.'

They sat down with the coffee. She laid a hand on his and felt the instinctive withdrawal but kept it there. 'Hugh, I need to know what you read in those papers.'

He shook his head.

'Tell me what you saw,' she said softly.

'Well, there wasn't much – an executive summary like the beginning of an official report. I thought it was a government paper of some sort at first. I read the first few paragraphs and stopped at that.'

'What did they say?'

'They outlined what he claimed to be a kind of takeover of British government by big business; the influence of these corporations was distorting government and they were secretly running the things that would normally be left to the civil service. Really there's nothing new in that. The newspapers have been saying it for a long time.'

'And?' she said, revolving her hand and smiling.

'There was some kind of system – ASCAM or ASCAN. It monitors people.'

'What else?'

'He talked about the inquiry of a parliamentary committee; I forget which one: ASCAM – or whatever it was – was formally denied by the government. A lie had been told. David was misled and in turn he had misled the committee and now he was setting the record straight.' He stopped. 'That's the gist of it.'

'Did he specify which corporations?'

'No, I didn't see any names I recognised.'

'How did he couch this? As one corporation, or many?'

Russell held up his hands in defence. 'I'm sorry, I . . .' He looked round doubtfully, as though to ask whether they should be talking in Dove Cottage.

'I think we're OK here,' she said. 'Eyam is dead. They've obviously been over every inch of the place and cleaned everything out.'

Russell didn't look reassured.

'Was there a table of contents in the report?'

'No, I don't think so.'

She let go of his hand. He sprang up and she followed him outside and removed her luggage from the Audi. He caressed Eyam's car affectionately and told her that the temporary cover had been fixed for her to drive it. 'She's a beautiful old thing.'

Kate nodded, wondering why cars were always female. 'Are you sure you're OK to drive back?'

'Yes, I'll be fine,' he said. 'Look, let's keep the conversation we had in there to ourselves.'

'Of course! Drive carefully. We'll speak tomorrow.'

He got into the Audi and smiled before the worry returned to his face and he drove away with a wave.

*

The three items she'd spotted stood alone on a shelf in the utility room, above two recycling bins: a bottle of Puligny Montrachet 2001, a box of dog biscuits and a cylindrical container of Italian cheese sticks. Propped up behind them was a postcard of a sunset. She took out Eyam's letter to her and read the last part aloud: '*I write on a patch of gravel garden in front of the cottage resting on an old metal table, which I inherited when I bought the place. I have a glass of Puligny Montrachet at my side; a neighbour's dog is making eyes at a bowl of cheese sticks. It has been a very hot day. The sun has set and the sky is bruising a gentle purple in the west. It is just past eight o'clock.*'

She picked up the containers in turn and examined each one – there was nothing unusual about any of them – then returned them to the shelf in their original order and looked at the postcard of a sunset over Skye, which she held up to the light. Nothing was written on the back and there was not the slightest indentation on the card's surface. The image itself seemed to hold no particular significance. She stood back to ponder the configuration, then looked into the recycling bins below, where Eyam had separated plastic and paper. Nothing. What the hell was he playing at? She poked around behind the boiler, felt beneath the shelf and searched along a skirting board but found nothing. Deciding to let the problem settle in her mind, she withdrew to look over the rest of the house.

Upstairs she lay on the clean white bedspread and gazed across the valley, propped up on one arm. She wondered what it would be like to wake to the reflected light on the ceiling each morning with Eyam beside her. The sense of him in the room was so strong that suddenly she could not think of him as dead but merely absent, and that overwhelmed her with a sudden sense of present love, which she tried to dismiss by again telling herself that Eyam was a selfish prig. A sweater and a pair of trousers were folded over the back of a chair; pairs of shoes were lined up by a wardrobe; a book lay on the bedside table. She swung her legs from the bed and went to the bathroom, where she laid out a few of her things and looked at herself in a shaving mirror that was fixed to the wall on a concertina bracket. Her skin was still firm and healthy but the magnification of the mirror showed the lines at the corners of her mouth and eyes. When did she get to look so tough? She grimaced at the effect and pushed the mirror away angrily. It sprang back and the disc spun round to reveal three photographs wedged into the rim of the flip side. She remembered the occasion immediately. They had been celebrating Eyam's award of the John Hicks Economics prize, a large group that started out with three punts on the Cherwell and moved to a sprawling picnic amongst the cow's parsley on Christ Church Meadow. Later just the three of them posed on a bench in front of the evergreen oak in the medieval cloisters of New College – her, Eyam and a tipsy-looking Darsh, and for some reason all wearing caps. She pulled the picture from the rim and the two others that were lodged behind it fell into the sink. One was of a group standing and sitting along a felled tree in a clearing in a wood. On the back was written, 'Some bell ringers'. She recognised five faces from the wake, including Alice Scudamore and Chris Mooney. Why had he given these people £125,000 in his will?

The third showed Eyam and Kilmartin at a reception in a garden. A modern brick building was in the background. Kilmartin did not smile but acknowledged the camera with a tolerant reserve that somehow reduced his presence to that of an onlooker without association to either photographer or fellow subject. The caption on the back read, *With 'Emile' – Peter Kilmartin, the man for every problem – Dinner at St Antony's College, Oxford, July 1999.*

The freshness of the colour of the first print suggested the photographs had not been wedged in the mirror for very long. Clearly Eyam was telling her something – maybe that all these people could be trusted. She took the photographs down to the computer in the sitting room with an idea that she might find the images on the screen, or maybe even determine when he had printed them off.

She turned the machine on with a vague feeling of trespass, but remembered what he had said. *All my earthly goods are now yours: my secrets too. Think of nothing as too private for your eyes. I am opening myself to you.* There was very little on the desktop, no files in the hard disk and a quick search of the email folders showed that nothing had been sent, received or deleted for a very long time. But since Eyam's broadband service still appeared to be working, she went online and typed in the word ASCAM. One reference on an American security website told her that ASCAMS stood for Automatic Selection

Correlation and Monitoring System. That would tie in with what Russell had told her.

It was two thirty. She took a walk on the hill above the cottage, passing on the way the newly installed water turbine on one of the torrents that ran down the hill. At the summit was an ancient barrow and it was from there that she dialled the office number of Isis Herrick, a friend of hers working in the British Mission at the United Nations. They'd seen each other a few times in New York, having met on a course in London more than a decade before. After Charlie's death, Herrick took Kate out for lunch and was candid about the life of a single woman working for SIS abroad. It was lonely and everyone in the embassy assumed you were available for sex, even the married men, and that made the job difficult.

Isis answered after she was put through by the switchboard and after an inquiry about Herrick's baby, Kate asked, 'Know a place called Kilmartin?'

'Yes, I think I know the place you mean,' Isis said. 'Why do you want to know?

'I'm thinking of a visit.'

'Right . . . well, I haven't been there lately but it's a reliable spot, very interesting and there's a lot to see. The best part is that it's very well-connected yet always so quiet. I can't recommend it more highly, Kate.'

'Really? This is a very important break I'm planning.'

'All I can say is I'd bet my life on it. The place is unique and totally dependable, but it does take a while to get to know.'

She hung up and dialled directory enquiries to get the number for St Antony's College, Oxford. The woman who answered in the Middle East Centre volunteered that Kilmartin was in London doing a broadcast for the BBC World Service about his book. She'd take a message and see that he got it by the end of the day. Kate told her that she was calling about the seed catalogues and left her name, but not her number.

She returned to the screen to research the best estate agents for the area. Just then, in the top of her field of vision she saw a large grey bird flash past the windows. A second later there was an explosion of small birds from the direction of some bird feeders at the end of the garden.

She sprang to the window to see a trail of feathers hanging in the air and the hawk make off with its prey towards the orchard. She moved to the front door to see where it went. Across the valley a patch of sunlight expanded and rushed towards her. Around the garden the wet branches of the trees glistened in the new light. Spring was in the air. She inhaled deeply and felt something of the magnificence of the place Eyam had left her. But how on earth did he expect her to live here? She turned and noticed an inscription above the door, *Le paradis terrestre est où je suis,* Paradise is where I am – a quote from Voltaire, which Eyam used to enter in people's visitor books, as though to say earthly paradise always happened to be where he was.

She returned to the computer and saw that when she'd jumped up to see the bird she had accidentally opened the computer's internet history. She began to scroll through the entries that went back to the previous autumn. The most recent date shown for a search was on November 22nd, when a dozen or so sites were visited, all of them connected with Goa or Sri Lanka. Had he been thinking of going east rather than to Central America? Or perhaps he suspected that his movements and communications were being observed and had left a false trail with the searches. She would never know and moreover, she told herself, it didn't matter. Nevertheless she continued to look at the history of searches. On November 14th and 15th he had used a train timetable, visited a site specialising in recordings of ancient music, read the *New York Review of Books* online, browsed through the lists of a second-hand bookseller named Hammonds, and consulted two American political blogs.

She was about to close up the history when she came to the drop-down lists for October 10th and 12th. Both contained hundreds of individual sites with coded headings or titles that meant nothing to her. She opened one that actually had a name: AppleOfMyEye. A magenta-coloured home page appeared with a postage-stamp picture of a child, which was quickly replaced by a panel demanding a pass-word, credit card details and an email address. She moved down the list. Each website was the same. Image after image flashed up, then was withdrawn as the site was blocked, either by the search engine or the absence of a password. But in these fleeting shots she saw enough to know she was looking at child pornography – hundreds of children, bewildered, lost, agog, splayed, crouching, sad, held fast in the dark ocean of adult depravity.

'Jesus Christ!' she murmured and without thinking turned the computer off and yanked the cable from the machine. 'Eyam didn't do this,' she said to herself. 'He couldn't do that – it isn't him.'

She sat back and gazed at the blank screen. The only answer was that the websites and those appalling images had been placed on his computer to incriminate him. What could be a simpler way of neutralising him? A middle-aged bachelor in a remote cottage with child pornography downloaded onto his computer, his credit card details stored like the images in his hard drive, would make conviction a certainty. The shame attached to the arrest, never mind prosecution, would discredit anything he had to say.

She stood up and headed towards the end of the garden to call Russell. Before she reached the spot where she'd seen him use his phone she heard a cry and saw Nock running down the drive. He leaped a low ornamental box hedge and ran towards her, pursued by a terrier and a lurcher.

'Is that a phone you've got there?' he called out. 'It's urgent.'

'What's happened?'

'It's Mr Russell.'

'What's happened?'

'There's been an accident. He's in his car. Across the road at the end of the track.' He stopped, his chest heaving. 'I think he's dead.'

10

A Wonderfully Private Institution

Peter Kilmartin rose from the small table in the stacks of the St James's Library where the new volume on the Akkadian language had absorbed him for the past hour. The book still lay open at a colour image of the bronze head of King Sargon. Kilmartin had always been convinced it was in fact a portrait of Naram Sin, one of the builders of the city of Nineveh and the subject of his own book. But identification seemed to matter less after the head had vanished in the looting of the Iraqi National Museum in Baghdad, which had been a moment of near physical anguish for him. The loss in those first weeks of the war over a decade before was incalculable – the jewellery from the royal tombs at Ur, tablets containing the first written poetry and one of the earliest accounts of the Flood, thousands and thousands of objects that had not yielded their secrets.

On the facing page was a map of Assyria superimposed on modern-day Iraq. Kilmartin stared at it, thinking about the fate of the antiquities of Mesopotamia. On the whole he liked Americans, but the trouble was not one of their bloody generals knew that if you sank a shaft at the site of Nineveh, outside the modern city of Mosul, you would travel nearly a hundred feet down before hitting virgin soil – a hundred feet that took you back to the invention of agriculture and the very first cities in the history of mankind. They parked their bloody tanks in the oldest civilisation of the world, and pleading military priorities and a kind of unembarrassed folksy ignorance, let the sacking of the museum commence.

His gaze moved to the rooftops on the western side of St James's Square. He'd do better to concentrate on the young woman he was about to meet. She didn't know what he wanted and after serving eighteen months in prison she would certainly be on her guard against being trapped. He hoped his friend the priest would reassure her.

He picked up the volume, tugged the light switch and walked to the end of the stacks in near darkness, his feet ringing out on the metal plates. Through the grid of the floor and the ceiling above him he could see one or two people working at small tables, or searching the bookshelves. He thought of King Ashurbanipal's great library at Nineveh and was somehow certain that it possessed the same bookish calm. He loved this place, particularly the stacks, which he thought far superior to the library's Reading Room. That was for people who wanted to sleep or work – not to think.

Before reaching the end shelves he dropped down and pulled a book from the bottom shelf and looked at the lending record at the front. It had been taken out three times since 1995. That wasn't good enough. Eventually he found one with a clean page, noted down its title and the library code on the spine and, having placed a postcard of a Samuel Palmer watercolour at page 150, returned it to the shelf. He left the stacks, stooping as he went through the door to join the carpeted stairway down to the hall. *Ishtar's Tongue* – not a felicitous title, by any means – was stamped at the desk where he had a few words with Carrie Middleton, who had been there as long as he could remember and occasionally stored one or two items for him in the rare books safe. He didn't leave immediately, but instead waited by the entrance for a cab to drop someone off at this corner of the square. The walk to St Mary's Church was no more than a few minutes, but taking a cab meant his journey was unlikely to be monitored. Even though he was working for the prime minister he'd rather not leave a footprint.

The drop-in centre at St Mary's crypt was stuffy and lit by strip lighting. The Reverend Roger Hopkins, his oldest friend, sat at a table in a dog collar and worn leather jacket with the young woman. As Kilmartin approached a small, sharp face looked up to search his without embarrassment.

'Hello there,' said Hopkins, throwing himself back. 'Coffee?'

'Tea, I think,' said Kilmartin. 'Thank you.'

'This is Peter – the man I was telling you about.'

'The spook,' said the woman with undisguised hostility.

'And this is Mary,' continued Hopkins.

'I've been retired,' said Kilmartin pleasantly, 'for quite some time now.'

'Once a spook . . .'

'That is what they say.' He paused. 'It's very good of you to agree to talk to me.'

'I'm not here to talk, just listen.'

'Fine, I am very happy to—'

'I want to know. Are you trying to set me up? I did my time. I lost everything – job, career, boyfriend, flat. It's total bloody shite, you know? My friends won't have anything to do with me. It's like I've got leprosy. I can't find work and I'm watched the whole fucking time. I wish I'd never got dragged into this business.'

In the unforgiving light of the crypt her face possessed an extreme, martyred beauty. She was short – no more than five foot two – with natural dark-brown hair and brown eyes. Her hands moved restlessly, sometimes seeking the shelter of the sleeves of her jersey.

'But as I understand it *you* contacted David Eyam,' he said quietly. 'You got in touch after the first committee hearing. Isn't that right?'

She shrugged. 'That's not true, not that it matters now he's dead.'

'I haven't come here to offer you sympathy, salvation or even a means of revenge, but I do believe that we share a concern and I hope to be able to do something about that by bringing to light some of what you gave our friend.'

'I can't tell you anything.'

Hopkins reappeared with the tea. 'I expect a healthy donation to the centre for all this, Peter,' he said jovially. 'It's very quiet here at this time; you shouldn't be disturbed.' He went off to deal with a young man who had slumped across a table at the far end of the crypt.

'You don't look fifty-five,' she said. 'More like late forties. Are you sure you aren't in government service?'

'I'm fifty-seven actually and feel it. Any illusion to the contrary is due to good genes. I have some Basque blood swimming about me.'

She appraised him. 'I had a visit last week. They came to tell me that if I said anything I would be put back in jail or prosecuted under the

97

Official Secrets Act *again* and given a longer sentence. My family couldn't take that. I'm taking a risk just talking to you.'

He nodded. 'Look, I have a certain remit. Let's call it an assignment from the very top. And that will explain to anyone who wants to know what I am doing talking to you. You're not the only one.'

'You write books,' she said accusingly. 'I looked you up.'

'Not on your own computer, I hope,' he said quickly.

'I'm not that stupid.'

'Good,' he said. 'I am at a slight disadvantage in all this. I was out of the country for the period of our friend's exit from government and then your prosecution. I missed most of it and because there was nothing in the media I'm afraid I was not aware of what was going on until a long time afterwards.'

'And now Mr Eyam's dead,' she said, sitting back and folding her arms. 'I mean, you have to admit it all looks pretty convenient.'

He gave a shake of his head. 'That's not my style.' He paused to drink his tea. 'Let me just remind myself about your part in all this.'

'Still,' she said, unwilling to leave the subject, 'they could have got someone else to do it – favour for favour. A shipment of cocaine overlooked, et cetera, et cetera. Nobody is exactly beating their chest over David Eyam's death. He's out of the way. He can't cause any trouble now.'

'Can I make an assumption? You were a high flyer. You must have been for them to entrust you with this information . . . with this project.' He had added that wording hopefully. 'But you see I'm at a disadvantage because I don't know what it was. There's no trace of a mention in the House of Commons Intelligence and Security Com-mittee Annual Report, but then of course you wouldn't expect that because—'

'Because the prime minister *with the consultation of the committee* excludes part of the report that would be prejudicial to the discharge of the functions of the intelligence agencies,' she said as though reciting something dull in class.

'Exactly,' said Kilmartin, saluting her good memory with a nod. 'And because the hearings are held in private there is no Hansard record. No journalists' notes. Nothing to say what was discussed in that committee.'

'So you've got nothing?'

'Well, there are the members of the committee of course, but a glance down the list tells you that none of the nine is sufficiently onside to encourage an approach of the sort I have in mind. Yet they must have been interested in order for them to ask Eyam about this *project* in the first place. If the thing were so off limits, the chairman, who is very much the prime minister's man, would have put a stop to it. So, I conclude that there was a move in the committee to examine whatever it was that you knew about, a move that may have been secretly frustrated.'

'Look, this isn't doing anything for me. I'm going.'

'Please don't, Mary,' he said firmly. 'We both understand how important this is. I am asking you to stay and hear me out.' She sat back and looked the other way. 'You said you were working for someone at the top. Why should I talk to you?'

'I told you that so you would know there was a way we could both explain this conversation if ever you or I were asked about it. Look, I was a friend of David Eyam's. I had complete faith in his judgement. I believe that what he and you did was the right thing.'

'Not in the eyes of the law.'

Kilmartin offered her a look of regret. 'I have managed to get hold of most of the transcript and I realise going through your case that you were not charged with passing anything to him; that there was no evidence that you ever met or communicated in anyway. But your lawyer made little of this.'

All the tension and angularity of her being flared in her eyes. 'Don't be so fucking dumb. You're missing the whole point. I was charged with copying certain documents and information; that was enough to send me to jail. They didn't have to prove that I passed the information to someone in order to demonstrate I was in breach of the Official Secrets Act. The mere act of copying was enough because it showed intent.'

'Are you saying you never met Eyam?'

She leaned forward with her face close to the table. 'Look, I can't do this. I don't know who the hell you are. If I admit anything to you they could charge me with the crime they never managed to bring to court – of actually leaking information.'

He drew back concessively and nodded. 'I do understand your fears, but this *isn't* about you.' He stopped and slid an envelope towards her. 'This is your membership of the St James's Library. I have paid for your subscription. All you need do is go along with these forms signed and collect your membership card. It's a private library, a wonderfully *private* institution.'

She said nothing. He picked up the postcard. 'On the back of this I have written the location and title of a book. If you want to talk, simply leave a message where you find a similar card in the book. If you wish to give me something, but fear leaving it in the book, ask for Carrie at the front desk and she will keep it. She is completely reliable. You will be able to devise your own means of disguising what you hand to her. A hollowed-out book may seem rather old-fashioned but I have always found it works perfectly in those circumstances.'

She looked down at the card.

'Please think about this. I need your help. But please also remember we're in the business of resistance, Mary. You will have to be very, very careful. Do not mention this to anyone. Memorise what's on the card and destroy it.'

She rose suddenly, scraping her chair on the floor. Then she leaned towards him with her delicate white hands splayed on the Formica of the tabletop. 'I'm going.'

'Please,' he said, gesturing to the chair. 'I want to say one more thing.'

She remained standing but did not leave.

'Unless we hit them, Mary, this will go on and people like you will be hounded and harassed for as long as they choose. We're fighting for something here. It's nothing less than the good order of government and freedom, two things I feel rather strongly about. I believe you do too.'

'Fine words, Mr Kilmartin, but that is the kind of sentiment that put me in jail. I don't know who you're working for and that is the only thing that interests me.'

'We need ammunition, Mary. I can do nothing without it.'

She began shaking her head. 'Sorry, I've really got to go.' Then she turned and hurried from the crypt, but he noticed that she had taken the form and the card with her.

Kilmartin looked at his watch. There were three hours before the discussion programme for the Persian service at the BBC World Service headquarters in the Aldwych. He rose and thanked Hopkins, handing him a cheque for £500, which he had written out beforehand. It wasn't the first, by any means. The income from his share of the family brewing business had become embarrassingly large and he saw no reason why the alcoholics who relied on Hopkins for shelter and support shouldn't benefit from the sales of Kilmartin's Ales, which under his brother's management had bought whisky distilleries and several other drinks businesses. Besides, Hopkins was one of the few genuinely good people that he knew.

He left the crypt knowing he could have handled Mary MacCullum better. But when so little was known about what happened at those secret meetings of the Security and Intelligence Committee, there was no other way. He had to break through somewhere even if it did mean scaring her a little and perhaps worse, showing his hand.

He came to a junction in Soho, and crossed to a newsagent where he bought one of the disgusting small cigars he occasionally succumbed to. He had two more stops before he was due at the BBC World Service in Bush House. He set off briskly down Charing Cross Road and headed across Trafalgar Square to Whitehall. A hundred yards before Downing Street he entered the familiar door marked Cabinet Offices and swiped his pass at the security door. The man at the desk recognised him and dialled the secretary to the head of the Joint Intelligence Committee without Kilmartin asking. Ten minutes later Andrew Fortune appeared in shirtsleeves, a figure of neat anaemic brilliance with almost white blonde hair and a ready smile. He took Kilmartin by the elbow and led him to a large office, where two young civil servants were clearing up after a meeting.

'Terrific review in the *TLS*, Peter. I was very pleased to see it.'

'I can't believe you've got time to read book reviews, Andrew.'

'My wife spotted it. Your publishers must be terribly pleased.' This was followed by a quizzical smile. 'You're not due in here are you? No crisis in the tribal areas that I don't know about? No Uzbek turmoil that has escaped the notice of the Joint Intelligence Committee?' Fortune was a career bureaucrat who went home to Hertfordshire most evenings and had never enjoyed serving abroad with SIS. He'd got himself into a couple of homosexual scrapes, one with a young Turkish art dealer who'd attempted to blackmail the happily married father of two with a photograph of him snorting cocaine. Kilmartin had helped him – saved his career probably – yet there was something about Fortune that he had never liked. He looked down at the beautifully ordered desk. 'I thought I'd pop in to ask you about one of your former charges on the South East Asia desk.'

'Is it important?'

'Not especially. I would value your advice though.'

'It's good to see you. Now who is it?'

'Her name is Kate Lockhart, formerly Koh. Used to do for us in Indonesia.'

'Yes, I remember her well. Her husband died and she moved on. To be honest, I never took to her much. A rather self-contained woman, though she turned on the charm for the job. Professionally, she was very good, when you managed to point her in the right direction. Trouble was she was schooled by McBride and she had learned a lot of bad habits from him. What's this for – a job?'

'No.'

'Then are you going to tell me what it *is* for?'

'Certainly. Is she reliable – solid?'

Fortune thought. 'God, I can't remember much about her. *Resistant* is the word that comes to mind.'

'I see. She was a friend of David Eyam's.'

Fortune's expression changed: Eyam's name was still radioactive. 'Really. Yes, well, that was all a very sad business. I mean his death, of course.'

'Just looking into the other matter – keeping an eye on it, you know. But I would like you to keep that ultra-quiet. Not a word, Andrew.'

Fortune's eyes narrowed while the smile remained. 'What are you up to, Peter?'

'As I said, looking into it.' He stopped. 'For the prime minister, Andrew.'

'But surely that's all over with – long gone?'

'Er . . . yes. But there are concerns. As you know, after things die down people are apt to talk because they think the toxicity of a particular situation somehow diminishes.'

Fortune placed his palm on his chest. 'Not me, Peter.'

'Of course not.'

'I don't quite understand what you're saying then.'

Kilmartin touched the back of the chair. 'May I?'

'Please do,' said Fortune, sitting down on the sofa. 'There's surely no danger. She's an ordinary citizen with none of the necessary knowledge. I mean, this stuff was *very* restricted. Very, very restricted. I didn't – don't – even know about SPINDRIFT.'

'Quite,' said Kilmartin. Now he had got the name of the project that had put Mary MacCullum in jail and caused Eyam's fall from grace. 'It's like this: I'm just standing in the outfield, Andrew. Should any ball be lobbed my way, I hope to catch it.' He paused. 'So, nothing comes to mind about Kate Lockhart?'

'Well, I gather she is of interest. I imagine that's who they are referring to, though I have not heard her name mentioned. There was some concern about his heir. Has she inherited his estate?'

'The heir could be a worry, I agree. It is – how shall I say – a possibility that his estate includes damaging material.'

'Well, exactly, and the situation politically is not good. Not good at all.'

Fortune was, unsurprisingly, on the other team, not an important player perhaps, but someone who saw the present government as the only solution to the nation's problems and either consciously or unconsciously had jettisoned the neutrality of a civil servant to become a party member. At some stage he would have to ask him about Eyam's time at the JIC and the events leading up to his fall, but now was not the moment. He looked around the room. 'This job must be tough. The sheer volume of material coming over your desk makes me feel faint. You don't need another headache. None of us does.'

'Well, it's not that we can't cope,' Fortune said hastily. 'It's just that this stuff is very sensitive and it has now become essential for the country's future.' The little bastard did know what SPINDRIFT was and he was a supporter. The country's future, my arse, thought Kilmartin and rose with a grave nod.

'You're looking very trim, Peter. Very fit indeed.'

'The result of almost ceaseless food poisoning in the East,' he said. 'But thanks. You're scrubbing up well yourself. There's nothing else you can remember about Kate Lockhart, is there?'

'It will all be in the personnel files at the office.'

'Yes, but they're dry as dust, as you know well. Never tell you anything really interesting, do they?' Fortune knew that he was referring to Ali Mustafa Bey and it would be enough to sharpen his memory. He thought for a moment.

'Drugs . . . maybe she used cocaine after her husband died. There was some suspicion of that when we interviewed her to see if she wanted to stay on.'

Kilmartin doubted that. It was typical of the office to mistake grief for chemical dependence. 'Really, how interesting. That may be of great help. Thank you. I'm glad I dropped in. I do hope I haven't messed up your afternoon.'

'Not at all.'

'And all this is very much *entre nous*. Let's keep a watch on this thing. Lunch next week?'

'Yes, I think I can.'

'I'll ring your secretary.'

Fortune gave him a boy-scout grin. Kilmartin smiled also and patted the untrustworthy little shit on the back. He had found what he came for: the name of the project and maybe the beginning of an angle.

An hour later he was crouched down marvelling at the bas-relief of a herd of gazelle in the Assyrian rooms of the British Museum when Murray Link joined him. He rose and handed him a paperback copy of *Assyrian Sculpture*.

'The DVD is taped to the inside back cover,' he said, looking round the hunting scenes from Ashurbanipal's palace in Nineveh and taking in the handful of people in the room at the same time. 'Seen any of this before, Murray?'

Link, a short man with a narrow, furtive face, unwrapped his scarf. A shelf of fine hair was brushed forward over his forehead and he blinked from inside the drained complexion of a night worker. 'It's the film that was on TV, as you said.'

'No, you idiot, I mean these sculptures. They were carved in 645 BC, or thereabouts. Astonishingly lifelike aren't they?'

Link shrugged. 'About the film,' he said.

'The DVD you've got there is a second- or third-generation copy so . . .'

'So, we won't be able to tell whether the camcorder wrote all the film to the original disc. You should have emailed it to me or used the post. It would have saved us both a lot of time.' Link looked at him hard. He knew there was something else Kilmartin wanted from him.

'It's good to see your face, Murray. Good to see you prospering in the private sector.'

Link shrugged. He had been removed from the Technical Department of MI6 after being found guilty of one too many lapses in security. He went on to set up Blink Forensics in East London. 'Only part of the film was shown in court and on TV,' continued Kilmartin. 'There's some material at the beginning before the main action. I want you to examine it and see if anything strikes you. We're looking for any known faces and anomalies – anything which tells us more about that afternoon in Cartagena and the death of David Eyam.'

'You think we killed him?'

Kilmartin gave a shake of the head. 'You've spent a lot of time analysing films of explosions from the Middle East and Pakistan, Murray. You know what to look for.'

'It wouldn't be the first time local hoods did our work for us.'

Kilmartin's eyes returned to the herd of gazelle – a male turned its head towards the sound of the king's men who were about to drive the herd into the arms of death – and considered the idea of David Eyam's assassination. 'The question is whether we believe David Eyam was more of an inconvenience alive, or dead. You could argue that he was more of a threat dead, because he had nothing to lose. A man like Eyam would not go gentle into that good night. He wouldn't take it lying down, Murray.'

'I'll look at the film over the weekend. Are you in a rush?'

'Yes.'

'Right, I'll be getting along then. Where should I send the bill for the analysis?'

'Of course! I'm sorry. I was forgetting you're in business these days. Would you like me to give you something upfront? Or you can send the account to St Antony's and I will settle up at the end of your work.'

Link looked embarrassed. 'I'd welcome something now. It'll come to about a thousand pounds – say half.'

Kilmartin moved to a small gallery off the main rooms where there were no other visitors, wrote out a cheque for the full amount and blew on the ink before handing it to him. 'There was something else, if you wouldn't mind sparing a little more of your time, Murray.'

Link folded the cheque and placed it in his inside pocket. His manner softened. 'How can I help?'

'I know none of us is meant to gossip; cross fertilisation between agencies is frowned upon. But we all know things are occasionally shared between the technical departments – the various specialists at the office and with MI5 and GCHQ. You get to know each other, you talk the same language, share your problems.'

'That's what they chucked me out for.'

'Yes, I know. But I wonder if you have come across the name SPINDRIFT? Have you ever heard it referred to?'

'Sounds like a fucking washing powder. No, I haven't.'

Kilmartin persisted. 'We're both grown-ups, Murray. We're intelligence practitioners – signed the Official Secrets Act. You're not passing anything to the enemy, to the outside. And you should know that I am working at the request of the highest authority.'

'Then why don't you ask that *high* authority?' said Link.

'That's not possible, but come on, Murray, your friends and colleagues must have heard of this, surely.'

Link eyed him for a few seconds. 'What scenario are we talking about?'

Kilmartin had an unreasonable hatred of the word 'scenario'. '*Context*,' he said without thinking. 'I have little sense of the context. But this is something the Joint Intelligence Committee is aware of.'

'Has it got a label?'

'What sort of label?'

'The one that says, "This will burn your fucking face off." I mean, if I go typing the name into Google it will set off government trip wires; next they'll be ripping my fingernails out before I know it, Mr Kilmartin.'

'See what you can find out anyway, Murray. Have a word with your friends. It's important.'

'If you say so; but I'll need paying for the information – properly.'

'Of course, Murray,' said Kilmartin, his eyes drifting to the two-and-a-half-thousand-year-old relief of a lioness speared and crippled, dragging herself through the desert sand.

11

A Creature of Habit

Kate moved gingerly to the side of the Audi, aware of the smell of petrol. It was much darker in the thicket of hazel and holly where the car had come to rest at an angle. The front had ploughed into the far bank of a ditch with a savage force, reared up then tilted at twenty degrees. There was a good deal of water in the ditch, which perhaps explained why the car had not caught light. She worked her way along the driver's side and, placing a foot on the trunk of a fallen tree in the ditch, looked inside the car. Held by the seat belt, Russell's body sagged over the passenger seat; his head lolled forward and his arms had dropped from the wheel. That struck her as odd. He would surely have tried to control the car until the last moment, unless he had passed out before hitting the brush. There was far less blood than Nock had made out. A lot of mud had come through the smashed windscreen. Russell was cut below his right eye.

She moved round to the passenger side, climbed down into the water and pulled the door open. As she examined the body, her mind replayed his amiable conversation on the way to Dove Cottage. He had spoken about family holidays in Scotland, the outing in June every year to the Opera at Glyndebourne and the annual weekend in France's vineyards with university chums. A creature of habit was the way he apologetically described himself, and she had liked him for that. His face had frozen in a look of mild expectation, almost a smile. Controlling her shock, she reached out and touched his neck with the hand that had shaken his in the cafe a little over twenty-four hours before. Russell was utterly cold. He must have died instantly, though she couldn't see what injury had killed him. Possibly it was the blow to the head from the night before: a delayed haemorrhage perhaps, which struck suddenly as he left the drive.

She was now aware that she was shaking and had a curious stale taste in her mouth. She stood up and controlled herself, withdrew from the car and went to join Nock in the road. There were no skid marks visible, no signs of any other vehicle being involved; merely evidence that Hugh Russell had swerved on the stony track as he approached the gateway and, rather than slowing down as he met the road, slammed his foot on the accelerator and careened through the stand of hazel on the other side.

Nock gave her a roll-up to smoke.

'Jesus,' he said.

She blew out the smoke and shivered. 'Did you hear anything? See anything?'

'No – my dogs noticed something had happened first. I wouldn't have seen it if the terrier hadn't dived in there.'

'Where are they?'

'They took themselves off back to my place.'

'Oh God,' she said, looking back at the car. 'Poor Hugh. This is awful.' She was still shaking and she held her hand very tight to stop Nock seeing.

Twenty minutes later the accident investigation team arrived and paced out the likely sequence of events under arc lights. There seemed no good explanation for his bolting across the road like that, and the skid marks on the gravelly incline puzzled them. It was as though he had shot off from a standing start. A pathologist arrived and examined the body *in situ* with a head torch, while murmuring into a digital recorder. When he withdrew his head from the passenger window Kate approached and told him about the injuries Russell had received in the attack at his office. The man listened carefully to her description and asked whether Russell had fallen forward in the attack. She thought not.

'Then my gut tells me that this man suffered some other kind of trauma. That's what I am feeling.'

Presently the body, wet and drenched in petrol, was removed from the car by two policemen and was laid on a stretcher where the pathologist examined Russell again. A few minutes later he stood up in the headlights of one of the police cars and called out to the inspector. 'You should see this. I believe this man was shot. The cut below his eye is a bullet wound.'

The operation to lift the Audi on to a flatbed truck was immediately halted and quarter of an hour later a .22 calibre bullet was found in the roof of the wreckage. That probably meant it had passed through the open window on the driver's side as Hugh Russell approached the road. The skid mark on the gravel marked the spot where he had been hit and his foot came down hard on the accelerator in reaction.

'I should have seen it before,' said the pathologist, pointing with latex finger to Russell's face for the edification of a group of officers. 'You see the stretch marks running like tears down the face away from the point of impact. That is always a classic sign of a gunshot. They follow the tension lines in the region of the eyes and the nasolabial folds. A bullet can freeze the face in the victim's most characteristic expression.'

And in this case, thought Kate, it had produced neither agony nor aggression but the straightforward cordiality of a country solicitor.

'And the exit wound?' asked one policeman. 'We didn't see any signs of it.'

'That was because the bullet exited beneath the bandage at the back of the victim's head. It simply lifted one corner of the dressing and continued on its way. The dressing fell back and covered the wound when the body dropped forward.'

A team of three detectives arrived and began to work out the geometry of the attack. The position and angle of the car and the line indicated by the exit and entry wounds and the final position of the bullet led them to believe that the killer had lain in wait about twenty paces below where the car came to rest. A large area was cordoned off so that a minute search could be conducted at first light. Then the site was cleared of people.

Just past nine, Kate drove the Bristol back down the track with a police officer in the passenger seat and Nock in the back. She was now sure that Eyam had been assassinated in Cartagena. The bomb must have been intended for him. He had known the risks, which was why he had planned his funeral, prepared a will and had taken steps to leave her the dossier. But why go to Colombia, where it would be a simple task for his enemies to disguise his murder? From what Swift had said, there was good reason to believe he'd left the country using a false passport, but then he checked into the hotel using his own name with a credit card in his own name, thus giving anyone looking for him an exact location. It didn't add up, but more than that this was not the kind of mistake the patient and calculating Eyam would make.

Russell presented a different problem to the killers. There was no time to fake an accident, or disguise his murder any other way. He had to be eliminated immediately because he was the one person who knew what was in Eyam's dossier, and they could not allow him to remain alive with that knowledge. The only conclusion to draw was that her last-minute decision to stay at Dove Cottage had saved her life. If she'd left with him, she would certainly have been killed too. She must accept that she was already a target, or would become one the moment they thought she knew the contents of that dossier.

Nock was questioned in the back of a police van parked in the drive, while she made an exhaustive statement to a detective inspector named Jim Newsome. She gave an exact account of her day from the moment Hugh Russell picked her up at the hotel to the discovery of the Audi by Nock. They went back over the funeral and her first meeting with Russell in the cafe. She kept as close to the truth as possible, but there was much she had to omit – her presence in Russell offices, all mention of the documents and of course the child porn she'd found on Eyam's computer. She filled out the day with plenty of detail about exploring the house, her walk and her calls to New York. Newsome nodded a lot and took down notes. He was polite, but she knew that any experienced investigator would sense the omissions soon enough, and Newsome had a hard, proficient air about him. He asked her a lot of questions about her decision to stay overnight at the cottage and let Russell drive back to town when clearly he should not have been at the wheel of a car. She answered that Russell had begged her to give the place a chance before putting it on the market and indeed during the afternoon she had begun to understand what Eyam had seen in Dove Cottage. It was very peaceful, she said.

'Peaceful but unlucky,' observed Newsome dryly. 'After all, the place has been associated with two violent deaths in as many months. We must at least consider the possibility of a connection. Can you think of any reason why both men were killed?'

'I don't see how there can be a connection,' she said.

'But if there is it would put you in the line of fire, wouldn't it? Because you are the common denominator.'

'Not in any real sense: Mr Russell was David Eyam's lawyer for a long time before I came on the scene.'

'But you knew them both, particularly Mr Eyam.'

'Yes, he was my closest . . . my oldest friend. We hadn't seen much of each other over the last two years.'

Newsome pondered this. 'And yet he leaves this place to you. Did you know he was going to do that?'

'No.'

'I hope you don't mind me saying, Miss Lockhart, but it seems odd that a relatively young man should make a will and leave every-thing to someone he hadn't seen for two years and not even tell her about it.'

'Mr Russell told me that David had been ill. Believe me, I was very surprised, and before you go there, I am pretty well off in my own right and have no need of Mr Eyam's money. To tell you the truth I find it an embarrassment.'

'You're very fortunate. These days there are few people who can say that. How much money is involved?'

'I'm not sure, but you can consult Mr Russell's partner Paul Spring. He will be in charge of the probate.'

'We will, Miss Lockhart, be assured of that.' He paused. 'Still, you'd expect Mr Eyam to tell you about his plans in the event of his death.'

'Why are you asking me about Mr Eyam? Aren't you interested in Hugh Russell? He was just here, in this room like you. And now he's dead – murdered. Why the hell are you talking about Eyam?'

'Why was it you left your job in New York so suddenly?'

'The pressure had been intense: I needed a break.'

'So it was a coincidence that you were here when you received the news about his death. Forgive me, Miss Lockhart; it all seems a bit convenient.'

She opened her hands. 'Look, I know what you're saying. You wonder if I somehow engineered Mr Russell's death, maybe also Mr Eyam's death, so that I could inherit this place. Let me just say I have no need of any of it. Look me up on the web and make your own deductions.'

'I will,' he said, looking down at his notebook. 'Do you mind telling me how much you earned last year?'

'Actually, yes.'

'Give me an idea. Over a million dollars?'

'It varies. Last year less than that.'

Newsome straightened. 'You must be very good at your job.'

She didn't reply.

'So, in effect this house is now yours, Miss Lockhart.'

'In theory,' she replied, 'though I don't know when I officially take possession.'

'Have you a copy of the will?'

'I thought I was here to answer questions about Hugh Russell's death, not my private affairs.'

'I'm just asking to see the papers he gave you before his death. You're a lawyer; you understand that the will is all part of the context of this murder.'

'If you want a copy of the will, you should apply to Russell, Spring & Co. His partner Paul Spring will happily expedite the request, I'm sure.'

'I will. So, you're going to sell up?'

'Yes, as soon as it is mine to do so. I couldn't live here with all the associations you mentioned. Anyway, it is impractical – I don't have the time to visit, let alone to deal with all the maintenance.'

'But you have Mr Nock for that.'

'Mr Nock was employed by David Eyam, then in his absence by Mr Russell. It's not my arrangement.'

'And you say you've never met him before today?'

'No, the first I knew of Mr Nock was when Hugh mentioned his name. I met him this morning when he dropped in.'

'Dropped in . . .' said Newsome.

'I think Hugh called him to tell him I was here, that's all.'

After an hour and a half, Newsome closed his notebook. 'We've got all we need tonight, Miss Lockhart, but we will want to talk to you at the station as the investigation develops.' He handed her his card. 'And call me if you think of anything that might be relevant to the case. Inform me or anyone at the station if you're going anywhere.' She rose with him. 'There will be a patrol car at the end of the drive guarding the crime scene. So, if you have any worries you know that officers will be at hand.'

When they left Nock came in and asked if she'd like him to spend the night downstairs. She poured them each a glass of Eyam's whisky and said she would be fine on her own, although some part of her could have done with his company: he reminded her of Cas, a record producer she'd had a brief fling with in New York, and, well, Nock was attractive.

He showed her the heating thermostat in the utility room and flipped the hot water switch. 'It gets pretty cold up here at night, even in the summer,' he said, 'and the beauty of this system is that it's nearly all your own power. You've got a shed load of batteries out back.'

They found themselves in the sitting room. She looked down at the computer. 'I guess you came to know David fairly well,' she said.

'Yep, we got on great. I miss him. I really liked the guy.'

'But he was having problems with the authorities.'

'Is that what you call it?' said Nock bitterly.

She drank the whisky. 'What happened in England, Sean?'

'No one was paying attention. Nobody gives a damn any longer.' He shifted and looked embarrassed and she wondered why.

'Did you know Eyam was under surveillance?'

He shook his big Viking head, passed a hand over the stubble on his chin, and looked away. 'I guess so. I came across stuff – sensors in the woods and that kind of thing – before he died. I think they were trying to monitor his movements to the cottage, especially visitors who drove here. There was a lot of activity after he died.'

'You think this place was bugged?'

'Maybe. There were some men here after his death. I think they had come to remove everything. I told Mr Russell about them.'

She looked around the room. The place could still be wired, in which case her conversation with Russell in the kitchen might have been overheard, and that might explain why he had been killed when he left.

'Let's go outside anyway,' she said quietly.

She lit a cigarette in the damp air and gave one to Nock, who inhaled and held his breath as though it was cannabis. 'And the computer?' she asked. 'Were they monitoring that?'

His eyes narrowed. 'Look, I don't know how much to say to you. It's difficult.' He looked away and his leg fidgeted.

'Sean, this is important – I believe the people who were watching David killed Hugh Russell because of what he knew. Do you understand what I am saying? Now, again, do you think they monitored or otherwise tampered with the computer?'

'Could be.'

'Did you know that someone put some illegal material on it? *Kiddy porn* I think is the right expression. They wanted to incriminate him and send him to jail, Sean.'

'You should destroy that,' he said, letting a stream of smoke into the cold night air. 'Can't be right to have that kind of thing in the house,' he added vehemently.

They went inside. Nock unscrewed the back, located the hard drive and extracted it with the help of a short curved crowbar and a hammer from Eyam's toolbox. The casing popped out and flew across the carpet to the other side of the room. He picked it up and gazed down at it with an odd intensity. 'Shall I do it?' he said, taking it to the flagstones by the door. She nodded and he dropped it onto the floor and hit it until there was nothing but a little pile of plastic and metal parts. He swept the remains into his pocket and said he would dispose of them on the walk home. Then he picked up his jacket and went to the door where he looked down at her, and believing he saw something in her eye, took her in his arms without permission or seemingly any doubt that this was the right thing to do. He was gentle and Kate felt something stir in her, but there was no question that she was going to respond.

'You'll be blaming yourself for Mr Russell's death,' he said as he let go. 'Don't. This isn't your fault. Know that, Kate. There are some real bastards out there and they will stop at nothing. Believe me, I know.'

'How?' she said, now much more interested in his tone than the rather awkward pass he'd made.

'That's for another time. I'll see you tomorrow. You've got my mobile number if there's any trouble.'

There was no trouble except in her dreams of the car in the ditch and Russell's body floating out of the window on a tide of filth and oil. She woke at first light and opened the curtains. At the bottom of the valley a ribbon of mist followed exactly the line of the stream down to the farm. The moon hung low on the far side of the valley. One or two birds had begun to sing and owls still called to each other across the valley. At the end of the garden a deer drank from the small pond, raising its head at regular intervals to the sounds in the woods.

She reached for her phone from the bedside table and sent the word 'today' in a text message to Darsh Darshan, then slipped from the bed and went to run the shower. After a few minutes the water was still cold. Cursing, she stumbled downstairs to the utility room in her T-shirt. Next to the switch where Nock had turned on the system the night before was a pair of manual timers in a box with a plastic window. Both the heating and hot water timers were set to come on between midnight and two in the morning. 'Who the hell needs hot water at that hour?' she muttered out loud. She tugged the window open and reset both to the right time – seven a.m. – then she shifted the buttons on the hot water timer so the immersion heater clicked into life. A steady hum ensued. It was at this point that she noticed that the action of turning the timers had caused something to drop from behind the wooden board on which they were mounted. She slipped a hand under the two clocks and drew out a cassette tape. In that instant she realised the timers were almost directly in line with the empty bottle of wine and the packets of cheese straws, and dog biscuits. Then she remembered the awkward phrase in his letter: 'You will find it all behind the times.' Eyam had set the clocks to the wrong time so that anyone needing hot water would release the tape. That person was likely to be her. Not bad,

116

she thought, looking at the recordings of Handel's *Sarabande* and *The Messiah*, sung by New College Choir. Not bad at all.

She turned it over and read the typed label stuck to the back. 'Press "Play" and "Forward" simultaneously.' She went into the kitchen, put on the kettle and began searching the cottage for a tape player. Then an idea came to her.

12

Red Admiral

Roughly twenty-five miles to the south of Dove Cottage, Peter Kilmartin sat in the old coach house and stables that he had recently converted to a magnificent study, looking out on the pewter forms materialising in his garden with the first grey washes of light. A lifelong early riser, he used these quiet hours to relish the freedom to potter about his garden and to browse in his library, the design of which had been in his head through his last four jobs in SIS.

Above the low schoolmaster's armchair were two quotations pinned to a green baize noticeboard. The first was a Chinese poem written some five thousand years before: '*When the sun rises, I go to work; when the sun goes down I take my rest; I dig the well from where I drink; I farm the soil that yields my food; I share creation; Kings can do no more.*' The second was from a long letter by Thomas Jefferson, a hero of Kilmartin's, chiefly because of the ingenuity Jefferson showed in organising his retirement at Monticello. '*I talk of plows and harrows, of seeding and harvesting with my neighbours, and of politics too, if they choose, with as little reserve as the rest of my fellow citizens, and feel at length, the blessing of being free to say and do what I please without being responsible to any mortal.*'

Kilmartin tore himself from the pleasure of watching the light bring his garden to life like a theatre set, to consider the first draft of a book review, but then the screen of his mobile lit up and the phone began to vibrate. He peered at it. No number was displayed, then he answered to Murray Link's voice.

'You're up early,' said Link. 'I thought I'd be leaving you a message. I have just finished looking at the material you gave me.'

'Yes, and what did you find?'

'Let's just say there's a lot wrong with it.'

'In what way?'

'Looks like two sections were written to the camcorder at different times, which is at odds with the date and time information you see when playing it. You've got to see it for yourself. I've done a full analysis that I want to show you.'

'Can you be more specific now?'

'One thing I can tell you is that the first section, the part that wasn't shown in court, was completely wrong. According to the dateline it was recorded just before the main section, but there's a lot of internal evidence – a clock on the bell tower, for instance, and the angle of the sun, to say that it was morning, not evening. It is pretty obvious stuff. And in the main section there are many weird jumps and pauses, which make me think the whole thing smells. Some of it has been expertly done. The rest is amateur city. It doesn't make sense.'

'Where and when can I see it?'

'Anytime; anywhere. I'll bring a laptop.'

'Someone will call you. Don't use this phone again.'

Sensing Kilmartin was about to ring off, Link said hurriedly, 'And there's the other thing you asked me about.'

Kilmartin coughed. 'I think that must be for another time,' he said quickly.

'Yeah, OK.'

Kilmartin hung up and sat back in the chair, with the tips of his fingers pressed together. If the film was a fake, only one of two people could be responsible, each with wildly different motives. If the solution he favoured turned out to be right, it seemed impossible that the Andrew Fortunes and Christine Shoemakers of the world were not onto it as well: if he had his doubts they would too. But then ten minutes later something changed his mind. He had crossed the cobbled yard to the house. His sister Helen was up and had just made a cup of tea. She turned on the radio to hear the news headlines at seven thirty a.m. The second item on what appeared to be a fairly slow news day concerned the murder of a local solicitor at the home of the former senior civil servant who himself had died by violent means in Colombia.

Two people were questioned overnight by detectives but weren't detained. Police sources suggested that the victim had been shot by a high-powered sniper rifle as he left the property in his car.

Although the address of the murder wasn't given, Kilmartin was certain the location had to be Dove Cottage, the place that Kate Lockhart had inherited. He returned to his study pursued by a knowing look from Helen and sat down to think. Perhaps they really were bent on eliminating everyone who knew about SPINDRIFT, in which case Link's discoveries were even more puzzling. He found the number for Eyam's landline at Dove Cottage and rehearsed what he would say. 'It's about the seeds you ordered from our catalogue, miss,' he said to himself. 'You must leave *immediately* to collect them.' No, that sounded bloody stupid. Before the number rang out he hung up. He would stick to his original plan. Kate Lockhart was capable of looking after herself.

She left Dove Cottage in the Bristol at eight and stopped by the police car at the top of the drive to tell the two officers she would be away from the cottage all day and that she had left Newsome a message on his phone telling him of her movements.

She drove slowly, taking her time to get to know the foibles of Eyam's forty-year-old car, the sluggish steering, the throatiness of the engine in acceleration and a mulish tendency to veer right when the brakes were applied sharply. The trip took just under two hours and at some point she became certain – as certain as McBride's law of instincts dictated – that she was being followed. Yet if pressed she couldn't say by which cars or where she first became prey to the sensation. Maybe it was the knowledge that for years the police in Britain had recorded every journey made on every major road with automatic number recognition cameras. She went through a routine to see if any cars were on her tail, slowing and accelerating and twice turning off the motorway and circling a junction roundabout to glimpse the traffic following about a mile behind her. But she saw nothing. She tried playing different parts of the cassette, but found only music on both sides. It didn't make sense. Why had Eyam gone to so much trouble? She decided to wait until she reached Oxford, where she could look at it properly and maybe buy a small tape player if the ancient tape deck in the Bristol was the problem. But when she arrived in the city from the south and drove into a car park near Magdalene Bridge she ejected the cassette, saw that she had failed to follow the instructions to press 'forward' and 'play' at the same time, and placed it in her handbag.

She crossed the bridge and walked up the High Street to a cafe near Queen's College. Kate was impervious to nostalgia of the white flannels and dreaming spires kind and never understood people who pined for their university days, but this cafe still held something for her. During one summer, the year after she had left, she came back to see Eyam when he was haunting New College, light-headed with indecision about his career. He had finished his postgraduate work and could not decide whether to stay at Oxford, accepting the offer of a post at the university, or to find a job in the outside world. She used to fetch supplies from the cafe while he lay on a couch like a doomed juvenile poet. They holed up in his rooms getting sloshed on wine and listening to early music and took some kind of oath of undying friendship, which in Eyam's case was accompanied by many extravagant quotes. The most unromantic and practical of these was Montaigne's observation that a good marriage resembled friendship rather than love. It was then that they slept together for the first time, a natural outcome of a day of messing about and also of their whole time at Oxford, and an affirmation of closeness but also – at least in her case – a night of erotic fulfilment never matched before or since. When they went in the rain to the station after four days of speaking to no one but the cafe owner, she to go back to London to her law studies and Eyam to his family in the north where his mother lay ill with cancer, she clung to his arm, certain from his manner that he was closing the door on her.

The cafe had extended the delicatessen side of its business. She ordered a cup of tea and placed herself at a corner table so she had a good view of the street through a display of hams and breads. She was on home ground. If there was a team tracking her they'd have to follow on foot and she knew the university well enough to lose them. Sipping the tea, she watched for ten minutes and saw nothing untoward. She left and walked towards the town centre, then took a right turn and made for Brasenose College. There were several places she could use to sift her wake for watchers. This she did twice with a slight sense of unreality before entering the maze of Blackwell's bookshop for quarter of an hour. Finally she headed down the canyon of New College Lane and stepped through New College's ancient door to find an old friend – the head porter, Cecil, who looked up from a clipboard and without missing a beat greeted her by name.

'Miss Kate, always one of my favourites: now, what brings you back?'

'Oh, I thought I'd look over the place and see a friend of mine at the same time,' she said.

Cecil's expression clouded. 'I was sorry to read about your Mr Eyam. You were his friend, weren't you? A fine young man he was too. There was always something special about him. You could tell that from the first.'

She nodded.

'A bad business to be sure,' he added.

They talked for a few minutes while she watched the lane. Cecil seemed to sense the alertness in her eyes. 'Something troubling you, miss?'

'I just wonder if you could keep an eye on who comes into the college over the next hour or so. I can't explain now, but it's very important that I meet this friend in private.' She paused. 'And that no one sees us together.'

'No problem – leave it to me.' He appraised her with an amused look. 'Heard you were doing very well in New York. Saw something about you in the college magazine.'

'And the photograph? I look retarded,' she said, smiling. Her eyes fell on a phone inside the lodge and she asked Cecil if she could use it. The woman answered at St Antony's Middle East department and she left a message for Kilmartin to say she'd be at New College for the next hour or so. She gave the number of her cell phone.

Then Cecil told her of a small panelled vestry between the chapel and the hall: they should go there if they wanted absolute privacy and quiet, and he would keep a lookout. Cecil's ability to spot a wrong'un, as he put it, had not dimmed with the years.

She passed into the Front Quadrangle, the first quad to be built in either Oxford or Cambridge, and turned left to the chapel. It was not quite noon, so she went through to the cloisters where students had walked since the time when the college was founded to replenish a priesthood ravaged by the Black Death. Little had changed in the twenty years since she had been there. The great European evergreen oak shaded a fifth of the grass courtyard; the bench where they'd posed for the photograph after Eyam won the John Hicks prize was in the same position; the atmosphere in the vaulted cloister was still heavy with the devotions of the past. At six on a winter Sunday the place had all the dismal foreboding of a nineteenth-century ghost story: even on a bright spring day its powers of suggestion were strong. She could almost see Eyam on the bench in the middle of the grass with a book. It was his bench – the bench where he read and thought and celebrated. That was why she went to the cloisters: to remember Eyam.

The clocks of the university began to strike twelve and she moved quickly inside the chapel, pausing in the ante-chapel to listen – no sound came from the main body of the building – then passing through the great screen into the chapel. She saw Darsh perched on a carved misericord in the stalls immediately on her left, the exact same spot where she had found the homesick and rather bewildered maths prodigy over two decades before.

He gave her a rueful look. 'You know what I was thinking, Kate? How my whole life was changed when you took pity on me that evening. All those people you knew became my friends – the sort of friends I'd never had before. Friends for life. I owe you.'

'What's come over you?' she said, grinning and sitting down beside him. His head was sunk in a thick orange scarf. 'That may be the first nice thing you've ever said to me. By the way, that was quite a show you put on at the funeral. I thought you'd be locked up for taking a swing at Glenny.' She paused. 'But I wanted to say you spoke the only true words of the service, Darsh.'

His face spread in a surprising smile. 'Glenny is a bastard. There were so many hypocrites at the funeral; so many complete and utter bastards!' His voice rang out in the religious chill of the chapel.

They made their way along the chapel to a door on the left and found Cecil's ecclesiastical cubbyhole. It smelled of a mixture of cleaning fluid and antique incense.

'Were you followed here?' he asked.

123

'I don't think so. What about you?'

He shook his head. 'I lost them in the Mathematics Institute.'

'You lost them with *that* scarf – it's like a beacon.'

No second smile. 'You know,' he said, 'since the funeral my rooms have been turned over by the police – everything searched and picked apart. Imagine, one of the great mathematicians of our time treated like a common criminal.' He said this without irony. 'I am followed everywhere and snooped upon at every turn and now I've had enough. England has become intolerable. I've decided to take up a position at Yale. I leave in June.'

She moved a vase and a broom and sat down on the edge of a table. Darsh arranged himself on a high stool that was covered with dried droplets of paint. The gloved hands brushed dust from his suit. His domed forehead glistened in the light as he directed a look of hooded inquiry at her.

'You should check your computer,' she said. 'Someone put a lot of child porn on David's.'

'I don't use computers of that sort,' he replied as though talking about public transport. 'David told me all about that. It was the moment he knew he was beaten; that they would stop at nothing to destroy him.'

She leaned forward. 'What the hell did he do? I mean, Eyam was like the head prefect, the chief boy-scout. He never stepped out of line. He was far too grand to be a whistleblower. Tell me, Darsh.'

'He made an honest man of himself. He took the ultimate test. His principles triumphed over ambition, vanity and the love of power.'

'How?'

'He went to a parliamentary committee and told them the truth about a secret that only a few know about. The committee suppressed it – naturally; this is England.'

She shook her head. 'Take it from the top, Darsh: I want the whole story.'

He sniffed and looked out of the window. 'All I know is he was asked by John Temple to become the head of the Joint Intelligence Committee while a new chairman was found.'

'Surely that job goes to someone who has experience in the intelligence services, someone much older,' she said. 'It takes a lot of skill to coordinate and make sense of raw intelligence for policymakers. Eyam had a few months' training in SIS, that was all.'

'I have no idea about these things, but you're forgetting his analytical powers. I once heard that he was respected even by foreign delegations for his agility of mind at the negotiating table. Temple trusted him and I guess he persuaded him to take up the position for a few months. That appealed to him. He was fascinated by the big strategic issues of power, food and water and maybe he felt he could influence the government on them.'

'Then what?' she said, realising how little she had known about Eyam's life in government, an ignorance only in part due to Eyam's discretion and reserve about his work.

'He was summoned by a parliamentary committee – I forget its name – and he was asked a specific detailed question and he replied with something that was not true, although he didn't know it at the time. Then he learned that he had been misinformed and he told one of the committee members he had more to say on the subject. They called him back and he corrects the record.'

'And you have no idea what this was about?'

'No, nothing was revealed by the committee. Their hearings are held in private. David was removed from the Joint Intelligence Committee and offered some inferior position – I believe it was in the Work and Pensions Department. He declined and left the civil service. Then his troubles began. He was followed, his flat was searched, his calls monitored. He was given a full security interview that lasted two days. He told me he could feel himself falling apart. They destabilised him – that was the word he used. Then he began to run.'

'Run? What do you mean?'

'He began running. He found it kept him sane. It also amused him to lose the people who were always following him. Eventually, he wrote a private letter to Temple pointing out that he had done nothing wrong; that he was not in breach of the Official Secrets Act because he had the highest clearance and he had revealed nothing to anyone outside government, apart from complying with his statutory obligations to answer the committee's questions truthfully. Temple understood that beneath the surface there was a threat. Eyam knew a lot of damaging things about Temple's government, things that weren't covered by the Official Secrets Act. The prime minister had no option but to make a deal. There was a meeting, just the two of them late one night in Downing Street. Temple agreed to stop the harassment if Eyam left London and went to live somewhere quietly and have no contact with anyone in the government or the media.

'So he went to live near High Castle and began to prepare his counter-attack – an account of official secrecy, and the government's capture by international corporations. That's how he described it to me anyway. I surmised his plan was to publish it before the general election, which people believe will be announced some time in the next six months. He told me nothing in detail. That was David all over. You see he didn't want to involve me. But you, Kate, you are a different matter. He wants you to wage his war. I can tell. I know the way he operated.' He stopped and examined her with his chin held high. 'Did you love him?'

'As a matter of fact yes, Darsh.'

'But you abandoned him. Why was that?'

'Maybe it looks like that but—'

'It does,' he said unsparingly. 'I loved him but I did not abandon him, Kate.'

'*You* were in love with Eyam?'

He looked away.

'I mean he wasn't gay, was he?'

'What a profoundly stupid question.'

'Darsh, he left me pretty much everything in his will. We were the best of friends, even if we did fall out from time to time.'

He peered up at the top of the window. 'No, he wasn't gay, as you well know. But I am and I loved him.'

'Look,' she said after a while. 'I'd like you to have anything you like from the house: books, pictures – anything. He'd have wanted it. And to be honest I have no idea what to do with it all.'

'He left it all to you for a reason.' His eyes returned from the window to settle on her. 'He wants you to fight his fight. That's why he left it to you. Not because he loved you but because among his friends you are the most resilient. A "demure, bloody-minded, headbanging bitch" was his expression. Did you know that's what he thought of you?'

'Thanks,' she said. 'So who's the villain – John Temple?'

'This isn't a fairy story with one villain and one hero; it's about a political condition; it's about Eden White and his companies . . .'

'I met Eden White after the funeral. He's like some kind of mani-festation – ectoplasm.'

Darsh ignored her and continued. 'It's about Temple and that creep Glenny and the Home Office, the state within a state; it's about apathy and fear; it's about the collapse of . . . look this is England . . . I don't have to explain the deep cultural complacency of the English.'

'Yeah, yeah. That's the kind of theoretical shit you read in newspaper columns, Darsh. Someone hounded Eyam from office and then persecuted him and planted child porn on his computer. That's illegal and wrong. Someone killed Eyam's lawyer with a rifle outside his cottage last night probably because he'd seen documents. The documents were intended for me.'

He shook his head with genuine sadness. 'We're getting to see that bastard side of life, you and I.'

'Yes, and the point is that David was murdered – by whom we don't know – and now Hugh Russell. It's not beyond the bounds of possibility that they are all connected. Have you ever heard of a monitoring system called ASCAMS? Do you know what that is?'

He shook his head but she knew he was holding something back.

'After the funeral Eden White gave a dinner in honour of David, a lot of government and corporate people. What was that about? Why was White there?'

He snorted an odd laugh. 'To make sure David was gone?'

'Is there any evidence to say that this all involves Eden White? His companies sell systems to governments around the world. We know this has got something to do with a monitoring system called ASCAMS. Was ASCAMS one of the systems supplied to the government by White?'

'These are things for you to find out,' said Darsh. He removed a boiled sweet from his pocket and unwrapped it.

'So, Eyam goes into exile in High Castle. What happened then?'

Darsh held the sweet between forefinger and thumb, examined it like a jewel and popped it into his mouth where it moved from one cheek to the other several times before he answered. 'I went down there to see him last summer. He seemed content – fulfilled even – and happy with this place you have inherited. He was contained, pregnant with some big idea. But then something went wrong. In a letter he told me he was under extreme pressure. I assume that by late October he had made his plans. He spent two weeks caring for his father before he died in late November. It was around then he discovered they'd tampered with his computer. He told me at his father's funeral – he asked me to go for moral support – and that he thought he would be arrested very soon. It was the last time I saw him. On December 8th he left for France.'

'For France!'

'Well, he couldn't buy a ticket here or leave this country without being picked up. I believe he crossed to France hidden on a private sailing yacht, with a friend. Then he flew to Martinique. I know because he sent me a postcard.'

'What was he doing there?'

'Kate, his father's business fortune was based in the Caribbean.'

She slapped her forehead. 'Of course, he went because of the money. That's why there was no mention of him in his father's will. He and his father must have arranged things so Eyam had funds waiting for him in the Caribbean.' She paused. 'Do you know someone named Peter Kilmartin, a friend of Eyam's? Attached to St Antony's College. Foreign Office before. He said he'd met you.'

'I saw him once with David. He wrote a paper on Assyrian mathematics and astronomy. I looked over the mathematics in the paper.' He shook his head with dismay, either at the crudeness of Assyrian mathematics or of Kilmartin's, she wasn't sure which.

'He comes recommended. Do you agree?'

'What I saw was a big, vigorous Englishman with higher than average intelligence, some culture and the unconscious brutality of the breed. I can't tell you *whom* to trust. Eyam has set you up to complete the job for him and you have to make these decisions for yourself. But of course you still have a choice. You don't have to do what David wanted. You can forget the whole thing and go on with your life.' He eyed her without moving. 'But if you do fight this thing I will help you, because I owe you. Darsh does not forget.'

He told her how to contact him through the Mathematics Institute, instructing her to use the name Koh when leaving messages. Then his attention moved to a butterfly struggling in a cobweb at the top of the window. Like a cat he sprang suddenly from his stool to stand on the table beside her and trapped the butterfly with one ungloved hand. With the other hand he peeled filaments of old spider web from the wings.

'Come on,' he said. 'Open the window. Quickly!'

She wrenched down the handle and banged on the old frame with the heel of her hand.

'A red admiral,' he said, having released it. 'They emerge from hibernation at this time of the year and are joined by butterflies that migrate from France. People assume they are dead, but with the first warmth of spring they wake.' He gazed down at her with an inquiring look.

'Thanks, I'm glad to know that, Darsh,' she said, closing the window.

He stepped nimbly onto the stool and jumped to the floor in one movement. 'So, we will be in touch.' And then he did something rather odd. He kissed her and held her hand for a moment. 'If you fight this thing there is much that will surprise and shock you, Kate Lockhart. Are you prepared for that? Are you prepared for the fight of your life?'

'I don't know,' she said. 'I don't know if I can do anything.'

'Well, I expect the answer will come to you soon enough. Let me know when it does. Let me know what you are going to do.'

'Is there something you're not telling me?'

'Just say the word. That's all you have to do.' He got up, arranged his scarf and slipped through the door.

She waited for five minutes after he left, then returned to the ruminative quiet of the Front Quad and went to the porter's lodge where she found Cecil with his head in a big notebook. 'They were here,' he said before allowing his gaze to surface over his reading glasses. 'The people looking for you: they didn't say as much but then they didn't have to because I can tell, see. There were three of them – two women and a man came in separately and looked around the public areas. One of the women said she thought her friend was in the college and she described what you were wearing – most insistent she was. I said I hadn't seen you.

'And this arrived for you,' he said reaching below a shelf, 'just a few minutes ago by taxi from St Antony's.' He handed her a small parcel. Inside was a cell phone with a note from Kilmartin, which instructed her to use the phone only to call the number already in its memory. He also had a clean phone, with no record of purchase or ownership. Conversation should be kept to a minimum without names, and the phone should not be used in a car or at a place that could be readily associated with her.

13

The Spreading Stain

Philip Cannon's gaze followed the government's chief scientific adviser's hand as it left the keyboard in front of him and drifted to one of four big screens on the wall of the new underground facility of Britain's Security Council.

'These satellite images were taken this morning, so they are the very latest information we have,' said Professor Adam Hopcraft, a tall, spare man in his sixties. 'The two left-hand screens show reservoirs in mid-Wales; and here we have photographs from Cumbria. In each you will see that the open water is stained with a reddish pink dye that spreads outwards in these frozen wisps. And this,' he said moving to another screen, 'is a time-lapse study of the North Bowland reservoir in Lancashire, which with others supplies Manchester with drinking water. The stain spreads over three days to colour about one third of the water, which shows these blooms of algae that we are seeing have a great deal of energy.'

He tapped some more on his laptop. Cannon looked round the room. Since moving from BBC News to take the job of director of communications at Downing Street, he occasionally marvelled at the government's ability to focus talent and brains on a problem. David Eyam had personified the system and, although Cannon always found him a mite arrogant, it was he who had showed him that at the very top of government you sometimes saw brilliant individuals working together and producing absolutely the right policy.

A permanent staff of fifty now worked for the council, which was intended to complement rather than replace the ad hoc COBRA committee. The new council was chaired by a retired admiral named

Cavendish Piper, who certainly looked the part with his close-cropped steel-grey hair and weathered features, but who was in Cannon's estimation among the dimmest government servants he had ever met.

Cannon wondered now if there were rather too many people in the room. Over and above the twelve members of the council present, there were three ministers and twenty or so co-opted specialists, counter-terrorist experts from the police and MI5, scientists from the government service and from the Ministry of Defence, public health officials, local government chief executives, epidemiologists and a group of marine biologists, environmentalists, microbiologists, phycologists – experts in algae – who had been brought in from the universities. It looked like overkill by the prime minister, but he trusted Temple's instincts: toxic red algae was about to knock everything else out of the news and become a popular obsession that might dominate the first half of a four-week general election campaign that he was certain Temple was planning. The prime minister had to get this one right.

'These harmful algal blooms – HABS,' continued Hopcraft, 'are not limited to marine environments. They are also found in fresh water lakes in Australia and New Zealand. The cyanobacterial blooms are by definition blue-green. This toxic red algae – TRA – is interesting because red blooms are mostly confined to oceans, not fresh water, so that may be some clue as to what we are dealing with. The important point is that the cell walls of this TRA contain a substance that causes gastro-intestinal, eye, skin and respiratory irritation. Consumed in large quantities, the algae will damage the liver and neurological systems of humans as well as animals.'

'How is it spreading?' snapped Temple, who was chairing the meeting while Admiral Piper sat doing his best to look decisive at the other end of the table. 'Should we investigate possible sabotage? Have we any idea where it comes from?'

Cannon recognised not panic in his master, but a raw political energy.

'We don't know how it's spreading, prime minister,' replied Hopcraft with a note that signalled he wasn't prepared to be bullied. 'The likely candidates are birds and humans – people travelling from reservoir to reservoir for recreational purposes perhaps: fishing, sailing, birdwatching. It could be anything. As yet we have nothing definite on this. However, we have established that the algae's genetic code most closely resembles types found in New Zealand's South Island. It seems to be intolerant of water with a high pH value. That much we do know.'

'But how did this get into our water supply? It doesn't just appear out of the blue.' Temple turned to Christine Shoemaker of MI5. 'Is there a possibility this has been deliberately introduced as an act of sabotage?'

'If I may, prime minister,' said Hopcraft, trying to head her off, 'I think that conjecture would be premature at this stage. These things do spread around the world and such organisms are capable of relatively swift adaptation in new conditions. It may have been here for some time; we have no way of telling. And we should remember that the new filtration systems with ultrafine membranes do stop this particular algae.'

Temple batted the last sentence away with his hand. 'Christine, are you aware of any groups that have the necessary capability or that are planning this sort of biological attack?'

'It's a possibility, but we have no specific intelligence that says the people we're watching have contemplated this kind of action, though of course it would appeal in as much as drinking water is a very basic resource. The idea of introducing naturally occurring toxins into the supply and causing widespread panic would be an attractive option to some of the groups.'

'Precisely,' said Temple. 'It must be understood that I'm taking this very seriously indeed.' He looked around the room. 'I want twice daily reports on all aspects of the situation – scientific, crisis management and security. The public is rightly very concerned about these occurrences and it is our duty to answer those concerns with explanation, reassurance and action. Philip will work on the media strategy this afternoon. We should aim for a full briefing of the press and broadcast media at five p.m. Adam, I'd like you there, but at this stage I do not wish for any speculation as to the source of this problem.'

He stood up and asked Cannon to remain behind, also Christine Shoemaker and Jamie Ferris, who advised Temple on security matters and came from MI6 via OSI, Eden White's business intelligence company – Ortelius Security and Intelligence. It took a few minutes for the room to clear, during which Temple walked up to the screens and examined the images. Piper attempted to ingratiate himself but was pretty soon sent on his way.

'Jamie has some interesting things to say about money transfers in the Caribbean, Christine,' Temple said without turning from the screens.

Cannon didn't need one of Temple's excursions into the intelligence world now. He had three hours to organise the briefing and coordinate the line from all government press officers, vital on a story that could easily get out of hand if one of the departmental spokesmen or a minister went off-piste. 'Do you need me for this, prime minister?'

'Please stay. I'll only be a few minutes. Jamie?'

Ferris coughed. 'Our information is that very sizeable sums were left in a number of accounts in the Cayman Islands and Dutch Antilles by Sir Colin Eyam, which as far as we know have not been included in his estate. Estimates put it in the region of ten million US dollars, but that is only the money we have traced. We believe there is much more. Sir Colin was a very rich man and a very organised one. After his death, several large transfers took place in the week before Christmas to the Inter-American Development Bank, Cartagena, into an account held in the name of Daniel H. Duval, the name of a passenger who left Paris for Fort-de-France in Martinique on December fourteenth. This was about the time that Eyam vanished. We have also traced debit cards held in a variety of names that were used in Colombia to draw on funds in the accounts in Cayman and Curacao. On January second the money began to leave the account in Cartagena in small packages of ten thousand dollars to many different destinations. We are talking about a sum of at least two million dollars, but again we cannot be sure of the exact amount. I should stress that the procedures followed were extremely sophisticated and on a par with the money laundering operations of international crime syndicates.'

'And when did this activity cease?' asked Shoemaker.

'There was a blizzard of transfers between Colombia, Curacao and Cayman leading up to January twelfth, the day Eyam was killed. The money went back and forth and every which way. But on the twelfth all activity stopped, except in the case of one debit card, on which regular amounts of five thousand dollars have been drawn every week since that date at the same bank in Cartagena.' He looked at some typed notes. 'This card, held in the name of Jan Tiermann, is being funded by an account at the Netherlands-Caribbean EuroBank of Curacao. We now have surveillance at the bank in Cartagena to see who is using the card. Most of the money is withdrawn over the counter so it won't be long before we identify the individual.'

'Is this any help, Christine?' asked Temple.

'Most certainly, prime minister. Clearly Lady Eyam has no knowledge of these funds, or at least if she does, did not control them, and anyway the abrupt cessation in the movements of money after the explosion would suggest this was solely David Eyam's responsibility.'

'Except for the debit card.'

'We think that is a local man, prime minister.'

Temple threw Cannon a mysterious look, both cunning and regretful. 'Find out all you can on this, Jamie. There is a feeling of purpose in Eyam's actions that is not at all clear to me. I want to know who is using that card and what connection they had to David Eyam.' He stopped and picked up the briefing papers from the Government Scientific Service. 'Right, Philip, let's go back to the office and sort out what we're going to say about TRA.'

When Kate pressed 'Play' at the same time as 'Forward' she realised that the action tripped a switch in the car's adapted tape deck, and caused the pick-up head to shift fractionally so that it read the unused strip of magnetic tape running between the two tracks of music. It was a technique developed in the Cold War for passing messages from the Communist bloc in adapted music cassettes. She had been told about it, more as a matter of historical interest than practical trade-craft, in the first weeks of the intelligence officers' training course. Presumably this was where Eyam had learned about it also.

The first snatch of Eyam's voice came as she crawled through the traffic on the outskirts of Oxford. She wound the tape back to the start and decided to take the long route through the Cotswold Hills back to High Castle. It would probably add an hour to the journey but she was in no hurry. As she cleared the city she played the recording from the beginning.

'I hope you're alone,' he began. 'If not, I suggest you wait until you are.' There was a pause, presumably to give her time to turn the tape off or to collect herself. She heard the sounds of rooks in the distance and the rattle of bare branches. He must have recorded the message in the garden of Dove Cottage during the winter. 'OK, Sis? Good. You found the tape – well done – and you're almost certainly in my dear old car, which is good. I checked it for listening devices myself.' Another pause – coughing.

'By the time you hear this, I will be gone and you will be the proud owner of Dove Cottage and the flat in London. I realise that this must all have come as a surprise to you and I cannot predict how you feel about my legacy. Despite the money I've left you I anticipate a certain irritation. Well, I apologise, Sis. You see – I can say sorry. I wish there was another way. But I had to keep my cards close to my chest. Practically every part of my life is now monitored. The house is bugged and all communication by phone and computer is impossible. I agonised for a long time about coming to see you in New York and telling you everything that you now know about, but I decided that it would be fairer to allow you to think about this once I was gone. I believe you may still be unhappily engaged in that process.'

'You're damned right,' she said aloud.

'The documents passed to you by Hugh Russell with my letter will give you a good idea of why I had to leave, and if you inspect my computer you will know why the matter became urgent. They played very rough with me – a measure of their desperation but also of the corresponding strength of the case against them – and there seemed a very good chance that I would be jailed as a child molestor. I could not endure that.

'You're a lawyer, Sis, and the first thing you will want to know is did I do anything illegal? The answer is no. But by opposing them I was certainly made to feel like a criminal and in the end I had to behave like one. There's nothing in the dossier that harms national security – in the true sense – and nothing that is illegal or morally wrong. But you must know that possession of the dossier, and indeed of this tape, may get you into a lot of trouble.

'You have a choice: if for whatever reason you have no interest in helping destroy the thing that destroyed me, that's fine, Sis. Really, I do understand. You've got a life in New York and you deserve peace and happiness. If, however, you're willing to help, you must be prepared to use all your cunning and resilience. You are equal to the job, but let me warn you that this will consume your life.

'OK, so that's the sales pitch over.' He gave an ironic laugh. 'As you've seen in my outline, I've assembled the case against the prime minister, Eden White and senior members of the government and Civil Service. When I use the word *assemble*, that's not quite right. Actually it is you who will have to assemble the evidence. I marshalled it over the course of the last two and a half years then saw to its dispersal in order to protect it. This evidence consists of original documents and copies of ones that cannot be contested. Even though I say it myself, there is no one better able to describe what has happened. Clearly, if I had left this all in one place – say with my lawyer, or at the Dove – it would have been vulnerable. So I've arranged for it to come together at an appropriate moment. But I will not say when or how because there are some things that it is better for you not to know now. There are other people in this thing – good people whose lives I do not wish to ruin. Only one has the whole picture and that person will make themselves known to you when it is safe and they are certain that you are committed.'

Eyam stopped and coughed, a dry chesty cough, which went on for some time. Kate paused the tape because she needed to concentrate on what he was saying. Fifteen minutes later she found an open gateway leading into some woods, reversed a little way down the track, turned the engine off and picked up where she had left off to hear Eyam clearing his throat away from the microphone.

'There's no point my going on about the dossier now. I know that you will already have mastered the contents, so I wanted to say some things I should have told you before now.' He paused. 'It's odd. I've been planning to make this tape for some time and thought I knew what I was going to say, or rather how I was going to say it, but now I come to it I find . . . well, that it's harder than I thought because I suppose it means I won't be seeing you again. I suspect that's why I've left it to the last possible moment. Remember that evening in New York? Our last meal together?'

Kate exhaled. 'Forget the damned restaurant,' she said out loud. 'Tell me about the bloody dossier.'

'I was thinking about it again today,' continued Eyam, 'and wondering why I behaved so idiotically. I suppose there was something in me saying, "Wait! Wait until we're both ready." That of course seems ridiculous.' He paused again then asked, 'Was that it? I still don't know for sure. I was absorbed by the discovery of DEEP TRUTH and it weighed on me. You see, I was about to take a leap into the dark with this thing, and I was dwelling on my part in it all – my responsibility and failure and hubris. I always knew how to control things, think round or finesse them, but then I found a situation that I couldn't manage in the usual way. I had a stark choice and I had to jump one way or the other, and there was no way I could avoid that. Yet instead of talking to my friend, asking her advice and resorting to her exceptional judgement I behaved like a bastard and belittled her.' He stopped again. 'I am sorry – I'm rambling. Forgive me. I'm pretty much at the end of my tether. We buried my father today and I've had a hard time of it lately. In a few hours' time I must leave the Dove. I will not sleep here again. That's quite a thought. It saddens me greatly because I've never felt quite so attached to a place or more inspired by a setting. I felt at peace here, Sis, and I wish now that you'd got to know it with me. It has an exceptional spirit. There's a quote from Wordsworth, which captures it well. I can just see that derisive smile of yours, but here it is anyway: "*I have felt a presence that disturbs me with the joy of elevated thought . . . A motion and a spirit, that impels all thinking things, all objects of all thought and rolls through all things.*" It suddenly strikes me that those two lines might easily refer to DEEP TRUTH.' He cleared his throat.

She took out a cigarette, lit up and stared at a line of wild cherry just coming into flower across the road. What was he talking about? 'What the heck is DEEP TRUTH?' she murmured.

'Here I am mumbling into a tape recorder on a freezing cold night, trying to make sense of things to you, so let me return to the matter in hand. The purpose of the material that will come to you is to expose how DEEP TRUTH was allowed to happen and who was behind it. The prime minister and Eden White are the key figures, but so are the home secretary, Derek Glenny, the deputy director of MI5, Christine Shoemaker, and one or two high-ranking officials in the Home Office and the police. I would guess that the total number of people who know about it is no more than twenty. It is a well-kept secret and always will be, and the point is that it is so well hidden that it cannot be exposed without the original documents and letters of instruction. Once you have everything it is imperative that you move as quickly as possible to place it beyond the reach of government and Eden White. I have no doubt that the most effective way of achieving this is by using parliamentary privilege. It is true that we have all got used to dismissing Parliament, but there are still some good people there and this course will enable the media to cover the story without restraint. I favour the use of one of the select committees, because there is much more opportunity to really go into detail. It will be your job to approach the MPs who will give the material the protection of Parliament by accepting it as evidence.

'My guess is that the election will be called any time from the first week of April, after Temple sends up the usual chaff suggesting he will run later in the year. He will call it and get it over with as soon as possible. So you should seek to publish as near to that date as possible. Timing is all. If you publish too early Temple can hold off calling an election until the autumn and spend the summer denying everything. He is a ruthless and gifted propagandist.' He stopped for a few seconds. 'But, Sis, I cannot hide from you the dangers that lie ahead. Here am I, sitting in my garden, with just a few of my possessions packed and ready to flee the country. I am beaten. That should be a warning to you. They will stop at nothing to obstruct publication. You cannot trust any computer. Be careful when using your cell phone. Do not log onto your work email address because they will break into the system using your password and read everything. Never seek to research any of this on the internet and never discuss anything important in public.

'There are a few people you can rely on. Emile – Peter Kilmartin, is one. I hope he has made himself known to you. Nock is a good man but has no idea of all this and lately . . . well . . . I have to say I have had some doubts about him. It's possible that he's been compromised in some way. Our old friend Darsh is however wonderfully loyal, reliable and discreet. Also, there is a fine group of people who I have come to know while living here who go under the general name of the Bellringers. Some may have already made contact with you. Never allow any of them to know of my plans. Oh, yes, one other thing: Oliver Mermagen will seek to make himself useful to you. It was slippery old Promises who brokered the deal with Temple that allowed me to leave London and live in the country. But do not trust him. All his business now relies on the patronage of Temple and Eden, and he must be regarded as the enemy.

'So, that's about it. My motto has been belt and braces. One way or the other, all the necessary material will reach you. Now it's up to you.

'I send my love to you, my true friend, with thoughts of all our times together. There is so much I wish to say to you now but the words are all tainted with the consciousness of my own shame and stupidity. I feel completely inadequate. Good luck, Sister. Destroy this tape at the earliest opportunity. Now, I must say goodbye.'

The recording didn't end immediately. She heard him walking across gravel and a door being opened. A cough then silence. Eyam had slipped away. Faded like some bloody ghost. He'd had the last word and hung up on her before she had time to ask all the questions that had accumulated during the ten minutes of the recording. 'Bastard!' she said, slamming a hand on the dashboard.

'Bastard Eyam! Don't do that to me!'

She got out of the car, her mind tearing at the substance of the tape, such as it was, and the references to DEEP TRUTH. Was this a project or some kind of operation? And then there was the will. Had he made it because he expected to be killed like Holmes and Russell, or was he ill? That cough sounded chronic and there was an air of resignation about the whole recording that was utterly unlike Eyam, whose optimism was the nearest thing he had to a faith. And how could he be so stupid as to assume that she'd got the dossier?

She climbed back into the car, and sat for a few seconds, over-whelmed by an anguished sense that through their entire relationship they'd kept missing each other, and that this was just another occasion when his voice, his need, went unanswered. With a tug of will she shook herself and pulled back onto the road, certain that if Eyam had been defeated she stood very little chance of success. Whatever virtues she might claim, fighting lost causes wasn't one of them.

14

Mother

It would be perfectly simple to give in now, put the bloody cottage back on the market and return to London, yet as she drove through the deserted Cotswold landscape, she recognised something was drawing her back – the unfinished decryption of Dove Cottage, the sense of abridgement in Eyam's tape, and her straight curiosity about DEEP TRUTH.

She stopped in a small town of honey-coloured stone houses for a bite to eat and bought some groceries. Sitting on a bench by the town's war memorial she worried at the problem with a bleak sense of her own impotence. Then she tried Kilmartin's number. There was no reply so she continued on her journey. Near Cheltenham she hit the traffic coming from the racecourse and swung north to cross the River Severn near Tewkesbury. On the road to High Castle she received two calls: the first was from the coroner's clerk, Tony Swift, who asked to see her that evening. 'Well, OK,' she said with a slight hesitation and a hope that the bull-necked Swift had not taken encouragement from a goodbye kiss.

He added, 'I'll have some friends with me. They want to meet you. Same place? Good.'

A few minutes later she answered to a voice that said: 'Darling?' Only her mother could deliver the word with such a note of crisp accusation. 'Are you driving? If so will you pull over? I need to talk to you now.'

Kate seldom thought of her family, but when she did a photograph often came to mind of the five of them standing round a table twenty years ago. On one side were Kate and her father, Sonny Koh; on the other her mother – pleated tartan skirt and twinset – her sister Laura in a similar uniform and brother Bruce.

The two sides could not have been more different. Her father, a gambler and disruptive genius, who killed himself a few months after Charlie Lockhart died, stood back with mischief dancing in his expression, the mixed ancestry of Indonesian Chinese, Indian and Dutch traders evident in his light, liquid eyes and the sheen of his black hair. He was better looking than any man Kate had ever seen and he provoked a passion in her mother that would never otherwise have surfaced in her rather formal personality. Her love for him was epic and, to Kate, redeeming, and when he overdosed in a hotel in the Sumatra leaving debts and an ex-mistress with a child she retreated into a granite stoicism, throwing herself into her work as a barrister, which would eventually lead her to the bench.

Stricken by her father's death so soon after Charlie's, angry at her mother's self-control, Kate found a kind of solace in the law too – it was the only thing they had in common. New York made it impossible to dwell on her loss, but the anger smouldered like a peat fire deep underground. Even before she talked to a grief counsellor, who despite her misgivings was actually quite good, she realised that the hostility towards her mother was in fact rage for her father. Like Eyam, he had left, vanished without the slightest thought for her or how she would survive without him.

'Are you still in the country, Kate?' her mother asked.

'Yes. Sorry I've been very busy,' she said as she pulled up.

'Were you going to ring, or were you just going to flit off again?' Her mother didn't wait for an answer. 'Well, I'm sure you were going to get in touch when you had time. I read about David Eyam's death and heard from Oliver Mermagen that you were at the funeral. That is one reason why I am calling.'

'Oliver Mermagen! What the hell's he doing ringing you?'

'It was the only way he knew how to get hold of you. He found me in the phone book. He told me that you had moved back to this country and were looking for a job. Is that true?'

'I haven't decided what I'm going to do yet.'

'But have you left your job in New York?'

'I left the job, not the firm.'

She cross-examined her for a few minutes while Kate wondered without much regret why all their conversations lurched from one misunderstanding to another. Her younger sister, Laura, and Bruce got on well with her and had obliged her with conventional marriages and the regular production of extremely dull, pale-faced children. But Kate and her mother always found themselves circling each other.

'The point is,' she said as though Kate had needlessly interrupted her, 'Oliver Mermagen has found you a job – a very well-paid post in London working for a man named Eden White.'

'I've already talked to White, Ma. He's a creep.'

'But he's influential and wealthy and he wants to see you again.'

'It would be like going to work for the Mafia, Ma.'

'Oliver says you would be perfect for his organisation. I gave him your number. Surely you realise that it's very considerate of him to go out of his way like that, don't you think? He was always a good sort.'

'Yes,' said Kate.

'Good, well I'm glad we've spoken. I was sorry to hear about your friend. He was evidently a very gifted person, if you believe what you read in the obituaries. But he went off the rails. Perhaps he should have married.' She stopped to underline that. 'I can just remember his face – very intelligent eyes.'

'Yes, that was Eyam.'

'I hope we'll be seeing you in Edinburgh soon, Kate.' She paused. 'Don't leave it too long, darling: we're becoming strangers.'

'I won't,' she said, caught off guard by the genuine appeasement in her mother's voice.

Tony Swift led her from the Mercer's Arms to a private room at the back of the Black Bear pub where five people sat round a table. She recognised the photographer Chris Mooney and Alice Scudamore. A tall man in his mid-forties got up and introduced himself as Danny Church. He was followed by Andy Sessions, a web designer who seemed to her the epitome of the word 'bloke'. The last was Michelle Grey, a therapist of some sort, who offered her a slender hand that jangled with bracelets.

Bottles of red and white wine were on the table. The atmosphere would once have been thick with cigarette smoke but now the private room smelled of the pub's food and the fumes of the coke fire in the grate.

Tony Swift grasped a pint of beer from a wide hatch that opened onto the bar, sat down and threw a hand out to the table. 'Who's going to start?'

Danny Church said he didn't mind, and stroked a soft beard streaked with grey hair. 'We're here to make contact with you and to tell you about us. With Hugh Russell's murder everything's changed. It's obvious he was killed because of his association with David Eyam and that makes us all feel really jumpy.'

'Threatened,' said Alice Scudamore.

'We think things are coming to a head,' said Andy Sessions.

'Everything is connected,' said Chris Mooney fiercely. 'Our lives have been made hell. They're trying to crush us – police, tax inspectors, bailiffs, local authority snoops.'

'Is that really true?' asked Kate pleasantly. 'Can you prove there is an organised campaign?'

'Not in the legal sense,' said Alice Scudamore. 'But it exists. They're gradually stripping my house because I refuse to pay identity card fines. They won't jail me because that would be too public. They just barge in, take what they want and leave. They can do that now you know.' She shook her head and looked down. 'I can't work, I've got no money and I'm stressed out. And the worst thing about it is that we all know they're listening to our phones. They're watching our email, monitoring our movements. They make it obvious. We see the same men outside our houses. They're everywhere. Rick and Andy's web company is falling apart because they've lost all their contracts. The tax inspectors are around every moment of the day. Their bank has withdrawn its loan facility. At least six of us have been charged with new offences. The VAT inspectors turned over Penny Whitehead's home and took her computer to try to prove fraudulent claims, and Michelle's partner received the same treatment at his restaurant.'

'But you can't prove it's a coordinated campaign. The authorities will argue that they're just doing their job properly, and most people would support them judging by what I read in the papers.'

'That's exactly what we were told by our member of parliament,' said Chris Mooney. 'We tried taking the story to the media, but we got nowhere. They're not interested – not even the local rag or radio station. They just think we're all being paranoid. The national media couldn't give a toss. The wankers down in London have no fucking idea what's going on out in the sticks. Do they ask what's happened to the rights of ordinary men and women? Do they give a fuck? No, because they're not being persecuted and pushed around like we are. They don't see what's happened and you know why – it's because they're part of the problem.'

Alice Scudamore began nodding. 'Look, just take our word for it: this is a campaign of persecution. They've practically admitted as much.'

Tony Swift took a long draught of his beer and looked at Kate. 'I didn't tell you about this the other night because . . . well, I wanted to consult these good people here and . . .'

'What he's trying to say,' interrupted Chris Mooney, 'is that they offered me a deal. They told me that everything would stop if I informed on the others. They gave me the names of the people they wanted me to watch, but I didn't turn them down flat. I mean, I've got to think of my family.'

'Have you any record of this approach? A tape or a phone recording or anything else?'

'No, they stopped me on the road because of a traffic offence and then after a few minutes this guy gets out of an unmarked car that's pulled up behind me and he leans in the window and tells me he wants me to inform on my friends. I mean, it's unreal.'

'Did this individual say where he was from?' asked Kate.

'No, I guess Special Branch or maybe MI5. I didn't ask. Look, they've got me by the fucking balls. I can't move without one of these bloody agencies giving me a hard time. I've had the VAT people on my tail, building inspectors, the police, some damned busybody from social services threatening us with a parenting order and a *home environment study* because my youngest is in trouble at school. My elder daughter's flat at university has been searched by the police twice – they say she's linked to some extremist environmental group. They know everything about my family. When the man offered me a deal he mentioned my wife's depression. That was like ten years ago. How would they know unless they'd looked at her medical records?'

'So what are you going to do?'

'I'll play along with them and just tell everyone in the group that I have to do this.'

'They'll offer the same deal to someone else who may take it,' she said, 'which means they will know you're stringing them along.'

Mooney opened his hands in dismay. 'Fuck it. I'm not used to this. I'm a bloody photographer, not a double agent.' He stopped. 'But you're a lawyer. Tell us what we should do.'

She thought for a moment. 'You need a narrative and a timeline of exactly what has happened to all of you. It's no good you fighting this thing by yourselves. You need to band together and make a convincing case – which takes in everything – and find other people across the country who appear to have suffered like you. Then go to a London lawyer who specialises in this area of the law and campaigning and make your pitch. Someone will take it on. Get it out in the public domain.'

Andy Sessions, who with Michelle Grey had not spoken, drummed his fingers on the table, leaned forward and said, 'Tell us about yourself, Kate. You arrive out of the blue and inherit David's house and all his possessions. We want to know who you are and where you stand on all this.'

The noise from the bar swelled and briefly silenced the group. Kate looked up and through the hatch saw the slender black man Tony had signalled to two evenings ago. He was standing at the bar between two young men, who looked like identical twins. Her eyes met the black guy's and he turned away to one of his companions.

'You know what?' she said. 'I'm not really in the mood to explain myself to a bunch of complete strangers. If what you say is true about your group being under surveillance it wouldn't really be sensible, would it? I am sorry about your problems but I'm no part of them. David Eyam is dead. Hugh Russell is dead. Forgive me if I don't get too worked up about your tax inspections and parking fines.'

'So you're not interested,' said Alice Scudamore, who had watched her with a private intensity that made Kate suddenly consider the possibility that she'd once been close to Eyam.

'I'm not interested in establishing my credentials for you,' she said. 'Yes, you have problems and yes, Merrie old England sometimes seems like it's becoming a shitty little dictatorship, but a case is what interests me and you don't have anything that resembles one.'

A silence fell on the group.

'Who are the bell ringers?' she said.

'Why do you ask?' said Alice Scudamore.

'David Eyam left money to the Bell Ringers of the Marches Society in his will. I never knew he was interested in bell ringing, but then again there was a lot I didn't know about David's life down here.'

'They're a group,' said Swift slowly. 'They rang the bells at his funeral. He was friends with some of them.'

'Good friends apparently: he left them a hundred and twenty-five thousand pounds. What would bell ringers want with that kind of money?'

'There are all sorts of expenses,' said Mooney. 'I'm a member of the group.'

'Well, you must be pleased,' said Kate.

Mooney grunted.

Not much more was said and a few minutes later they began to get up and leave separately through the bar. She looked at Tony Swift, seated with his pint and his immovable, owlish self-containment.

'So tell me what that was all about?'

'They wanted to have a look at you and see where you were at.'

'*Where I'm at*, Tony!' she said, putting down her glass. 'And you, Tony? Where are *you* at? Does all the information you hear get passed up the line of the Citizen's Watch? Or are you a paid-up member of the High Castle chapter of Paranoia International?'

'Let's get out of here,' he said, getting up and draining his glass, apparently unfazed.

Outside she said, 'You didn't answer my question.'

'Me? Where am I at? Oh, I just do my job, keep my nose clean and try to help people when I can.' He stopped and looked at the moon sinking through some cloud above the castle battlements, then hitched up his trousers and buttoned his enormous black coat.

'There's something very familiar about you, Tony. I can't put my finger on it.'

'It's because I seem like every middle-aged bloke you've ever met. We're the same the world over.'

'No, that's not it. There's something else.'

They began to walk.

'The black guy in the bar with the twins – who is he?' she asked. 'I know you know because you nodded to him the other night.'

Swift smiled. 'You'll meet him one day. His name is Miff.'

'Miff?

'Yes, Miff is a friend.'

'And the twins?

'David and Jonathan: they're Jehovah's Witnesses.'

'In a pub? Jehovah's Witnesses? It doesn't seem very likely. Who are they? Why does this Miff character shadow you?'

Swift stopped and looked up at the moon. 'We're living through some strange times here. But I prefer to think of them as an eclipse, Katy; not the beginning of the long night.'

'You called me Katy. I haven't been called that since my first year at Oxford.'

'Sorry, it somehow seemed natural.'

'And Miff – why does he follow you?'

'We have business together.'

'Business. What kind of business?'

'It's of no interest.'

'You were saying about the eclipse and the long night.'

'I believe this is an eclipse because I'm an optimist. However, I am also a realist about myself. I'm just a coroner's clerk: no more than that. I have to move at a speed that is in keeping with my station in life. You're an extremely clever woman, as well as a very beautiful one, I might add. But don't embarrass me by asking me to explain things to you.'

'I didn't.'

'Ah, but you will,' he said, quietly turning to her. 'You will. We have to keep our powder dry.'

'What powder?'

His hand found her shoulder. 'There you go asking questions. I am going to say good night, Kate. Sorry.'

He looked long and hard at her, then turned away and took his thoughts off to what she assumed was a loveless bed, unless Miff was waiting there for him.

She got lost trying to find Dove Cottage in the dark, but after an hour eventually came across the spot where Hugh Russell had died. There was no police car, just tape cordoning off a portion of the road and the area where the Audi had ploughed into the bank. She reminded herself to phone Paul Spring the following day to ask how she should approach Hugh Russell's wife.

Inside Dove Cottage there was such a desolate air that she nearly turned and left for the hotel. But she unpacked the groceries, lit a fire and read a note from Sean Nock saying he would come in later to see she was OK. What now? she thought, looking round the kitchen. Make herself at home? Play house by making those minor adjustments that would put her stamp on the place? Start thinking about replacing the floribunda pattern curtains, which reminded her of her mother, or the tapestry cushions in the sitting room? No, Dove Cottage was still indisputably Eyam's, and it always would be. She could not assume ownership even if she wanted: it would be like wearing someone else's clothes.

The sitting room warmed up quickly, and she sat by the fire with a cup of soup and crackers thinking about the group she had met in the pub. Her eyes moved to the bookshelves. It was a while since she'd done any serious reading away from the law and the occasional detective mystery. And now she had the time and all Eyam's library at her disposal. That was quite an interesting prospect, but what the hell was she going to do with the library that Eyam had asked her to look after? There must have been at least twelve hundred volumes in the sitting room alone.

She swept the shelves, making a rough calculation. At regular intervals, he had pushed the books back to accommodate various objects on the shelves – a photograph of his mother in a silver frame, a fragment of a Greek amphora, a little terracotta Roman head, a Russian icon, an old brass microscope – knick-knacks, most of which she recognised from his flat in London. Occasionally, instead of an *objet d'art* breaking the line a book had been turned so that the front cover showed.

And then she gasped, because there was the book: *The Story of a Shipwrecked Sailor* by Gabriel García Márquez, the book Eyam had been reading in the bar in Cartagena and gave to Detective Bautista before he died; the book the detective had flourished in front of the camera and claimed was some kind of good luck charm: the last gift of a true English gentleman, he had said. She put the bowl down and went to fetch the book – a slim volume, first published in Spanish in 1970, then in English translation in 1986. She read the first sentences of Márquez's preface about the eight crew members being washed overboard from the Colombian destroyer *Caldas*, which had been bound for Cartagena; how the search for the sailors was abandoned after four days but one sailor had lived to crawl up a deserted beach in northern Colombia, having survived ten days without food or water, drifting on a raft in the ocean. His name was Luis Alejandro Velasco. García Márquez described him as looking like a trumpet player, not the national hero he became; a man who had natural instincts for the art of narrative, an astonishing memory and 'enough uncultivated dignity to be able to laugh at his own heroism'.

She flipped through it. About halfway through, the top of one page had been turned down, a sure sign that Eyam had been at the book. There didn't seem to be anything of particular significance on that page but maybe that wasn't the point. The point was this: if Eyam had already read the book, what was he doing with another copy in Cartagena? Eyam had a miraculous ability to absorb the written word, barely forgot anything he read, and was able to quote whole passages from years before. His comprehension and memory for the written word were of a very high order indeed, and he did not re-read books because he didn't need to, especially books with such an elementary story.

She sat down and began to read the hundred-odd pages with the attention normally applied to a complex legal case. The vitality of García Márquez's tale and of the storytelling impressed her, but when she put the book down an hour later she had only one thought. When the sailors were washed overboard everyone in Cartagena believed Velasco was dead. As they prepared his funeral he was out there on the ocean sipping seawater and catching seagulls to eat. When he was found and news reached Cartagena it was truly as though Velasco had come back from the dead.

She poured herself a glass of whisky and checked herself: brought herself up short and tried to think of something else. But it wasn't as if she was imagining all this. The same book was there, clear as day in both the tourist recording and the interview with Bautista. Not the Spanish edition, mind you, but the English translation in paperback with a cover that looked very much like the one she held in her hand – an ocean with a warship steaming towards the horizon.

She put on a jacket and went into the garden to ring Nock's number. 'I'm back,' she said. 'Can you come round? I want to ask you something.' Then she dialled her message service and worked through the accumulation of new messages until she reached Eyam's and listened to it again. 'Hello there, sister – it's me. Eyam. I felt like having a chat, but it seems you're busy and I now realise it's not ideal this end either, because I'm sitting outside in a street bar and a bloody wedding party has just appeared so you wouldn't be able to hear much anyway. But, look, I miss you and I'd really love to see you when I get back. Perhaps we should meet in New York.'

An ordinary message but one with a secret, she was sure. At the end of a list of options she was invited by the automated voice to key eight for message details. There was no record of a telephone number, but the message had been left at five thirty-eight p.m., Saturday, January 19th – not January 12th, the date of the explosion. So when Eyam called she wasn't in the office working on a deal, but staying with Sam Calvert and his wife. She went into the phone's calendar to make sure. January 18th–20th was marked off with the words *Calverts – country*. It was the same weekend she'd told old Sam Calvert she wanted to leave and he had shown her into his den on that Saturday afternoon and persuaded her to take a few months off, then join the London office. He didn't want to lose her but he reckoned it was time for her to get her bearings in her personal life, by which he meant that she should get a personal life. Hell, he'd even pay for a cruise or finance a pro bono section in the London office if it meant she'd stay. She could have a baby on the firm, if she wanted. Whatever it took, she only had to say.

She checked the GPS facility, which rather unnecessarily in her view kept a record of the phone's precise location for every minute it was switched on. She entered January 12 and an approximate time, and a map of Manhattan came up with the address on Sixth Avenue in a panel below. Right, she was in the conference room and the phone would have been on the table beside her and switched on; she would have answered. She did the same for the following weekend. There was no record of the phone's location in the afternoon because it had been switched off, but for that morning it gave an address in Connecticut.

There was no mistaking it – the call had come a week after he had died, and yet Eyam had taken care to locate and time the message by mentioning the policeman and the wedding party passing in front of him. She turned towards the lights of the cottage with a profound sense of bafflement. There could only be two explanations. Either the automated message service had made a mistake on the date of the call, which seemed highly improbable, or Eyam was alive and moreover meant to convey that astonishing fact by obliquely alerting her to these discrepancies. That of course was absurd – impossible. But just pretend it's possible, she said to herself. What would the phone message mean? He was saying, yes, I am in the film that was shot outside the cafe but I wasn't killed by the explosion. The presence of *The Story of the Shipwrecked Sailor* was an internal clue, planted there by Eyam, who could be sure that she would search the cottage high and low after his letter. Her mind reeled. She stood shivering in the cold, staring vacantly at her breath clouds, which were lit blue by her mobile. If Eyam had faked his own death there must be others involved – Detective Bautista for one. And Darsh for another: she remembered that odd look he gave her when he talked about the red admiral butterfly, the butterfly that hibernates then comes to life in the spring, or flies north from France. Was he saying Eyam was still in France? Did Darsh know and if so was he dropping a hint to see if she had any suspicions of her own? His theatrical display of grief at the funeral might also contain its own message – the prayer he quoted about the inward man being renewed and the things that are not seen being eternal.

And it wasn't just Darsh who was dropping hints during the service. She went inside, found her bag in the kitchen and drew out the order of service for the funeral that Eyam had planned with such care and prescience. On the back was the poem entitled *The Death of Me*. She read the second verse: '*I may be gone for now, sister, For others say I've died. But I'll wait for you here, sister, 'Til we take the waters wide.*' This wasn't an anonymous American folk song, but verses Eyam had knocked up himself and with some gall placed on the back of his own funeral service. She stared at the words and whispered, 'Eyam, you fucking bastard.' Gripping the booklet, she sat down heavily and struggled to get a hold on her thoughts. Until this moment, disbelief, hope and joy had competed to overwhelm her but now the hardening conviction that Eyam was alive sparked a sense of what? Betrayal seemed the best word. He had deceived her, used her unscrupulously without thought for the grief and remorse she would experience, jeopardised her life and caused the death of an innocent man. Faking a death was somehow the ultimate lie and Eyam had done it in order to pass all his troubles to her and escape the responsibilities of the cause he seemed to have created. Cowardice was the other word that came to mind, but she had no time to refine her thoughts further because Sean Nock was hailing her from the open front door.

'Come in,' she said, getting up.

Nock was in a loose lumberjack shirt and steamed in the cold. He had run all the way. 'You sounded worried on the phone.'

'I'm fine,' she said coolly. 'I'm going to ask you a question and I want a straight answer.' She picked up *The Story of a Shipwrecked Sailor* and handed it to him. 'This book was placed facing outwards from the middle of the bookshelves. Did you put it there?'

'Maybe it was moved during cleaning,' he said innocently.

'I don't have a cleaner.'

'Yes, you do – it's me.'

'You're an engineer, Sean, not a cleaner.'

'I was paid to look after the place and that included doing a bit of dusting and vacuuming.'

'Sean, did you put that book there so that I would see it? Were you told by anyone to do that?'

'I don't think so – no.'

'Don't fuck with me, Sean. Did you put it there?'

Nock gave her a look of bewilderment. 'Really, I don't remember moving it.'

'You stay here. I'm going to make a call outside. When I come back I want some answers.' She snatched up her bag and left for the end of the garden where she took out Kilmartin's phone and dialled his number. He answered after the first ring. 'We need to talk as soon as possible,' she said.

'Yes, I agree; we have much to discuss,' said Kilmartin, 'but I can't speak now. We should meet tomorrow. Town or country, which suits you?'

'Country. Near here.' As she said it she saw several headlights slashing through the trees at the top of the track.

'Good. I'll call first thing,' said Kilmartin and hung up.

Now she saw a flashing blue light. A few seconds later three police cars plunged into Eyam's drive, pulled up and disgorged several uniformed police officers. Then came two unmarked cars and three men in civilian clothes got out. One of them was Newsome. The uniformed police ran to the front door and opened it without ringing. Then through the sitting room windows she saw them seize hold of Sean Nock. There was some shouting and a tussle in which Nock threw two of the officers across the room. Without thinking, she switched off the Kilmartin phone and placed it into one of the flower pots stacked at the corner of Eyam's vegetable patch and placed another pot on top. Then she summoned the call register on her own phone, worked her finger across the screen until she picked 'Received Calls' from the menu and kept pressing the screen until the number of the last call received was ringing.

'It's me,' she said when her mother answered. 'I need some help. Can you call Sam Calvert at Calvert-Mayne in New York, and explain that I need the best defence lawyer in England. He'll know who that is. I think I'm about to be taken to High Castle police station. Got that?'

'Yes, I'm writing it down, darling. High Castle . . . police station.' For once Kate was grateful for her mother's composure. 'Will Mr Calvert be readily available?'

'He has an assistant called Amy Stovall. Tell her who you are and explain it's urgent. Look, I must go now. Thanks, Ma.'

'Got it. Good luck. Call me if you can.'

She waited in the dark watching the police race through the house, searching for her. She dialled her message service and went back to delete the voicemail from Eyam, then turned off the phone, dropped it in her pocket and walked towards the front door. Newsome turned at the sound of her crossing the gravel. 'Kate Lockhart, I am arresting you in connection with the murder of Hugh Arthur Russell on March 13th. You will come with us.' A woman officer took hold of her and led her to the unmarked car. Sean Nock, by now bound with blue wrist ties and sporting a gash to his eyebrow, was taken to the back of a police van.

15

The Edit Point

Kilmartin arrived at the Isambard Hotel on Edgware Road at nine thirty p.m. and went to a room reserved by a New Zealand national named Owen Kennedy, having paid for it with a credit card and shown a passport in the same name. Murray Link followed him a few minutes later, having received a text with the room number. He set up a laptop on the desk while Kilmartin withdrew a couple of miniatures from the fridge and sat down on a chair beside Link.

'Christ, what's that you're wearing, Murray?'

'What do you mean?'

'The aftershave.'

'My wife gave it to me. I'm trying it out.'

'God, I've met yak herders who smell better,' said Kilmartin and tipped the whisky and vodka miniatures into two glasses.

'Do you want to see this, or not?' said Link testily.

'Yes, please go ahead.'

'OK, so this is a right dog's dinner,' he said gleefully as his fingers scurried across the keyboard. 'What do you know about camcorders, Peter?'

'Very little.'

'Right, well, the camcorder that made this film was a pretty sophisticated model that records not onto discs but straight onto a hard drive that can store about five hours of footage. It contains a number of interesting features that are rarely appreciated by the average punter. It stamps the film with metadata known as EXIF – Exchange Image File Format, to give its full name – hidden information which allows you to know the make and model number of the camera, the time and date the film was made, even the camera settings. This particular model is also fitted with a GPS device that tells you where the camera was when the film was made.'

'Good Lord! You mean you can tell all that from a DVD that is maybe a third-generation copy?'

'Absolutely, but you have got to know what you are doing.' He clicked on an icon. 'Now this is the part of the footage that wasn't played at the inquest. It shows the party of tourists in the port area of Cartagena and also visiting some kind of memorial by the sea. You can see the city in the background and by the way the GPS code indicates that they were in that spot when the images were shot.'

They watched the trio of tourists walking in the port, then standing in front of a large stone slab carved in the shape of a book. On the cover were written the words '*Gabriel García Márquez – Relato de un Náufrago.*' The camera focused on the rest of the inscription. Kilmartin translated the whole with little difficulty. '*Story of a Shipwrecked Sailor. Who was stranded for ten days in a raft without food or water. Who was proclaimed a national hero. Kissed by beauty queens and made rich by publicity and later hated by the government and forgotten for ever.*'

'How can he be forgotten for ever if they set up a bloody memorial to him?' asked Link.

Kilmartin smiled absently and made a note in a small red book. 'I wonder why this wasn't shown at the inquest.'

'I'm coming to that,' said Link. 'OK, so now we get to the main action,' said Link. 'I want you to notice a couple of things. The tourists are all wearing the same clothes, but there are one or two minor differences. The blonde woman with the red spotted shirt has a large plaster on her knee which does not appear in the first part of the film.'

'So what? She probably hurt herself sometime later that day, before they got to the cafe where Eyam was killed.'

Link shook his head and brought up a still of the group by the memorial and magnified a section around the woman's left knee. Instead of a plaster, a graze could be seen, surrounded by an area of untanned skin. 'So this sequence in the port, which was thought to have come from the morning of the bomb, was in fact shot much later – maybe two or three days later. Notice that the man is wearing different-

158

coloured running socks with his trainers – blue not white – and the group as a whole is much more tanned than in the bomb footage.'

'You're right. What about the hidden data in the film of the cafe and the bomb going off?'

'That's the odd part. The EXIF metadata is kosher in the port and the memorial scenes – it says the filming took place on the morning of January 12th in Cartagena in conditions of extremely bright sunlight. When we come to the scene at the cafe the data has been tampered with, which is possible with a special programme, although you've got to know your onions. In some parts there's no data and in others another date pops up – January 19th.'

'So what's that mean?'

'Someone was screwing around, trying to remove the information about date, time and location in the film, but did a crap job. For instance, parts of the film are geo-coded for a position that is outside the city of Cartagena, by about twenty miles. I've checked. But that's not everything. There's a jump in the film, a bloody great chasm, which is obvious when you play it through. I can't understand why no one noticed. You'll see what I mean.'

He ran the footage from the moment when the camera dodged from a bell tower to a balcony to settle on the three tourists drinking beer. Eyam and Detective Bautista were in the background. The whole sequence was much faster than Kilmartin remembered, but then he recollected that the coroner's clerk had kept on starting and stopping the film. The edit point, as Link put it, came after Eyam's exchange with the policeman and his phone call. He paid for his drink and walked across the street into the alleyway. There was a moment of stillness and then a jolt, indicating that the camera angle had been slightly altered, or the camera had dropped fractionally on its stand. Kilmartin thought that the clerk must have stopped the film at that moment, otherwise he would have seen it. The position of the detective lounging in the chair remained the same, but the people in the foreground had shifted slightly.

'So this is where they cut a whole slice of time out of the film,' said Link. 'How long is anyone's guess. I did some work on the watch that the man in the foreground is wearing – I'd say we're looking at ninety seconds to two minutes. There is no other internal evidence to give an exact time and all the hidden data is missing from this section.'

'So Eyam potentially had time to get clear of the gas bomb?'

'Exactly – only it wasn't a gas bomb. If you place footage of this bomb alongside a video recording of a bomb from Iraq seven or eight years ago, the two just don't compare. A bomb using pressurised gas containers with gas leaking into a large area set off by a core of explosive is a powerful weapon, which would have killed everyone in that street, a little like the fuel-air bombs used by the American military. The blast wave is spectacular. But this explosion was something much less devastating.' He pulled up a still of the white van as it entered the alley and activated a graphic that lifted the van and spun it around. 'The main explosive pod was probably laid in the middle of the back of the van in plastic bags. Around this would be a mixture of petrol, viscous oil and diesel, probably contained in drums. The petrol causes a spectacular fireball, which is followed by clouds of black smoke created by the oil and diesel. I'd guess that small charges were rigged to the doors, to the right-hand side of the chassis to flip the vehicle over and maybe even to the engine block.' A grubby finger touched the screen at different points. 'These were the pyrotechnics of an action movie, Peter. In fact I think the whole thing is a kind of movie set up. It looks real because most people's experience of explosions is limited to Hollywood pyrotechnics. They don't have access to footage of real explosions.' He showed Kilmartin a clip of an experiment involving a pick-up vehicle and an improvised fuel-air explosion performed by the US military, in which the shock wave could be seen moving out over a very large area. There was no comparison between the two explosions.

Kilmartin moved his chair back and stared at the wall.

'David Eyam wasn't killed in Colombia that day,' said Link.

'Oh, I'm not sure we can go that far,' said Kilmartin.

'We can,' said Link. 'He wasn't trying to disappear for ever. There are too many inconsistencies in the metadata. If someone knows enough to alter the EXIF, they do it properly, but here they've made a complete Horlicks of it. I guess this fellow was trying to tell anyone who looked at the film properly that it was all phoney. Maybe he knew you would be that person.'

Kilmartin shrugged. 'Too risky – our former employers were just as likely to get hold of the film and run the tests you did.'

'Not if DNA evidence established that Mr Eyam's remains were found at the scene of this explosion. I looked up the inquest reports. DNA samples underpinned the coroner's verdict. No one had any reason to doubt that your man had died. With DNA everyone rolls over and suspends their critical faculties.' His eyes twinkled. 'I'll tell you one thing – this had to be an inside job. Someone in the coroner's investigation fixed that DNA evidence. That's the only way all this could have worked.'

'You're running ahead of yourself, Murray.'

'No, I'm not.' He turned back to the computer and clicked on another icon. 'I was looking at the metadata in the final seconds of the film and this is what I found in the very last image.' The letters **EYAMALIVE** appeared on the screen. 'Eyam Alive, or I *am* alive. Take your pick, but either way it means the same.'

At that moment the cell phone rang in Kilmartin's pocket. Without surprise he answered to Kate Lockhart's voice. As he agreed to a meeting in the country the following day, he wondered how much she knew. But now his problem was the man sitting beside him. Link wasn't stupid: he would realise he was in possession of information with a very high market value. Kilmartin regretted asking him if he or any of his colleagues had heard of SPINDRIFT because that told Link why Eyam's faked death would matter so much to the government, or to anyone else he might try to sell it to – Eden White's intelligence outfit, for example. His request about SPIN-DRIFT might contextualise what was discovered in the film and although Murray Link might not yet have reached the point in his own mind when he'd be willing to sell Kilmartin out, sooner or later he would.

'And the other thing you mentioned – SPINDRIFT?'

'Oh, I think we'll leave that for now. It isn't relevant to this and I think I've had enough excitement for one night,' said Kilmartin and handed Link the outstanding part of his fee. 'This is on the under-standing that I have not only bought your technological genius, Murray, but your silence. I do not want this getting out. Do you hear?'

Link nodded.

'I mean it, Murray. I don't want any cause to feel angry with you.'

'Understood. You're the guv'nor. You paid for all this.'

16

Interrogation

Kate submitted to it all: to the media, which had been tipped off about the arrests and was waiting as the convoy of cars slowed at the rear entrance of High Castle police station, allowing cameras to be pressed to the window of the car she was in; to the humiliation of 'the Cage', where suspects were held; to being searched and having her clothes removed for forensic examination; to the replacement white forensic suit and black canvas shoes; the incompetence and woeful gaze of the custody officer who informed her of her rights but then did not seem to know how to fill in the computerised custody form; the universal cheerlessness of the place with its unforgiving light and the minatory tone of the notices addressed to suspects; to the wilting heat and airlessness; to the whistling of constables in distant corridors; and to the astonishing fact that she was arrested and deprived of her liberty and was for a period of one and a half hours locked in a cell with a brushed steel lavatory that smelled of urine: to all this she submitted with a cold, silent fury.

It was in the early hours before the police doctor determined she was fit in body and mind to be interviewed and legal representation was assigned from the duty calls centre – Jim Wreston, a fresh-faced man in his late twenties with a loosened tie knot and scuffed shoes, who seemed hopelessly in awe of the police. She was taken to the interview room where Newsome was waiting with the officer she had seen overseeing the security operation in the square on the day of the funeral. His name was Tom Shap and he was a superintendent. Newsome recited a legal caution and for the tape recorder's benefit gave their names and that of an officer of unspecified rank, referred to simply as Mr Halliday, who sat tipping the back of his chair against the wall.

They began with her relationship with Eyam. She told Newsome again how she learned of his death, about her attendance at the inquest and the funeral, the intervening weekend and being approached by Hugh Russell in the Green Parrot cafe. She described her astonishment at his news about the will and then went on to say how Russell had told her on the following day about the theft of documents and the attack on him. Her account was clear and poised, even though her mind was still racing with the possibility that Eyam might still be alive. She worried that this vast, unconfirmed secret would communicate itself as guilt, and the one thing she needed now was for the police to let her go. But it was clear Newsome and Shap were laying the foundations for a long interrogation. Wreston sat mute beside her, occasionally glancing in her direction as if he understood the drift of the police questions, which she knew he didn't.

Shap, whose manner had not improved since her first encounter with him, asked about 'the lost hours' between Russell's departure from Dove Cottage and the discovery of the car with his body inside at the end of the track. She was getting to know the property, she replied, thinking about what she would do with all Eyam's possessions. She recalled phoning the office in New York and then she mentioned using the computer, which she instantly regretted.

'I'll to come to that later,' said Shap.

'In the meantime,' said Newsome, 'perhaps you would explain these.' He drew some still photographs from an envelope but held them towards his chest.

'You haven't disclosed this material,' said Wreston.

'I am doing so now,' said Newsome.

'Let's get on with it. I have no objections,' Kate said.

He handed the photographs to Wreston.

'You told us,' said Shap, 'that Hugh Russell informed you of the break-in at his office and the attack he suffered and that all the time you had been in the hotel.' He laid down the four CCTV images of her standing outside Russell's office and one of her pushing the door open. Newsome described the images for the tape recorder.

'These place you at the scene of at least one crime,' said Shap. 'We conclude that Mr Russell didn't see who hit him because he was struck from behind. We know you were in the building at the time of the attack, though you omitted this important fact from your story and this leads us to believe that having failed to kill him on that occasion you lured him to the cottage where your accomplice, Sean Nock, finished off the job for you.'

'That's ridiculous,' she said.

'Then how do you explain your behaviour over the weekend and on the evening of the attack? One resident whose garden backs onto the alleyway known as the Cut recently installed CCTV to deal with the problem of burglars. He has film of you making your way along that alley once over the weekend and then early on Tuesday evening.'

'I did go to see Mr Russell at his request,' she said after a while.

'At last we're getting somewhere,' said Shap unpleasantly. 'What were you doing there?'

'Mr Russell asked me to take delivery of the documents.'

'Why didn't he mention this to the investigating officers when they took his statement?

'Because I asked him not to.'

'Why?'

'Because he said the documents were sensitive. He came to Mr Eyam's wake at the Bailey Hotel. He was flustered and said he wanted to give them to me immediately. I didn't know what was in them of course, but I thought I should take delivery as discreetly as possible. When I got to the offices the door was open and after a few minutes I went upstairs. I was halfway up when two men attacked me. I saw very little because of the light. I was hit several times and fought back. When they left the building I continued upstairs and found Mr Russell unconscious. The safe was open. When he came round he confirmed that the documents were missing.'

Shap sniffed. 'Come on, Miss Lockhart, do you really expect us to believe this? The story about the two men is pure fantasy, isn't it?'

'No,' she said quietly as an idea struck her. 'Do you want to see the injury I received?' She lifted up the trouser leg and showed them the cut on her ankle. They were unimpressed.

'There was no other reason to explore that alley two days before the break-in,' continued Shap. 'You were finding a way of getting to his office unnoticed, weren't you?'

She met his eyes. 'What possible motive could I have to attack a man I had not met until that morning?'

'You tell us. Maybe it was Mr Eyam's will,' said Newsome.

'I am the main beneficiary of Mr Eyam's will. That is true, but the will's authenticity can be established by simply looking into Mr Russell's records and consulting his partner. It was witnessed by Mrs Spring, whom I've never met. As I told you, I have no need of money, inspector. I am not the kind of person who goes round forging wills. I still have a very well-paid job and considerable savings.'

'The will is being examined now,' said Shap.

'You took it from my purse?'

'Together with the letter that purports to be from your friend David Eyam. Tell us a little about that. It seems a strange document. Not the sort of letter you would want a friend to read after your death. It seems, well, so vague and . . .'

'And whimsical? Yes, David was like that sometimes. To tell the truth I only read it once because it made me so sad to think of him gone. We had been friends for a very long time. Maybe he was a little drunk when he wrote it. I believe he was ill. There is a lot that is painful to me and still unexplained.' Halliday had stopped rocking his chair and let his hands drop to his knees.

'Quite so, Miss Lockhart,' said Newsome. 'What do you think he was trying to convey in that letter? It's almost as if there was a coded message in it.'

'It did seem a bit odd, I agree. I don't know what you mean by a coded message, but then I haven't had time to think about it.'

'Because you spent all day on the road,' said Shap. 'Where did you go?'

'I am sure you know, inspector. I went to Oxford to see a friend in college – my old college.'

'Do you mind telling me who?'

'As a matter of fact I do – it's personal.'

'Look, Miss Lockhart, unless we get your cooperation on these matters this will go very badly for you. We will learn the truth one way or another, I can assure you of that.'

'What truth is it that you want? That I hit Hugh Russell over the head, but failing to kill him, inveigled him out to Dove Cottage the next day, having arranged with another man I'd never met before to have him gunned down just a few hundred yards from the cottage, so putting me at the scene of the crime? Is that what you believe? Is that really your theory?' She looked from one face to the other. 'Or are you holding me here on the pretext of the murder inquiry while you go through my phone, computer and personal belongings?'

Newsome stretched and then locked his hands at the back of his head. 'You seem anxious, Miss Lockhart.'

'I'm not anxious, but I'm extremely angry at the way I'm being treated. Has it occurred to you that if I'd been in that car I would have been killed also? Does it matter to you that while you question me the real killers are getting away? The two men who attacked Hugh and me are clearly the prime suspects, yet you put no effort into finding out who they were. There is not one shred of evidence to say I killed my friend's lawyer. You have nothing and you know it. You have no alternative but to let me go.'

'You're not going anywhere. Even if we didn't have the film of you entering the building, we'd still know you'd been there. Your DNA and fingerprints have been found on the safe door and I am confident that we will find fibre evidence to match the clothes you were wearing that evening. We know that you left by the rear door and that you retraced your steps to the hotel by the Cut because we have film of that too. That is compelling evidence of your intentions that evening and the following day, Miss Lockhart. You will certainly spend the rest of tonight in the cells.'

She looked at Wreston. 'Then this interview is at an end,' she said. 'I read the code of practice while I was waiting. You have already failed to give me proper rest and nourishment. If I recollect rightly it says that, *"Breaks from interviewing should be made at recognised meal-times or at times which take into account when the suspect last had a meal."'*

'That's at my discretion and if you refuse to answer questions an adverse inference may be drawn by a jury.'

'By a jury! There won't be a jury because you can't charge me, and I very much doubt you have even enough to keep me here. But go ahead – ask your questions. I am not saying anything more until my chosen legal representative arrives. I am informing you that I am tired and that if you continue with this interview I will formally lodge a complaint about your oppressive behaviour.'

Wreston woke from his trance. 'I think my client is indicating that she needs rest. It *is* nearly two thirty. Under the guidelines, she has a right to reasonable treatment.'

Newsome switched off the tape recorder. After forms were filled in and two tapes ejected from the machine the three policemen left without a word. A few minutes later she found herself in a cell with a sandwich, banana, milk chocolate wafer biscuit and a cup of tea.

She slept fitfully for a few hours and woke early with thought of the book on the shelf and what it meant. If Eyam was alive, there were only two motives that might have caused him to leave England – straightforward evasion or a more sinuous and ultimately mystifying diversionary plan. As she lay on the foam mattress, a glimmer of daylight showing through the bottle-glass cell window, she decided it was more likely to be the second. If Eyam had intended to vanish for ever, it would have been simple for him to remain hidden and find a new life on his father's fortune. But he had left clues that he was still alive, including a barely coded confession in the order of service for his own funeral, which might just as easily have been spotted by someone else – Kilmartin for instance – or any of Eden White's more alert associates.

The way to make sure that only she saw those lines in the song would have been to leave it at Dove Cottage or with Hugh Russell. But, no, he had put this clue in the most public forum possible. Why? There was no clear answer, at any rate none that she could readily find, huddled in a paper suit under this thin blue blanket with the dreadful smell of piss in the air. But she did keep on reminding herself of Eyam's exceptional skills of manipulation, his foresight, the obsessive organisation of his affairs. Eyam was a planner, a list maker, a ticker-off of things done. None of this was an accident. If he was dropping these rash, schoolgirl hints about his secret, he wanted someone other than herself to become suspicious so they would start investigating his death, his whereabouts and his intentions. Perhaps he was laying a trail, setting up a diversion while evidence against Eden White and the government was published? If this was the case others must have known of the plan to fake his death before she had come anywhere near suspecting it. At least one person had been to the cottage while she was away and left the copy of *The Story of a Shipwrecked Sailor* so she would see it. But why hadn't he been more explicit in the tape? Maybe she'd missed some clues in it. She wouldn't have another chance to hear it because the people who must now be looking at her computer and phone and drawing a precise picture of her life and associates would probably also find the tape in the car and subject it to the same kind of scrutiny.

But the first priority was to get herself released. Nothing would be solved inside High Castle police station. She needed time, fresh air and a bit of quiet to think everything through and decide a course of action which it seemed to her must now completely detach itself from David Eyam – either the memory of him or the reality of his continued existence.

At seven thirty a.m. they brought her tea and something that resembled a toasted sandwich, which was glued by melted cheese to the biodegradable box. She was allowed a shower, but no toothbrush or paste was available. At nine she was taken up from the cell and shown to a new interview room, which was slightly larger and equipped with two cameras. Wreston was there and she asked if there had been any word from her own lawyers. They replied no. After the formalities concerning the two interview tapes – one of which was sealed for the record – and a caution delivered by Newsome, he started the interview. He went back over everything exhaustively, picking holes in her story, finding significance in the slightest hesitation or inconsistency.

Shap sat saying little. It was an hour before he asked, 'When you were in the cottage after Mr Russell left, where was Mr Nock?'

She groaned. 'I've no idea. He went off for some kind of meeting – I don't remember what he said. Next time I saw him was running down the drive after he discovered the car. He had a couple of dogs with him, which later disappeared.'

'You say you had never met before that day?'

'Yes.'

'Or had contact with him?'

'I had no knowledge of Mr Nock's existence before I came to High Castle.'

'But he was at Mr Eyam's funeral.'

'So were a lot of other people. I didn't notice him.'

'So what were you doing all that time?'

'I told you last night.'

Shap looked at some notes. 'Using your phone and the computer in the house. Mr Eyam's computer, right?'

'Some of the time, yes.'

'That's odd because we've examined the computer and found no hard drive. How could you have been using it?'

She looked at him coolly. 'That's because I removed the hard drive and destroyed it.'

'Removed the hard drive?'

There was no point lying. She was sure they would already have checked with the internet provider or looked at Eyam's search engine records and learned that there was some traffic from Eyam's account that afternoon. 'By chance I found some things on that computer which I did not think worthy of David Eyam. I knew he could not have been responsible for them and I decided to destroy the evidence.'

'What sort of things?'

'Pornography – illegal pornography.'

'You're talking about child porn?'

She nodded.

'You know that your action amounts to an offence. You were destroying evidence of criminality. What do you say to that?'

'It is my computer now and David Eyam is dead. You can hardly prosecute him.'

'Mr Eyam's death does not excuse the destruction of the drive. Those images may have contained valuable evidence about victims and perpetrators of crimes who are still alive. Did that not occur to you?'

She shook her head. 'Are you questioning me over a computer hard drive, or a murder?'

'For all we know the two may be related,' said Shap.

'Don't be stupid,' she said. 'You know perfectly well they aren't.

Those images were planted on Eyam's computer as part of a campaign of persecution, which he suffered after leaving his job in government. They were going to be used to prosecute a man who had become an embarrassment, or even a threat to the present government. He had no alternative but to leave the country.'

'What proof do you have of any of this?' asked Newsome.

'Of course I don't have proof.'

'Then how are we meant to believe these allegations that you make so freely?'

Just then there was a commotion at the door and a very large man in his late-fifties came in and stood looking at the three officers, his huge bulbous features registering civilised horror. 'I am John Turvey and Miss Lockhart is my client,' he said. He looked at Wreston. 'Thank you, sir, for holding the fort. Now, if you wouldn't mind, I'd like a consultation with my client in private.'

'I mind very much,' said Shap getting up. 'I mind very much that you walked in on this interview.'

Turvey looked at him from under his brow, then produced four or five newspapers, which he let fall onto the table. 'And while we have that consultation perhaps you would care to look at these. My assistant has already highlighted the parts of the coverage that are designed to blacken my client's name.' Kate caught a glimpse of a couple of headlines – TOP US LAWYER IS MURDER SUPECT; TWO HELD AFTER 'HIT' IN RURAL PARADISE. The second was accompanied by a photograph of her taken as she was driven into the police station. 'A letter has already been dispatched to your chief constable,' growled Turvey.

'We are not responsible for the media's coverage,' said Newsome.

'But you are for the statements issued by a Superintendent Shap, which I assume is you.' He looked thunderously at Shap. 'These statements all but say my client is guilty. If she is guilty why has she not been charged?'

'We are conducting an investigation into a very serious matter – the murder of Hugh Russell. You have no right to barge in here and start making accusations.'

'Accusations?' said Turvey. 'This prejudicial coverage is a fact, just as

170

the incomplete custody record for my client is a fact. Now please oblige me, superintendent.'

At length they were shown into a room for their consultation and Turvey went over everything she had been asked about by the two officers. At the mention of the CCTV stills he left the room to make a phone call to instruct the members of what he called his team, which included a former Scotland Yard officer who had arrived in High Castle in the early hours.

An hour later they went back to the interview room where Turvey sat with his hands folded across his stomach contemplating the two officers with a gaze of professional dismay. There was hardly a moment when he did not fill the room with disdain for the proceedings, and he amused himself by treating Halliday, whom he'd told her was an observer from Special Branch, as some kind of office junior who was there to open the window on request or fetch a jug of water. Turvey intervened only a few times, when Newsome made remarks about Kate's character, but mostly he seemed to be content for the pair to exhaust themselves. The hard drive of the computer obsessed them because it was the only evidence of Kate's criminality. Turvey had instructed her to play a straight bat, to hit every ball back to the bowler, as he put it, without flourish or feeling. She was certainly capable of looking after herself, but she was encouraged by the monumental steadfastness sitting beside her. They got nowhere on the computer or the child porn. At four they took a break and Kate was returned to the cells.

When she was taken back an hour later Shap was holding a piece of paper and displaying some of his former swagger, but they had to wait for Turvey, who had used the break to have a sandwich with his team. He came back into the room hugging his briefcase to his chest. No sooner had he lowered himself to his chair – an action that was accompanied by a good deal of sighing – than Shap disclosed that he would show Kate an ID supplementary form filled in by her at the Bailey Hotel on the evening before Russell's murder. 'The form contains misinformation and in certain parts has been defaced.'

Kate laughed. 'You can't be serious.'

'You do realise that this is a criminal matter,' said Shap. 'For a lawyer you display remarkably little respect for the law.' He showed her the form. 'Were you requested by the hotel management to comply with the law by filling in this form?'

'Before you answer that question, Miss Lockhart,' said Turvey, 'I must ask these gentlemen the relevance of this to the inquiry into the murder of Hugh Russell.'

'We suspect that Miss Lockhart was attempting to conceal information about herself because she knew that she would be involved in the matters we are investigating today – namely the murder of Hugh Russell.'

'That's absurd,' she said quietly. 'The hotel already had my passport and credit card details and mobile phone number. This form was superfluous and I treated it as such.'

'You had shown your passport,' growled Turvey without looking at her. 'Then there can be no question of relevance in the matter of Mr Russell's murder. She was not hiding anything, and as far as I can see she complied with the law. The hotel was being officious, superintendent.' He reached for his briefcase and fixed Shap with a look of dreadful black intensity. 'Perhaps it is time for me to make my own disclosures. Your entire case against Miss Lockhart rests on some CCTV footage of the entrance to Mr Russell's offices in Mortimer Street. Is that right? This footage comes from the town's surveillance system, which is operated by the police. Is that also correct?'

Neither of the officers reacted, but Halliday shifted in his chair and leaned forward, suspecting that Turvey was about to show his hand.

'Your images come from the police street surveillance system. But these days there are many such cameras operating and not all of them belong to the police. In that vicinity there is also a system run by a bank, which covers the front of the premises and looks out across the street, as it happens, onto the entrance of number six: there is a high-definition camera fixed inside the transom of the bank's front door. My associates have now been able to retrieve images from this camera that show two men entering Mr Russell's office about twenty minutes before my client and then leaving in some hurry. They went in carrying nothing, but, as you will see, one of them is leaving holding a file and the other is clutching his face. He is clearly injured, a fact that tallies with my client's account of what happened inside that building. We have checked with Mr Russell's secretary and found no appointments for two men of their appearance. She does not recognise them as clients of the late Mr Russell. And his partner, Paul Spring, says that he has never seen these individuals before.'

He paused and swept off his glasses. 'I suggest to you that these were Mr Russell's assailants – the men attacked him, broke into his safe and stole documents that were intended for my client.' He placed the photographs one by one on the table, ending with a shot of the two men leaving the offices. 'The point that won't escape you, nor – if I may say so – the media, is that exactly the same footage, though perhaps not of similar quality, lies in the police system. Yet you did not think to view all the film available from that evening, an odd decision since it would have confirmed my client's story.' He raised a hand against Newsome's protest. 'The second part of your allegation, that Miss Lockhart arranged to travel to Dove Cottage where Mr Nock killed Mr Russell, does not stand up to examination either. Mr Nock has an iron-clad alibi for the period of an hour either side of Mr Russell's death. As you very well know, he was in the local hospital seeing a specialist for torn ligaments in his shoulder. My associates have checked with the doctor and his receptionist, as have police officers from this station. He did not return home until four fifteen, by which time Mr Russell had been dead for nearly two hours. It was then that he took his dogs for a walk. Do I need to continue, chief inspector? No, because you know all this and yet you continue to deprive my client of her liberty and make these wild allegations against her when she herself could very easily have been shot too. Last night and through today you have leaked details about her life to the press, details that have come from this very room, super-intendent. You have treated her to all the indignities of official suspi-cion, and at the same time shown scant regard for her safety or for the proper conduct of this case.'

His voice had risen steadily but now it fell to almost a whisper as he pushed a photograph under Shap's gaze. 'For it must be clear that these men are the only suspects in your case; that they are still at large and in a position to harm my client, who was the intended recipient of the documents they stole.' His great hands pressed into the desk and he leaned forward so that his head was no more than a foot above the photograph. Kate was struck by the magnificence of his profile, like the head of an emperor on an ancient coin.

'They killed Mr Russell because, while they had taken the documents, they suspected that he had some acquaintance with their contents. That is the only conclusion to draw.' He looked at his watch. 'Unless my client is released, these images will be issued to the media within the next half hour together with a press release drawn up by my office in London, explaining that instead of pursuing the obvious suspects you have hounded a potential victim. There will be a full discussion of the documents and what they may or may not contain. Given they once belonged to the late David Eyam, it seems likely that the media will show not inconsiderable interest in this angle, and I should imagine that this will also concern your masters at the Home Office.' He drew back with no hint of the anger leaving his expression. 'Now perhaps you gentlemen would like to consider my client's position in the light of the evidence that I have laid before you. This country may have taken a lurch into the Dark Ages as far as due process is concerned, but some standards are still observed and there remain many remedies open to me.'

Shap had gone white with anger. 'You think you can come in here and threaten me?' he said.

'Oh, make no mistake about it. I *am* threatening you and Chief Inspector Newsome here with immediate exposure for incompetence and possibly even negligence. How else would you describe the failure – deliberate or otherwise – to look at the complete footage from Mortimer Street?'

'You are attempting to influence the course of a police murder inquiry!'

'What murder inquiry? You haven't started yet, and that is what I propose to tell the media.'

The first reaction to this came from Halliday, who got up and left the room furiously but without saying anything. Then Newsome went through the routine with the tape recorder while Shap and Turvey stared each other down.

As they left, Turvey called after them, 'Half an hour, gentlemen, that is what you've got. One half of one hour.'

'That was impressive,' she said. 'I realised that they would have pictures of the men going in and coming out of the building.'

'Of course you did, my dear – a clever lawyer like you. Of course you did. But much better that you let me defend you: it's never easy to defend oneself.'

'But it was a good ace beautifully played, Mr Turvey and I am grateful to you for coming all this way. I will call Sam Calvert and thank him when I get out of here.'

'Oh, good Lord, Miss Lockhart, what on earth makes you think I've played my ace? That is for another time and I certainly don't propose to use it on this occasion, nor even to tell you about it.' He waved a hand airily towards the pair of black hemispheres fixed into the grid of ceiling tiles above them.

17

Book Lovers

Late on Friday afternoon Peter Kilmartin slipped into St James's Library, caught Carrie Middleton's eye and followed her gaze to the row of catalogue computers in the Issue Hall, which he went to consult. A few minutes later she bustled over in her neat, old-fashioned grey twinset to stand at the screen next to him. She said nothing, but searched the screen for a few seconds then took a scrap of paper from the holder beside the screen and, having noted down a reference number, left with the paper in her hand. Clever Carrie. A piece of paper remained on the desk with indentations of her writing clearly visible. Kilmartin's hand absently drifted to retrieve it and then he wrote his own reference down, taking care not to obscure the furrows made by Carrie's stubby little pencil. She was waiting at the far end of the stacks, sitting quietly at a small, unlit table. As he approached through the religious gloom, he reflected that he was far from protected against her charms, which came in a rare combination of warmth and brisk formality. Carrie had brown hair, dark eyes and a neat, womanly frame, always in his experience played down in somber-coloured outfits that were bought with an eye for quality during the January sales. She had the best taste of any woman he knew; at any rate it spoke to his eye.

'You are naughty using the library like this, Mr Kilmartin,' she said. 'You'll have us all locked up.'

'I am sorry, Carrie,' he said, sitting down opposite her, 'but I wouldn't ask if it wasn't important. And please stop this Mr Kilmartin business. We have known each other far too long. Peter, please.'

'All right, Peter, but it does seem strange. Anyway, I did want to talk to you because that young woman you told me about came in this morning and completed her membership. She asked for me by name and said she wanted to see the stacks and I showed her. She seemed very anxious. I asked what the matter was and she said she was sure she'd been followed. Anyway, we found the book together – *Babylon* by Eckhard Unger, last borrowed in December 1998. Your marker is still here on page a hundred and fifty.' She opened the book and read, '*Meiner Frau Hawiga in Liebe un Dankbarkiet Gewidmet* – to my wife Hawiga dedicated with love and gratitude – how romantic. I wonder where Herr Unger and his Frau are now . . . anyway.' She looked up and smiled. 'Mary MacCullum told me that if she was caught it would mean years in jail and she knew what that was like because she had already done eighteen months. For some reason she felt she could confide in me. We agreed that she couldn't risk leaving these papers so that anyone could find them.'

'Oh well, I quite understand,' said Kilmartin. 'Thank you for telling me.'

'Typical man,' said Carrie. 'You didn't wait until I'd finished.'

'Sorry, please go ahead, Carrie. I do apologise.' It occurred to him that she was flirting and he reciprocated with what he suspected was a rather foolish smile.

'So we agreed that I would hide the book in a place where only I could find it. Here's the title and place.' She handed him a piece of paper. 'It's been there just five minutes. No one will be up in "Religion" at this hour.'

'Thank you,' he said, pocketing the paper. 'That really was beyond the call of duty.'

'I felt sorry for her and I wanted to help.' She leaned forward and placed her hand on his arm. A mixture of Chanel, and for Kilmartin the equally intoxicating scent of books, came to him. 'You're not going to get her into any more trouble, are you, Peter?'

'I certainly hope not, Carrie,' he murmured.

'I changed the book because it wasn't large enough to conceal the envelope. It's one of your hollowed-out jobs.'

'OK, I'd better go and see what she's left.'

'I'll come up in about half an hour or so. Will that be enough time?'

'Yes, I should imagine so. Thanks, Carrie. I am very grateful to you.'

He left for the main staircase, passed through 'Literature' into 'Religion' and quickly located *The Religious History of New England*. He sat down at a table overlooking the roofs behind the library. Black clouds moved from the west; the light was fading fast: he tugged at the light-cord and a line of fluorescent tubes flickered in relay along the bookshelves.

Inside the book were six sheets of paper folded into the size of a cigarette packet and held together by an elastic band. He undid them and found four sheets of an uncorrected transcript of secret evidence presented to the Intelligence and Security Committee for a date almost exactly two years before – March 20th. The top sheet of the transcript named the chairman and nine committee members. There were some opening remarks by the chairman. The next page was marked '20'. This was Eyam's moment of gallantry, the moment when he gave up everything to tell the truth. His eyes ran down to the name Sidney Hale MP.

Sidney Hale: Thank you, chairman. As you know, this committee has a particular onus of scrutiny owing to the conditions of secrecy in which we operate. We report to the prime minister but our primary duty is to Parliament and to the people of this country. There is a fine line between the interests of the state and of security and the interests of the people and good governance. I will make no attempt to draw conclusions before we have heard Mr Eyam's evidence, but I think it's important that we listen very closely to what he has to say.

Chairman: Very well, let's get on with it. Mr Eyam, would you like to step forward?

Mr Hale: Thank you, Mr Eyam, for agreeing to appear a second time. On the last occasion we were in this room you were asked about a project called SPINDRIFT. Is that correct?

David Eyam: Yes.

Mr Hale: As acting chairman of the Joint Intelligence Committee and an important member of the prime minister's staff in Downing Street responsible for strategic security issues, you assured us that – and here I think it would be helpful to quote from the record – 'No such thing as SPINDRIFT exists and I have never heard of the name.' Is that true?

Mr Eyam: It is true that I said that, yes.

Mr Hale: But was your assertion true?

Mr Eyam: Yes, I had not heard of SPINDRIFT because it is an unofficial name given by my predecessor at the Joint Intelligence Committee to a project that was officially described as DEEP TRUTH, although I should perhaps make it clear that that name is rarely used. You see I had not understood that they were one and the same thing and so I misled the committee, for which I apologise.

Mr Hale: Would you care to tell the committee what DEEP TRUTH is? After all, we have heard other evidence from officers in the Security Service, which backs up your original remarks that no such thing exists. You seem to be taking issue with some very creditable witnesses, Mr Eyam.

Mr Eyam: I cannot tell you what it is because I am only here to correct the false impression I gave last time I appeared before you. I am here to assert that it does exist.

Mr Hale: Is that all?

Mr Eyam: Essentially, yes.

Mr Hale: But you believe this to be an issue of sufficient importance for you to come here and correct the record.

Mr Eyam: Yes.

Mr Hale: But if this were the important matter you suggest surely Parliament, or at least this committee would recognise one or both of the names. There would be some cognisance of this matter and we would know what you were talking about.

Mr Eyam: I suggest that there is some knowledge of DEEP TRUTH, which is why I believe I was asked the question the first time I came before you. I believe that indicates that there is – how shall I put? – limited awareness of DEEP TRUTH and therefore disquiet, among a very few people in Parliament.

Mr Hale: And was this done with Parliament's knowledge? Was there any legislation specific to setting up SPINDRIFT or DEEP TRUTH, whatever that might be?

Mr Eyam: I believe it was brought into existence without the knowledge of Parliament. Members of this committee will know that there is an increasing trend towards granting wide discretionary powers to departments and ministers when a bill is going through Parliament, which means much passes into law without debate or publicity. A lot comes into being without public awareness.

Mr Hale: Are you saying that it has no statutory basis and that this was done without the knowledge of the members of either chamber?

Mr Eyam: It would not be the first time.

Chairman: But surely these days there is an issue about expenditure. To your knowledge, have large amounts of public money been spent on SPINDRIFT?

Mr Eyam: I cannot say.

Mr Hale: Cannot say, or will not say?

Mr Eyam: I cannot say accurately what expenditure is involved.

Mr Hale: Is money your principal concern?

Mr Eyam: It is always a concern, but if you ask my personal opinion, no it is not my principal concern.

Chairman: I believe we are in danger of straying into the realms of fantasy here. We seem to be talking about something that has no agreed name and has never been sanctioned by Parliament or discussed in the secret proceedings of this committee. Mr Eyam will not say what it is; merely that this thing exists. It all seems a little too theological for this day and age. I mean, haven't we got more important things to think about?

Mr Hale: Mr Chairman, if I may, you are forgetting that Mr Eyam comes from the heart of the political establishment. He's not a journalist in the grip of a conspiracy theory. He believes in the effective power of the state, as he told us before, but clearly his presence here indicates he has some concern.

Mr Eyam: My beliefs are unimportant. I am simply here to correct the false impression I gave during my previous appearance. That is my legal duty.

Chairman: Well, I think we will all agree that you have complied with that obligation. Thank you, Mr Eyam.

After reading the exchange again, Kilmartin pushed the papers away and sat back with his arms folded. Eyam had consciously given very little away but the admission of the existence of the entity known as SPINDRIFT or DEEP TRUTH held its own significance and was enough to get him into trouble. There were two more sheets of paper. The first was the record of evidence given later that day by Ms Christine Shoemaker, the deputy director of the Security Service. She was asked what she had to say about Eyam's assertion and whether she could enlighten the committee about DEEP TRUTH. No, she said, she wasn't aware of anything of that name and could not imagine what Mr Eyam was referring to. She confessed that she did not understand why Mr Eyam had been so anxious to appear in front of the committee a second time and then said so little. The last page of Mary MacCullum's bundle was an email to Christine Shoemaker from Dawn Gruppo, one of the prime minister's principal aides whom Kilmartin had met a few times.

From: Dawn Gruppo <DGruppo@no10.x.gsi.gov.uk>
Sent: 20 March 15:45
To: Christine Shoemaker <CDSCDS@Secserv.ugn.gov.uk>
Subject: (no subject)
Christine,

The balloon has gone up at the ISC. D. Eyam admitted to 4-2. We need you to get over there now and give robust evidence to the contrary. They are expecting you and will make time for you during the afternoon.

Sorry this is short notice but essential that this is knocked on the head quickly. JT most concerned.

Best, DG

He looked up as the first fat raindrops of the storm began to splatter against the window. The email probably proved JT – John Temple – and Shoemaker knew of SPINDRIFT, DEEP TRUTH or 4-2 and were actively involved in the denial. Whatever this entity was. But what about Eyam? Why hadn't he released all this when it had happened? Clearly he had the evidence at that time because otherwise he would not have gone to the committee. If he had qualms about doing so as a member of the Civil Service who'd signed the Official Secrets Act, surely those would have vanished once he had been sacked? Any number of websites would have published the material without a second thought, especially with supporting documents. Instead he had buggered off, leaving a whole lot of bloody stupid clues. If Eyam had had a plan it was now certainly unravelling.

He turned to the sound of footsteps coming rapidly across the cracked brown lino from the direction of the main stairs. In seconds Carrie was in front of him; her eyes and brow in upheaval. She tugged the cord to switch off the lights.

'Four men have just come into the building and have asked to look around. I wasn't in the Issue Hall when they arrived so I don't know who they are. Brian at the door doesn't know but thinks they are MI5.'

Kilmartin got up, folded the papers and pocketed them. 'It's frightfully important they don't see me here, Carrie.'

'Then you'd better leave by the fire escape on the fifth floor,' she said. They stole up two short flights of stairs to a green door. She pushed the bar down to open it. An alarm sounded in the distance.

'Don't worry, I'll explain that to them,' she said.

Kilmartin found himself on a flat roof. He leaned into the wind and made for the side of another building fifty feet away. The rain had turned to hail and several times he lost his footing on a carpet of pea-sized hailstones. He reached the wall and looked down a fire escape that descended in stages to the first-floor level, then hooked right out of view. He should be at home considering the prospects for the weekend, not scampering around London's roofscape like some delinquent novice spy, but he took his time because the fire escape was visible from different parts of the library and lights were coming on in sequence as the men toured the upper floors. He didn't see them, but he spotted Carrie with her back to a window gesturing to someone, so he waited until she had gone before taking the last two flights on the escape and running full tilt to the point where the escape way disappeared behind the northern walls of the library. Even if they saw him now it would be too late. Masons Yard was below and in no time he would lose himself in the genteel evacuation of St James's in readiness for the weekend.

18

Great Lord Protector

'So, what was your ace?' Kate asked Turvey as they walked towards the Bristol, which had been impounded for forensic tests the night before and was now waiting in the street near the police station for collection.

The great man wheezed his irritation. 'Let's just make sure everything is in order with the car, shall we?'

'Mr Turvey, I'm your client; I need to know.'

'Sam Calvert is picking up the bill. That makes *him* my client, but I accept that you do have some rights in the matter.'

'The bill's not an issue. I'll pay it. If you have any doubts I can call Sam now.'

His eyes were watering in the cold and his hands had acquired a purplish hue. 'Miss Lockhart, I am going back to London,' he said firmly. 'It was a very early start.'

'I may need this information to protect myself.' Her mind was half on the tape in the car and wondering if they had found Eyam's message; that and the vast discovery of the night before. There was now absolutely no doubt in her mind that Eyam was alive.

'To protect yourself? No, this information won't protect you. Indeed there's every reason to suppose that it will have the opposite effect. And anyway, my dear, it must be checked and that is what my people will do when we get back to London.' He stopped. 'You should leave here. Let things cool down a bit. The reason I insisted the police bail did not specify that you stay at Mr Eyam's residence was because it is unsafe. I was not being frivolous, Miss Lockhart.'

'But this information may have a bearing on things that you are unaware of – implications that you can't possibly know.'

'I have no doubt about that. I sense a dark hinterland in this affair in which I do not wish to trespass. Still less do I want my firm to go to a place whence it may never return, Miss Lockhart. You should extricate yourself from these matters as soon as possible.'

They had reached the car. Turvey pulled off an emissions penalty notice stuck to the windscreen and gave it to her. 'It seems you have not made the proper adaptations to this vehicle.'

She unlocked the door and placed the ticket on the passenger seat with her computer, which had also been seized by the police.

'You're right – there is much more to this than you understand.' She smiled up at him. 'Come on – trust me: one lawyer to another.'

Turvey banged the car door shut. 'There is almost certainly a listening device in there now,' he murmured. 'You must be careful who you talk to while you are using it and guard against indiscretion in what you say on the phone.' He began to make motions to the car and driver waiting a little distance off. 'There's no doubt in my mind that they are targeting you for a reason. I urge you to leave for London as soon as you can.'

'I'm going to collect my things and see Paul Spring and ask him to handle the sale. He was Hugh Russell's partner.' The offices of Russell Spring appeared in her mind. 'I know what it is!' she exclaimed. 'It was something on the film, wasn't it? The CCTV from Mortimer Street?' He considered her and shook his head despairingly. 'You or your team recognised one or both of the men,' she continued. 'You've got a name, haven't you?'

'A name that I do not as yet know: identification must be established beyond reasonable doubt.'

'Then will you give me a copy of the film?' she said.

'This is not your property – it is the bank's.'

'Mr Turvey, I cannot tell you how important this is. I believe the men you've identified work for the government. Look, I have to have something to fight them with.'

' "Give me the tools and I'll finish the job." '

'What?'

'That's Churchill. Are you familiar with another quotation of his? "Courage is what it takes to listen." '

184

'I insist, Mr Turvey. I need that film.'

He opened his briefcase and gave her a DVD in an envelope. 'Copyright belongs to the bank, of course.'

She took it with a broad smile. 'I'll credit them.'

'Sam Calvert said you'd moved over here to work in the London office. He says he's going to miss you in New York; he speaks highly of you.'

'That was nice of him.'

'Normally I might seek to lure you away from him, but I think you're too hot to handle, Miss Lockhart.' He smiled. 'I hope that I have the pleasure again, but perhaps in less fraught circumstances.' He offered her a great soft hand and nodded as though indulging a mischievous teenager.

'And you will give me the name?' she said.

'We'll see: the real question is whether the police made the same identification as my man did. I suspect they did because that would explain why they folded in there so quickly.' He stooped and whispered. 'But they don't know we know. That's my ace. So let's keep it that way.'

He let go of her hand. '*A bientôt d'avoir de tes nouvelles*, as the French say, Miss Lockhart: I look forward to hearing your news.'

She got into the Bristol and started the engine. John Turvey gave a little royal flick of the hand and then moved with the purpose of a locomotive engine to the waiting car.

For much of the next twelve hours she slept. Nock insisted on bedding down for the night in the sitting room, having told her again that he had not moved *The Story of a Shipwrecked Sailor*. She waved his protestations away and apologised for being grumpy and obsessive. The book didn't matter, she said. Again she was aware that Nock would make a move if he knew how, or was bold enough. He looked at her with an odd, rather amateurish hunger and once laid his hand on hers but quickly withdrew it and looked away. Another time she might have allowed things to progress, but there was too much on her mind just now and Eyam's tape, which she had retrieved from the car, had warned her about Nock. She left him downstairs with a duvet she had found in the airing cupboard.

Next morning he rose early and to her amazement baked a loaf of bread, which he left outside her room with butter, marmalade and coffee. He called out to her that he'd be back later to do some work.

Sitting cross-legged on the bed in Eyam's bathrobe, she breakfasted with a new clarity. As the beneficiary of a faked death, she was now absolved of responsibility for Dove Cottage. And with that also lifted the weight of guilt about her failure as a friend, which seemed quite absurd to her now. Eyam had cold-bloodedly used her, but worse he had made a fool of her. Of all the people he knew he had chosen her to be his patsy, and that made her very angry indeed.

She put the tray aside and began to write with a fluent objectivity in a notepad that Eyam kept on his bedside table. She must assume firstly that Eyam's cover was blown or at least that his story would not hold for very much longer, because the clues would be picked up by others. The call he made to her a week after his supposed death would probably have been revealed during an examination of her phone and its records while she was in police custody. Even though the message had been deleted, it probably existed somewhere in the phone company's system and a record of the call from Colombia – or thereabouts – would remain. And once that had been discovered, they would go back into the inquest and the whole fraud would be exposed. That call was a problem because it would inevitably lead those investigating Eyam's case to conclude she was involved, but there was very little she could do about that.

She must also assume that every call she made on her phone and all internet use would now be monitored. Moreover it would be a folly to believe that the people working with Halliday – the Special Branch officer who sat mute throughout her interviews – had not discovered and listened to the cassette when examining Eyam's car. Yes, it might serve to show she hadn't been involved from the start, but that would make no difference. Hugh Russell appeared to have been murdered merely on the suspicion that he had seen Eyam's dossier.

As a lawyer she was in the habit of sharing her distillation of a case with colleagues – Ralph Betts and Ted Schultz, particularly – and she missed them now because, despite her reputation as a loner, the truth was that she functioned best in a group. So did Eyam, which was what made her think of the way he had planned this daring fraud and who else might be involved. Were all those people in the pub part of it? She thought not. But what about Tony Swift, who had organised the interview in Colombia, led the coroner by the nose through the film and arranged for the fraudulent matching of Eyam's DNA? It had been a huge risk to send the remains back to Britain, where they might be examined again, but they were only tested for drugs and then Swift had made sure they were delivered to the coroner's office before sending them on to the funeral director. Eyam and his collaborators had thought of everything, right down to the dressings worn by Detective Bautista in the film. She wondered how much he had accepted from Eyam; whether Swift was also being paid or if he was doing it all from conviction.

What mattered to her was that she was now free of any obligation to Eyam or his cause. If he had wanted to enlist her help he should have been straight with her instead of attempting a kind of entrapment. She certainly wanted to see Eyam again, if only to give him a piece of her mind, but it would have to be on her terms and she could not allow herself to be used any more. Her raging curiosity about Eyam's plans must not get the better of her or give the impression that she was part of the conspiracy. She didn't have much on her side except the DVD of the two men leaving the offices of Russell, Spring & Co. That was worth some leverage with the authorities, at least for the time being.

She put on jeans, and a pullover, an old suede jacket and Wellington boots she found by the back door, and set off into the woods behind the cottage with Kilmartin's phone, which she had retrieved from the flowerpot. She considered the possibility that, like the tape cassette, it had been discovered and left in place for her to use, but instinct told her not.

The morning was bright and sweetened with the smell of new leaves and flowering willow. She walked a couple of miles through the woods that ran along the ridge above the valley and then dropped down on the other side to find a bank of violets, whose scent released sudden vivid memories of her childhood. Staring down at a clump of purple and white flowers, she called Kilmartin. Even if he was working for the other side, she could use him as a conduit to explain she had no part in Eyam's disappearance or his crusade.

'Are we still meeting?' she asked.

'Yes, I think that would be a good idea, but I'm not sure when. Maybe tomorrow; certainly Monday. I'm tied up at the moment.'

'Tell me when and where and I'll be there.'

'In the country; I'll come to you.'

'Is that wise?'

'We'll arrange something. I'll let you know.'

She waited a beat. 'You do *know*, don't you?'

There was a silence at the other end. At length he replied, 'Yes, I believe I *do*. How long have you . . . ?

'A day or so,' she cut in.

'The phone is encrypted – it'll last a few days – until they know you're using it.'

'Still . . .'

'Yes, you're quite right. We'll be in touch.'

She hung up and walked back to Dove Cottage where she used her own phone to call and thank her mother, who told her that she was coming to London to see her sometime over the next week. Kate held off committing herself but clearly there was no escaping the reunion. Her mother closed with, 'Do ring Oliver Mermagen.'

This she did immediately, because Mermagen represented another line into the other side. He was in his car. 'Is this a bad time?' she asked.

'No, it's fine; actually I'm just on my way to Chequers.'

'You move in high circles, Oliver,' she said, wondering why the prime minister would want Mermagen at his country residence.

'To tell the truth it's a bit of a bore. I had something fixed for the day – a client of mine was taking me to Deauville. Still, it's important that I'm there.'

'My mother said you rang, but I imagine that any interest you had in my legal career has waned after my night in custody.'

'Not in the least: I knew the police were being idiotic. These things happen – no blame attaches to you, Kate.'

'Tell that to the newspapers.'

'Our cross to bear in this country: they get worse as they get more desperate for sales. Look, I rang because Eden White wants to meet you for a longer session. He's interested in acquiring your services.'

'Yes,' she said. 'That seems rather surprising.'

'I'll see him at Chequers and—'

'At Chequers!'

'Yes, he'll be there and I'd like to be able to say that you'd be willing to have a chat with him next week, while he's still in London. He leaves on Thursday.'

'That sounds fine,' she said.

'Great news! I know he'll be pleased.'

'Oliver, do you mind me asking what you're doing at Chequers?'

'The election, Kate! Temple is taking soundings before making his decision when to go to the country. It's one of the great advantages of a political system without fixed terms.'

'For the man that calls the election, yes.'

'A finely balanced judgement, as you say.'

She smiled at the vintage Mermagen return, which typically failed to acknowledge her point; a technique that always provided Mermagen with the account of the world that suited him best. 'Then I'll expect to hear from you,' she said.

There was just one more communication with the world outside Dove Cottage that morning. A postman arrived, parked his van at the track and delivered a bundle of letters, bills and mail-shots held together by two red rubber bands. When she took it from him in the garden, he said: 'Good to see the old place being used again. You will be wanting to look at the first one now – it's special delivery.'

On top of the pile was a plain white envelope without a name or address.

'The issue is this,' said Temple, looking round the Great Hall at Chequers. 'Should we wait for better signs in the economic indicators, or play our hand now?'

Philip Cannon surveyed the prime minister's group of political intimates – the men and women he relied on to keep him in power. Each served a distinct purpose in Temple's life, though this seemed to be rarely appreciated by the individual. He had scooped up and shed individuals over the last two decades, gradually refining the inner circle with a cold certainty that he would one day be holding court at the Elizabethan manor that had been left by Arthur Lee to the nation for the sole use of the prime minister. There were the stalwarts from the beginning of his political career like his constituency agent and chief whip; the admen, media strategists and pollsters; and the people from Number Ten, Temple's chief of staff and head of strategy and his chief economic adviser, the head of his Policy Unit and Temple's principal private secretary Dawn Gruppo. There was no overlap, no repetition and little love lost between them.

Set apart both physically and in status from this group, which had gathered on the sofas at the centre of the room, were Eden White, sitting by the great window that looked out on the remains of the Tudor courtyard, and the press baron Bryant Maclean, who had sunk into a chair underneath the portraits of Charles I and Queen Henrietta Maria in the corner of the room, and watched the proceedings with a look of rubbery, wrinkled impatience.

No one heard Temple's opening remark because June, his second wife, a former weather girl and latterly television cook and author of the bestselling *Discreet Charm*, a study of modern etiquette, had allowed the business of welcoming the guests to spill into the meeting. She moved around the room, lightly touching people's shoulders with the end of her splayed fingertips. Tall and athletically trim with a helmet of blonde hair and a particle-beam smile, she possessed a glamour that was both remote and neighbourly. As one of the junior press officers in Cannon's department had observed, she was one of Temple's key assets, because women wanted to be like her and men wanted to have her. Whatever they thought of Temple, they admired him for laying siege and winning the hand of his Teutonic beauty. And of course June Temple had totally erased the memory of poor Judith Temple in her dowdy suburb near Leeds, her problem children and her career in sociology.

'Thank you so much, dear,' Temple said, the parentheses spreading wider than usual to emphasise that the glow of a newly married couple had not dimmed. June clasped her hands in an expression of hospitable satisfaction and took herself off. 'The election,' he said, 'is upon us.'

Cannon's heart sank. Weekends at Chequers were like the bonding sessions for the BBC's management he used to attend in hotels that always seemed to be near Watford. In fact this great square room with its chandelier, heavy table lamps and June's flower arrangements very much reminded him of the lobby of one of the posher country hotels. At Chequers he was reduced to an inmate, at the beck and call of the prime minister, unable to take a walk when he wanted, go for a pint without permission, have a nap or flick a fly over some unsuspecting trout. But he stayed in the job and put up with Chequers because of a straightforward fascination with Temple, who was in many ways the weirdest human being he had ever encountered. And at the end of it all would be a damned good memoir, a pension and the speaking circuit, where he would reveal John Temple, the man who took time off from the affairs of state to watch a daytime TV chat show, who once went missing at a G20 summit and was found – by the US Secret Service – in a railway museum, who wanted nothing more than to turn Britain into a republic and replace the monarchy with a president, presumably with an eye to his own retirement.

He drained the lukewarm coffee and withdrew into himself. Everyone in the room would have their say and to a man and woman they would opt for an October election. It was the orthodoxy, the unchallenged product of group-think: you couldn't find anyone in the media or political establishment who favoured an election now, although six months before the spring offensive had been all anyone talked about. Cannon knew that, the prime minister knew that, but still they had to sit there on a beautiful morning as the bloody economic adviser went through his predictions for lending activity and interest rates, food and oil prices, public spending, growth and employment in the second half of the year.

From his chair beside the arcaded minstrel's gallery he gazed at his boss with objective wonder. Like Lloyd George, Churchill, Thatcher and Blair, John Temple had energy and endurance. Having spent most of the night up with the American secretary of state, he'd completed forty lengths of the indoor pool donated to Chequers during the Nixon presidency, read all his papers and made notes for a speech. He did not stop and he never looked down – or back, perhaps another characteristic shared with the big names that had spent their weekends on this Buckinghamshire estate.

Two hours elapsed. No drink, no food. Thank God for Bryant Maclean, who rose to leave, but said he was doing so knowing that the prime minister had got the answer he wanted: October was the only sensible choice.

'I'm not persuaded of that,' said Eden White from the window. 'A spring election looks very doable.' The voice was flat and curiously unimpressive. This was the answer Temple wanted. He needed to dive off the high board now, get it over with and settle into another term. Heads swung round. The two titans looked at each other across the room, grinning not with humour, but relish. Cannon remembered a poem by Ted Hughes about two wolves that meet in a forest – 'Neither can make die the painful burning of the coal in its heart till the other's body and the whole wood is its own.'

White was utterly still; his face was polished alabaster in the reflected light from the courtyard. 'From both the security as well as economic points of view,' he continued, 'I believe it's better to go now. Prime minister, you know the circumstances you have to deal with, the criticisms you will face. Things are already beginning to improve. After years of the slump, difficulties with lending, there are signs that the public is feeling a little safer economically, yet they are still afraid for their physical well-being – two powerful reasons to support the status quo.'

'That's not what my papers have been saying,' growled Maclean. 'The polls are bad; the country is beset by problems that never get any better. You've got riots; you've got rot – a total breakdown of society in some of the big cities. You've all read what the bloody liberal columnists are saying about the country's malaise. Look, John, people are beginning to like you; they appreciate your calm and competence. It's taken time for them to get to know you, but now they are daring to think you're doing a good job. But you need more time to prove it.' He turned, shrugged and slipped a hand inside his cashmere jacket to knead the back of his hip. 'And don't forget you still have the option to go to the country next year.'

'That would be a death wish,' said White.

'Not half as dangerous as going now,' returned Bryant, and then he looked back at Temple and grinned. 'But hey, prime minister, it's your picnic; you choose the ant hill.'

Was that a threat, or was Maclean disowning his power in the land? Everyone in the room knew that if Maclean were not onside the election would probably be lost, and if he defected to the Opposition with the full panoply of broadcast and print media plus the range of 'independent' attack dogs that he financed in the blogosphere, Temple would be crushed. But they also knew that Bryant Maclean faced scrutiny of his tax status as well as a monopoly inquiry if the Opposition won.

A couple of beats later – the famously unnerving Temple pause – the prime minister rose with an unreadable expression. 'You're right to say what you have, Bryant. I appreciate your candour and your wisdom. You know how much we all value your advice. It was really very good of you to come all this way.' He took him by the elbow and steered him under the minstrel's gallery. 'Are sure you won't stay for lunch?'

'No, I gotta be going. Gotta talk to the Chinese.' Then he called out as they disappeared from view. 'Cheerio, Eden. See you soon I hope. My regards to your wife.' The wife that Eden had unceremoniously ditched after she suffered a nervous breakdown several years before.

Cannon got up and followed. At that moment he was not so much dismayed as mystified by Temple bringing his two main supporters – both of whom lived abroad and so rarely saw each other – to come face to face and fall out. Now, whichever way he jumped he'd risk angering one of them. For a reason that remained totally obscure to Cannon, Temple seemed to have decided that would be Bryant Maclean.

They reached the entrance. Temple signalled for Cannon to stay back and walked Maclean over the lawn to his helicopter. They stopped short of it, about a hundred yards from the house. Temple was having the last word, gesturing and craning to look Maclean in the eye. Maclean stared at the ground, then at the trees and after a minute or so began shaking his head. This he did not stop until he reached the door held open for him by one of the helicopter crew.

Later, during the abysmal lunch of sandwiches in the Great Parlour conference room, the chief pollster used two screens to show the results of secret polling from the marginal constituencies, which – though few knew it – had been financed by Eden White. Because of the peculiarities of the British electoral system, the election would be decided by between 120,000 and 200,000 voters. The pollster team had names and addresses for that target group and every detail you could wish to know about their lives, from the brand of toothpaste they used to the number of times family members had visited hospital in the last four years. He knew the religion, the performance of the children at school, where they went on holiday, their commitment to the community – a particular obsession in these days of pro-social programmes for the responsible citizen. It was, he said, the most refined voter profiling in the history of elections: if you could get to these people – and there were ways of doing that which he wasn't going to bore the prime minister with – he could guarantee a workable majority of twenty-five to thirty-five seats.

They rose at three p.m. and all except Eden White, who went off to his room, moved to the western end of the Long Gallery for coffee. Through the window decorated with coats of arms, June Temple could be glimpsed beyond the bare trees flying about on the tennis court with a female member of the security detail. Temple watched fondly. It was Cannon's moment.

'Am I going to have to calm Maclean's people down?' he asked. 'We don't want them jumping all over this in tomorrow's papers. Maclean is a hack first of all and he'll leak if you parted on bad terms.'

'Yes, I imagined he would,' said Temple without interest.

'Then we are going to have some trouble if he believes you're going to call a snap election.'

'Yes,' said Temple, 'but we needed to prepare the country somehow, even though a spring election has always been on the cards. Might as well have Maclean do it.'

'You don't want those bastards going over to the other side. I can talk to a couple of political editors this afternoon.'

Temple put down his cup, spun the nearest of a pair of antique globes and gave an imperceptible nod of his head. 'You look like you need a walk, Philip.' He moved to the bookcases and opened a panel of shelves lined from top to bottom with dummy books. Behind it was an old linen-fold carved door, which he unlatched and closed behind them.

Before the rest of the party knew what had happened they had vanished into a corridor of portraits. Cannon had seen the trick before and was amazed at the pleasure it still seemed to give Temple. 'I'd like one of these in Number Ten – in the Cabinet Room preferably,' he said.

They stopped by Robert Walker's portrait of Oliver Cromwell in armour. 'I need to get going on Maclean now,' said Cannon. 'If he's really pissed off he will start running stuff on the web tonight.'

'Yessss. I suppose he may be a little irritated because he doesn't like being boxed in.'

'How's he boxed in? He is one of the most powerful men on earth. He doesn't look boxed in to me.'

'Put it this way – he's now got all three major parties wanting to scrutinise his business empire in Britain.'

'You threatened him with an inquiry – Jesus!'

'I said it was on the political agenda and that being the case we obviously might have to respond to what was being said by the two Opposition parties. That was all. I didn't threaten him.'

'That was a threat, if you don't mind me saying so,' said Cannon. 'And what can you possibly gain from it?'

Temple worked his jaw as though chewing on this. 'Well, he knows that he hasn't got time to run to the other side and anyway it is the one thing the Opposition parties agree upon, so they are unlikely to go back on their word to gain his support at this stage. There's nowhere for him to go.'

'I hope you're right.'

'I am. If all three parties are threatening him it will affect his share price and Bryant cares a lot more about that than politics – or when I choose to hold an election.'

'Or losing to Eden White?'

'That too.' He looked up at the picture of Cromwell. 'The Great Lord Protector – an odd title to choose, don't you think? Prime minister, first minister, president – none of these occurred to him. Yet I see what he meant. That is exactly what you feel leading the country: an acute desire to protect the people. I admire Cromwell more than most of the men who have occupied this house, you know.'

'Really?' said Cannon. 'Standing there in that armour and sash like the Black Prince, he looks more royal than the king that the Parliamentarians beheaded.'

'The armour is symbolic, Philip. They'd given up wearing full armour in battle by that time because of firearms. It's a symbol of his readiness to defend and protect the Commonwealth.'

Ten minutes later they were striding with three protection officers up the hill to Cymbeline's Castle, an ancient earthwork not far from Chequers. From the summit there was a good view of the local village and the parish church, but no sooner had they got there than Temple set off southwards across the rolling grassland.

Cannon hurried to catch him up. 'Will you tell me exactly when you are going to call the election?'

'Certainly Philip – on Tuesday March 26th. The election will be held a month later on April 24th. That will give us about four and a half weeks of campaigning.'

'Then I'll go back to London tonight, if you don't mind. There's going to be a lot to do.'

'Not quite yet, if you don't mind,' he said firmly. 'We've got one or two more meetings and I want to show you something over there.'

A few hundred yards on they reached two large, round tanks, one covered and the other open to the air – the water supply for Chequers. Around the open tank several men in protective gear were sampling the water. A Range Rover was parked nearby, from which appeared Harry Tombs, the prime minister's *de facto* personal photographer, who was always on hand at Chequers. Temple started putting on one of the suits worn by the men and then made his way to the edge of the open reservoir.

'When President Nixon visited Edward Heath in the seventies,' he said, peering into the water, 'the Secret Service tested the water supply. They were right. Did you know that as of this morning, we've got six more reservoirs affected by TRA?'

'Yes, I read that.'

'That's ten in all – and they have only just begun checking. We may have a very large problem on our hands. So we'll get some pictures taken and you can distribute them this evening.'

'Is that wise?' asked Cannon out of earshot of the others. 'It looks like you're stoking a crisis and that may not be the wisest thing to do with an election in five or six weeks' time. And this tank hasn't got a trace of red algae – or has it?'

'No, but you're missing the point. This will show that I'm taking the crisis seriously. We all have to.' He lowered a plastic visor from the safety helmet. 'Remember Cromwell's armour. This is symbolic, Philip, symbolic of my protective role.'

19

Country Matters

A few moments after the postman left, Nock appeared carrying a toolbox and an engine in a sling.

'So you've got your first post – word soon gets about the place is occupied.'

'Right,' she said, looking down. 'What's that?'

'The pump for your water supply, which needs some attention: I'll use the workbench out the back if that's OK.'

She sat at the table and smoked, wondering about Nock. Presently she took out the unmarked envelope and looked at the contents. There were two sheets of unsigned paper. One warned that everything she did or said at the cottage was likely to be monitored and that on no account should she send an email or make a call that she wasn't happy to be seen or heard by a third party.

On the second sheet there was a map reference, which she went to look up on Eyam's Ordnance Survey map of the area. The spot was several miles to the north-west of Dove Valley. The instructions told her to come alone at any time over the weekend, tell no one where she was going and avoid being followed, which would mean leaving under cover of darkness. Beneath it was typed a sentence: 'Leave from that which is named for the Silures and walk back through time to those that remember the Ordivices.'

The code – or in her opinion a damned silly riddle – had something of Eyam about it, and it was only that which made her contemplate deciphering it and following its instructions.

'Who or what are the Silures and Ordovices?' she asked Nock when he appeared with the motor.

He blinked at her. 'I think they are Celtic tribes of Wales. One lived in the north, the other in the south. But don't take my word for it. I only know about them because their names were given to rock groups. I did a little basic geology as an undergrad.'

'Rock groups,' she said and thought of the run of geology volumes beneath the shelf where she'd found *The Story of the Shipwrecked Sailor*. She found *Geology of the Marches* and returned to the garden bench. The book was peppered with Eyam's notes – summaries of what he had read, together with the dates that he had explored different parts of a landscape that had begun life 500 million years ago, sixty degrees south of the equator. The story of its migration north to collide with the landmass that now forms Scotland interested her, but she found nothing to decode the sentence. At length she laid the book aside and made sandwiches, which they ate with a couple of bottles of beer at the end of the garden. Even at this distance from the house their conversation was murmured.

'You fix the pump?'

'Yep.'

'It must be nice to be so practical.'

'Well, I can't figure all this out,' he said.

'You mean Hugh Russell's death. How much did David tell you about his own problems?'

'Not much, but I knew it got serious before he left. He just went out of range, if you know what I mean.'

'I am struggling with some of it myself.' She stopped and looked into his tranquil blue eyes. 'You're not hiding anything from me, Sean, are you?'

'I don't think so,' he said, holding the beer bottle to his lips.

There was silence between them. She lifted her face to the sun and closed her eyes. Eyam was right. Nock wasn't kosher.

'I believe he came close to telling me something but never got round to it,' he said eventually. 'I wish he had now. It would explain things – why he went off without saying goodbye. To tell the truth I was a bit hurt.'

'I know the feeling,' she nodded.

'But you understand more than I do?'

She shrugged.

'That's cool with me,' he said with an odd, agonised expression. 'Don't tell me. I came out here for a life of peace.'

'I wasn't going to. What were you doing before, Sean?'

'I was a researcher with the Earth Science and Engineering Department at Imperial in London – dam structures and stuff – then I got sick of London and there was some trouble with the police and I ended up here.' He swept his hand across the view of the valley. 'You can have a good life here if you don't mind the quiet.'

'Possibly,' she said. 'Look, I've got to be going.'

'You want company?'

'No thanks.'

'And you won't tell me where you're going?'

'Nope.'

'Well, stick to the back roads and you should be all right. You've got my number?'

'Yes, I'll be fine,' she replied, moving to the car and thinking about Hugh Russell leaving a few days before.

The day was slipping away from Philip Cannon. It was now clear to him that he would not get back to London until late that night or even the next morning. Temple expected him to attend two more meetings and a dinner.

The first of these took place in the Great Parlour conference room and went under the heading of a scientific briefing, in effect an un-minuted meeting of the Security Council without – unsurprisingly – Admiral Piper. A procession of scientists wearing casual clothes gave their views on TRA. It soon became obvious that those who suggested the problem was not the threat to public health claimed in the tabloids, or that it could be handled with less hysteria, were not as welcome as those armed with theories about the likely cause of the algae and its means of spreading. These were treated to an intense cross-examination by the prime minister, who had mastered a little of the science of harmful algae blooms and several times used the word *anatoxin*, which he unnecessarily explained was a compound that caused convulsions – a kind of neurological meltdown and respiratory paralysis. The latest data was that fifteen reservoirs and lakes were now affected; the algae seemed to be able to travel hundreds of miles and leap over the quarantine lines that had been set up.

Adam Hopcraft, the government chief scientific officer, listened with aloof interest, his hands thrust into the pockets of a lightweight cardigan worn under his jacket. He made notes, he nodded at his colleagues' opinions and he sucked air through his teeth with only the mildest disdain while gazing up at the plaster frieze of hawthorn trees. For a full hour he kept his own counsel. Then Temple turned to him. 'Well, what do you make of it now, Adam? Can you really deny that we have a crisis on our hands? One that threatens to engulf the entire water supply of the country?'

'I agree that it seems alarming, prime minister, and I must say I have been impressed with the contributions made so far. The point remains that, while we may not yet be able to contain the algae, we can deal with it effectively with ultrafine filtration. We have flown scores of these plants from the United States. More are on order and we believe that we can cope.'

'I wish I could have your confidence,' said Temple, turning away.

'And there is another point,' persisted Hopcraft. 'At this stage I do not think it's wise to ignore where this thing has come from. I suggest we consider two possibilities. The first is that the algae has been with us for longer than we appreciate; that it has bloomed with the rising temperatures of spring, having spread unnoticed through the course of last year and maybe even before that. There are four thousand species of marine red algae; algae spores can travel great distances on the wind.'

'None of that makes any difference to the nature of the threat,' said Temple. 'We are where we are. We have to respond to give the public confidence.'

'Quite so, prime minister, but it may be wise to allow for the possibility that this algae has not spread through any malign agency, but is either the result of climate change and global travel – a combination of the two perhaps – or has been released by accident from one of our own environmental laboratories. Such algae are being studied at the Marine Environmental Research Station at Ashmere Holt and also by the biological weapons people at the MoD.'

'As I understand it, Adam, the genome is different to anything we've seen before.'

'Well, that is true, prime minister and . . .'

Temple turned to Christine Shoemaker. 'Would you sketch out the analysis you've been doing in the past couple of days?' She began speaking immediately so that few heard Hopcraft add that organisms adapt and evolve, and that this freshwater red algae might be a variant of an algae being studied at the Ashmere Holt lab.

Shoemaker, in black trousers and an olive-green jacket, and a new hairstyle that Cannon thought made her look like a cosmetics sales-woman, took them through a list of questions, her head arcing through 180 degrees to engage those sitting at the end of the conference table. First, was it possible for a group to infect the water supply with samples of algae? The answer to this was most certainly yes. Reservoirs in Britain were easily accessible. Second, had this kind of attack been considered by terror groups? Yes, there was a lot of evidence to say that at least two groups under surveillance had researched the possibility of harming the water supply. Third, was it within the capability of such groups to mount an attack? Yes, she reported that MI5's scientific officers had concluded that once samples had been obtained and possibly modified it would take nothing more than a good-sized garden pond for the algae to multiply in sufficient quantities.

'Is work being done to connect the occurrence of TRA with the movements of any of the individuals you are watching?' asked Temple.

'I was going to touch on that, prime minister,' she said crisply, 'but you will appreciate the security aspects of this matter.'

He squeezed his eyes together with understanding.

'But we may expect some arrests over the next few days under terror legislation,' she added, 'which will allow us to thoroughly examine premises in the Midlands area that may be the source of this attack. But I do emphasise to those present the highly sensitive nature of this information: nothing of the police operation should pass from this room.'

By degrees, the slight possibility of the water supply being poisoned by terrorists became first a probability, then by the end of the meeting a near certainty. Cannon watched Hopcraft make interventions to try to regain a sense of proportion and scientific reason but nobody listened and, before long, tea was being served in the Great Hall. Temple had got what he wanted; not a decision or a new course of action, but an orthodoxy, which had been implanted and would be played back to him for as long as needed.

Cannon went to the room on the north-east corner of the house where the younger sister of the beheaded Lady Jane Grey, Lady Mary, had been imprisoned for marrying without the Queen's consent, a billet that he always seemed to be consigned. He sat on the edge of his bed and phoned two political editors at Bryant Maclean's newspapers to talk about the algae crisis meeting. As he expected, both asked him about the possibility of a snap election. He explained that the prime minister was keeping his options open and that he would make his decision on the merits of the case – a vacuous pomposity, if ever there were one – without allowing such things as red algae to play any part in his thinking. These untruths told, he swung his legs onto the bed, closed his eyes and thought of the young woman locked up in the room for two long years at the pleasure of Her Majesty, Elizabeth I.

Kilmartin left the constituency home of Sidney Hale MP disappointed. Hale was not the same person who had engineered David Eyam's second appearance at the Intelligence and Security Committee to establish the existence of Deep Truth. A union man, a left-wing diehard with thirty years of bare-knuckle politics behind him, Hale had suffered a series of small strokes during the winter. He kept his illness secret but it was obvious he could not continue as an MP. He had welcomed Kilmartin warmly at the little house on the outskirts of Rugby and offered him a drink, but Kilmartin saw that the proceedings of the ISC all but eluded him: Hale couldn't remember the circumstances of Eyam's second appearance, what had preceded it, who else was involved, or why he had been so taken up with the subject. Meetings from his early years were still clear, but more recent events were blurred. He told Kilmartin with a smile that these days he could barely keep awake, which wasn't necessarily a disadvantage in Parliament.

At the door Hale stood pathetically stooped and fumbled a handshake, but then a gleam of the old light appeared in his eyes. 'The man you need is the fellow from Carlisle. Good sort even though he's on the government benches.'

Home beckoned. He set off cross-country towards Herefordshire. With a clear road he'd make it before dark, but ten minutes into the journey he received a call from Dawn Gruppo, who said that Temple wished to see him at Chequers that evening. He made excuses but Gruppo said that the matter was of the utmost urgency. He gave her his car registration number for the security gate at Chequers, took down directions because she told him that it would not come up on the satellite navigation system and drove south towards the Chiltern Hills.

Within a few hundred yards of the track leading to Dove Cottage, a silver BMW fell in behind the Bristol. It must have been waiting in a gateway at the bottom of the hill. She saw two men in her mirror and immediately put her foot down. The BMW did not keep pace with her; either the Bristol was now fitted with a tracker or the BMW's satnav told the driver that there was a long straight track ahead of them and there was nowhere for her to go, unless she decided on the suicidal option of turning left at a hairpin bend and climbing a steep incline through some woods. It was the road she had mistaken for the approach to Dove Cottage a couple of nights before. She took her foot off the accelerator before the bend so her brake lights didn't show. With a solid, antique agility the Bristol took the corner well, indeed a bit tighter than she anticipated because the rear wheel ploughed up the bank sending a shower of earth into the air. She rose through the woods with surprising speed, the light and shadow of the trees strobing in her left field, and reached the top of the hill, at which point the tarmac road hooked right and petered out into a track where several rusting pieces of farm machinery were parked. She spun the car round with a handbrake turn to face the direction she'd come and, with all the anger of the last few days metabolising to aggression, she raced forward to the top of the hill to see the BMW coming towards her.

The instructor of Evasive Driving Skills For New Intelligence Officers would certainly have disapproved of her next course of action, which was to aim the Bristol at the BMW. She did so knowing that hers was the much heavier vehicle and the revamped V-8 engine would probably protect her from the impact of a head-on collision. But this was not to be. As she ran down the hill at a mere forty mph, the nerves of the BMW's driver faltered and he adjusted his line to take in a strip of grass and the edge of the ditch. As the cars approached each other his front wheel slipped into the ditch and before she knew it the Bristol had barged past, scraping the length of his vehicle and causing his back wheel to follow the front. The Bristol received one or two knocks and some paint damage but nothing more. She glanced in the mirror and saw two men scramble out of the car, which had come to rest at an angle. It made her let out a peal of laughter, the first in God knows how long, and it lightened her whole being.

In High Castle she parked in a side street and walked up to the square, where she knew that the CCTV cameras would pick her up but doubted anyone was watching. Anyway the coverage of the town centre was by no means total and she reckoned she could do what she needed without being seen. In an alley off the square she bought some new underwear, then visited an estate agent and asked about the local property market. Seemingly satisfied with the manager's answers she took a card and said that Paul Spring would be in touch the following week.

The next shop was a newsagent, where she carried a brown padded envelope and a newspaper to the counter and asked for some postage stamps.

The man looked up from his laptop and smiled when she approached.

'Rossy must have sold you that scarf,' he said.

'This?' she said, lifting the end of the scarf. 'I bought it in the square last week.'

'Yeah, from Ross Iyer: hope you didn't pay over the odds for it?' He grinned.

'I hope not too, but I like it so . . .' her eyes moved to the screen in front of him. 'What's that you're doing there?'

'I deal in coins,' he said, turning the laptop towards her. 'I make more money from that than running the shop now. I wonder why I bother any longer.'

He showed her a page of coins struck at the time of Alexander the Great. He was bidding on one recently found in Macedonia. She was in no hurry so she listened. Besides, an idea had occurred to her as she looked down at the computer, which would require her to get to know this man a little better. He was in his mid-thirties with an unsuccessful goatee beard and black hair brushed back. There was a tattooed star on his earlobe. They talked for a while and he lit a cigarette. 'It's my shop,' he said, 'and I'll smoke where I damned well like. Screw them.' He flicked the spent match neatly through the open door.

'Quite right,' she said.

'I recognised you from the newspapers,' he said. 'Seemed like they were clutching at straws.'

'They were.'

'I knew Hugh Russell. Everyone did. He was a good man. He acted for Rossy once. Hope they catch the bastard.'

'Yes.'

He rose from his stool and offered her his hand. 'Hi, Nick Parker.'

There was no one in the shop; they talked on for a few minutes until she looked at him steadily and said, 'I am having a bit of trouble – it's my computer – and I was looking for a place where I could upload something to the web.'

His eyes narrowed with the last exhalation of the cigarette and he leaned down to extinguish it on the side of a metal waste bin.

'Perhaps I could help,' he said, working a knuckle in his eye.

'I don't want to put you to any trouble.'

'No worries; I've got to sit here for another hour anyway. What is it?'

'A piece of film – a piece of CCTV footage, to be precise. You will see for yourself. It was taken outside Hugh Russell's offices and, well, it could be very important for the investigation. I just want to make sure it's somewhere safe.'

'Jesus. That's serious stuff. Have the police seen it?'

'Yes,' she said.

He gave her a sideways look. 'But you don't think they're going to make use of it?'

'It's hard to say. But look, if you don't want to do it, I'll understand: you don't know me. I'm a stranger.'

'I wasn't saying that. Anyway I know who you are and you look trustworthy to me. Have you got it with you?'

206

'Nick,' she said touching his sleeve. 'This is very important. I can trust you with this?'

'Absolutely,' he said, looking her straight in the eye. She gave him the DVD.

'Right, I'll put it up on my site – Uriconcoins.com – there are a couple of pieces of film up there already. Maybe it will help the number of hits I'm getting.'

'Maybe,' she said. 'Are you sure about this? Let me pay you for your trouble. Would you accept some money?'

He shook his head.

'Go on, I'd feel better about it.' She handed him one hundred pounds in twenties, which he accepted graciously. 'I was going to post the DVD in this envelope to my office in London. Could you do that for me once you've put it up?' She addressed the envelope to herself at Calverts. 'I just want to park the footage for the time being so no one sees it. Can I call you when I know what I want to do with it?'

He gave her a card.

'And it would be great if you didn't tell anyone about this for the time being.'

'No problem,' he said and added, 'No worries.'

Cannon napped for half an hour, took a bath and emerged to catch sight of himself in a mirror. In the three years that he'd been in Downing Street, his hair had turned grey and thinned, he had lost all his muscle tone and become soft in the middle. He hardly recognised himself – this sad, tubby, out-of-condition liar. But it was the expression in his face as he stood there, one of grizzled habitual slyness, that shocked him most and he was suddenly seized by the fantasy of resigning and spending the summer on the chalk streams of southern England, getting fit and rising early to work on his book about Temple. Then his mobile phone rang. He was needed in the sitting room off the Great Hall as soon as possible.

In the room with Temple were Eden White, Christine Shoemaker, Dawn Gruppo and Jamie Ferris. Something inside Cannon recoiled from them but he said hello as cheerfully as he could.

'Close the door, Philip,' said Temple. He was already changed for dinner and his manner was solemn – more Number Ten than Chequers. 'Mr Ferris here has come across some remarkable information. Perhaps you would explain, Jamie.'

Ferris was sitting at the writing table in a tan suit, a pale-blue shirt and striped tie: a neat, reassuring figure from the overlapping worlds of consultancy and intelligence. He leaned forward, hands clasped between his knees. 'It appears that David Eyam staged his own death.'

'You've got to be joking,' said Cannon.

'I'm afraid not,' said Ferris. 'I think you were in the room when I went through the activity of various offshore accounts held in the Caribbean, so I won't explain again.'

'But all that ceased on the date of his death in January except for the use of a debit card.'

'Indeed,' said Ferris. 'We have done a good deal of work and we believe we've found another, well-funded account which is still very much active and has been used many times since that date.'

'Maybe someone else is spending the money?'

Ferris shook his head. 'No. You see we now know he faked his death – the whole thing was a carefully worked out plan. We've hard evidence which I am not at liberty to disclose to you.'

Cannon sat back. 'You are aware that if this becomes public know-ledge it will wipe everything else off the front page? The web will be a riot of speculation.'

'That is why you are here, Philip,' said Temple. 'To advise us on how to handle this.'

'There isn't any way you can handle this! It's a fucking nightmare because everyone is going to ask why he did it. How long have you known?'

Ferris looked at Eden White, then at Temple before answering. In that moment it occurred to Cannon that Eden White's presence in a room was almost insubstantial, like some kind of spectral manifesta-tion. The most he'd ever heard him say were the few sentences in support of a snap election that morning. 'We learned last night,' said Ferris. 'And things have become clearer today with a viewing of the evidence.'

'Viewing,' said Cannon. 'Are you talking about that film from the inquest?'

Ferris didn't answer.

'So what do you want me to do about it? Actually, more important is what the hell are *you* going to do about it?' He looked round the room but the question was aimed at Temple.

'*Do* is probably not an option at the moment since we don't know where he is,' said Christine Shoemaker. 'He may be in France but we don't know.'

Cannon's mind was spinning. 'Does this have anything to do with the murder at his place in the country? A solicitor I think it was. How does that fit into the picture?'

'There are many criminal aspects to this whole story,' said Ferris. 'The murder may indeed be one. We understood from the police that Eyam left the country to avoid charges over child pornography.'

'I can believe many things of Eyam,' said Cannon, 'but not that.'

'This is what we *know* to be the case,' Ferris said. 'And then there has been avoidance of death duties on his father's estate. That is a criminal matter that the police will need to investigate.'

White let out a sigh.

'I agree with Eden,' said Temple softly. 'We're straying from the point. Which is, Christine?'

'That he couldn't have done this alone,' she said. 'He must have had help from many people. We're looking into the handling of the inquest, though we do not expect to have much before Monday. We realise he must have built a support network in the Caribbean and Colombia and here in the UK.' She stopped. 'But to what end was this very complex, expensive plot hatched?'

'Clearly he plans mischief of a very high order,' said Temple. 'What do you think we should do, Philip?'

Cannon felt that they should be sitting in an office, not round a coffee table bearing daffodils, magazines and a book on British dog breeds. 'Well,' he ventured. 'You could head him off by going to one of the papers and telling the whole story. Once an arrest warrant has been issued a police inquiry can be announced and an international manhunt can begin – standard fare for the media.'

'Yet this is more than a presentational issue,' said White, fingering the lapel of his suit. 'More sensitive, more intricate, more connected.'

'Connected? How so?' asked Cannon.

'Mr White means that this is not simply a matter of someone on the run who has faked his own death,' said Gruppo, happy to act as tutor. 'Eyam was one of us and because of the difficulties we had with him he could prove a very great danger to the state. There are grave implications.'

'To the state?' said Cannon, shifting in the oval-backed chair. 'How? He was no risk before he disappeared. Once that business with the Intelligence and Security Committee was over, no one heard from him. There were no leaks. He was the perfect civil servant – discreet to a fault.'

'He was always a risk,' said Temple. 'He is in possession of important state secrets and the fact that he staged his own death must mean he plans to reveal what he knows. That is where you come in. It will be important to have a strategy in place to deny, rebut and refute the allegations that he may make.'

'If Eyam presented such a big threat, what was to stop him making these disclosures when we thought he was dead? Maybe he has no intention of saying or doing anything at all. Maybe he was just evading the police on the child porn.'

'I wish we could believe that,' said Temple.

'There's another point. If I am to go out there and deny allegations of a substantial kind I have to know what they are likely to be.'

'It is in the nature of this problem that they are unknowable, Philip. We cannot anticipate in this affair,' said Temple. Someone put their head round the door behind Cannon. Temple nodded and rose. 'A media strategy is what we need on this.'

Cannon wasn't having that. He rose quickly and followed Temple into the Great Hall where five men, none of whom he recognised, were waiting in a group. They carried laptops, briefcases and folders. There were also people from Number Ten who had just arrived. June Temple hovered.

'A word, prime miniser?' Cannon said to Temple's back. 'I can't develop a strategy for the unknowable. I've got to have an idea what I will be defending and to know whether the allegations that are levelled at us – the government or whoever – are true.'

Temple didn't respond but gazed right through him. Then his eyes followed Eden White who had slipped out of the room and was passing behind Cannon.

'And if this thing with Eyam is really big,' Cannon continued, 'isn't it worth waiting until the autumn for an election?'

'The election will be next month; nothing can change that. Eyam's appearance makes it imperative that we hold the election now.' He moved off to welcome the group without another word, leaving Cannon startled by the iciness in his manner. Without thinking he moved towards the door of the little sitting room. It was slightly ajar and he heard Ferris say: 'Well, it's true that a man who has already been declared dead cannot be killed again.'

Instead of entering, Cannon went to his room to fetch his coat. He was going to have that pint, alone in a pub away from the house that Arthur and Ruth Lee had so generously given to the nation, because he wanted to phone his wife, to mull things over and consult what he gloomily regarded as the rump of his conscience.

20

The Otherness of the Other

After arriving at Chequers, Kilmartin was kept waiting for an hour sitting on a Jacobean chair in the Stone Hall beneath the portrait of an unidentified Edwardian woman. Scotch and water, a bowl of cashew nuts and magazines were brought to him on a tray by a member of the Chequers staff. It was hardly the atmosphere he expected. The place was quietly frantic. At least two meetings seemed to be in progress. Doors were opened and closed. People passed from room to room, nodding to him on the way. He stretched his legs and looked at the paintings. When he asked if he could see the Chequers library, he was told it was being used for a presentation.

He had rather old-fashioned notions about the English country house weekend, a sense, particularly at Chequers, that the affairs of state should be conducted at a more leisurely tempo with good conversation, wine and ideas – the big picture. Even in wartime the place had been maintained as an emblem of English civilisation. Hitler strutted before the inflamed skies at the Berghof while Churchill pottered in the Rose Garden in his siren suit. But Chequers in the twenty-first century had become a hive filled with the dreary hum of consultants and technocrats who knew nothing but work and targets and their own ambition. As he came through the front door, he had noticed a room on the left filled with young people working at screens. The security procedures at the gates and at some bollards, which rose automatically in the middle of the drive as he approached the house, had been unusually heavy.

He was on his guard and when Dawn Gruppo asked him to follow her to a large conference room, and with the certainty that the prime minister did not want to consult him on the politics of Tajikistan, he girded himself as though for a difficult border crossing. In fact Temple did not want to talk to him at all. In the room, sitting in four adjacent seats on the far side of the table, were Andrew Fortune, a man who introduced himself as Ferris, Christine Shoemaker and another man of about forty who gave only his first name – Alec.

Producing a show of bonhomie, Andrew Fortune gestured him to a seat opposite them and offered him a drink, which Kilmartin declined.

'JT will be along shortly,' Fortune said, 'but he did just want us to have a word by way of preparation. Sorry to have kept you. Things are rather hectic.'

Kilmartin nodded amenably.

'This is in the nature of catch-up. The prime minister has asked us to find out how things stand.'

'In what way?' asked Kilmartin. What bloody amateurs they were. If they wanted to lull him into indiscretion they shouldn't arrange themselves like a board of inquiry; if they hoped to force some sort of confession from him, Chequers was not the place. What he read into this hastily convened interrogation was panic.

'On the thing you came to see me about in my office last week.' Fortune grinned and looked down at some papers. 'David Eyam and this woman who used to work for SIS – Lockhart.'

'Yes,' said Kilmartin. 'The prime minister asked me to keep an eye on things.'

'And?' prompted Shoemaker.

'This was only a week or so ago, as you know. I attended the inquest in High Castle.'

'Indeed,' said Fortune. 'Did you get anywhere with it all?'

'As a matter of fact yes, I did. But what I have learned is for the prime minister's ears only.'

'I think you'll find that we are in his confidence on these matters,' said Shoemaker briskly. She looked round to suggest they would hardly be there without Temple's blessing. 'Would you mind telling us what you've discovered?'

Kilmartin looked at her. Of course they knew. He must assume that Murray Link had wetted his bed and sold to a higher bidder, forgetting that the information was not his to sell.

'The film shown at the inquest didn't seem quite right to me,' he said. 'I noticed a peculiar jump and one or two anomalies. Put together with the remarkable coincidence of the explosion being filmed, it did raise one's suspicions. As you know, initially the prime minister asked me to look into the matter and make sure that there was no suggestion of the British government assassinating Eyam. But my inquiries led me to believe that Eyam was alive. I thought it would be wise to have it checked since no one else seemed to have questioned its authenticity and I got in touch with Murray Link, formerly a technical support officer with the Secret Intelligence Service. He came back to me with the evidence that the film had been faked.'

'Why didn't you tell us immediately?'

'I wanted to make sure. I felt it would be useful to find out Eyam's motives and what sort of help he'd received.'

'But this information was plainly very urgent,' said Shoemaker.

'In what way urgent?' he asked innocently.

'It must be obvious to you.'

'Not really, though I do agree that it is sensational news, which is different: that is why I wanted to be sure of my facts. I don't know how much work you have done in the field Ms Shoemaker, but it is my practice to make sure something is as accurate as possible before making a report.'

'When were you going to make that report?' asked Ferris.

'Well, the summons to come here seemed to be a perfect opportunity.'

'Not before?' said Ferris.

'No,' said Kilmartin, drawing the DVD of Murray Link's analysis from his pocket and placing it in front of him. 'You will find all you need here.' He had an idea what was coming next but wondered who would ask the question. Fortune? No. Fortune knew very well that Kilmartin remembered every detail of his adventure with Ali Mustafa Bey. Fortune did not want to be there. In the event it was Alec who spoke. Kilmartin guessed him to be a senior officer with the Security Service. A thinker and a planner, a man who didn't object to six weeks in a room asking the same questions over and over.

'But you weren't simply inspired by the notion that Mr Eyam's death had been elaborately faked?'

'I am not sure about the word elaborate – there are clues he left in the film that give the lie to the whole exercise, which I find rather baffling.'

'That's as maybe,' said Alec. 'I am interested in what else you have taken upon yourself to investigate.'

'I didn't take anything upon myself. I am still actively working for the prime minister, as he will confirm, and I view the assignment in a wide context.'

'Which includes talking to convicted criminals?' said Alec.

'If you mean Mary MacCullum, yes. But I'm afraid she told me nothing about Eyam and the Intelligence and Security Committee, which is obviously the key to this matter. Despite my reassurances she would not talk to me.'

'But you made a second arrangement to rendezvous with her.'

'No, I met her just once.'

'Twice: the second time at St James's Library yesterday. Both of you were seen there.'

'Coincidence. We were not there to meet, though I would have been happy to have talked to her and in public.'

Alec lifted the top sheet of a stapled document. 'We have no report of you leaving the library.'

'Oh really?' said Kilmartin. 'Evidently I did leave because I am here with you.'

Alec did not look up for another minute. 'You see,' he said at length, 'we don't understand what you're doing.'

Kilmartin stared at him dully. Perhaps he did recognise him. There were so many like him in Britain's intelligence establishment; bureaucrats who commuted to the Home Counties each night, and drew a pathetic self-esteem from official secrecy and their ability to reach into other people's lives. The man was utterly average – brown hair with a little grey, parted on the left; small square glasses; an ordinary, passionless face, crimped into neat regular folds at the eyes and mouth. He knew Alec, though he had never seen him before.

'I came here to see the prime minister and that is what I am going to do. If he is unavailable I will leave.'

'Not just yet, if you don't mind,' Alec said. 'We would like to ask you a few more questions.'

'What is the wide context you speak of?' said Shoemaker.

'Why?' asked Kilmartin.

'What do you mean, why?'

'*Why* did he do it? *Why* did he go to all this effort? What motivated him? Who else is involved and *why*? I believe I am beginning to have some success.'

'In what way?' said Ferris.

Kilmartin's gaze settled on Ferris. 'Are you allowed to hear this sort of thing?'

'He is empowered,' said Shoemaker.

'Who by? You? Is Mr Ferris a civil servant, or just some overpaid part-timer?'

Ferris grinned but Kilmartin saw him shift in his chair with discomfort.

'Then I will ask the question,' said Alec. 'In what way are you having success?'

'That's between me and the prime minister. But, yes, I think I am beginning to get some understanding of this.'

Shoemaker was nipping at her cuff. She turned to Fortune and gave him what was clearly an unwelcome cue. Fortune cleared his throat. 'Last week, Peter, when you came to see me you mentioned SPIN-DRIFT.'

'As I recall, it was you who gave the name to me, Andrew. You see, I had never heard of SPINDRIFT before you mentioned it. As you know, I have spent a lot of time out of the country on various projects for the prime minister and have been rather out of touch.'

'You told me that the prime minister had asked you to look specifi-cally into that area, whereas the prime minister says he said no such thing.'

'He asked me to dig around and find out what was being said. Those were his words. I made a note after our conversation, as I always do. It helps to remind us both of the mission. I usually send him a private memorandum so that he has the opportunity to correct, expand or refine the assignment, and this I did last week. He told me to keep my ear to the ground and mentioned there would be an election this year and the undesirability of allowing conspiracy theories to breed. You can check for yourself: the memorandum is on record. At that stage no one – least of all the Security Service, it seems – questioned the authenticity of the film. That was my work, but since none of you asked to see the analysis in this DVD, or have even asked about the hidden messages discovered at the end of the film, I must conclude that you've already seen it. Either Murray Link came to you, or you got to him. To be frank, it makes no difference to me, but do please give me the credit for advancing this investigation to its current state. Now, if you have problems with what I have been doing, please take it up with the prime minister.'

Fortune gave him a persevering smile. 'It's odd. I distinctly remember you being specific about the programme.'

'It was you who mentioned SPINDRIFT, Andrew. Perhaps you would like to see my note of our conversation as well?'

'It was a private conversation!'

'Andrew, please don't talk to me about respecting people's privacy. Not here, in this room, in this company. You told me about SPINDRIFT but I have no idea what it is. I might add, nor interest either.'

'And the woman, Kate Lockhart,' said Shoemaker hastily. 'You agree that you mentioned her name to Andrew?'

'Yes, indeed: I explained that I saw her at the inquest and then at the funeral. You were there. Perhaps you missed her, Christine. I talked to her because I recognised her from SIS. I asked Andrew about her past.'

'Have you been in touch?'

'Not yet, but I certainly plan to.'

'You haven't phoned her?'

'No, but I have her number. As you know, she was arrested in connection with the murder of that solicitor outside Eyam's home, which the more I think about it seems to be an increasingly important part of this affair.'

There was a silence.

'Don't *you*?' Kilmartin said, sweeping the group.

'There are many criminal aspects to this case,' said Ferris. 'That is one of them.'

'Why did you go to see Sidney Hale this afternoon?' Alec asked.

Kilmartin shook his head with real incredulity. 'Did the prime minister order this surveillance of my movements?'

Alec avoided his eyes and said nothing.

'Please answer my question!' he said with the menace that he rarely allowed himself to show.

Alec's eyes lifted with the calm of an obdurate booking clerk. 'It's no good using that tone with me, Mr Kilmartin. We are merely allowing for all eventualities. These are very serious matters.'

'Is the prime minister aware of your operation to monitor my activities, or not?'

There was no answer.

'Then I must assume he is. And that leaves me no option but to terminate my work on his behalf.' He rose and stood looking down at them. Ferris reached for the DVD, but Kilmartin was too quick for him and returned it to his pocket.

'We would like that,' said Shoemaker. 'It may be important.'

'Come on, let's not pretend: you've got a copy of your own. This is mine and I paid for it.'

'But you must understand that—' she began.

'If you want this, you will have to go to court for it, Christine. Is that clear? In the meantime, you can be confident that this information will go nowhere. By the way, Sidney Hale's recollection of events is not as sharp as it used to be. He could tell me nothing about David Eyam's motives in returning to give evidence to the ISC. But no doubt you know that too.'

He moved towards the door, but before reaching it he turned to them. 'In everything I have done over the past week, I have had the prime minister's interests at heart. My time and dedication, both in this matter and in past assignments, has now been rewarded by suspicion, doubt and unwarranted surveillance. I will make this clear when I explain why I can have no more to do with this affair.'

When he opened the door Gruppo was standing there with her hard little face turned up with a look of inquiry.

'The prime minister's ready for you,' she said.

Kilmartin regarded her. 'I am afraid I have to go.'

'But you can't. He's coming now.'

'I will be happy to explain to him in a letter.'

He moved past her.

'I'm sorry,' she said. 'It would be totally unacceptable for you to leave now.'

'I'm not in the habit of subjecting myself to this kind of inter-rogation, and nor am I content to allow my movements to be watched.' Wondering if he was overplaying the indignation, he began to walk down the corridor. Gruppo skittered after him but soon he was taking the stairs down to the ground floor. At the bottom, he ran slap into Temple.

'Peter says he has to go,' piped Gruppo from behind him. 'I explained that you've set aside time for him.'

'Going, Peter? But you've only just arrived. And I do need a word with you.'

'Prime minister, if I may . . . Look, I don't take kindly to the sort of treatment I just received. I won't tolerate it again.'

'Tolerate what, Peter?'

'Being given the third degree by Christine Shoemaker and her little gang; I didn't sign up for that. I'm more than happy for them to take over this work but I must ask that the surveillance on me is lifted immediately.'

'I don't know what they said to you but clearly they have overstepped the mark. Look, come and have a drink. I've got half an hour and I want to ask your advice on all this.'

Kilmartin was happy to go along with the fiction that Temple was ignorant of what had happened. He almost suspected that the prime minister had been given some kind of a nod, possibly a call from Shoemaker's cell phone, or had even listened to the whole thing himself. Kilmartin allowed himself to be led to a room that Temple used as a study, where they sat in armchairs facing each other.

'These are very difficult times, Peter. I've just been talking to the president and we were reflecting that the pace of events seems to quicken every day. You know, it is only from this job that you have true perspective of the world. It's enough to give you vertigo.' This commonplace of statesmen over, he appraised Kilmartin. 'I'm sorry that you were irritated by Christine and her colleagues but I want you to know that we are all working for the same thing – stability and the security of the state. They plainly misunderstood my instructions, but you do see that Eyam could make a lot of mischief at this moment?'

Kilmartin nodded. There was nothing for him to say. Both looked round the room.

'I love this place, you know,' continued Temple. 'It has bestowed immeasurable benefits on British public life. Chequers gives the prime minister breathing space. It allows decisions to be made more rationally.' He stopped. 'You know that when Winston stayed here after he lost the forty-five election he wrote *Finis* in the visitors' book?'

'No, how interesting,' said Kilmartin, wondering why it was that prime ministers felt able to refer to Churchill by his first name. Perhaps the job conferred retrospective familiarity with greatness: a club where people referred to each other by first names.

'But it wasn't *finis*,' continued Temple. 'Winston came back in fifty-one. I plan to come back too.' He stopped, got up and went to his desk where he aligned a leather blotter and a book. 'This business about Eyam: what do you think he wants? What's your opinion, Peter?'

'Motive is always difficult to read,' he replied. 'We make a rational assumption about someone's behaviour based on what we would, or would not, do in the same circumstances, ignoring the *otherness of the other*. We consider only influences that make us what we are and impose those beliefs on them. It is the classic mistake of intelligence analysis.'

'Which Eyam never made; he was very good at that job, though I know he hated the JIC.'

'What I'm trying to say is he may not mean anyone any harm.'

'Yes, that's one argument I've heard today, but you don't agree with that, do you? You think that we haven't worked out what his intentions are because we're not seeing things from his point of view. Is that what you're saying?'

'Perhaps. But certainly that is the right approach.'

Temple returned to his chair and pressed his fingertips together. 'I want you to continue to look at this, Peter. Find out about his friends – plug in and see what you can discover. See how organised they are.'

Kilmartin began shaking his head. 'In the circumstances, I don't think I can.'

'Why is that?'

'Because I'm not prepared to work under the constant supervision and monitoring of the Security Service, or anyone else that may be involved, like Ferris.'

'That was all a misunderstanding.'

'To be frank with you, I felt I was used to flush out information, prime minister. I prefer to work alone. I do not function effectively when second-guessed or monitored. It's a matter of personality, I'm afraid.'

'That's what I like about you, Peter. You're your own man; you have no allegiances. That was why I took to you all those years ago when I was in the Foreign Office and no doubt making a hash of things.' The false modesty allowed him to pause and make an astonishing statement. 'It's vital that I'm re-elected this year. Without me, without our policies, I truly believe that the nation will be less safe. I must see things through. Another term. That's all.'

Kilmartin did not say, '*Après moi le déluge*,' but he very much felt like it.

'I respected Eyam,' continued Temple. 'I've sat next to him in countless negotiations and watched that mind at work. Everyone who's seen it at close quarters is in awe. His grasp of a problem is immediate: he thinks ahead, helping the other side to reach a more moderate position without them realising. If they proved less than cooperative, he was brutal, remorseless.' Temple's lips spread into a wide but humourless grin. 'A mind like that deployed against the state represents a very considerable threat.'

'Against the state, prime minister? I'm not sure you're right about that. David loves this country. He's quietly very patriotic.'

'We think we know people, Peter. But we don't. In this job you really see that. David was about to be charged with child pornography before he skipped the country. Did you know that?'

Kilmartin shook his head but allowed no other reaction to this unbelievable revelation. 'If he was about to be charged,' he asked, 'why would he come back? Why would he leave clues and hints that his death had been faked, instead of vanishing for ever?'

Temple leaned forward with the drink cupped in his hands. 'You are the best person to answer those questions. You've already had a lot of success: I expect you to have more.'

Was Temple admitting he knew what he had said to Shoemaker half an hour before? 'But I will not be your mechanical hare, prime minister. I won't be pursued and watched while I do my job. If I have your agreement that all surveillance on me is suspended, and I put that in writing to you, I will continue. I hope you understand.'

Temple's eyes flinched then hardened, giving Kilmartin a sudden glimpse into the dismal vault that contained the prime minister's soul. 'Of course, if that's what you want, Peter. Now go and find the otherness of the other for me.'

'*The Hawtrey Arms in Better Times*' was the caption of the framed black and white photograph of the hunt meeting outside the pub in 1910. Kilmartin idly examined it as he waited for a steak and new potatoes in the pub close to Chequers. A voice sounded behind him. He turned and recognised the prime minister's chief spokesman, Philip Cannon. He was also looking at the photograph.

'What did Virginia Woolf say about human beings changing for ever in December 1910?' asked Cannon.

'Exactly that, though I was never sure why 1910,' said Kilmartin. 'Do you want to join me?' He'd met Cannon a few times at Number Ten and had always thought of him as a decent sort, perhaps overwhelmed by the pressure of the job.

'For a minute or two,' said Cannon sitting down opposite him. 'I've been here long enough as it is. Are you going to Chequers, or have you just been?'

'On my way home. Thought I'd get a bite before I hit the road.'

'I'm not going to ask you what you were seeing him about, but I've got a damned good idea.'

Kilmartin smiled pleasantly but said nothing.

'I've had ten calls, none of which I have answered,' said Cannon, looking at the screen of his phone. 'And more emails than I can count.'

'I don't envy you,' said Kilmartin. 'Is there a big dinner up there tonight?'

'Not especially,' replied Cannon. 'A few cronies. He calls it a *huddle*. Trusties. No outsiders. Can I get you a drink?'

'No thanks – driving.'

Cannon nodded. 'I had the idea you were a fisherman, but maybe I'm imagining that.'

'Very rarely: my brother occasionally invites me to the Dee.'

'Lovely! Good spring fish, even these days of factory ships scooping up every living creature in the sea and salmon farms screwing up the stock.'

'I believe so,' said Kilmartin, 'though I rarely lay a hand on one.'

Cannon looked morosely into his drink. Kilmartin thought he'd had one or two too many. 'I've got a couple of days booked on the Spey in ten days' time but I'm bloody well going to have to cancel.' He sighed. 'This time of year – there's nothing better.'

'I'm sorry to hear that. Work?'

He nodded. 'I'll try for May after the election.' He stopped and took a long draft of his beer. 'That's a state secret so keep it to yourself, but I don't see how he's going to the country with this panic over red algae.'

'I was reading about it.'

Cannon grimaced, then his face clouded. 'You are aware that we are strangely bound together, Peter?'

'How so? Not on red algae, I hope.'

'Eyam,' he said, lowering his voice and talking at the table. 'I assume you know Eyam is alive and that we're looking for him. A lot depends on him being found and all that being wrapped up without too much fuss. It's the sort of story that obsesses newspapers, even in their depleted, feckless state.'

'More than red algae?'

'Yes. What do you make of the Eyam business?'

'Not easy to know, and I'm not sure we should be talking about it here.'

'But you're on the inside, Peter. JT trusts you; he likes you; respects you.'

'No more than Christine or Jamie Ferris or *Alec*.'

'So you've seen Shoemaker's familiars. Did you know they've all worked for Eden White? Alec Smith still does.'

'Smith – does he indeed? White is quite the *éminence grise*.'

Cannon's index finger followed the grain of the wood on the table-top. 'You see, my problem is that I will obviously have to handle the Eyam story, but I have no bloody idea how. When I saw you come in it struck me that we might be able to help each other.'

Kilmartin's steak arrived. 'What d'you have in mind?' he asked when the waitress had gone.

'I'd like you to give me heads-up when this thing is going to blow. JT thinks I can drop my trousers and perform without any bloody foreplay.'

'He wants it all to come out?'

'No, he knows it's just something we're going to have to deal with now that Eyam is—'

'Yes,' said Kilmartin quickly and cut into the steak. 'There's no guarantee I'll be able to give you much advance notice.' He looked at Cannon and noticed that the bottom of one eye was bloodshot and that his ears were flushed. Cannon was in his forties and wasn't wearing well. 'It is, after all, a very novel situation.'

'I'll say. Now, what can I do for you?'

'Nothing yet, but I'm sure I'll think of something. I'd like to know of any developments you hear about in connection with Eyam – what that fellow Ferris is up to. And the election is interesting.'

They exchanged cards. 'Probably better if I ring Number Ten once in a while,' said Kilmartin. 'Cell phones can be unreliable.'

Cannon rested his chin in his hand, pushing the flesh of one cheek up. 'You're not an assassin, are you, Kilmartin?'

Kilmartin continued eating for a little while, then put down his knife and fork and wiped his mouth with the napkin. 'No, I am not an assassin,' he asserted quietly with a look that ought to have made Cannon apologise and change the subject.

'I heard someone today say you can't kill a man who's already been declared dead. That worried me. And the murder of that lawyer at Eyam's place made me wonder if this is all going to turn ugly. We need to protect the PM from that kind of madness. He's basically a good man, the best prime minister we've got; the country needs him.'

'Yes,' said Kilmartin.

'Forgive me for asking that, but you know what they say about governments these days – they are run either by gangsters or spooks.'

'Yes, I have heard it said, though it seems a little on the simplistic side.'

21

Avalonia

Just before six, she left Dove Cottage by the back door. It was still dark: the air was cold and there were little patches of frosted grass that whispered under her boots as she walked along the track away from the road. An old canvas knapsack she remembered once seeing in Eyam's rooms in New College twenty years before was slung over one shoulder. In it she had packed two Ordnance Survey maps, a compass, the second edition of *Geology of the Welsh Marches*, Eyam's waterproofs, a torch, a bottle of water, a flask of coffee and some hastily made sandwiches. She took with her a long hazel walking stick, found by the back door, and tucked in the pocket of the old suede jacket were a pair of binoculars.

Rising early and stealing a march on the day made her feel strong and optimistic, a mood heightened by the last of the Blue Mountain coffee. The route to the map reference, about eight miles north-east of Dove Cottage, followed the ridge behind the cottage then plummeted down an escarpment into a narrow valley where two small rivers met below a village. She reached the escarpment by the time the sun rose, and sat on an outcrop of limestone, scanning the path behind her with the binoculars. Nothing moved. Then she swept the landscape ahead of her, probing the blue haze for a small hill, which was marked on the map by a disused quarry. Once she had found it she set off again, her mind filled with the beauty and the unusual emptiness of the countryside, and the hope that she would see Eyam.

As she drew near the quarry, moving cautiously along a sparsely wooded hillside, she began to focus on the note she had in her pocket. The map reference only provided a starting point. No destination was given, merely a direction that she had worked out by using a map in the *Geology of the Welsh Marches*, which showed the bands of different rock groups. She waited ten minutes then moved down to a lane, which passed by the quarry, and followed it until the entrance appeared on her left.

The quarry was renowned for the fossils that had been laid down in the tropics as the Welsh and English landmass had crept north on the journey from a point sixty degrees south of the equator to its present position sixty degrees north. The message had said: 'Leave from that which is named for the Silures and walk back through time to those that remember the Ordivices.'

Having transferred these boundary lines to the Ordnance Survey map, she saw there was only one way she could walk to cut across all the different strata, and that was more or less in a westerly direction. The strata in the quarry dated to the age named after the Silures tribe – the Silurian, which from her reading of the night before she knew to have been about 420 million years ago. If she followed a line westwards along a stream the rocks became progressively older until she reached outcrops from the Ordovician period, 450–500 million years ago, named after the Ordovices tribe that had lived in North Wales. That was what the note meant by going back in time. Clearly whoever wrote it had drawn from the same source, for the book specified that in a little over an hour the amateur geologist could see examples of shale, sandstone, flags and limestone, and along the way pick up fossils of trilobites, though only usually their tails, which apparently shed as the animal grew. She stopped at the quarry but saw nothing except a fox darting among scrub and gorse bushes.

After a tractor passed along the lane she left the quarry, found the stream and began to walk westwards, recalling the tedium of geography field trips at school. The air became cooler when she entered the gloom of a steep wooded valley that was more like the wilder Celtic fringes of Britain than Shropshire. The stream was in spate and where it had broken its banks and flooded the path she was forced to climb up and pick her way through the dripping undergrowth. The rational and lawyerly part of her character suggested that this whole adventure was ridiculous. As much as she was desperate to see Eyam and settle things, she was also aware that she should have listened to Turvey's advice and returned to London. Instead she was running round the countryside with her little daypack like some love-sick Girl Guide.

She stopped, leaned against a tree and lit a cigarette which she realised she didn't want. At the moment she dropped it in the mud she heard a report above her as a stick gave under the weight of something or someone. The noise came from a patch of dense pine about fifty feet up. As she stared into the gloom she coldly reasoned with herself that if she were to be picked off by the same sniper who'd killed Russell, she wouldn't have got this far. She waited, resisting the primeval fear of the forest. No sound came for thirty seconds, then a gentle rustling as whatever it was withdrew up the hillside towards a bluff of rock, which could just be seen above the treetops. She slid round the tree and moved to the water. The stream was swollen and the current strong, but on her side she could just see the bottom. She crouched and put one boot into the icy water, then the other, and stood. Water rose above her knees. Probing the bottom with her stick, she moved into the centre of the stream and felt the rocks and shingle shifting under her feet as though they were on a conveyor belt. Four more uncertain steps brought the water to her waist. She lunged forwards, seized hold of a bough, hauled herself to the bank and clambered onto dry land where she shook the weight of water from her boots. She turned and peered up into the trees. From the new vantage point she saw that two bulky figures had moved above the pine trees and were looking down at her. Their faces were in shadow but there was an intent about them that made her jump up and push through the undergrowth towards the disused rail track that she'd glimpsed once or twice over the last hundred yards. For some reason she remembered Eyam's lines from the funeral – 'And I'll wait for you here, Sister, till we take the waters wide.' And then she swore.

Between her and the old railway line was a strip of open ground about thirty feet wide. She sprinted across it, threaded her way through the silver birch saplings that colonised the slopes of the embankment and arrived on the open track. She glanced left and right, wondering which way to go. To continue on the westerly route seemed foolhardy, particularly as there were a only a few villages and farmsteads shown on the map, and these were some distance away; but to return in the direction she had come would not guarantee her safety either, even though there was a hamlet about half an hour away. Cursing her desire to see if Eyam was really alive, she crossed the track under the calls of some ravens circling high above her, and dropped down the other side of the embankment, where the ground was firm and offered good cover from the far side of the valley. Deciding to maintain her original course, she set off at a jog.

Fifteen minutes later she'd put a mile or so between her and the two men, but the ravens seemed to have kept pace with her. She stopped, drank from the water bottle and dully watched the birds through the trees. Then she became aware of the faint ringing of Kilmartin's phone and fumbled for it in one of the side pockets of the knapsack.

'Yes,' she said,

'Where are you?'

'On a walk, trying to dodge some men. I'm about eight miles from our friend's place.'

'A rendezvous?' asked Kilmartin.

'I guess so, though I don't know who with or where. Do you want to meet? I'm being watched at the cottage. I had to push two of them in the ditch yesterday.'

'Look, they're onto our friend,' Kilmartin continued. 'I've just been at Chequers.'

'Did you see my friend Mermagen?'

'I don't know him but I imagine he was there to talk about the election. Temple is going to call it very soon. But the important point is that they know everything. You understand? The situation has become more urgent than I anticipated and I sense an enormous effort is going into tracing Eyam. Every possible agency is involved. We need to meet.'

'Right,' she said, taking out the map. 'There's a town called Long Stratton not far from here. I can probably reach it on foot.'

'I know it.'

'Between six and seven this evening?'

'I'll find somewhere beforehand and let you know where on this phone.'

She was about to hang up when she heard the unmistakable crack of a rifle shot from behind her. She dropped down, clutching the phone to her ear and looked around.

'What's going on?' asked Kilmartin.

'Someone's shooting.'

'At you?'

'No, I don't think so. Maybe at some birds.'

There were two more shots in quick succession, which seemed much closer.

'Are you there?' demanded Kilmartin.

'Yes,' she whispered and raised her head above a bramble bush. There were two men dressed in khaki, camouflage jackets and calf-length lace-up boots standing beside each other. One aimed a rifle with a telescopic sight at something in the sky, using the branch to steady the barrel. He was no more than thirty feet away. A fourth shot followed, then he lowered the rifle, slung it over his shoulder and the two men made towards her. With considerable astonishment she recognised the twins from the pub.

Kilmartin's voice was still in her ear asking if she was all right. 'It's OK – I've got to go,' she said. 'We'll speak later.' As she pocketed the phone she heard a loud clatter behind her as something hit the railway embankment.

'What the hell was that?' she shouted.

'The drone that's been following you,' replied one of them.

'A drone!' she said incredulously. 'How the hell did it know where I was?'

One twin brushed past her with a solemn expression and vanished up the embankment, then reappeared holding a machine, which measured about a metre across and possessed four rotors, one at each corner of its light plastic frame. Two were still spinning noiselessly. 'There are four cameras on this little bird,' he said. He dropped it on the ground in front of her and heaved a rock onto the globe at the centre of the rig. What remained was crushed under his boot. Come on, we've got a car waiting over there.'

'I thought you two were Jehovah's Witnesses. What the fuck are you doing running around like a couple of paramilitaries in the woods? What happened to Life in a Peaceful New World?'

'The government happened,' said one.

'You coming?' said the other.

She looked from one to the other. They were slight and dark with thin elfin features and fine black hair. 'They'll be coming to see what happened to their machine. They will know its last location.'

'Where are you going to take me?'

'To see Swift. But you stay here if you want. They'll be along to find this thing.'

She shrugged and they set off, keeping to the cover of the pine trees. After half a mile they reached a shelter where a long-wheelbase Land Rover was parked with no more than an inch or two to spare under the corrugated iron roof. One of the twins slung the drone into the open back with a look of distaste and told her to get in.

Inside there was a smell of diesel and dogs. A litter of chocolate wrappers, empty drinks cans and cigarette packets filled the dashboard tray in front of her. The one with the rifle sat with the gun between his legs and the other, who had collected the drone, started the engine and, pumping the accelerator, turned his head to reverse out of the shelter.

'I was followed. I saw two men.'

'Ours. You met one of them in the pub – Danny.'

'Shit, so I needn't have crossed the stream.' She looked down at her wet trousers.

They pulled away from the shelter and followed a bumpy wooded track up to a bridge where they stopped and cast the drone into the torrent so that it was hidden under the bridge.

'Hold on and mind your head on the metal roof. We're about to hit some rough ground.'

'How far are we going? I've got to be at Long Stratton by six.'

Neither answered until they had reached a fork in the track were squeezing the Land Rover up a rutted path towards an open gateway. 'I doubt you'll make your meeting,' said one.

They travelled over an area of moorland for about three miles, during which she hit her head more times than she could count. Though he was competent at cross-country driving the driver got stuck twice and he had to engage four-wheel drive by pressing a yellow knob to lift them out of the potholes.

'You can be seen for miles up here,' she shouted above the roar of the engine. 'Aren't we a bit exposed?'

'Yes, but this old banger belongs to the farm over there,' said the driver, who was clearly enjoying himself. 'Nobody will bother to look twice at it.'

They drew up in an untidy farmyard and she was told to get out.

'OK, that's us done. We'll be seeing you,' said the passenger twin. The Land Rover roared off. She looked around the farmyard.

'Over here,' she heard a voice call out from shadows of the barn. It was Swift. He stepped into the light and put his hand up to shield his eyes and walked towards her.

'It's good to see you – we wondered whether you'd make it.' He stopped and revolved through three-sixty degrees, inhaling the moorland air with relish. She noticed the sound of larks high above them and grouse calling across the heather. 'I never tire of it up here,' he said. 'You know this lump of rock we're standing on is Precambrian – over five hundred and fifty million years old. It comes from the ancient continent of Avalonia.' He pointed to the north. 'And those hills over there are made from the eroded material of rocks where we are standing. That's the oldest beach you've seen, I'll bet.'

'You're the geologist?' she said.

'No, I've just picked up a bit from friends.'

'Eyam? Tell me where he is,' she said.

He gazed at the landscape and said nothing.

'They know. I've just heard they're onto this scam of yours. And that means they'll be looking at that inquest.'

'We expected that.'

'Where's Eyam, for Christ's sake?'

'In good time.'

'Why the delinquent twins and the gun?'

'You saw what happened to Russell.'

'If they'd wanted to kill me they could have done so long before now.'

'Yes, that did make us wonder if you'd gone over to the other side. The police seemed to let you go rather quickly.'

'Because I had a damned good lawyer: and by the way, I'm on nobody's side. You should know that. And that coded note, for heaven's sake: what were you thinking of?'

'We had to find a way of contacting you without Nock knowing. Nock is working for them. That's why we went in for that rigmarole with the postman and the note.'

'Nock is working for whom?' she demanded.

'Most likely the Security Service, or perhaps Eden White's outfit – OIS. Who knows? We believe White had Russell killed. Once they knew he had seen the documents, they moved.'

'Then who turned *The Story of the Shipwrecked Sailor* round so I would see it?'

'That was me,' he said. 'Clever of you to work it out. I was all for telling you, but we just couldn't trust anyone and we weren't entirely sure about you. Coming to the cottage and just breaking the news wasn't an option either. There are listening devices everywhere, which is how they knew Russell had seen the documents.' He shook his head. 'We realised Russell must have told you something at Dove Cottage.'

'And this morning: how did they know I'd left?'

'I guess there are micro-cameras up there.'

'They were removed.'

'Who told you?'

'Nock told Russell. It surprises me – basically he's a decent man.'

'They've got some kind of hold on him.'

'Did Nock put the porn on Eyam's computer?'

'Could be. We don't know for sure, but it is an academic point now. Anyway, we don't have time for this. Your ride's here.'

'What're you doing this for?'

'I told you in the square the other night – this is some kind of last chance. We have to fight what is going on.'

She looked at him. All the affability and mildness had left his face. 'You were talking about an eclipse. That implies a kind of optimism.'

He smiled to himself and turned to her. 'Maybe, but we're still run by a few big corporations and a fifth-rate government.'

'And you don't mind breaking the law!'

'Don't be so bloody prim. This is more important than breaking a few laws.'

She looked away. 'You helped fake a death and then distorted the process of the inquest. Nobody forced you to do that.'

'What is it with lawyers? You only think about the law, not right and wrong. Where was the law when Hugh Russell was gunned down? Eh? Where was the law he respected his entire life? A good man like that. Where was your law when they took you in for questioning, because they wanted to pry into every part of your life? You know that was the reason.'

'If Eyam hadn't faked his own death and you hadn't helped him, Russell would probably be alive today.'

Swift began walking. 'You think we killed him?'

'Don't be stupid. I'm saying that when you tamper with the truth innocent people get hurt.'

'We'll see: we'll see what you think in twenty-four hours.'

They rounded the corner of a barn. Waiting twenty yards away was a man in a gunslinger's long black leather coat, black cargo pants and a pair of scuffed trainers. He was in his late forties. Longish, rather straggly blonde hair curled over his ears and back into a kind of point at the nape of his neck. He wore several rings and a small cross on a gold chain. A delicate pair of sunglasses was propped on his forehead. He looked like a member of a fairground crew, or a veteran roadie.

'Meet Eco Freddie,' said Swift. 'He is your driver today. He'll take you where you need to go.'

'To see Eyam, right?'

Swift didn't answer.

'Good to meet you,' said Freddie. 'Now let's be having you.'

A little way off stood a large, low-slung, metallic-grey saloon with an oval radiator grill that reminded her of a fish's mouth. The alloy wheels had been sprayed matt black and the tyres were thin and wide. Mud was splashed along the flank of the saloon, and the windows were blacked out. Like Freddie, the car had a look of honed criminal practicality.

'This,' he said with a flourish of his hand, 'is the Maserati Quattro-porte – still the finest and fastest four-door on the market. It's the 2009

Sport GT model with a new gearbox. My best baby. Hop in the back and *attachez votre ceinture*, my dear. You will find something of vaguely human form in the front seat. That is Miff. Take no notice of Miff. He's a useless pestilential gangster, aren't you, Miff?' He banged the roof of the car and they both got in.

The handsome black face from the pub turned to her and a hand was held out between the two front seats. 'Pleased to meet you,' he said in gentle voice. 'Aristotle Miff.'

'Call a child Aristotle and what you get is a subnormal crack addict,' said Freddie. 'That's right, isn't it, Miff?'

'Take no notice,' confided Miff with a hand fluttering doubtfully in front of his face. 'Freddie has *issues* of the white supremacist kind. The broken home, the childhood dyslexia: we make allowances even though he does not like to be seen with a person of colour.'

'It's no fucking good greasing up to her, Miff. She's not gonna tip you.'

He started the engine and moved off very slowly so that the grassy ridge along the track would not damage the bottom of the car.

Miff switched on a small laptop, put on a headset and handed one to Eco Freddie. 'Lucky you didn't bring Eyam's car – sticks out like a camel's dick.'

'And this doesn't?' she said.

'Plus it's like driving a fucking Chippendale wardrobe.'

'Thomas Chippendale didn't make wardrobes,' said Miff.

'How would you fucking know?'

'He made mirrors, tables, chairs, cabinets, bureaus, but not fucking wardrobes, Freddie.'

'Wouldn't that be *bureaux*, not fucking *bureaus*?'

'Why the laptop and headphones?' she asked.

'That's how we get you to your destination without the filth spotting us with their cameras. It's a kind of specialist navigation system put together by a cooperative of public-spirited individuals, like Miff here, who don't see why the authorities should know every flaming move made by the citizenry of these fair islands. Every time a number recognition camera goes up it's added to the system on the web. It's technological war against the Old Bill.'

'But they surely don't put cameras out here?'

'They've got them everywhere. Out here it's to catch the sheep shaggers.'

'And the headphones?'

'That's coz my baby moans when she enjoys herself and I gotta hear Miff, though it's a mighty pain to listen to him.'

They dropped down from the hill. Looking along the valley she could see the ancient rock formation rise from a patchwork of small fields like the vast rounded back of a whale. They came to a tarmac road. Freddie put his foot down and the car shot forward. The noise of the engine was like the roar from a furnace door being opened.

'Right, one hundred,' shouted Miff. 'Fork left . . . humpback bridge two hundred . . . dip one hundred.' He continued in this vein from the roads of the Marches into the narrower lanes of Wales, his eyes never leaving the map on the computer that registered their position with a slowly pulsing light. They travelled for about half an hour until they reached a kind of depot with a broad concrete forecourt.

'This is where you get out,' said Freddie.

'Here?'

'Yes, here.'

Miff hopped out and opened the door for her, still wearing his headset. She swung the rucksack onto the ground, got up and unstuck the damp trousers from her legs.

'Can I ask you something? Why Eco? What's *eco* about this car?'

'He joined Greenpeace in the nick,' said Miff, beginning to rock with mirth. 'And he's vegetarian, aren't you, Freddie?'

'Shut the door, darling, before Miff wets hisself.'

Miff got in, waved, and then Freddie sharked off into the empty lanes with a growl from the Maserati's four exhausts.

She turned to the nearest shed, which looked as though it had been used to house heavy vehicles or agricultural machines. Around the entrance, where two large sliding doors shuddered in the wind sending an occasional dull reverberation through the building, the concrete was stained with diesel and engine oil. Either side were piles of oil drums, stacks of tarry railway sleepers and coils of fencing wire. From inside the shed, she heard the chirp of sparrows echo in a large, empty space. The air of doleful abandonment was total. She looked around and then approached a small door cut into the side of the shed where a safety notice flapped in the wind, pulled it open and peered into the gloom. She called out, but hearing nothing let the door slam shut. Then a voice came from behind her. 'Hello, Sis.'

22

Witless Familiarity

She spun round and saw Eyam standing twenty feet away. She stared at him, utterly perplexed as to what emotion she felt or what her reaction to him should be, and took in the gauntness of his cheeks, the sunken eyes – as well as their feverish intensity – and the long hair. The beard had gone.

'Where did you spring from?' she said evenly.

'Sorry, did I make you start?' He gave a sheepish smile.

'No, I'm quite used to the living dead.'

'Thanks,' he said. He walked towards her and now she noticed that he carried a stick; that his clothes were hanging off him and that his grin revealed many more of his teeth than she remembered. But none of this formed itself in her mind as anything more than an impression of Eyam looking somewhat younger.

He reached her and held out his hands, dropping the stick in the process. It clattered on the concrete. He glanced down and when he looked up, still wearing a slightly unworldly grin, her hand caught him on his left cheek. 'What the hell were you thinking?' she said in a murderous whisper. 'I grieved for you, Eyam. I cried for you. I was mortified – ashamed and furious with myself for failing you. It was like Charlie dying, though worse, because I felt I'd abandoned you. How could you have done that to me, Eyam? I was your friend. How could you have been so heartless? How could you not tell me?'

His eyes registered her anger and maybe he nodded with understanding, though she didn't care to notice it, nor for that matter did she consider the veins that bulged at his temple and in his neck. 'I am sorry,' he said at length. 'I had no idea how this would go.'

'Crap, you wanted me to believe you were dead. You used me, knowing that if I believed you everyone else would.'

'Not true,' he said, bending to get his walking stick and at the same time looking up into her eyes. 'I left as many clues as I could think of to say I hadn't died in the explosion, clues that only you would understand. I didn't want to put you through the pain.' He placed a hand on her shoulder and she shook it off. 'Once this thing started it was very difficult to control.'

She gazed at him, aware only of the crashingly obvious thought that had been with her since she had first begun to suspect he was alive. 'In all those years, despite everything – our differences, the bad timing and let's face it, the competition between us – I rashly assumed that you loved me, as a friend or a sometime lover or . . . Christ knows what. I thought you loved me just a little, Eyam. Do you understand what I'm saying?'

He nodded, and she wondered if he could possibly understand. She shook her head and looked down, which is to say she looked into herself. Was relief part of her anger? Was some glimmer of love still there? Her eyes moved and searched his face. 'The thing is, no one who loved another a person could treat them like this. That's what I take away from your behaviour. You used me like any other fucking man. You exploited my love and loyalty for you. And do you know what the worst thing is? I let myself be exploited: for that I can't forgive you.'

'I know,' he said quietly. 'But honestly, Sis, I wanted to cause you no pain. There was no other—'

'That time you phoned me,' she cut in, 'the Saturday after the explosion. Were you going to tell me then?'

He shook his head silently.

'Even if you had spoken to me?'

'No.'

'But you said on the tape that you had agonised about coming to New York. Were you going to tell me, or not?'

'I decided not. Certainly not on the phone.'

'Why?'

'Because you never know who's listening, especially on a call from

Colombia. I knew you would work it out, and you did.' His eyes pleaded with her, but there was also something resilient and determined behind his expression.

'Have you gone mad? How could you expect this to work?' She stopped and looked at him. 'They know – they know you're not dead. Kilmartin phoned and told me a couple of hours ago.'

He took the news calmly but asked, 'Were you using your own phone when you talked to him?'

'No, mine's switched off and I wouldn't have taken the call on my phone. What do you think I am? Some kind of moron?'

'They will have a trace on both by now.'

'Kilmartin gave me a phone, OK? It's clean. It's got encryption. But that is hardly the point, is it? I mean, Hugh Russell was killed because of this bloody stupid game of yours. You used him and now he's dead. I could have been shot in the car with him.'

'I wonder if I could ask you to turn the second phone off. They'll be monitoring all traffic from this area.' He was looking into her eyes, trying to connect with her. 'And I think we should continue this conversation elsewhere.'

'Tell me one good reason why I shouldn't leave now.'

'Because you have no alternative: whether you like it or not, you're involved. And because I am doing the right thing.' She hit him again, good and hard, and connected with the side of his head. But this time the anger flared in his eyes and he caught hold of her arm as it withdrew. 'Will you stop that, Sis? You've made your point, OK?'

She was unrepentant. 'You're so damned manipulative. From the moment I showed my face at the inquest you knew I would be marked.'

'Actually, I didn't know you would come. How could I have predicted that you were going to give up your job in New York?'

'But you knew I would come to the funeral.'

'Not necessarily – we were on pretty bad terms. I emailed you several times and got no reply.'

She started shaking her head. 'Oh, give me a break – you knew I'd come. Hugh Russell was looking for me on the day of the funeral. You left me a bundle of documents about the government's activities. I mean, those were state secrets, Eyam. You must have realised they would stop at nothing to get them back.'

'They're not state secrets – they are the secrets of a corrupt cabal. There's an important difference, Sis. Look, there's a lot I want to tell you but I'd rather not do it standing out in the open. By the way, do you know if they think I'm in the country?'

'I've no idea: Kilmartin didn't say, but they used a drone to follow me to the valley, so I guess they hope I will lead them to you.'

'Maybe. Look, I really must leave here.'

'How did you fake the film?' she said quickly.

'With a lot of trouble: did you look at it closely?'

'Why would I, for Christ's sake? I took it at face value until I saw the book and then I started to think about what you were really saying in that poem on the back of the order of service. But the film fooled me, which is what it was meant to do.'

'It's just there were one or two messages hidden in it for you which you might have found amusing but I won't bore you with that now.' He looked at her. 'Right, Sis, it's time to go. Are you coming, or not?'

'As you point out, there's not much else I can do.'

She followed him to the back of the sheds where a two-seater quad bike was parked at the head of a wooded track. She wanted to ask why he moved with such difficulty, but he cut her off. 'How's the Dove?' he asked. 'Isn't it a wonderful place?'

'Which part is wonderful? The isolation and proximity to a murder scene, or the quaint little building with more mikes than a recording studio? To tell you the truth, I didn't see its charm.'

He smiled to himself, climbed onto the bike and wedged his stick between his leg and the machine. She did likewise with hers and gripped the handles either side of her, but when they shot off up the track she had to move her hands to his shoulders, and it was then that she grasped how painfully thin Eyam was. They travelled for about thirty minutes, shooting along Forestry Commission pathways and never once having to resort to a public road or stop to open a gate. The noise of the engine made talk impossible so she sat on the back looking up at the countryside and conceded that one of the greatest minds of her generation was also good on a quad bike.

They reached a bluff of rock where there were trees growing out of the faults and crevices in the strata. Beneath it was a wooded dip in the landscape and from the rock face projected a flat, grassy shelf. Eyam stopped, then turned the bike down a narrow pathway and slowly tacked into the dip, at which point Kate saw that the shelf was a roof supported by walls made from stone hewed from the bedrock. A large cattle shelter had been elaborated to make a cabin with a bay for the bike and a wood store. He told her to get off, then reversed the bike under the shelter and stopped the engine. She walked a few paces and looked about. 'What is this? Robin Hood's lair?' She turned. Eyam was leaning against a post, looking drained. 'What's the matter with you? You look as though you're on drugs.'

'I'm fine,' he said brightly. 'Just a bad night, that's all.'

'I'm not surprised if you're sleeping out here.'

'Lunch?'

'Lunch! I'm meeting Kilmartin at six o'clock. Forget lunch. I want an explanation. I want to know what this is about. How long have you been here?'

'A few days: it's fine when you get used to it, but the Dove has a better view.'

Despite her protests he went inside and returned carrying a loaded tray, which he placed on a bench that ran alongside the cabin.

'Come, sit and we can talk,' he said. 'I even have wine.'

'I'm getting a really bad feeling about this. It's like you've become insane. For God's sake, tell me what this is about.'

He uncorked the bottle and handed her a tumbler of red wine. 'OK, so this is about a system, an incredibly powerful monitoring system, which was introduced secretly and which continues to extend its control of society through every official computer, every database and every surveillance system. Some call it SPINDRIFT – a nickname given it by Christopher Holmes, my predecessor at the Joint Intelligence Committee. By the way, I am certain that Holmes' death was no accident, that he was murdered with his wife, and that will become clear when my evidence is published. It is also known as DEEP TRUTH, which originally described the product of the system – the official knowledge of each one of us.'

She took a mouthful of wine and looked away to avoid the annoying intensity of Eyam's expression.

'DEEP TRUTH, if we are to call it that, is the evolution of another system called ASCAMS, which stands for Automatic Selection Correlation And Monitoring System.'

'Russell mentioned it,' she said.

'Yes, he must have read the dossier. He told me wouldn't but . . . Anyway, ASCAMS was introduced back in 2009 to watch terrorist suspects in the build-up to the Olympics. Instead of the Intelligence Services picking targets, the system trawled all relevant transactions and behaviour and made deductions about their intentions. For example, it correlated all those who bought a ticket to Pakistan, or any Arab State, who made telephone calls to particular numbers or certain purchases on the web, or who were in the habit of travelling to certain places. It searched for certain profiles and patterns of behaviour.'

'In other words, your basic data mining package,' she said.

'No, you don't understand,' he said, looking exasperated. 'This thing monitors everyone! Everyone, Kate! And everything they do! It uses incredibly powerful software to sift the behaviour, not just of suspect individuals, but of the entire population.' He looked away and inhaled deeply. 'Soon after ASCAMS was introduced someone had the bright idea that it could be used to identify criminality. Then the Police National Extremism Tactical Coordinating Unit and the Forward Intelligence Teams deployed it to watch activist groups. And so the system gradually expanded – as these things do as a law of nature – to the point where it seemed sensible to monitor the entire population. But before that could happen DEEP TRUTH needed organisation, money and new software. That is where Eden White came in. His companies provided the upgrade for ASCAMS. Once they had everyone's important data – this so-called *deep truth* – it was a relatively simple matter to add the software that made the connections and provided the evidence to different government agencies of wrongdoing, or *suspected* wrongdoing. For example, declared incomes are matched with expenditure on airlines, hotels and so forth and when there's a disparity between the two the Revenue is informed. Then it went one step further to identify troublemakers, those that seemed disposed to anti-government beliefs, which of course these days is read as *anti-state* activity. The system even identifies people who merely appear to "harbour intentions" and nudges one or other government agency to take action.'

'But the public assumes this sort of thing goes on, don't they?' she said. 'I mean, this isn't new.'

'The British public hasn't got the slightest idea how far DEEP TRUTH has penetrated each life or what power it gives the government. It has never been debated or discussed and the beauty for the government is that it is totally deniable. There's no single computer, no facility or building where the operation takes place, and it doesn't have a dedicated staff. DEEP TRUTH lives in the system – in the software of every computer belonging to government agencies. It infests government communications and suggests ways of updating itself, of pulling in more and more data and setting new tasks for itself. For instance, it taps into social neworking sites to make use of all the information people volunteer about themselves. It knows where they go, what they buy, their friends, their salaries, the performance of their children at school, when they stay in a hotel or visit a doctor – just about everything. And like all databases, it's capable of the grossest errors, which are never rectified because no one knows why they have occurred in the first place. No one challenges the wisdom of these automatic decisions. It's a monster because of its size, its reach and the determination of those who protect it, not because of any innate intelligence. Its power resides in its witless familiarity with the lives of every one of the sixty-five million people living in this country and its ability to make connections between different people and groups and to probe almost every aspect of the personal realm.' He stopped and looked at her. 'You must see that without anyone knowing this thing has altered society profoundly, Sis.'

'Of course I see the threat, but I just wonder how you hope to outflank the government and the world's most sophisticated surveillance system from a broken-down hovel in the back of beyond. You probably don't even have electricity here.'

'Actually, I do – it comes from the farm below.'

'And they don't mind?'

'I own it.'

'You can't own a farm – you're dead.'

'A foreign company that I own controls the farm – a good investment with the price of food these days.'

'How long have you spent setting all this up?'

'Two and a half years.'

'So you started before you went to that committee?'

'Yes, before my second appearance in front of the ISC. I was on the inside, Kate. I know the nature of the beast. Temple, Eden White – I know how they think. I planned for a long time.' He looked down. 'I have pickle, bread, ham, tomatoes, olives. I've even got some cheese for you. It's made on the farm – quite good, I believe.' He leaned against the cabin and straightened his legs. Dappled sunlight warmed the wood of the window frames and bench, which made gentle creaking sounds.

'You never told me the whole story because you wanted me to get hooked on the problem you set for me. You manipulated me, Eyam, and Darsh was part of it – all that talk about butterflies waking from the dead or flying up from the south.'

'Butterflies?' said Eyam, mystified.

'Yes, the red admiral: look, I'm not going into it, OK? Darsh was talking in riddles because he wanted to know if I suspected you were alive.'

'He was aware of my hopes; that I wanted to return – yes.'

'It's the same thing.'

He turned to her with a mild expression. 'Look, you can sit here bitching, or we can talk.'

'What happened to you, Eyam? You look like a derelict.'

'I was coming to that. You see, Sis, I didn't know whether I *would* be able to return to England. That's the point.'

'Because you might be arrested abroad?'

He shook his head patiently. 'I didn't know if I'd make it.' She began to say something. 'For God's sake shut the hell up and listen, will you? I didn't know if I'd make it because I have cancer – Hodgkin's – cancer of the lymph system. I was diagnosed last year. Do you understand?'

245

Logic engaged before compassion. 'Then why fake your death?' she asked.

This really amused him. 'You haven't changed, that's for sure.'

'Look, you have cancer,' she said, and with the words absorbed the reality. 'I'm sorry – oh Christ, you know what I mean. Why fake your death if you thought you were going to die?' She stopped and said quietly, 'Are you going to die?'

'Probably,' he replied.

'How long have you got?'

'Who knows? I've been lucky. I found a new doctor and got a different course of chemo and things began to improve. But at the moment I'm not *on drugs*, as you put it.'

'God, I'm sorry. I'm a heartless idiot.'

'How were you to know?'

'But I did,' she said. 'That's what makes it worse. Hugh Russell hinted you had health problems and there was a finality about the tape. I knew something was wrong. You said as much.'

He sipped his wine and breathed deeply. 'When I left in December I didn't think I'd see England again. I was given a matter of weeks and I sure as hell wasn't going to spend them in jail as a suspected paedophile. I hung on for my father. He helped me make the financial arrangements abroad, devising ways of keeping all the money in his estate hidden but accessible by me. I left immediately after his funeral.'

'So, why fake your own death? Nobody knew where you were.'

'I *advanced* my death, as it were, so that I could control things before I actually died. I wanted them to think I was out of the way while activating the process of disclosure, for which in large part I hoped to rely on you. I needed to pass everything on to you in the will and put you in place.'

'That was a risk. How did you know I would help? We were hardly on good terms.'

'I relied on your sense of justice. I needed you to put it together and I believed that you would when you saw it all. Then I began to feel better and thought I couldn't leave it to you. I decided to come back,' he said.

'Are you on the new chemo now?'

'Not at the moment: I have to be able to function, Kate.' Their eyes met and for a moment they didn't speak. 'I'm sorry,' he said, 'I know it's all been difficult for you.'

She brushed this away. 'And Russell, did he know?'

'No.'

'But he must have, because of the funeral service: the poem could only have been inserted when you knew you were in remission.'

'That's sharp of you. Yes, I sent him a letter just before Christmas and I made some adjustments to the will and funeral service.'

'It didn't occur to you that I might get killed with Russell?'

'*It didn't occur to me* that they would start shooting people.'

She put her glass down and rose. 'This all seems so vague and chaotic. I repeat my question. How the hell do you think you are going to beat the government from here?'

He studied her as though for the first time. 'You look different. Less New York: yes, you seem rested, clear-eyed: somehow more open. Really, you're looking great.' He paused. 'But to answer your question, I think we have a fair chance now I'm back. However, I still need your help.'

'Of course you do, because you can't go to Parliament in your shabby clothes looking like a zombie and tell them everything you know about DEEP TRUTH, because they'd lock you up. You want someone to do it for you. That explains these lame attempts at charm.'

'You're perfect for the job.'

He smiled but she didn't return it. 'Tell me something: I am curious about how one fakes a death these days. What about the body?'

'That belonged to a male victim of another bomb who was never identified.'

'I grieved over those remains,' she said, shaking her head. 'There's something very dark and premeditated about sending charred body parts across the world for your friends to weep over. It makes me think you are capable of anything. When I found that child porn on your computer I immediately thought that someone was trying to incriminate you, but, hell, now I'd seriously ask myself if you were responsible.'

'Sis, I am *not* a paedophile.'

'Have you any idea of the number of offences you and Swift have committed?'

'Some,' he said, letting his head fall back to the wall of the cabin. 'But this is very important. The stakes are greater than you can imagine.'

She noticed the surfaces of his eyes were covered in an oily film, and his skin, though tanned, seemed stretched across his face. 'You're exhausted,' she said.

'I'm fine – really.'

'So what are you going to do now?'

'Watch Temple make his moves, then make mine. I believe he's already started.'

'Kilmartin was at Chequers. He didn't say why. But he said there's talk of a snap election.'

'Bryant Maclean's newspapers both came out strongly against it today, which makes me think that Maclean has heard something he didn't like.'

'Does it really matter? Why don't you just publish everything about DEEP TRUTH on the web? You could have done that while you were in Colombia.'

'Because the material would have been dismissed as conspiracy theory: they would deny it, ridicule it and spin it into non-existence. No, the actual documents must be laid before Parliament and given the protection of Parliamentary privilege, because that's the only way people will take any notice.' He stopped and closed his eyes again. 'And there is the symbolic importance of returning power of disclosure to Parliament. But timing is all: we need to put this in the public domain at the point when Temple can't go back on calling an election, yet Parliament is still sitting.' Suddenly he grimaced and moved forward as if he was about to spring to his feet. But he waited on the edge of the bench, concentrating on something in the distance. Then he relaxed. She put her hand to his shoulder. Charlie had worn the same expression in his final months. 'What is it?'

'I'd better lie down.'

They went into the sparse, gloomy interior, where there was a table and a bed and a sink. It was larger than she had expected and cleaner. Some clothes were folded into square piles. There were half a dozen books on the table and a music player. Eyam sat down on the bed, then lowered himself so that he lay on his side with his legs folded. She gave him some water and perched on a crate at the end of the bed and watched him fall into a fitful, feverish sleep. There was no sound except the birds outside and the creaking of the wood as it warmed in the spring sun.

23

The Oxford Plotters

He woke with a start half an hour later. 'Sister!' he exclaimed, moment-arily astonished to find her sitting beside him. He ran a hand through his damp hair and rubbed the back of his neck. 'I get these damned sweats when I sleep.' He lifted his head and blinked. 'What we need is a cup of tea.'

She used a camping stove beside the sink to boil water while Eyam lay with one arm crooked behind his head staring at the ceiling. They talked about who he paid and how he faked the film and where he'd been hiding, all of which gave her an entirely fresh image of Eyam as someone who could put up with a lot and was comfortable with risk.

He looked a little better: his colour had improved and the habitual smile, which did so much to emphasise, win over and prompt as he spoke, returned to his face. She picked up the box of lapsang souchong teabags and looked at him with eyebrow cocked.

'There are some things a man on the run cannot travel without,' he said. 'I still have a stash of Colombian coffee, but I'm saving that.'

'When did you leave Colombia?' she asked quietly.

'When I knew that my death was being taken seriously. There was a lot to arrange. A man from the embassy – we assume SIS – was sent to check out the explosion and interviewed Luis Bautista. We passed that test. Then I began to feel a lot stronger because of the chemo and I hitched a ride back to Spain in a private plane using false French ID. I made my way to the French side of the Pyrenees – to a charming farmhouse in the Ariège where I stayed for a few days – then travelled north and crossed the channel by yacht, the same way I'd left. Bloody awful crossing though. I was seasick for the first time in my life.'

'So where does Tony Swift fit in?' she said, fishing out a teabag.

He looked at her hard. 'I'm not sure how much I should tell you yet.'

'Look, you idiot. If they know you faked your death they'll figure out his involvement. He's as good as charged. Even he gets that.' She held out one of the mugs. He raised his head then moved his feet to the stone floor and took it. 'The last time we were holed up in a room like this,' she continued, 'was at the end of your time at Oxford.'

'I remember it well.'

She turned to him. 'I guess that's when I fell for you.'

He looked up. 'You had an odd way of showing it – going off and marrying someone else.'

'Oh come on! You weren't interested.'

He inhaled deeply. 'It wasn't that. My mother was dying and I was in a funk about my career. Bad timing. You could have waited.' He looked up. 'But, Sis, we've had the closest possible friendship.'

'Not recently: I got tired of your rules. You always manipulated the situation so it was impossible to say what I really felt about you.'

He shook his head and sipped his tea.

'People always know when they're behaving like shits, and *why*.' She meant to say it lightly but heard the bitterness in her voice. 'Why did you use me, Eyam? Why?'

He shook his head. 'I had to, and I genuinely believed that you would see the importance of all this.'

'Is that all you can say? How can you expect me to help you when you simply won't engage?' she asked.

'Engage? That's an odd word to use, Sis, given the extent of your self-absorption these last few years.'

She looked at him, astonished. 'Oh, for Christ's sake. I had an important job to do. Responsibilities! I had to bloody well concentrate.'

'But your life in Manhattan was something else – so . . .'

'I was a success, dammit.'

'But you weren't a success as *you*: that's what counts in life. You were a self-obsessed phoney.'

She looked out of the window then turned to him. 'You're a

251

pompous, cold-hearted bastard, you know that? If I am so self-obsessed, why would you trust me to carry out this great mission of yours?'

'I mistakenly thought you would be outraged by what has happened in Britain. You should be appalled at what is being done here.'

'By people like you.'

He conceded this with a Gallic nod to his right, then grinned. 'I suppose I was relying on the awkward libertarian traits I thought you inherited from Sonny Koh.'

This surprised her. 'I don't remember you meeting my father.'

'I did at Oxford one weekend, then at your wedding.'

'When he got drunk.'

'He was sad at losing you, Sis. He was one of the brightest and most amusing people I've ever met. There's a lot of him in you.'

'God, he was funny, wasn't he?' She was suddenly disarmed by the memory of her father's speech at the wedding. 'He'd see the absurdity of you sitting in this shack planning the downfall of the prime minister.'

'Maybe,' he said, his eyes clouding. 'Yet I have never been surer of what I have to do.'

'Christ, Eyam, I wonder about your grip on reality. They know you're alive so there is literally nothing else they need to know. Don't you see that? Now it's simply a matter of tracking you down, killing you or arresting you on any number of legitimate charges. You're finished.' She got up and placed the tea mug by the sink. 'I don't understand why you didn't wait for the election to be called and reveal everything then. A senior official – the head of the JIC no less – going public with that kind of material would have been far more devastating than someone who has allowed himself to be incriminated as a paedophile, flees the country and then fakes his own death. You have absolutely no fucking credibility, Eyam.'

'But the material does.'

'Maybe, but why did you have to behave like a criminal? What the hell happened to you? You could out-think anyone; you played the long game. Nobody could beat you. But this skulking about looking like death warmed up . . .'

'Thanks.'

She reached for him automatically, but failed to touch his shoulder. 'What I meant was—'

'I know what you meant. But there's a point when you can't go on faking it.' He let the hand fall from his chin. 'Are you familiar with Hannah Arendt's writing?'

'Some,' she said impatiently. 'I'd have thought she was a bit woolly minded for you.'

'I happened to read something by her which struck me as profoundly true. "No cause," she wrote, "is left but the most ancient of all, the one, in fact that from the beginning of our history has determined the very existence of politics, the cause of freedom versus tyranny."'

'This isn't a tyranny.'

'No, it isn't a tyranny yet. But DEEP TRUTH is the perfect totalitarian tool.'

She sat down, leaned forward and slapped the top of her thighs with frustration. 'Nobody cares, Eyam. That's the whole point. Nobody gives a shit as long as they feel safe, they can feed themselves and watch TV. Most people have no higher political aspiration than a snail. The public buys the idea that these things make their lives easier and safer.'

'But they haven't been given the choice! Officials and politicians lied. Public money was spent without Parliament knowing.'

'That's hardly a first. The whole point of governments is that they take decisions about issues the public don't want to think about. That's what you spent your life doing.'

He got up, walked to the door and looked out. 'Tell me you haven't become as dumb and cynical as you seem,' he said.

She shot to her feet, picked up the empty mug and flung it at him, missing by several feet. 'God, you can be so bloody rude and patronising, Eyam. That's why I didn't reply to your emails.'

He turned. 'I'm sorry: that *was* rude, I apologise. But you don't seem to see that this isn't a game: Eden White ordered the deaths of Holmes and Russell to protect his system.' He moved to her and put his hands on her shoulders. Again he said he was sorry. 'But their deaths are as nothing,' he continued, 'when you really understand that this system has begun to presume to know the intentions of every mind in the country and is penalising tens of thousands of people with increasing vindictiveness. You see, it allows no private realm. People can't exist inside themselves. It is totalitarian because it dominates and terrorises from within. Once a government has that kind of power it not only develops extremely brutal characteristics as a matter of course, it becomes grossly inefficient because it is no longer accountable and its actions are never held up to scrutiny.'

She shifted under his hands. 'I don't need an elementary course in government studies.'

'We all do,' he said, 'because this is the classic totalitarian sickness of the twentieth century, updated for the twenty-first century.'

She looked up to the rafters. 'Oh please God – save me from this. You were the one who helped Eden White, the man who threatens to destroy the very system you cherished.'

'Exactly.'

'You set up the Ortelius Institute for Public Policy Research – his think tank.'

'Yes.'

'You gave him credibility. He used your brain, your ideas and policies to get to the most powerful people in the land and become one of them himself. You made it possible for him. He bought you.'

'Let's not forget White developed into a murderer and tyrant by proxy long after I worked for him.'

She freed herself gently from his hold and they stood looking at each other.

'Look, I have to get out of this damp shirt.'

'Be my guest,' she said.

He went over to the sink, took off his jacket, sweater and a plaid shirt and washed himself in cold water with a flannel. He was tanned and there was little spare flesh on him. 'You look fit,' she said.

'Thank you, Sis.'

'I meant you've lost a lot of weight.'

'A couple of stone since I began running: actually that's why I didn't notice I was ill. I put my fatigue down to the running. Would you hand me the towel?'

She went over to him with the towel and dried his back. 'I will help you,' she said to the back of his head, 'because you are sick and you are my friend and well, you know . . . for old times' sake. But there are conditions.'

He turned and reached for a shirt on top of a neat pile. 'That's my girl,' he said.

'You have to tell me everything you know. Where possible I want to see the documents and the proof. If I think that there is no case to answer, or that your evidence is insufficient, I reserve the right to withdraw my support.'

He nodded. 'I'll tell you everything, but as you know the proof is dispersed and hidden. What made you change your mind so quickly?'

'You can be sure it wasn't your lecture on twentieth-century totalitarianism. It's the illegality of it all – the two murders and the fact they tried to incriminate you as a paedophile. I'm a lawyer: I believe in the law and the rule of law.'

'Carry me over floods, Sister, carry me to the other side.'

She smiled despite herself. 'Look, I'm meeting Kilmartin later. I need to think about getting to a place called Long Stratton.'

'Don't worry about that: Freddie will take you, but I want you to meet somewhere else – a village called Richard's Cross.' He picked up a walkie-talkie, which she hadn't noticed, and spoke: 'Give us about an hour.'

'OK,' came a voice.

She switched on Kilmartin's phone. 'I'll just text him.' But before she could compose the message the phone vibrated with an incoming text, which she read to Eyam: '*Meet 5.00–6.00 – where?*'

'Tell him the parish church in Richard's Cross. It's a little way out of the village. We'll look after the arrangements. Freddie will get your stuff from the Dove and he'll take things from there.' He sat down rather heavily on the bed, then lay back and propped himself up with a rolled sleeping bag.

'You don't look so good.'

'I'm fine,' he replied. 'Another cup of tea would be appreciated.'

As she made it, he began to set out the case against John Temple and Eden White. His narrative was clear and unswerving: he did not stray or repeat himself and only paused to drink. He was the best witness that Kate had ever heard and as she listened she knew that he deserved all her help.

The guests at June Temple's lunch moved slowly along the southern wall of the rose garden in front of Chequers looking at a new collection of narcissi planted by her the year before. Philip Cannon ambled behind the group smoking a cigarette, which caused some annoyance to the prime minister's wife, who claimed the smell would spoil the scent of the flowers.

Cannon had had his fill of the weekend and took no notice of her, yet he conceded to himself she had done a fine job over lunch, charming a group of well-known guests that included a dramatist with a hit at the National Theatre, a historian, a TV anchorman, an actress, the Astronomer Royal and Oliver Mermagen. Over lunch they had talked of cultural renewal and the government's campaign against pornography. The guests wore the slightly flushed and thrilled expression that Cannon was used to seeing on the faces of those who approached the centre of power. In his experience it was almost always accompanied by a manner of exaggerated fascination, no matter what the politics of the individual.

Cannon stopped and looked over the wall at the four protection officers with automatic weapons, who discreetly shadowed the prime minister's movements in the open ground beyond the garden, then glanced back at John Temple and Eden White, who had paused at the centre of the parterre to listen to Mermagen. White glanced towards the main group, underlining what Cannon had noticed at lunch: Eden White had a weakness for celebrities and particularly the petite dark-haired girl who had made it big in Hollywood on the back of an art house movie.

The tour of the garden was a signal that the lunch party was over and soon the guests were departing. The prime minister beckoned Cannon. Inside, the garden girls and other members of staff were packing up and carrying laptops and files through the house to the cars parked at the rear of the building that would take them back to Downing Street.

Cannon followed Temple and White – but not Mermagen, who was somehow shed by White along the way – to the Long Gallery. As they arrived, a large Aerospatiale helicopter in burgundy livery and carrying White's corporate logo – a version of the Eye of Horus – landed on the ground to the north of the house and disgorged three men.

Temple sat on one of two sofas facing each other and gazed intently at the blue and white chintz pattern, while waiting for the noise of the helicopter's engine to subside. Cannon looked out of the window at the light on the trees against the black clouds in the north and remembered the skies of his boyhood in the Yorkshire Dales.

'Do you play croquet, Eden?' asked Temple.

White shook his head.

'We should play more croquet at Chequers this summer. It nurtures the strategic instinct. You know that Harold Wilson dreamed up the idea of a Commonwealth peace mission in Vietnam while playing croquet here?'

'It doesn't say a lot for the game,' said White. 'Wilson was a clown.'

'Came from France,' said Temple.

'What?'

'Croquet. It was originally called *jeu de mail.* The Irish made it into the game we know; the Scots made golf out of it.'

'I don't play that either,' said White.

'You see that bastard Maclean has been talking to the Leader of the Opposition?' continued Temple, but in the same idling tone he had used about croquet. 'Met with him in London last night, though he said he was going to China.'

'He's pathetic,' said White. 'He can't take his support to the other side now. And the Opposition can't go back on their word to reduce his influence in British national life. They are both in a bind. Call the election. He'll live with it.'

'What do you think, Philip?'

'Maclean has been around a lot longer than any of us. There aren't too many governments that get the better of this guy. He's a snake. Business is always first with him. He could make some kind of concession to the Opposition parties that placates them but saves most of his interests, and then in exchange give them his backing. You're seven points ahead in the polls and rising, but he could turn that around with a campaign against you.'

'Maclean's not going to do that,' said White softly. 'Look at it logically, John. The only reason Maclean is angry with you is because he thinks you have a better chance of winning in six months' time, and that's obviously because he *wants* you to win and *needs* you to win. If he goes against you, you'll still win. And where does that leave Maclean? I guarantee he's thought of that.'

'I hope you're right,' said Temple.

'But you can stop all this debate by calling the election immediately.'

'You mean next week?'

'Why not?' said White. 'It would forestall the other problem.'

Which other problem, wondered Cannon – Eyam or red algae?

Temple turned to him. 'Philip?'

'In principle there's no reason why you shouldn't go next week. The Easter holiday will fall earlier in the campaign, which will mean it won't start properly until afterwards.'

'A good thing,' said White.

'The manifesto can go to press this week,' Cannon continued. 'The advertising slots are booked, the websites geared up. Financially it won't make any difference. The party is as ready as it ever will be. And finally there has been no really adverse reaction to the revelation in Maclean's papers this morning that you were considering a spring election. People are resigned and seem to want to get it over with.'

'You're right. Have you got a diary?' asked Temple. 'Remind me of the dates.'

Cannon pulled out his phone and caressed the screen. 'You were thinking of April the twenty-fifth; if you call it this week you can hold the election on the eighteenth.'

'The eighteenth it is, then. I will go to the palace on Wednesday.'

'You have a meeting with the president of the European Commission that morning,' said Cannon.

'Then I'll see HM at midday,' said Temple. 'But I want to retain the element of surprise. This information must be kept completely restricted.'

There was a sound at the end of the Long Gallery. 'Are we disturbing you, prime minister?' It was Jamie Ferris and the two men he'd brought with him in White's helicopter.

'No, come along and join us,' Temple called out without turning round.

Ferris arrived at the pair of sofas with the men, whom he did not introduce. They wore business suits and conservative ties. The larger of the two had a thin white plaster covering an injury on his cheek. 'I felt I should bring you up to speed in person on developments concerning David Eyam, sir.'

'Yes – we were expecting you.'

'We know he's here in Britain.'

'Has he been sighted?'

'Not as yet, but the money trail has led back to the UK. One of the accounts in the Dutch Antilles transferred half a million dollars to the account held in the name of Pirus Engineering on Friday. The company had connections to Eyam's late father.'

'Anything else?'

'GCHQ picked up two calls from the Milford Haven area a week or so ago. Both were made from a point a few miles off the coast. We have checked with Customs and the Coast Guards and now believe Eyam was put ashore by a tender to the private yacht Picardy Rose, which set out from Barfleur in Normandy two days before.'

'I see,' said Temple. 'Has he contacted anyone?'

'The first call was made to a cell phone in the High Castle area.'

'To this woman you have been watching?'

'No, we know her number. It was someone else.'

'But she is his friend – the same person Peter Kilmartin is making contact with.'

'That's right, Kate Lockhart.'

'And she is his main contact?'

'No, I wouldn't say that by any means. We know that communications between them have been infrequent over the last two years. We have learned that she failed to reply to several of his emails before he even left government. There appears to have been some kind of falling out. However, he did leave his property and a considerable sum to her in his will, which would seem to indicate that she is an integral part of his plans. He phoned her after he had faked the explosion in Colombia. A call shows up in her American phone records. The Americans have let us hear it.'

'Still, it is difficult to read her part in all this,' said White almost inaudibly. 'Mermagen knows her and has been in touch with her. I hope to see her next week.'

'Really, is there anyone Mermagen doesn't know?' asked Temple.

'They were all at Oxford together,' said White.

'All of them?'

'Yes.'

'The Oxford Plotters,' said Temple. 'And there's also that mathematician who was about to get something in the Birthday Honours. He is at Oxford also.'

'Yes, Professor Darsh Darshan,' said Ferris. 'He's being watched. They are a very talented group of people. Kate Lockhart was in SIS, which suggests she is capable of a high degree of deception.' He paused. 'And there is one other.'

'Oh yes,' said Temple.

'His name is Edward Fellowes, star history graduate and university actor who left Oxford for a short service commission in the army and then went to the Foreign Office.'

'I haven't heard the name.'

'No, sir. It seems that using the name Tony Swift he inhabited the more humble role of the clerk in the coroner's court in High Castle. He is a few years older than the others. He met Eyam again at the FCO.'

'Good lord, so he was responsible for fixing the inquest. This is evidently a very well-planned conspiracy.'

'Indeed.' Ferris waited for a second then said: 'The Security Service says it's a matter of time before Eyam is tracked down, prime minister. They are concentrating on the area where he lived because he is known to have many associates there. These individuals are all being observed also.'

'I understood the network is thought to be quite large,' said White.

'We're not sure,' said Ferris. 'MI5 have a lot of catching up to do since the discovery forty-eight hours ago that Eyam was alive. Christine Shoemaker's team is working round the clock on it.'

'I am certain this means that Eyam seeks to affect the outcome of a legitimate electoral process,' said Temple, 'which as prime minister I cannot allow.'

'But he can't possibly know that you plan to call an election,' objected Cannon.

'True, but I am concerned that we don't have a proper understanding of his group of supporters, what he plans or the means available to him.'

'Oh, I think we have a pretty good idea of what he will try to do, John,' said White. 'As to the means open to them, well we can make a guess. He has the media and the internet, but it will be possible to make a very strong case that his accusations are the ravings of a desperate and vindictive paedophile. And he has Parliament. If you call the election next week, Parliament will be dissolved and all parliamentary privilege ends, so there is no hope of him gaining protection for his allegations.'

'Then he can be arrested and charged,' said Cannon, 'at which point you close him down.'

'What about the police?' asked Temple. 'Have they been informed?'

'Not yet, prime minister,' replied Ferris. 'There is a question of . . . how shall I put it – strategy? – which we three were discussing earlier.' The men beside him nodded. 'There are several options.'

White looked at Temple. 'These are operational matters, surely, John. You don't have to be concerned with the details. Leave it to Christine and Jamie. Jamie will keep an eye on everything and let us know of the important developments.'

Cannon coughed.

'Yes, Philip,' said Temple.

'If the police are brought in on this now, Eyam can be discredited immediately. They simply announce they are searching for a paedophile on the run who has faked his own death.'

'In due course that will be the decision reached, I am sure, but meantime we ought to leave it to the experts, Philip. We have an election to think about.' He looked up. 'Thank you, Jamie. That will be all.' Ferris and his two associates, whom Cannon now regarded as extremely sinister, made their way to the end of the Long Gallery in step, causing the floorboards to protest.

Cannon had the sense of being brushed off like a small child, but he knew exactly what had passed. You can't kill a man who's already dead, Ferris had said. That was what they planned because there would be no risk of a hearing in which he would be free to tell his story in the privileged conditions of the court. Ferris and his men intended to get to Eyam before the law did, and the implications of that were enormous for Philip Cannon. It was unthinkable that such an act was being plotted at the heart of government, yet this was what he had been witness to, even though the operational details had been glossed over. And there was something else that had struck him during the conversations about Eyam over the weekend, but especially listening to Temple and White in the last few minutes. At no stage had anyone declared that what Eyam had to say was untrue. That explained why they were so worried. David Eyam had returned from the dead to tell the truth.

He had a sudden desperate desire to take Temple by the shoulders and shake him. This was not the man he'd signed up to work for. Instead he said simply: 'You know that even if Eyam is out of the way you still have a problem with the group. We have no idea how many there are, or what they know.'

'You are quite right to point that out, Philip,' said Temple evenly. 'But you are forgetting that we have a developing national crisis with the spread of TRA.'

'Which MI5 assert may be the work of terrorists,' said White on cue.

'I don't understand,' said Cannon. 'I thought we were talking about Eyam's friends.'

'The Civil Contingencies Act 2004 grants the government a very wide range of powers in times of emergency,' said White.

Cannon felt himself swallow. 'You are going to call an election and then invoke the Civil Contingencies Act?'

'The other way round,' said Temple. 'The act will be invoked to deal with TRA tomorrow when I will make a statement on TV, then we'll follow that with the election announcement on Wednesday. It is important to leave a day between the two to let it all sink in.'

'God! Won't that seem rather extreme – panicky even?'

'No, more like the smack of firm government,' said White. 'By the end of the week the public will understand that John Temple is a prime minister who is prepared to deal with a crisis expeditiously at the same time as guaranteeing the democratic process in difficult times. It is the perfect strategy because Maclean can't oppose it.'

'You must have been playing croquet, Eden,' said Temple, springing to his feet.

24

Evensong

Kate had no idea why she suddenly called him David, when he finished his account and lay back. 'Are you sure you can do all this, David?' she said, then corrected herself to his great amusement. 'I mean, you don't look really up to it, Eyam.'

'We're not going to have to wait very long,' he said. 'I feel sure he's going to take the plunge this week.'

'But he won't if he knows you're in Britain. He will want to get you out of the way first.'

'No, he's a gambler, Sis, though he doesn't look like it. He'll bet that his people can take me first.' He stood. 'You know what I'd like to do – let's take a walk.'

'If you're up to it.'

He picked up the stick and went through the door. Outside, vast black clouds had assembled in the north although the sun still lit the land around them. 'This is my favourite time of year at the Dove. I'm glad I got back for spring.'

'It's so unlike you,' she said. 'You never seemed to notice these things before.'

'I wish I had.' He pointed vaguely at his chest. 'This has made everything much sharper and much sweeter.'

'Darsh said you had a breakdown.'

'Not quite, but I was unravelling. I didn't know how rough it was going to be to be thrown out, but the running sorted it all out. Burned off the toxins, so to speak.'

'But you knew you were going to be pushed.'

'True, but being ejected from the charmed circle after so many years is hard – nobody wanted to know what I thought any longer.'

'Ahhh! Poor Eyam. Nobody listening to his wisdom.'

He grinned ruefully. 'It was pathetic but there it is.'

'There's something I don't understand. You must have known about this system a long time ago, way before you appeared at the Intelligence and Security Committee the first time. You were right in the middle of it all – a trusted intimate of White's and the prime minister's. You had to know.'

He stopped. 'Well, yes . . . ah look, here's Tony.'

Tony Swift was making his way up the track swishing at the grass with a branch.

'Tom Sawyer and Huckleberry Finn,' she said, folding her arms. '*Dem two boys gonna take down dat big bad ole ger'nment.*' She turned to him. 'You had to know about all this stuff, Eyam.'

'General surveillance did increase in the slump because of fears of large-scale demonstrations and then there was an enormous spurt in the run up to the Olympics – that we all knew. But the installation of DEEP TRUTH was a different matter.'

'So you found him,' Swift called out.

'Yes.'

'And how's the reunion going?'

'It would be better if bloody Eyam here wasn't dodging my questions. But it is good to see him alive . . . I suppose.' She stopped. 'So now you're both here let me ask you about your organisation. How many people are involved?'

Swift glanced at Eyam, who nodded. 'All told about a thousand "Bell Ringers" – about twenty-five in the inner circle.'

'How long have they known about David?'

'Most of the inner circle have been told – the others don't.'

'How the hell do you communicate? We know they're watching the group in High Castle.'

'A procedure known as *onion routing* invented by a guy called David Chaum at Berkeley nearly thirty years ago. It's old but it serves our purposes. There are also means of signing on a website with zero-knowledge proof which the professor would be better able to explain for you.'

'Darsh! Of course, I should have guessed. Stick with the onion routing. How's it work?'

'Onion routing is a procedure by which you send a message to David that you have encrypted with a series of public keys belonging to randomly selected intermediaries. This creates many layers of encryption. The message is passed through these intermediaries, though they have no means of being able to read it. They simply decrypt the outer layer and pass it on until it eventually arrives at David with the core of the onion exposed. He applies his key and reads your message. All over the country there are people who offer their service to the syndicate. They don't know who you are and you sure as hell don't know who they are. It makes it impossible for the government to know what's going on.'

'You don't imagine that GCHQ might have penetrated your little syndicate long ago and is peeling your onions as we speak?'

'The intended recipient has a code which changes daily and which he acquires from an innocent-looking website. It can be a phrase from any website. If that code is not in place before the message is decrypted by his key, it destroys itself.'

'Sounds impressive, but they have ways of getting round things. Alice Scudamore told me she had her computer seized. They must have examined it thoroughly.'

'It made no difference. There was nothing on it.'

'Why didn't you use encryption to communicate with Hugh Russell?' she asked Eyam.

'I didn't want to involve him in any kind of cloak and dagger stuff – but I did give him a memory stick which is somewhere in his office, unless they found that too.' He stopped. 'But we're past that. Poor Hugh.' Then he looked at Swift. 'Kate has got word that they're going for the election. So that means we're on. She's going to meet Kilmartin and we'll pick her up from there.'

'Will he be followed?' asked Swift.

'I don't think so. He's used to this kind of thing.'

'Right, let's get going then,' he said, pulling a walkie-talkie from his jacket pocket. He pressed a button twice. A couple of seconds later the radio squawked twice in return. He turned and made off down the track. 'Freddie will be along in a couple of minutes,' he called over his shoulder.

They went back to the shed to get her bag. Inside Eyam spun round and took her in his arms and kissed her.

'What's this?' she said, drawing back so she could see his expression.

'Overdue.'

She reached up and brushed his cheek with her fingertips and kissed him once, her eyes never losing his. 'Is this part of the charm strategy?'

'I didn't know I was going to do it,' he said, holding her a little away from him. 'It just happened.'

'Yeah, right.' She kissed him again. 'But I'm glad you did.'

'If I used you . . .'

'You did.'

'It's because I believe in you.'

'With good reason.'

'I'm more grateful than I can say. I wonder what Charlie would say.'

'That's an odd thing, to bring him up now. Charlie? Well, Charlie would be on your side. He was an old-fashioned liberal conservative. He would approve and he's half the reason that I'm doing this. There was so much I regretted after his death.'

'Yes, I knew that,' he said. Then they kissed more passionately and for much longer. And when they left Eyam's wretched cabin and walked down the grassy track under clouds that looked as if they would fall onto the earth in an avalanche she held his arm, and all the tension between them had gone.

Later, after they had separated, Kate sent Kilmartin a text – Dick's X – for Richard's Cross – +O – the symbol for a church on its side. She knew he would understand, and quarter of an hour after she was left at the covered gateway to the cemetery by Eco Freddie, Kilmartin pulled up in a Citroen hybrid, and ran the twenty yards from the car through the sudden downpour.

He wiped the water from his face, dried his hand on the inside of his jacket and withdrew some rolled-up documents from beneath his coat.

'These are copies of emails sent between the Security Service and Number Ten in relation to Eyam's appearance at the Intelligence and Security Committee. There is also a transcript of his evidence.'

'You're presenting your bona fides?'

'Not really – we are both perfectly well aware that I might be using these to gain your confidence. The truth is that I am giving them to you because you will need them, even though they do not say much about this system. I don't expect you to tell me anything in return. I assume you've seen Eyam but I'm not interested to know where he is. Look, let's get out of the wet and talk. There's a light on in the church. It's bound to be open on a Sunday.'

The noise of the ancient iron latch echoed in a whitewashed nave. A woman emerged from the vestry near the altar and called out good evening. Kilmartin asked if they could stay until the rain stopped, then put several coins into a collection box that was let into the wall by the door. Kate looked up and saw the remains of a medieval painting high up in the nave wall, faint red scrolls and the head and shoulders of a saint opening his hand in supplication to an unseen deity.

They went into the back pew beneath a noticeboard that told of good works in Africa.

'The faith of generations is concentrated in places like this,' said Kilmartin. He unfolded a large handkerchief and wiped his glasses, then looked at her. 'They know Eyam's alive.'

'You said.'

'And it's a matter of time before they track him down.'

'Right.'

'I assume he's somewhere in this area, and they will draw the same conclusion. I don't have to tell you about the enormous resources they will now apply to this task.'

She nodded.

'It is clear that an election is to be called. Eyam must go for it now.' His eyes travelled from the woman arranging flowers at the altar to Kate's profile. She felt the insistence of his gaze. 'I cannot stress too much the importance of him placing whatever material he has in the public domain now.'

'He agrees. We are going to move as soon as we can.' She turned to him.

'We?'

She ignored him. 'Eyam says you are to be trusted. So does a friend of mine in New York – Isis Herrick. You know her?'

Kilmartin nodded. 'How is she? I knew her father too.'

'She's had a baby with Robert Harland, who also worked for the office.'

'Yes, Harland. A very good sort.'

'I hope they're right about you. If someone like you is on the other side, I know this country's lost.'

'They are.'

'Eyam is ill – very ill. It's Hodgkin's. He's not receiving treatment at the moment. I'm not sure how long he's got.'

'That's terrible news.' He was genuinely shocked. He slid down in the pew a little.

'Another reason for urgency,' she said bleakly. 'He is also convinced that an election is about to be called, but his health is the other determining factor. He's made the journey back. Now he wants to see it through.'

They sat silently for a few moments with the weight of Eyam's illness between them. 'What does interest me,' said Kilmartin at length, almost in a conversational way, 'is that the police aren't searching for him. It's a simple matter to tell the public that Eyam faked his own death in order to escape paedophile charges and get everyone in the country looking for him. But there's been no announcement. No news bulletins. Nothing.'

'Why do you think that is?'

He looked at her over his glasses. 'We have to consider the possibility that they plan to kill him. He's already been officially declared dead, which certainly makes things a lot easier if they do take that view.'

She let out a grim laugh. 'How does anyone get themselves into quite such a fix? He's *dead* and he's dying and yet he's still got people wanting to kill him.' She leaned forward. 'Look, we need to talk practicalities. How long is Temple going to believe you?'

He told her about his interview and cross-examination at Chequers and Temple's assurances about surveillance. He had made it plain that he would attempt to contact her to find out what he could, but he insisted that he wouldn't be followed or his calls monitored. 'I have a little time,' he concluded. 'They are pretty taken up with the election and David Eyam, as well as TRA.'

'Good, so I can tell Eyam you are able to help?'

He leaned forward to rest on the pew in front of them, as though he was going to pray. 'Yes, I think so. Clearly you need to know precisely when he's going to call the election and I will do my utmost to find that out. It won't be tomorrow. But it could be Tuesday.'

'I hope not. Look, there are a couple of areas in Eyam's plans that are fatally incomplete. The first is that an assembly point must be found – somewhere people can make deliveries. We will need photocopiers and a binding machine. Do you know of an office we can use overnight?'

Kilmartin gave his glasses another polish. 'I might have an idea, but I'll have to make some inquiries.'

'It has to be outside an area of high surveillance but within reach of Parliament.'

'I'll let you know tomorrow morning.'

'The second much larger problem is to persuade one of the parliamentary committees to hear the evidence of a man who has come back from the dead, or at least convince the committee to accept the evidence.'

'That is assuming you can get him to London and smuggle him into the Houses of Parliament without you or him being apprehended or shot.'

She handed him a print-out of the schedule of parliamentary committees for the next week that Eyam had given her. Kilmartin ran a finger down it. 'So we are looking at the Treasury Select Committee on Tuesday morning,' he said, 'the Home Affairs in the afternoon or the Joint Committee on Human Rights, which starts later that day.'

'I'm not sure Eyam is going to be well enough to appear.'

'Well, someone's got to do it. Failing Eyam, it probably should be you. How does he look?'

'Drawn and he has that bright, fierce look of the consumptive. You know? He needs a lot of rest. He didn't expect to be well enough to return.' She rubbed her hands together against the ecclesiastical chill. 'What's your story about me? I mean, you need to go back to Temple with some information. You can't just say she's enjoying the country air and is hoping to bump into her old university pal David Eyam.'

'I'll think of something.'

She got up. 'OK, so we'll be in touch tomorrow. The committee is the key, but I don't have to tell you that.'

He looked up at her with a steady gaze. 'The child porn on Eyam's computer. They are making a lot of it. There's nothing in it, is there?'

'No,' she said contemptuously. 'They downloaded it to frame him. When I found it I destroyed the hard drive.'

'It was still in his home?'

'Yeah. I guess they planned to arrest Eyam and seize the computer at the same time. That's the normal procedure in these cases.'

'The allegation could still sabotage his case, whatever its strength. The important things he has to say would mean nothing if there was the slightest suspicion that he had downloaded pornography of that nature.'

'Eyam is no paedophile, Peter.' She sat down again on the edge of the pew and at an angle so she could face him. 'I was his lover once. I know him like that.'

The glasses had slipped down his nose. He pressed them into place with his index figure and gave her a sideways look. 'But not recently.'

She looked away. 'Well, not exactly, but I know. People's natures don't change.'

'It is just that David is known to have catholic tastes, and made no secret of it. Something of Richard Burton about him.'

'I'm sorry? I miss the reference.'

'Burton, the Victorian explorer. The translator of the *Kama Sutra* and *Arabian Nights*. He experimented. He was a man who liked pain, transvestites, young men, prostitutes. Everything, as far as we can tell. David was a little like that.'

She looked at him with total disbelief. 'Are you sure? I thought Eyam got his kicks listening to the Ring Cycle and reading Cabinet papers.'

'Yes, I am sure. His private life was never any danger to him because he made no secret of it – except apparently to you – and he was so very good at his job. But if that experimentation strayed into an illegal area at any time, even in purely voyeuristic terms, that would be catastrophic for him and anyone involved in this business. What I'm asking is can they throw anything else at him? We have to know whether there is anything else out there. He owes us a straight answer.'

'I'll talk to him,' she said. 'But paedophilia is for inadequates, and whatever Eyam might be he is not that.'

'There is something else,' said Kilmartin. 'I need to know one or two important parts of what Eyam is going to say.'

'Why?'

'Because I will have to win over someone in Number Ten as well as the MP: I want to be able to give them a taste of what is about to come out. Something big; something shocking.'

'You can have two,' she said. 'John Temple is on Eden White's payroll – has been for years. Same with the home secretary, Derek Glenny. Of course, they are not actually receiving money now, but they will when they leave office. In each case an amount is being set aside for them offshore. That means the British prime minister is the paid servant of a foreign national. White isn't even a British citizen. He's an American.'

'Good lord. Where did he get this material?'

'He seems to have spent the best part of two years investigating it and he was building his case a long time before he left government. There is a more sensational revelation concerning Christopher Holmes, the man that Eyam replaced at the JIC. He seems to have been murdered because he was about to go public on what he called SPINDRIFT.'

'Has David got proof?'

'A handwritten memorandum from Holmes' personal files and a pathologist's report about head injuries suffered by Sir Christopher and his wife. They were very likely dead before the fire was started, but the report was suppressed. It was never heard at the inquest.' She gave him the copy of the slim dossier Eyam had handed to her earlier, but kept the summary at the beginning. 'That's what Hugh Russell died for. There's a lot in there.'

Kilmartin glanced down. 'What villainy! People aren't going to want to believe it.' He rose and looked at the altar. The rain had stopped, or at least was about to stop. Sunlight was streaming through a window behind them to strike an arrangement of spring flowers halfway up the aisle. 'The public will regard it as corrosive and seeking to influence the outcome of an election.'

'But at least they will have the facts before they vote.'

'If this doesn't work, we'll all end up in jail – maybe worse. The public won't be allowed to hear this without a fight. There are no rules any longer, Kate. They have killed twice and they will kill again if they need to. Are you prepared for that?'

'Yes, I am. It is that that makes me want to help Eyam. Having listened to him this afternoon, I know he's right. Now there's nothing in my life that is more important.'

'Good for you.'

'You know, I always thought you were on the other side,' she said with a grin.

'I was,' he said. 'I actually liked Temple and once I admired him quite a bit. But I now see that this affair is a product of his character. It took me a while, but I got there.'

She stood up and followed him to the door where he took her hand and wished her luck. They looked out on the almost black sky above a spring landscape lit by golden light and bridged by a double rainbow. The sides of some of the gravestones along the pathway were beginning to steam.

'England!' he said with wonder and some exasperation. He unwrapped the cellophane of a cheap cigar, lit up and strolled down the path and vanished through the gateway. She sat down on one of the stone benches that ran along the insides of the vaulted porch and heard a blackbird sing out in the bone-littered grounds of Richard's Cross parish church, as birds had done for over eight hundred years.

'Bloody England,' she said to herself.

25

The Bell Ringers

She consulted her watch and sent a text message to Freddie. No reply came. She sat waiting and wishing she had a cigarette, or had asked Kilmartin for one of his cigars. Nicotine allowed her to think clearly. In New York she was occasionally driven to join the assistants and staff of the mailroom skulking outside the main entrance to the Mayne building. Rarely did she return to her department without a new insight or an idea of how to proceed. A cigarette gave her a rush of optimism, a feeling that there was no problem she couldn't tackle, which was exactly what she needed now as Eyam's vast case against the government teemed in her mind.

Just before five thirty she glimpsed a small group of five or six people make their way up another path and enter a door in the bottom of the tower. A few minutes later a peal of bells shattered the drenched calm of the evening. She stepped out of the porch and looked up at the tower. The bells had a deep declaratory note – a summons was being issued in no uncertain terms: they were richer and more commanding than seemed likely in this modest parish church.

Turning round, she noticed several cars in the car park and by the sound of it more were arriving. People were hurrying up the other path. Then she saw Miff approaching across the grass with an odd, city lope. 'You should go inside. We'll be out here until you need us to take you to London.'

She went into the church and saw the woman who had been arranging flowers at the altar in the middle of a small group that contained Diana Kidd, Chris Mooney and Alice Scudamore. Kate nodded to them. The bells stopped and from the stairway leading to the belfry emerged other faces she recognised – Danny Church and Andy Sessions. They introduced her to their fellow bell ringers – Penny Whitehead, Rick Jeffreys, and Evan Thomas, the short intense Celt whom she had encountered at the wake and who ran a book bindery in High Castle.

Over the next ten minutes about thirty people had assembled in the pews at the front of the church. Tony Swift came in followed by Eyam, who nodded to the group but said nothing. Most of them seemed unsurprised by his presence. Swift moved to the centre.

'OK – thank you all of you for coming. As you know, we haven't got much time so I'll just get on with things. I've talked to each of you individually and you all know what you are going to be doing over the next two days. The sections of David's large dossier – all the original documents – are hidden and only you know where they are. It is now your job to retrieve the packages and bring them to London as soon as you can. This should not be difficult, but if any of you have doubts we would very much like to hear them now.'

Chris Mooney raised his arm. 'It would help to know where we are aiming for in London.'

'I know. It will be on the website as soon as we've made arrangements. Each of you has a clean phone: the website address will be emailed to you.'

'What happens if some of us don't make the delivery?'

'We have a complete record of the dossier in electronic form but obviously we prefer – in fact *need* – the original document. You just have to do your best.'

'Where's Michelle Grey?' asked Danny Church.

Swift cleared his throat apologetically. 'We have taken her out of circulation for the next few days. She was approached by individuals from White's OIS or MI5 – we're not sure which – and I believe she was about to agree to work for them. I talked to her and asked if she would voluntarily go into hiding. She agreed. We have retrieved the package and it is safe. She had no idea of its contents.'

'She must have told them what is planned.'

'She didn't know,' said Swift.

'What about our names?'

'I am afraid most of our names are already familiar to them, which is why we must all welcome the chance to act now. But I stress they have no idea what we plan – you are doing nothing wrong.'

Chris Mooney made a grunt. 'None of us knows what is in the packages,' he said, looking up to the beams above them. If these documents are secret, can we be charged with breaking the Official Secrets Act?'

'The packages are sealed, and in each case you can prove that you don't know what you're carrying.'

'That's not really good enough, is it? I mean, I have a family and a business to look after.'

'Chris,' said Swift patiently. 'We have been through this before. It isn't a problem if you withdraw at this stage, as long as we have access to the package David gave you and you agree to put yourself into quarantine for the next few days. Let me know at the end of the meeting. Is there anything else?' He looked around. 'No? Right, so I'll hand over to David now.'

Eyam rose and moved up the aisle to stand between the two groups of people. He smiled at Kate then looked round, seeming to engage each face in turn. 'Thank you,' he said quietly. 'I never dared to hope that I would see any of you again. I am more pleased than I can say to be here and receiving your help.' He paused and folded his arms. 'I have an apology to make to you all. I know some of you are angry about the deception that Tony and I were responsible for, but I want you to understand two things. When I left Britain I knew I was going to be arrested. I didn't have the strength to fight criminal charges, my illness and the government all at once. I needed a way of buying time so that I could regroup and get treatment while I waited for the moment to hit back. If I was declared dead I expected they would let up, which is exactly what happened. However, there was always the slight possibility that I would be able to make it back. I didn't want to close the door on my old life, which is why I wanted to let a few people know that I was still alive and actively concerned in fighting this regime. In retrospect I think it was rather foolish and confusing. I regret the lack of clarity in my purpose, and I hope you will forgive me.' He stopped. 'But I have a far greater regret and that is the death of Hugh Russell. It was avoidable and I take full responsibility for it. I cannot forgive myself for allowing that to happen.'

He walked a few paces up the aisle and inhaled so that his shoulders rose. He held up his right hand with the thumb and forefinger a centimetre apart. 'We now have the slenderest of opportunities to prevent this country's slide into an utterly new species of vindictive technological totalitarianism. The case against John Temple and Eden White is as powerful as we can make it. With the original documents, letters and accounts it will be impossible to ignore. We can prove beyond doubt the existence of a super system known as DEEP TRUTH, which has been covertly installed in all government computers. I won't go into it all now but the public will be left in no doubt about the power at the disposal of a very few people. The country will learn how the system has moved against thousands of people and ruined their lives. From your own experiences, many of you understand precisely how that works. Tony and I have put measures in place to make this graphically clear to the entire population, but only after every last page has acquired the protection of parliamentary privilege. Some of you have expressed doubts about this strategy. Why not publish it all on the web, you say? The answer is that in this de-physicalised world, the real documents are infinitely more convincing than anything we can do on the web. They contain handwriting, DNA, fingerprints and some will bear the printer codes that will allow the actual machines on which these documents were printed to be traced. If we take the trouble to present it all to Parliament and run all the risks entailed, none of this can be dismissed by government rebuttal. This way they have to refute the allegations. And the moment they start doing that, they will be in trouble.'

Evan Thomas put up a hand. 'I'm not sure I undersand what you hope to achieve. Relying on Parliament seems a pretty risky strategy. Is that all you've got up your sleeve?'

'That's a good question. What we hope to achieve is a step change in the public's understanding of DEEP TRUTH, how we are governed and the nature of the people who rule us. Everything will be published on the web, even if we don't get Parliamentary privilege. If any of us is charged the material will back up a public interest defence and we have the money for serious legal help. There's a big fund.'

'But such a case might be held in camera.'

'True, but by that time it will be picked up by the foreign press: even Temple is sensitive to criticism from abroad. But the important point is that there are some good people in Parliament. They've been waiting for something like this for years.' He stopped. 'Before we go our separate ways this evening I want to thank you all. I believe we are embarking on a historic mission.'

'What if no one notices?' Kate asked. The words were out before she knew it. 'By any analysis, the public must have some responsibility. When all this started in the Blair years no one paid it any mind. No one cared about the database state. When they were told that all their communications and movements and their private lives were open to inspection by the government, they didn't give a damn. They carried on thinking that the government was making them safer. Have you thought that people just don't care, or don't want to be disturbed, or believe they've got more important things to think about?'

'We don't have time for this now,' said Swift, who had moved to Eyam's side. Suddenly the memory of an actor in the Oxford Union Dramatic Society during the vintage years came to her: a postgraduate student who was about fifty pounds lighter than Tony Swift. He was five or six years older than the rest of them, a tall man with a shaven head and rower's physique who displayed an unexpected delicacy and range on stage. They had met once in the JCR and he'd called her Katy. What the hell was his name?

She tore her eyes from Swift to listen to Eyam who said, 'Some of what Kate says is right, but I believe the detail, the names, places, money, meetings and secret agreements – laid out clearly will prompt people to take notice. You talk about the apathy of the ordinary people. But look around you, Kate. I don't think that we should make assumptions about the public.'

At that moment she heard the iron latch of the main door being worked and then Freddie's voice.

'What is it?' asked Tony Swift.

'Just got word that a chopper's sitting on the farm. There's a fair bit of activity on the roads in that area too. They're not far behind.'

'OK,' said Swift quietly. 'Everyone knows what to do. We'll see you all in London. There shouldn't be any problem if you leave and go your separate ways without haste.'

The church emptied in under a minute. Anyone observing Richard's Cross parish church would have seen a congregation leaving in an orderly fashion having received the blessing for the week ahead. Cars, vans and a truck moved off into the village to take different directions at an intersection a little distance from the church. Kate followed Eyam to Freddie's car.

'Best if we don't travel together, Sis. We'll all take different rides and meet up tomorrow. Freddie knows where to take you.'

'Ed Fellowes,' she exclaimed. 'That was Swift's name when we were at Oxford, wasn't it? He was an actor.'

'So you remembered,' said Eyam. 'He was a great Pantagruel. He should've gone on the stage, but thank God he didn't.' He glanced at Swift trundling down the other path. 'Instead he went into the Defence Intelligence Service and was seconded to the FCO, which is where we hooked up again. He's a profoundly good man.'

They stopped short of Freddie's car. 'Look, I couldn't go into too much in there but I'll tell you everything in London.'

26

A Basket of Danish

Cannon was in his office by six on Monday morning with the two deputy heads of communications at Ten Downing Street, and a young woman from the party campaign manager's office. Each held a copy of a draft of a speech to be given by the prime minister that morning at the Ortelius Institute for Public Policy Research. It was headed 'Water Security and Britain's Resilience'. In bold type below was an instruction to the media. 'Check Against Delivery.'

One of Cannon's deputies, George Lyme, read the speech aloud as Cannon made notes and coffee. Then they went through it line by line excising the passages that painted a picture of total catastrophe in the water supply. Cannon's instinct was to concentrate the science in one part of the speech, having checked every statement with the known established facts. A briefing paper from the Special Committee for Water of the Security Council had arrived by email half an hour earlier. The facts on TRA were these: over thirty reservoirs were showing signs of contamination. Filtration systems were being rushed from a warehouse in Hounslow to every part of the country, but while they were being installed some areas were experiencing water shortages. Six towns in the north-west had no water and would be supplied by army tankers from noon that day. In Yorkshire the supply to Leeds and York was threatened. London was so far unaffected but special security measures had been taken to protect the main reservoirs and pipelines that fed the capital.

'So', he said, 'the PM should not speculate on the means of transmission, but merely state that this crisis needs to be met with the full panoply of scientific and technical responses. All this stuff about terrorism is conjecture and it will land him in trouble if TRA is found to have occurred naturally.'

George Lyme removed the pen from his mouth. 'Or worse still, it escaped from the government research station at Ashmere Holt.'

'Where did you get that from?' snapped Cannon, aware that until that moment such a suspicion had been restricted to the un-minuted proceedings of the Security Council.

'It's at the end of the briefing document from the Security Council.' He then read from a print-out of the email. 'The DNA profile of toxic red algae is sufficiently close to a species used in experiments at Ashmere Holt to warrant further investigations into the bio-security at the laboratory. While the first reported outbreaks of red algae occurred at fifty miles distance from the facility at Ashmere Holt it should not be concluded that these were chronologically the first to occur. The Swinton and Kirby reservoirs, which are nearest to the government research station, have both been found to have well-developed blooms of toxic algae. Given the documented growth rate of these algae, it may be concluded that the Swinton and Kirby outbreaks were established before the first identification fifty miles away at Crannock.' Lyme let the email fall from his hands onto the desk. 'They're doing some more work on this angle and are going to report more fully. You know why this is at the bottom of the paper? Someone's covering their arse. Probably the government's chief scientific adviser: he fucking hates the prime minister.'

'Possibly,' said Cannon, picking up the paper. 'This is a classified document and I don't want the contents discussed with the press or with anyone else in the Communications Department.'

'But there can only be three possible causes of the outbreak,' Lyme said reasonably. 'One: it has been spread by terrorists. *Unlikely.* Two: it has occurred naturally. *Maybe.* And three: it has been imported or spread accidentally by an unknown agent – probably a bloke in waders from the research station. *Almost Certainly.* With the record of lapses someone is bound to ask about Ashmere Holt.'

Cannon dictated a formula that embraced all three of Lyme's possible causes and sent the amended speech back to the prime minister's private office. When the woman from the campaign headquarters disappeared, he leaned forward in his chair.

'So we have a busy day ahead of us, lads. The home secretary is going to invoke the Civil Contingencies Act. The PM and Glenny are doing a joint press conference at midday followed by a statement to the house at two thirty.'

'Christ,' said Lyme. 'Have you got any idea what's in that act? There are enough powers to dismantle democracy overnight.'

'Who said we live in a democracy?' muttered the other deputy.

'But not all those powers have to be used,' said Cannon. 'You'd both better look at the act this morning. There's a digest on the government website.'

Lyme snorted contempt. 'Glenny will take anything he can get. He's a total fascist.'

'It's our job to persuade the media otherwise. Our line is that this course of action is proportionate to the crisis the country faces.'

'But if these new American filters neutralise the algae and make the water safe, what's the problem?' asked Lyme. 'Where's the crisis? Haven't we got enough real problems without inventing another?'

The same thought had occurred to Cannon in the middle of the night but he said nothing and instead swivelled in his chair to face his secretary, who had just arrived, and told her to arrange a meeting of press officers from all the government departments concerned with the water crisis at ten o'clock. Then his phone vibrated with an incoming email. He read it, drained the last of his coffee and made for the door.

'What a bitch of a day this is going to be,' said Lyme to no one in particular.

'It may get a lot worse,' said Cannon, who suddenly veered from his course and bent down to Lyme, whom he trusted and liked despite the ceaseless stream of complaint and sarcasm. 'David Eyam has come back from the dead,' he whispered, 'and it looks like he's going to cause trouble.' He straightened and looked down at Lyme's stunned expression. 'Keep it to yourself, boyo. Don't even think of telling the others, OK?' Lyme nodded. 'Right, I'll see you at ten.'

*

Temple had taken a chair at the far end of the Cabinet table. In front of him was a Thermos jug of coffee and basket of pastries. Christine Shoemaker had just arrived with a folder of papers under her arm and a young male bag carrier from MI5, who pulled out a chair for her. Jamie Ferris sat at the table with one other man. At the far end of the room was the home secretary Derek Glenny, who was staring out of one of two windows with his fists planted at his hips.

He had just said something about the early spring and Temple was nodding with his automatic smile. His eyes moved to Cannon and he gestured to a seat next to Ferris. Cannon sat down but didn't draw up his chair to the table, a conscious but oblique signal that he did not want to be there and considered the Cabinet Room a hallowed space that should be barred to the likes of Jamie Ferris and baskets of Danish.

'The director of the Security Service again sends his apologies,' said Glenny without turning. 'I sometimes wonder what we employ him for.'

'But we have Christine here,' said Temple brightly, 'and Mr Foster-King has a lot on his plate at the moment. I understand we will see him at the Security Council meeting in an hour.' As usual, Temple was crisp in appearance and unruffled in manner. At some stage in the last twelve hours he had managed to acquire a haircut. His skin had a moisturised sheen, which, like his whitened smile, Cannon put down to June's ministrations. He remembered the title of June Temple's next book – *Love in the Middle Years* – and wondered how his successors would handle its publication.

'Good,' said Temple, taking a last look at the front-page newspaper photograph of himself at the Chequers reservoir. 'We have half an hour so let's get on with it. Christine, where are we?'

'David Eyam is going to be a problem,' she replied. 'Last night a farm with extensive outbuildings was located in Wales – we believe that Eyam has been there for at least the last five days. The farm belongs to a company which is ultimately owned by Eyam's late father's holdings. We are not sure at this stage how many people are helping him, but by midday we should have an exact list of names. About a dozen people we've been watching have all vanished over the last twenty-four hours. None of the standard means of remote surveillance – ID card verifications, email or internet usage, credit card use, phone activity or the ANPR recording of the movement of vehicles registered to the subjects – has picked up anything. This is extremely unusual and it leads us to believe that all these individuals are involved in some kind of operation and have consciously dipped below the state's radar. Some of them will test positive for tracer chemicals released by drone at Eyam's funeral last week, but that is a pretty haphazard means of ID-ing people.'

'You talk about remote surveillance,' said Temple. 'Don't you have anyone on the ground keeping tabs on these people with their own eyes?'

'You will understand that there are many calls on the Security Service's watchers, prime minister. Up to now we have tended to keep an eye on the group at High Castle intermittently, believing them to be disaffected but not ultimately a menace. We've been testing the water by placing intensive surveillance on an individual for a week or so then moving on, allowing the automatic monitoring and scrutiny systems to take over. But we do have someone on the inside.'

'That's more like it.'

'We expect to hear from her today. We believe that she, like the others, is due to collect a package that Eyam asked her to store for him.'

'So you know what's in the package?'

'No, because she has never looked inside it and we have only just managed to acquire this woman's services. She has been able to retrieve the package without raising suspicion, the same reason we have not heard from her over the last day.'

'But you've got other names from her?'

'Yes, and some important information about the coroner's clerk, Tony Swift, who is clearly responsible for orchestrating the fraud of David Eyam's death. He has gone missing too, but the coroner is now being interviewed.'

'I thought we had control over the coroners' courts these days,' said Glenny, who had belatedly sat down and flung an arm around an adjacent chair.

'We do,' said Shoemaker, 'but I gather in this case it was thought prudent to give the coroner a free rein in a public hearing so that there could be no suspicion that David Eyam was murdered on the instructions of the British government.'

'You see,' said Temple to Cannon with a note of hurt. 'We make a commitment to openness and transparency and people abuse it.'

Cannon grunted, not in agreement with Temple, but at his delusion.

'Where are we on Kilmartin and the woman he was going to see?' asked Temple.

'Yes, Kate Lockhart,' said Ferris with a glance to Shoemaker. 'Eyam's friend and it now emerges sometime lover. Kilmartin has yet to be in touch but we know that he met her at a remote country church outside the village of Richard's Cross for twenty-five minutes yesterday.'

'You observed this?'

'No, a tracking device was fitted to his car when he was at Chequers. Previously we were relying on the Automatic Number Recognition camera network. We assume he gave a lift to her afterwards because she had not been seen at Eyam's cottage, and that they departed south together. The car did not stop until it reached London last night at ten.'

'Where are they?'

Ferris frowned. 'The car is in a car park in the Bayswater area. There is no record of Kilmartin having an address in London. The short answer is we don't know.'

'What about his phone?' asked Glenny.

'Switched off,' said Shoemaker.

'And hers?'

'Also switched off.'

'Well, get hold of him somehow,' said Temple. 'Let's have him in this afternoon after my statement to the House. Is there anything else I should know about?'

'Mr White is planning to see the Lockhart woman if she can be tracked down,' said Ferris, who was discreetly consulting the screen of a smart phone beneath the Cabinet table.

'He mentioned to me that Oliver Mermagen had made an approach,' said Temple. 'He seems to think he can prevail on her in some way. Maybe she can be turned. It seems unlikely but I've no objections. If he does meet with her, presumably you can keep watch on her from that moment.'

'Yes,' said Ferris, who had stopped scrolling through his emails and was reading one message intently.

'Good, let me know if anything important happens.'

Cannon raised his hand from the Cabinet table. 'What about the police, prime minister? Surely this is the time to bring them in. They can make arrests on the basis of everything that is known about Eyam and this man Swift, who is clearly guilty of distorting a public process.'

'That is all in hand, Philip,' said Glenny. 'The police will be making arrests.'

'But surely there will be some kind of statement expected from the government?'

'Not at this stage,' said Glenny.

Ferris put away his phone and pushed his chair back. 'Prime minister, I wonder if I might . . .'

'By all means do leave, Jamie; we've all got a lot to do.'

The night went badly. Kate was dropped off in a side street in west London by Freddie after Miff received a message on his laptop. The engine of the high-powered car bringing Eyam through the ANPR mesh that surrounded London had blown up after a chase through Hertfordshire involving two saloons. Eyam's driver, an associate of Eco Freddie's from Essex, had shaken off the pursuers at speeds of 130 mph but now the car couldn't travel above forty mph and they had abandoned it. The driver, navigator and Eyam were holed up in an agricultural shed ten miles north of St Albans. Freddie went off to collect Eyam while Kate, knowing that there could be no official record of her short-term let at the apartment block in Knightsbridge, simply hailed a cab and went home.

She now had three phones, the third having been provided by Eco Freddie to match the ones distributed among the group at the church. On waking at seven thirty a.m., she switched it on together with Kilmartin's phone and put her own phone on charge. She made coffee and listened to the BBC's *Today* radio programme while taking a bath. Much of the programme was devoted to the developing water crisis and the government's action. The coverage was linked to the speculation about a general election that had appeared over the weekend. Quoting

Downing Street sources, the BBC's political editor said it seemed unlikely that an election would be called when the government could not predict when the water crisis would be resolved. There was also a firm view from one of Temple's main supporters, Bryant Maclean, that an election would be easily won in the autumn.

Kate loaded the washing machine with her laundry and went down to a newsagent nearby to buy a newspaper and a packet of cigarettes. She strolled in the gardens behind the block of flats for a few minutes and then returned to the flat. It was just past nine when she heard one of the phones ringing as she put her key in the apartment door. The face of Eyam's phone was illuminated. She snatched it up and answered.

'Tony's been killed,' said Eyam's voice.

'Oh God! How?'

'They were hit from behind by a truck loaded with sand last night. They didn't stand a chance.'

'Christ, I'm sorry.'

Eyam tried to say something.

'Don't,' she said.

'Chris Mooney was with him. Tony took him because Chris was having doubts.'

'Jesus! He had a family.'

'The truck came from behind and flattened the car. There's a picture on the BBC website.'

'Are you certain it was them?'

'Yes, apparently Mooney had ID on him. It was found in the wreckage. The police were on his wife's doorstep this morning.'

'And what about the package?'

'They were on a stretch of road in Berkshire so they had made the collection. We must assume it's lost or destroyed.'

'Where's the driver of the truck?'

'Vanished. There were no witnesses. It happened in the early hours.' He paused. 'The sand truck used to be notorious in the Balkans as a means of assassination. That's the type of country we're now living in,' he added bitterly.

'How important are the documents in the package?' she asked.

'Very. Freddie is going to try to get a look at the car. It was registered in his company's name so he stands an even chance of being able to search it. We'll see.'

'Are you OK?'

'No,' replied Eyam. 'But that's not important.'

'Tony was your friend.'

'Yes. I loved the man but we've got to continue. I am going to have to rely on you now. Are you making the arrangements we spoke of?'

'I will do,' she said. 'How did they track yours and Tony's car?'

'I don't know, but I've got a good idea.'

'And the others?'

'They all arrived in London safely. Where are you?'

'In my flat – it's a company let. Secure and anonymous.' She gave him the address.

'I'll see you later. I have things to do.'

'Are you going to be OK?' she asked, but Eyam had already gone.

She lit a cigarette and paced the flat for a few minutes, convinced that the sand truck – like the sniper's rifle that killed Hugh Russell – was not a means that the British government would employ. It was much more likely that the two killings were organised – if not carried out – by OIS, which was leeching information from the state's surveillance systems. The important part of the night's events was that the cars carrying Eyam and Swift had both been targeted. Eyam said he had an idea why that was, which must mean that he suspected that one of his group was a traitor. If there was an informant, he or she must have sent a message after the church meeting because only at that stage would it have been clear which cars Swift and Eyam were travelling in. A simple text with the two registration plates was all that was necessary. Somewhere along the route Eyam's car had been picked up by new ANPR cameras, whose position hadn't been put into the system his navigator had been using. Swift and Mooney, who did not have a navigator, must have been tagged from a very early stage in the evening.

She picked up the knapsack and took out Eyam's paper on Eden White, which she had all but forgotten, together with the papers Kilmartin had given her – the transcript from the Intelligence and Security Committee and the emails in response to Eyam's evidence, and also the executive summary from Eyam's dossier. She put the paper about White aside and sat down to read the transcript and the emails, but then had another idea and reached for her purse. Nick Parker's business card for Uriconcoins was still lodged amongst her credit cards. She took it out and dialled the number of the part-time coin dealer in High Castle.

'Hit back,' she said to herself. 'Hit the bastards hard and low.'

Parker answered.

'It's Kate – the woman who was in your shop on Saturday with that piece of film that you stored on your site.'

'Yes,' said Parker unenthusiastically.

'Is there something wrong?' she asked.

'A mate of mine – Chris Mooney – has been killed.'

'I heard.'

'It's been on the local radio. He advertised his business in the shop. He had a wife and two children. It's brutal.'

'Yes,' she said. 'I want you to release that film. I believe the film has some bearing on Mr Mooney's death.'

'You mean . . . Chris's death and Hugh Russell's are connected?'

'That's what I believe, yes.'

'Jesus! What do you want me to do?'

'Put that film on the most public site possible – we need people to see those faces. But wait until you get emailed copies of transcripts and emails from a firm in London. Just get it out there and try not to leave a trail of any sort.'

'This is big.'

'It's very important, but don't add any of your own comments. Just let people make up their own minds about this.'

'I'll wait for your email.'

'Thanks,' she said. 'I'll call you when I can.'

Then she dialled one of the partners in the Calverts London office and asked his secretary to collect a package from her address, scan all the contents and send it to the email address written on the top. After that the originals should be returned to her. As she spoke she started making rapid notes on a pad, which she continued when she hung up. With Swift dead and Eyam ill and weak, there was much work to do.

*

Kilmartin had, of course, taken copies of the emails and the proceedings of the Intelligence and Security Committee, and it was these that he pushed gently across the desk towards Beatrice Somers with his fingertips. Baroness Somers of Crompton, a title she had chosen after being ennobled for her thirty-year service in SIS during the Cold War, and much else besides, did not touch or look at the papers but fixed him with hooded eyes which in her eightieth year still displayed unnerving acuity. Beatrice Somers was old-school: no memoirs or indiscretion had flowed from her pen since retirement and she had contempt for those that let slip the slightest detail about the workings of SIS. She had been at the top of the service when Kilmartin was a young man and she was still one of the very few people who could make him feel uncomfortable. He shifted in his seat, wondering if she was going to acknowledge what was in front of her, or not.

'You could have gone a lot further in your career,' she observed, 'if you hadn't been trying to be two things at once. You can't be an academic and an intelligence officer: I always told you that, Peter.'

'You were probably right.'

'Yes. Still, I suppose all of us have to make accommodations with our natures. Talent, character and ambition – you had the first two but not the last. With most intelligence officers it is the other way.' She shook her head with affectionate despair and the dewlaps beneath her chin and the folds of skin where her cheeks ended at her mouth shuddered. 'I suppose that you wouldn't have been happy stuck in the office.'

'That's certainly true – I had a good career in the field, Lady Somers.'

'Don't be such a silly ass, Peter. Call me Beatrice like everyone else does.' In a hundred years he would not be able to bring himself to do that. 'And you have been working for John Temple, I hear.' She continued looking out of the window. 'As some form of special envoy?'

He nodded.

'Yet now you come to me out of the blue with tales of conspiracy and surveillance systems and more acronyms than a person of my age wants to hear. It seems rather disloyal of you.'

'Maybe, but the evidence is very persuasive and the witness, whose name must remain a secret, is one of the most reliable people I know. I offer my personal guarantee on that.'

She placed her un-ringed left hand on the papers and drew them towards her. She gave Kilmartin one more penetrating look, then put on her glasses and began to read. He watched in awe at the speed with which she seemed to absorb the contents of the pages. Her intelligence was always beautifully camouflaged by a vague manner and her taste for capacious two-piece suits that reached two thirds of the way down her calf. No more than five foot five, she had surrendered to dumpiness at an early age, although her skin and the pale-grey eyes gave some idea of the pretty young woman who had been sent to the British Embassy in Moscow in the late fifties. Her entire career in the field was spent in the communist bloc or in countries threatened by the Soviets. When she returned to the old SIS headquarters at Century House in Lambeth to take up a senior desk job, her colleagues found to their cost that they had made the same false assumptions about Beatrice Somers as the agents of so many foreign powers had done. She possessed a fierce political acumen that had served her well in SIS and was occasionally seen in the proceedings of the Lords and Commons Joint Committee on Human Rights.

She put down the papers and stared from the window across the Thames. 'I can do little for you on the basis of this evidence,' she said.

'It is nothing like the entire case,' said Kilmartin.

'I have to have more to persuade my chairman.'

'The documents cannot be made available until the committee agrees to hear the evidence.'

'Well, that isn't on, Peter. I am sorry but I am not prepared to allow this committee to be used. And I can assure you that will be the first thought of my chairman, who is a member of the governing party. I want the name of this witness and as much as you know of what he is going to say and how it affects the business of my committee.'

Kilmartin addressed her demands in reverse order and started by making the case for putting the committee in the forefront of the fight for civil liberties in Britain. She was unmoved by this. Her interest only picked up when he expanded on what she had read about Eden White's penetration of and influence in the highest councils in the land. At length he revealed that David Eyam had faked his own death and had returned to Britain.

She listened without surprise or emotion, her hands resting together on a cream silk blouse just beneath her bosom, her eyes only once straying to the photograph of a young military cadet in a small silver frame on the windowsill. After forty-five minutes Kilmartin found that he'd allowed an old lady who wasn't too good on her pins to pick his pockets almost clean. She hadn't pulled rank on him; she was just damned good at her job.

However, there was one piece of information he managed to keep from her and that concerned the pictures of children found on David Eyam's computer.

Cannon was the warm-up man and the press were having some fun with him about the prime minister's schedule for the week, which had suddenly suffered a number of cancellations. He insisted that the time the prime minister had made available at the end of the week was to oversee government operations to clean up Britain's water supply. No, he said in answer to three questions, he could not say whether an election was going to be called because he was not privy to the workings of the prime minister's mind.

It was the insufferable vulgarity of the British media that Cannon hated – that and the almost total indolence when it came to research and checking facts. The journalists moved on to June Temple's reported remark that half the Cabinet were overweight and that they would all make better decisions if they took exercise before the Cabinet meeting.

'What sort of exercise has she got in mind?' asked a woman from the tabloids. There were more questions: would June be leading the Cabinet in an aerobics class? Given the title of her new book, did she recommend that ministers make love before Cabinet meetings?

He denied that she had made any such remark and answered no, no and no again. Then he closed his folder and stepped away from the rostrum. A minute later the television lights switched on and Temple arrived with Derek Glenny. Grasping either side of the lectern, the prime minister stood tall and surveyed the representatives of the media with a look of unbowed seriousness, an expression that Cannon thought he did rather well.

'Ladies and gentlemen, this morning I have had meetings with the

292

Security Council, with the heads of the intelligence services, the government scientists and all the departments concerned with the deepening crisis in our water supply. Since I spoke at the Ortelius Institute for Public Policy Research, the situation has altered. We now have eight towns in the north of England without water, and three more are threatened. Well over forty reservoirs are affected and we cannot say how many more will join those that must be quarantined, treated and fitted with special equipment from America. In a moment the home secretary will speak to you, but it is important that the public understands that the government is taking this crisis very seriously and that we are applying the full might of the state's power to deal with it. That is why I will be making a statement to the House of Commons to explain that I am invoking the emergency powers laid out in the Civil Contingencies Act 2004, and why I will address the nation later on today. As a government, we believe the mechanism known as the "triple lock" has been satisfied and that the temporary powers will, as required by law, answer the requirements of *gravity* and *necessity* and will be applied with geographical *proportionality*, which in layman's language means the power will only be exercised where we think the water supply or the public are at risk. Britain's traditions of civil liberties are at the heart of our discussions and we will take all steps to protect them as well as to ensure the public's safety. Now before I hand over to Derek, I will take a few questions on this issue only.'

A reporter from one of the tabloids raised a hand. 'You say you have had a briefing from the Security Service, prime minister. Is there any suspicion that the red algae is the work of saboteurs, maybe even terrorists?'

'The important thing in these kinds of situations, Jim, is not to spread alarm. Terrorism is certainly one of the possible causes that we have been looking at. The Security Service has knowledge of at least two groups who have actively considered such an attack in Britain.'

'So you believe that TRA is the result of terrorist action?'

'No, I am not saying that. This is one line of inquiry.'

'But that is your favoured solution?'

'What I believe has no relevance. I am simply saying these are the facts. We have two groups capable and willing to poison Britain's water supply. That is enough for us to take action.'

'Is there any information about these groups?'

'No, I'm afraid not at this stage. You must understand that the priority is to catch these people and MI5 needs to maintain operational security. But I again stress that this is only one line of inquiry.' He picked up the glass of water next to the lectern but rather than drinking, held it up to the room, so triggering a pulse of two dozen camera flashes. 'Our main concern must be the scientific and technological response to this crisis so that in a few days every person in the country can drink a glass of water like this without fear.'

All the work Cannon had done on the speech that morning, balancing the three possible causes and making Temple seem calm and statesmanlike had been undone. Half the journalists in the room left or started typing the line about a terrorist attack into their laptops and phones. He looked down at the paper that had been knocked up by Lyme and the chief of press at the Home Office that morning and wondered how Glenny was going to present the sweeping powers that the government was taking for itself.

Glenny stepped up to the lectern and directed a businesslike grin at Temple. 'You will all have a copy of the special measures that we are taking under the Civil Contingencies Act 2004 so I won't detain you by going into a lot of detail. But before I start I would just like to underline what the prime minister has said about the seriousness of this situation, and add that we invoke these powers with a sense of duty to the constitutional rights of every citizen in this country. Security is our top priority, however. As section twenty-two of the act makes clear, emergency regulations may make any provision that the person making the regulations – in this case me – is satisfied is appropriate for the purpose of protecting human life, health and safety.' That sentence was enough to put the room to sleep. Glenny did not make speeches; he intoned in a lifeless bureaucratic plainsong, and never would it be put to effect better than now, thought Cannon, as he watched him begin to read.

'The powers that we introduce provide for, or enable the requisition of property; provide for, or enable, the destruction of property; prohibit movement from a specified place; require or enable movement to a specified place.' He stopped and looked round. 'We further plan to prohibit assemblies of specified kinds at specified places at specified times and make use of the part of section twenty-two that allows for the creation of an offence of failing to comply with provisions of the regulations or a direct order given under the regulations.'

Glenny's list took under five minutes to read. He ended with an apology for the technical language and an assurance that the powers would last for one week only. 'If the government believes that it needs an extension then we will of course have regard to the requirements of the triple lock safeguard,' he said.

There was a silence in the room. Then a young journalist whom Cannon didn't recognise stood up. 'Am I right in thinking, home secretary, that you have in effect suspended the Constitution?' He looked down at his notebook. 'Confiscation of property without compensation . . . destruction of property et cetera without compensation . . . banning movement . . . banning assembly . . . the creation of new offences . . . these are the decrees of a police state, not a parliamentary democracy.'

Glenny shook his head affably. 'The prime minister will address the issues you touch on in the House this afternoon but I would just point out that these powers were passed by Parliament after many hours of debate and scrutiny in 2003. And when you talk about civil liberties let us not forget that the primary human right is the right to life.'

He removed his glasses, nodded to Temple and they left together.

27

The Devil's Quilted Anvil

Three hours later, Cannon returned with the prime minister from the House of Commons. Temple was in buoyant mood: the House had pulled together and listened to him with solemn comprehension of the crisis now facing the nation. Only a few speakers had dissented from his argument of necessity, and those reservations expressed about civil liberties were hedged with so many salutes to Temple's calm and responsible speech that they had little impact.

As Temple's car entered Downing Street, Cannon asked: 'Have you had further thoughts about when you're going to announce the election?'

'I'm minded to leave this to sink in for a day and go to the palace on Wednesday morning.'

The car stopped and its doors were opened by Temple's bodyguards. They got out.

'It may look as if you are bouncing the country into an election at a time of crisis,' said Cannon as they passed through the front door of Number Ten.

'I am satisfied these emergency powers are going to do us a lot of good,' replied Temple. 'The problem will be over in a week or so, once these filters are installed. We will have been seen to have acted decisively and we can get on with the campaign.'

'And the emergency powers?'

'They'll be lifted in due course. Big picture, Philip! Big picture!' He left Cannon with an equally meaningless light punch on the shoulder, a habit he had picked up from the American secretary of state.

In the Communications room Cannon went to Lyme's desk, pulled up a chair and sat down next to him. 'It's Wednesday – he's definitely going on Wednesday.'

Lyme's eyes didn't move from the screen. 'Then he's going to have to deal with this.'

'What have you got there?' asked Cannon.

'Just a few emails from inside this building, a transcript of the secret proceedings of the ISC, an interesting document which describes the installation of a secret super-surveillance system and some CCTV film of two blokes leaving a building.'

'What are you talking about?'

Lyme turned the screen to face Cannon and moved the cursor to a blank panel and clicked on the arrow. A caption appeared. *CCTV THE POLICE DON'T WANT TO SEE OF SUSPECTS LEAVING THE OFFICE OF MURDERED LAWYER HUGH RUSSELL.*

Cannon watched the two men going into the building followed by a woman. Thirty-five minutes later they hurried out. One was carrying a file, the other clutching his face. The woman did not reappear before the ambulance and police. The film ended and the panel was filled with two stills of the men blown up.'

'Oh Christ,' groaned Cannon.

'What?'

'Those men were with Jamie Ferris at Chequers yesterday.'

'You sure?'

'Positive. Ferris brought them on Eden White's helicopter.'

'Was JT in the same room?'

'Yes.'

'Not good. What were they doing in High Castle?'

'I don't want to know.'

Lyme looked doubtful. 'You may have to – there's a lot of speculation on the web. The lawyer was shot outside David Eyam's home, the transcript is of Eyam's evidence at the ISC and the emails about Eyam come from JT's private office. But this surveillance thing sounds creepy. Know anything about it?' He stopped and waited for a reaction but none came. 'The thing you told me about Eyam this morning, Philip: that could be really big. We don't need it now. All the usual sites are pumping out conspiracy theories.' He paused again. 'How many people know he's alive? Does anyone have an idea where he is?'

Cannon was silent for a moment, then went to his own desk and picked up the phone and dialled. As the number rang he swivelled his chair to face the window.

'You know that business we discussed in the pub,' he said when Kilmartin answered. 'I think it may be time to meet.'

'The Travellers Club at six?'

'Six thirty?'

'Fine.'

Cannon saw John Temple once more that day. He was summoned by Dawn Gruppo to the prime minister's sitting room at four p.m. He arrived late with a sheaf of papers and print-outs. Temple was at a desk in the corner of the room talking on one of three phones. Gruppo was standing next to him with her usual look of fierce concern. Shoemaker, Alec Smith and Andrew Fortune were on the sofas, while Jamie Ferris was at a round table covered with pictures of June and Temple's three children from his first marriage.

Temple handed the phone to Gruppo, who murmured something before hanging up and hastening from the room.

'Jamie was just bringing us up to date with the developments,' he said as Cannon sat down opposite the large mirror.

'About twenty members of the "Bell Ringers" – that is their name for themselves we think – met in a church near the village of Long Stratton. Our informant says that Eyam was there and he addressed the group but did not look well. We now have all the names of the people who were there. We believe there may be one or two others involved, people from Eyam's past in Oxford. All those at the church—'

'Let me just get this straight,' interrupted Temple. 'They have been using churches to meet. Isn't there some sort of law against that?'

'They are all part of a bell-ringing society. Bell ringers use churches when services aren't being held – an ideal place. They use half a dozen churches in the area,' he said. All those in the church were asked to retrieve packages they were keeping for David Eyam and bring them to

London immediately. These are to be assembled and used at some sort of press conference at an as yet undisclosed location.'

'A press conference,' said Temple. 'Have you heard anything about this, Philip?'

Cannon shook his head.

'So twenty individuals or thereabouts,' continued Ferris, 'left in various vehicles from the church last evening and made their way to London, presumably after picking up the packages. One car, carrying Tony Swift, the coroner's clerk and Eyam's right-hand man, was involved in a collision last night. Mr Swift and his passenger were killed. The police will be asked to search the vehicle and the bodies for any papers, as a matter of urgency.'

'What about this informant? Have you got her package?'

'We have only recently acquired the services of this woman, but we have seen what was in her package and copied it.'

'And?'

'It's relatively harmless material – embarrassing if it came to light but not a disaster.'

'So where is Eyam?'

'We must assume that he is in London, but if I may just go back to the church. An hour or so before the meeting, Kilmartin met Kate Lockhart for twenty-five minutes at the exact same place. This only emerged when the data from the tracker on his car was tallied with the information received about the church meeting. I thought you ought to know that, prime minister.'

'So we are to believe Kilmartin is in league with Eyam?'

Alec Smith spoke. 'He may have a reasonable explanation why he met Lockhart there, but it does seem as you suggest. After all, that is what we suspected when we acquired the analysis of the film from Colombia.'

'Do we have an idea when Eyam is going to move?' asked Temple.

'No, but we can assume in the next day or two.'

'We have all their details,' said Temple. 'We know their names, which means we know what they look like and that means they're going to find it very hard to move about the capital. Your people are working on this I take it, Christine?'

'Yes, now we have the names,' she replied.

'What are we going to do if Eyam does go public. Philip?'

'He already has, or at least someone has,' replied Cannon. He got up and distributed the print-outs of the web pages Lyme had found and a still from the CCTV footage of the two men.

'We've seen this,' said Shoemaker. 'We believe the documents come from Mary MacCullum. We are looking at the site and taking steps to remove the information.'

'But the CCTV film is the point, Christine,' said Cannon sharply. 'That man is the same one who came with Jamie to Chequers yesterday.'

'The identification is not at all clear,' said Ferris without concern.

'But you're not denying it. This man has been caught leaving the scene of a crime. If the police were doing their job he would be a suspect in a murder case. And then you bring him to Chequers.' He turned to Temple. 'This is very serious, prime minister.'

'You may have a point, Philip, but the priority now is to get hold of Eyam and his material and prevent him and his associates disrupting the democratic process. That's where we are now; that is what matters now.'

'But you're not going to be able to suppress this information, prime minister. The transcript from the Intelligence and Security Committee can't be denied. It is out there now. And people will wonder what this surveillance system is about. Even if Eyam is arrested or silenced this will become an issue.'

'Oh, I don't think that is necessarily true. The public knows that the government has the means to fight crime and terrorism and sometimes these things must remain secret in order to be effective. Do you hear people complaining about them? Do you hear people saying they feel less free? No, because they understand that one of the primary duties of government is to protect the public.' He rose from his desk and moved into the centre of the room, his eyes never leaving Cannon. 'We have come through a lot, Philip. You above all appreciate that people want a strong state. They want to know that there's someone at the top taking the tough decisions. And oftentimes they don't want to hear about the agonies of government – what we go through.' Shoemaker and Alec Smith nodded. 'Look, for a day or two this may be ticklish but it is your job to make sure that it doesn't last longer, Philip.'

'Ticklish is not the word I'd use, prime minister. If these revelations continue people will begin to think that their constitutional rights are threatened. This system will be portrayed as a monster – a technological hydra. They weren't consulted about it but it was their money that paid for it.'

'Philip! Philip! Let me tell you something: they don't *want* to be consulted about every complex piece of government apparatus. This system makes the country safer from all the problems that have plagued us.'

Cannon could feel himself about to lose it. He looked down to his feet and counted to three. Then he looked up. 'Everyone in this room knows the power of this surveillance system, I'm sure. I'm merely giving you my reaction as someone who has only come to know about this today. This system breaches constitutional rights and destroys lives.'

'I don't agree, but the point is that these matters are of the utmost secrecy, Philip, and the government cannot discuss them. You will think of a way of dealing with it without going into detail.' The parenthetic smile lines began to form and the eyes squeezed shut. 'Now if you wouldn't mind we have one or two more things to discuss. I just wanted you to understand where we were, and give you notice of this problem.'

Cannon got up feeling oddly relieved. As he left the Great Lord Protector with his favoured generals, he felt something clear in his mind.

At six twenty-five p.m. Kilmartin was handed a note by the porter at the entrance of the Travellers Club. He turned back into Pall Mall and took a cab to Madagascar, a lounge and dining club off Charlotte Street, where he found Philip Cannon in the corner of the bar with a broadcasting trade paper and pint of bitter.

'They've got a tracker on your car,' he said when Kilmartin had ordered from the waiter.

'Really?' said Kilmartin, looking around at the membership of the Madagascar – middle-aged advertising and TV people dressing too young.

'And they know your phone number, so it's reasonable to suppose that they're monitoring your calls.'

'You think so?' said Kilmartin with puzzled innocence.

'Oh come on, Peter, you don't have to play the spook with me. They're onto you. They know you met the Lockhart woman at a church where Eyam addressed his troops an hour later. They know about the Bell Ringers. They know the churches where they met. They have their names; they've got their photographs; they know how many people are involved. They've sprayed them with chemical dyes. And . . . they've got someone on the inside.'

Kilmartin did not let his expression change. 'Who?'

'A woman: I don't know her name. They've only just got their hooks into her.'

'Why are you telling me this?'

Cannon took a sip of his beer and thought. 'I had lunch in the House of Commons today,' he said eventually. 'It was before the PM's statement on the emergency powers. On the walls of that dining room are portraits of Charles James Fox, Edmund Burke and John Wilkes, three heroes of English democracy and as it happens three heroes of mine. They reminded me that they stood for the things I stand for – or did before I took this job.' He drank some more. 'I looked round the room and realised there wasn't one politician there who had the slightest doubt about these emergency powers. And I was right – not one of them spoke in the chamber. Not one, and yet there is absolutely no need for these powers. They are being used to impress the public and give Temple a lift in the polls. And maybe they will be used against Eyam.'

'I wondered about that.'

'They call it function creep.'

'Yes, I've heard the phrase.'

'You saw the documents and CCTV on the web?'

'Yes,' said Kilmartin. Kate Lockhart had warned him earlier and he was worried about Mary MacCullum.

'Well, here's the news. The men coming out of that building where the lawyer was attacked and robbed were at Chequers over the weekend. I saw them there and I am pretty sure they work for Jamie Ferris at OIS. They may have had something to do with Russell's murder.'

'Almost certainly,' Kilmartin said, keeping a check on his surprise. 'It does seem extraordinary that they were at Chequers. You know another two people were killed last night in a car crash?'

'An accident, yes. I heard about it, but Temple wouldn't have had anything to do with that. I know the man.'

'So do I, but we are talking about two men here, aren't we? John Temple and Eden White. What was it that Webster said? "A politician is the devil's quilted anvil; he fashions all sins on him and the blows are never heard." '

'And Eden White is the devil.'

'Let us say they help each other. There is an exchange from the coffers of corporate and political power that benefits both of them.'

'Still, Temple couldn't have known about this. He wouldn't be that stupid.'

'And he didn't know about the death of Sir Christopher Holmes, the late head of the JIC, and his wife either, but it happened just the same.'

'Are you sure about that?'

'I haven't seen the evidence but it is believed the inquest was fixed. A pathology report about injuries by the couple sustained before the fire wasn't presented.' He looked at Cannon. 'When's he going to call the election, Philip?'

Cannon was still shaking his head but he answered without hesitation. 'Wednesday – sometime during the morning.'

Kilmartin placed his drink deliberately in the centre of the table and studied him for a moment. 'Tell me something. Do you believe in what we are doing?'

'In as much as I know about it, yes. But everything is against you. The emergency powers mean that they can arrest anyone and detain them; the fact that they know the names of everyone in Eyam's group; the surveillance in London, which is now the most comprehensive in the world and includes facial recognition technology that will be primed by the ID card photographs of all the members of Eyam's group. And I haven't even begun on David Eyam – the man who faked his own death to escape paedophile charges; the millionaire who dodged paying death duties on his father's fortune and has used it to finance an operation to destabilise an elected leader at a moment of grave national crisis. Do you need me to go on? To answer your question, no, you don't stand a chance.'

'But you believe Eyam is right?'

Cannon gave a reluctant shrug.

'Then you have to delay Temple on Wednesday. We need the entire morning.'

Cannon pressed his hands together in prayer and touched the tip of his nose. 'If you really believe it's necessary, I'll try. But the best I can do is eleven thirty, maybe midday.'

'Midday,' said Kilmartin as though he was driving a bargain.

And then he felt one of two phones in his pocket vibrate with a message. He took it out and read the text from Kate Lockhart. 'David collapsed. Call me.'

He returned the phone to his pocket. She hadn't used his second name, which was good. By now every computer at GCHQ in Cheltenham would be sifting the calls and text messages and emails for the name Eyam.

'We're glad of your help, Philip,' he said. 'You do understand this is an endgame of sorts. People will get hurt. You are certainly risking your job.'

'Perhaps, but there are fish to catch and I have a book to write, and I won't miss the British press . . . or June Temple.'

Kilmartin nodded and began to rise. 'You know to be circumspect if you call?'

'Yes, there is one other thing. Bryant Maclean doesn't want this election and he'll be spitting tacks if Temple goes ahead without his blessing. That means he will take revenge because he can't be seen to be letting people get away with defiance. Just a thought.'

'A good one,' said Kilmartin.

28

Night Moves

Eyam was found slumped, but conscious, on a park bench in Kensington Gardens by a Spanish student. He was holding his phone. With his remaining energy, he asked the woman not to call an ambulance but to contact his friend whom he was trying to phone. She did both. He was taken to Accident and Emergency at St Mary's, Paddington. Half an hour later Kate joined him in a curtained cubicle, where she sat watching his tormented sleep and the ceaseless movement of his hands across his torso. He woke fifteen minutes later and turned to her.

'How did I get here?'

'You passed out in the park.'

'Damn!' he said softly.

'What the hell were you doing?'

'Miff and Freddie went to try to get access to Tony's car. We need those packages. I decided to find my own way to your place – rather foolishly perhaps – taking a walk in the park.'

A young nurse put her head round the curtain. 'How are you feeling, Mr Duval?' She looked at the notes. 'It's Daniel, isn't it?' She smiled at Kate and drew the curtain back. 'You look better than when you came in. The doctor will be with you when the results from your blood test are back.'

They waited for half an hour gazing on an average collection of London's wrecked humanity; a hostile young woman who had been punched in the face, a taxi driver stabbed in the hand, a confused old man who was demanding tea and shouting that he hadn't served in the army for eight years for this, and a large well-dressed Nigerian, whose

English wife explained that he was a manic depressive who had been drinking solidly for the last twenty-four hours.

The nurses spoke as though everyone was deaf. People came, wandered round and went – relatives, ambulance personnel, police officers, social workers, cleaners and porters.

'I think we'd better go,' said Eyam, but then a young Chinese man in jeans and a white coat arrived at Eyam's side and began to examine him. He reeled off the treatment he had received over the past year for the cancer – the radiotherapy on his right side, the combination of drugs known as ABVD – Adriamycin Bleomycin Vinblastine Dacarbazine, as Eyam insisted, and its side effects – nausea, vomiting and loss of appetite, and the chemotherapy he'd been given in Colombia.

The doctor sat down and looked him in the face. 'The level of your white blood cells is very low. You are likely suffering from an infection so I'll prescribe antibiotics for that, but you should have injections of growth factor to stimulate the production of white blood cells.' He paused to prod Eyam's stomach. 'To be honest, sir, I cannot tell whether you simply need general support or if the cancer has spread. That is my worry. I want to keep you tonight for observation and then you should have a scan and see a specialist tomorrow.'

'No, I need you to get me through the next couple of days. It's really very important.'

'What can be so important that you risk total failure of your health, maybe even death?'

'Trust me, this is vital. I want you to help me, doctor.'

The doctor consulted his notepad and thought. 'OK, it is lucky for you that I have some experience of this illness back home. I will do a deal with you, Mr Duval. There are three different types of drug that will need to be taken at strictly regular intervals during the day. But this is only a Band-Aid, Mr Duval. They won't do you any good in the long term.' He nodded vigorously to impress upon Eyam the seriousness of the situation. 'I will also include a prescription for sleeping pills so that you get more than intermittent rest over the next two or three nights. These may help with the night sweats too. In return you must agree to come back here within the next forty-eight hours. Is that understood?' He put out his hand to shake on the deal, then Eyam's eyes closed.

He beckoned Kate outside the cubicle. 'Your friend is at the stage where he needs constant treatment and monitoring. Do you understand? The cancer will spread unchecked without chemotherapy and he may lose his life unnecessarily.'

She nodded.

'I don't like doing this, but I know they're pretty stretched up in Oncology. If you think you can look after him, I can just about agree to his discharge.'

Twenty minutes later the drugs were brought up from the pharmacy and Eyam was wheeled to the hospital entrance where they picked up a cab.

At her apartment she gave him the pills, put him to bed and left him to sleep. After an hour of pacing up and down the sitting room, she buzzed Kilmartin up.

'How is he?' said Kilmartin when he came through the door.

'Not good.'

Kilmartin grimaced. 'This isn't going well, is it?'

'We'll see.'

'I dislike the good-news, bad-news formula, but I have both. We've got a slot in the Joint Committee on Human Rights – that's the committee that includes members of both houses. No one takes any notice of its reports of course, but it does have the power to accept the material and hear David in an open session.'

'And?'

'The bad news is that they seem to have got an informant on the inside of Eyam's little operation.'

'They know everything?'

'That's about the sum of it, yes.'

'God, we won't last until Wednesday when Eyam's in such poor shape.'

At that moment the door opened and Eyam shuffled in. 'I'm not dead yet,' he said.

She turned to him with a smile. 'Make up your mind: that's not what you were telling us last week.'

'The first thing we need to do is to get this man a suit and haircut,' said Kilmartin before embracing Eyam. 'Welcome home, dear boy.'

Kate was surprised by the delight flooding Kilmartin's usually cagey expression. She dispensed more pills and gave Eyam a glass of barley water, an article of faith in her mother's book of medical care, and stood by him with a matronly air while he swallowed the pills.

Eyam sat down on the edge of the sofa. 'You heard about the two killed last night?' he said flatly. 'That's three deaths I'm responsible for. I have to make this work.'

'Yes,' said Kilmartin. 'It sounds brutal, but for the moment we've got to ignore them and keep going, eh?'

'It's not so easy. Tony was a good and dear friend and a wonderfully interesting person. We used to go walking together in the Pyrenees. He was a great naturalist too, you know: very good on plants and birds. Taught me a lot.'

'Yes,' said Kilmartin. 'Look, I've found you an assembly point.'

'Where?'

'They've got an informant, David. So I'll keep this to myself for the time being, but I think I also have a means of getting your material into the House of Commons.'

'How did you find out about her?'

'You said *her*. So you knew?'

'It's Alice Scudamore: a beautiful and decent young woman put under intolerable pressure. Her sister is Mary MacCullum – the woman who helped me and was sent to jail.' Kate glanced at Kilmartin, who was looking extremely concerned. 'You see, Alice kept her married name after her divorce and because she always refused to give all her personal information to the National Identity Register, the government never made the connection. But when they did put it together they told her Mary would be sent to prison for another two years unless she worked for them.'

'Did you know they were sisters?'

'No, I never met Mary. Naturally, I saw her photograph in the papers but there was very little similarity except that they are both extraordinarily pretty. I didn't know until Tony Swift told me last week, when he thought she was just about to go over. He was a natural at this game, much more than I ever will be. Anyway, he got her to return the documents I'd asked her to keep for me at the end of last week. He replaced the contents of the package: you see, no one knows what is in their envelopes because they are sealed. Tony told her a cock and bull story about what we planned to do – a press conference at a large hotel in central London. He had the wit to book the room in the name of the Bell Ringers.' Eyam sighed. 'Last night we had someone with her all the time – Andy Sessions, one of our best men – so we didn't think she would be any danger to us. But clearly we were wrong. And now Tony's been killed.'

'But she couldn't have known he would be killed.'

'No, of course not.'

'However,' murmured Kilmartin, 'she could prove useful over the next day or two.'

'Maybe,' said Eyam. 'Have you got a drink, Sis? I mean a proper drink?'

'Do you think that's wise?' She heard her mother's voice as she said it.

'I'm feeling better.'

'Right,' she said, unconvinced. 'I thought you were dead when I saw you on that bed in A and E.'

'I needed sleep: that was all.'

She uncorked a bottle of red wine. Eyam held the glass up to his nose but did not drink.

'There is something we need to settle, David,' said Kilmartin, shaking his head to the offer of a glass and sitting down. 'If they don't catch you before, they are going to destroy you with this paedophile accusation. I am beginning to think the only reason that they haven't gone public on this and the story of your faked death is because they would prefer to get you out of the way quietly. But if you manage to start making your allegations they will hit you good and hard with it.'

'So?'

'You know what I am asking.'

'Did I download images of children being abused?'

'Yes.'

'Would it make any difference to your position if I said yes?'

'Yes, on the grounds that you would not be the best person to appear in front of the committee. I have given personal guarantees as to your good character and reliability.'

He looked into Kilmartin's eyes. 'No, of course I didn't, Peter.' There was silence.

'Is there anything else illegal we should know about?' asked Kate.

Eyam shook his head. 'I think you both have a rather exaggerated view of my activities.'

'There were stories,' said Kilmartin.

'The stories that circulated about me were intended to harm my reputation. Was there any truth to them? Well, yes there was, but I've never done anything that would shock your neighbours in Herefordshire, Peter. As anyone knows, eroticism is a declaration of an individual's sovereignty.'

'Anyway, there's no proof,' said Kate, seeing that Kilmartin was embarrassed, 'because the hard drive no longer exists.'

'They've almost certainly got records from the internet provider, or they may have accessed your hard drive remotely,' said Kilmartin. 'They will make the case stick if they want to – even now.'

Eyam ran a hand through his hair and looked at them in turn. 'Tony thought that they'd planted my DNA at the location of a crime. They had access to Dove Cottage. It would have been a simple matter to pick up a few hairs, as indeed they did when they were seeking to match my DNA in Colombia.'

Kilmartin slapped his hand down on the table. 'Let's forget this. I'm sorry for raising it. There's a lot to go over and I don't think I should be here too long.'

'The more important thing,' said Kate, 'is that someone has to replace Tony as the hub of this exercise.'

'It's got to be you,' said Eyam. 'We'll swap phones – mine has got all the group's numbers and email addresses on it.'

She took it. 'And encryption?'

'Up to a point,' he said.

Kilmartin and Eyam began to talk about the dossier. She went into the bedroom to make two calls. The first was to her mother and lasted no more than a minute. Again she was grateful for her mother's puzzled but brisk compliance. The second was to a cell phone number in the High Castle area. It lasted much longer and required all her skills of persuasion.

George Lyme was still out at the Security Council meeting when Cannon returned to his desk at nine thirty-five p.m. on that Monday evening. He sat down and scrolled through the emails in his inbox, occasionally firing off terse replies. After dealing with a dozen or so he came to one forwarded from the press officer at the Department of Health with a message written in the subject panel: 'Read this viral', then below in the email: 'Philip, no idea where this comes from but it seems better-informed than usual. If all that stuff at the bottom is true, very damaging. Best Geoff.' Below was the title *Who is Eden White?*

Cannon jumped to a section halfway down and read the account of the founding of the Ortelius Institute of Public Policy Research. It began with the allegation that Eden White set up his think tank specifically to infiltrate and influence the British political establishment and press home the sale of systems to government departments. The article described three stages to White's operation. Ortelius Intelligence Services – referred to as OIS – researched the personnel and policy issues inside government using former civil servants and spies to gain access and information. When they had identified the business opportunity, the think tank created a policy task force, which commissioned research papers and gave grants to friendly faces in Whitehall and the academic world. The policy was drafted. At the moment the policy was published, lobbying and PR companies – owned or part-owned by Eden White – swung into action, gaining support among politicians and in the media. At a time when the country and civil service were short of funds, Eden White was always there with generous grants. He held networking parties and hosted all-expenses-paid conferences abroad.

Seven separate systems had been sold to the government in this way. White's first big campaign was ASCAMS, introduced to secure the Olympics. There then followed systems sold to the Inland Revenue, the health service, the police and the Departments of Defence and Work and Pensions. The total surveillance system known as DEEP TRUTH came later and was designed to draw on the data collection underway with the other systems. Allies of White's people who spent time in one of Ortelius' research projects or who had been given generous research grants under the think tank's 'Mapmakers' scheme were spread throughout the civil service and government agencies. The list included the names of twenty people Cannon recognised – Derek Glenny, Christine Shoemaker and Dawn Gruppo were among them. John Temple had also been involved from an early stage. All those mentioned, said the email, continued to be paid by White and were effectively in his employ. The email ended with a promise of further revelations and documents to support them.

Cannon let out a low whistle and scrolled to the top to read about White's early years in Africa, his involvement with arms dealing, the arrest warrants, his subsequent flight from Kenya to Switzerland and business school then to the United States and a job working for a gaming magnate with links to organised crime. The account of his business dealings, the remorseless attacks on competitors, his treatment of business partners and the mother of his three children made Bryant Maclean look less threatening than a choirmaster. Feared and hated in American financial circles, White reformed his image in Britain through skilful publicity stunts and charitable donations, research grants and the foundation of yet another organisation called Civic Value, which sponsored various projects of community cohesion.

The intimate portrait of White had to have been written by someone who saw through the 'hypocritical sociopath' who went under the guise of social reformer and philanthropist. He was struck by the elegant bite of the article and he knew exactly where he had read that style before: in some of David Eyam's policy papers.

He dialled the press officer who'd sent him the email and was still speaking when Lyme returned from the Security Council meeting and appeared at the side of his desk. Cannon indicated it was going to be a few seconds before he could hang up. Lyme scribbled a note. 'Fancy a walk around the block?'

They left Downing Street ten minutes later. 'What is it?' asked Cannon when they had gone a little way up Whitehall.

'What the heck's going on? Correction: I mean what the *fuck* is going on, Philip? There was nothing in the meeting about where TRA came from, nothing about the science or the damned filtration systems. Nothing! It's like they're preparing for a massive terrorist attack. All police leave has been cancelled. They're constructing holding areas.

What the hell are *holding areas*, for Christ's sake? They are even threatening to use army patrols on the streets and to guard all major installations.'

'Who was chairing?'

'Glenny. Temple is out at the meeting of world finance ministers.'

'Yes, I know,' said Cannon. 'Dawn Gruppo told me he'd be using the next twenty-four hours to work intensively on the themes of his major election speeches. And where is he? Swanning around at a bleeding party. He always disappears when there's something unpleasant going to happen.' He paused. 'Who's going to be using these holding areas?'

'Police. They expect large numbers of arrests in central London, and get this: there's no plan to process these people through the courts – not immediately, anyway. All they talk about is securing major buildings and installations. That's banging people up without charge or trial.'

'We already do that,' said Cannon.

'Yeah, under terror legislation, but this is under emergency powers – a much more obscure process. It's not clear these people will have committed any crimes, or present any kind of threat at all. One or two of the securicrats even seemed a bit doubtful about it all.'

Cannon stopped and looked into Lyme's worried face. 'Who's pushing this? Where are these large numbers of people coming from?'

'It was all a little vague. MI5 has found some kind of site. Shoemaker said that people who log on are being told to go to London over the next twenty-four hours. Three thousand have gone into the site with passwords over the last day or so, but they appear to be communicating with each other using very sophisticated multi-layered codes.'

'And they are saying these people are responsible for spreading red algae – involved in some kind of plot concerning the water supply?' Cannon said incredulously. 'Have they gone off the deep end?'

'No one made a definite link between TRA and the site, but that was the implication. There was one context to the discussion. I repeat, what is going on, Philip? Has all this got something to do with Eyam . . . or what?'

Cannon didn't answer.

They turned left as they reached Trafalgar Square, passed under Admiralty Arch and walked in silence. Then Lyme mentioned the name of one of Bryant Maclean's editors. 'I had a pretty hostile call from her. They don't dish out that kind of shit unless Bryant is behind them. She asked whether the emergency powers were an election stunt. She also said the paper was investigating the outbreak of TRA and that her science editor would be putting some tough questions to the environment spokesman tomorrow.'

'Good luck to them,' said Cannon. 'To tell the truth I've had enough of today. I'm going home and I'm going to switch off my bloody phone.'

'What should I do?' asked Lyme a little plaintively.

'Nothing,' said Cannon. 'On second thoughts, take Gruppo out for her usual gallon of cider. She's got a soft spot for you. Everyone knows that. See if you can find anything out.'

'About what?'

'Don't be dim, George. About all this, for Christ's sake!'

He walked off in the direction of St James's, but before switching off his phone he dialled Peter Kilmartin's number.

Kilmartin listened to the two sentences spoken by Cannon and hung up. He was at his usual table in Ristorante Valeriano, a reliably good Tuscan restaurant he'd used for the best part of a quarter of a century. What was unusual about the evening was that he was sitting opposite Carrie Middleton, who had arrived in a flawless outfit of dark-blue with a tight skirt and high heels that made the old patron's eyes swerve to heaven.

'I'm sorry about that call,' he said, laying the phone aside, 'and also for asking you out for our date so late.'

'Stop apologising,' she said. 'It's lovely to be here. I was all on my own so I couldn't be happier.'

'I wanted to ask you a favour, Carrie.'

'I thought you might,' she said amenably. 'Is there something special you want me to store for you at the library?'

'No, I need to lie low for a few hours or so.'

'But of course,' she said. Her eyes sparkled. 'You can stay with me. My flat's small but you're welcome to the spare bedroom.'

'Normally I would use a little hotel in Kensington, but on this occasion I need to remain completely below the parapet.'

'This has something to do with the men who came to the library and that young woman.'

He cleared his throat. 'You wouldn't be doing anything illegal. I'm not on the run or anything like that, but I do need to be sure that my movements cannot be traced tomorrow.' He stopped as the waiter placed a dish of antipasti between them. 'Some more Prosecco?'

She smiled. 'That's settled then.'

'There was something else I wanted to mention. You see, the authorities probably suspect I received some information from that young woman – Mary MacCullum – and that it was passed to me at the library. That information has now been made public. I believe she will be arrested and may be forced to say what she did.'

'Poor woman.'

'We may have a chance of getting her released if things go well over the next forty-eight hours. It is a delicate situation. To be honest, things could go either way.' He coughed. 'But what I wanted to say was that with present exigencies, I may have been guilty of fostering the impression that the library was the proper place for their attentions tomorrow.' He looked at her.

'The library! What will it mean?' He had touched a nerve.

'Not much – all those buffers returning volumes of Disraeli's letters and Fulke Greville's poems over the next days will be subject to rather more scrutiny than usual.'

'The members, Peter! I mean . . .'

'Well, it's about time some of them were brought face to face with their government as it is, not how they think it is.'

She put her hand on Kilmartin's. He felt a surge of desire that was mixed with awe for Carrie Middleton's decency and good sense.

'Let's talk about something else,' she said gently. 'I want to remember this evening. Tell me about your new book.' If there was one way to distract Peter Kilmartin, it was to ask about the civilisation of Ashurbanipal II and his predecessors, and Carrie Middleton showed every sign of fascination.

Later they took a cab in the rain to Cavendish Court, a large 1930s block of flats on the edge of Pimlico, and passed through Parliament Square, where the road was reduced to one lane. Army vehicles were lined up along the Treasury building, and riot vans were disgorging uniformed police with shields and batons who were being filmed by TV news crews.

'People won't like this,' she said.

'That's the pity of it, Carrie: they'll think the government is protecting them. They'll be reassured.'

Eyam and Kate watched the television news in silence – footage of helicopters circling reservoirs in the North of England; people queuing to fill water canisters at army tankers in Blackburn and behind trucks in Humberside where six-packs of drinking water were being dropped to the pavement; aerial shots of the red algae; reporters interviewing scientists in anti-contamination gear; armed patrols of reservoirs near Heathrow; and riot police in Westminster. Then came Glenny and Temple at the news conference, Temple making a statement to the House of Commons and a televised address to the nation filmed at Number Ten that afternoon.

'He's enjoying himself,' remarked Eyam. 'It's interesting that nobody is asking where this thing came from. They have the best scientific advice available. I know most of the people involved. They should have got to the bottom of it by now.'

'It's bloody convenient that he's taken these powers just as you're about to go public. I wonder if they've cooked up all this stuff about toxic algae.'

He considered this and pressed the TV remote. 'No, Temple's an opportunist and a gambler – he's just using it.' ·

She leaned forward from her chair so that her face was just a few feet away from Eyam's. 'But the point is, *idiot*, it's going to be doubly difficult for you to get into the House of Commons if they've got police and armed soldiers guarding the buildings.'

'I'll make my arrangements tomorrow. Freddie will have some ideas. I have one or two.'

'You put an awful lot of faith in that man: where did you find him?'

'He found us. Fredde is a gangster of decidedly liberal hue. A member of his family had been misidentified by the system, or was at any rate being persecuted in the usual way, and he started to look into it and eventually got in touch with Tony Swift. A lot of people out there are very angry now that they understand what's been going on.'

'They know?'

'Oh, they know all right. They've just been keeping quiet.'

'So your project has become an open secret.'

'A closely guarded secret among hundreds of people.' He smiled and her heart turned over.

'You do look better,' she said.

'I feel it. I can't imagine what's in those pills.'

'Raw opium, I suspect.' She slid from her chair and leaned against the sofa where Eyam was lying. 'I want to talk about what you're going to do tomorrow.'

'Disappear,' he said. 'We shouldn't be together. If they arrest me you can go ahead with Kilmartin in Parliament.'

'You want to be found slumped on a park bench again?'

'If they don't find me I'll be there on the day,' he said. They both turned their heads to the window that was being pounded by rain. An explosion of lightning right overhead made her jump.

'Jesus! I think that must have hit the church spire.' She went to the window, looked out, then turned to face him. 'I've got this feeling I'm missing something, David. What's the deep truth about you?'

'Ah, you called me David.'

'Don't get cocky – in my mind you're still *Eyam* – the object of my eternal scorn.'

He grimaced. 'Generous.'

'I'm serious. There's something you haven't told me. You're so good at avoiding the subject.'

'What do you mean?'

'Something essential.' Her hands rested on the windowsill. She launched herself forward and walked a few paces to stand over him. 'You were at the centre of things before you took over the JIC; you must have known about this system. It would be impossible for all that money to be hidden without you knowing about it.'

'Oh, they're very ingenious at manipulating accounts.'

'When someone is concealing something from me I've noticed that they pick me up on the detail of a question. Forget the particular, what about the general? Did you know, or not?'

'I knew about DEEP TRUTH from the outset, yes.'

'So why didn't you stop it, or go public earlier? Why did you allow Mary MacCullum go to jail?'

'I didn't allow her to go to jail. I did nothing to encourage her.'

'Were you part of the planning?'

'I was embroiled, yes, tangentially.'

'You can't be tangentially embroiled.'

'Look, I was part of the decision-making process. At the very beginning I wrote something on the bottom of a memo and then forgot about it. Of course it wasn't called SPINDRIFT or DEEP TRUTH then. It was simply presented as a rationalisation of all data collection systems. You've no idea how fast you have to react in that position, or the number of papers you read. Day after day of crisis, policy made on the hoof, a hundred different briefs to master. There's no time to think. One day blurs into the next. You remember nothing.'

'But the idea of spying on everyone in the country – that's not a crisis decision. It's a long-term project to give the state power over the people. From ASCAMS to DEEP TRUTH is one fluid movement. You're not dumb. You understood where the process would end.' She folded her arms, but catching sight of a disciplinarian image in the mirror, let them drop and hooked her thumbs in the pockets of her trousers. 'You know what pisses me off? When you came to New York and lectured me about the pointlessness of corporate litigation you were actually involved in the planning of DEEP TRUTH.'

'By then I was trying to think what to do. There was just one memo, which I had forgotten about. I didn't even make the connection at first.'

'And you, the great liberator, the slayer of the database state! So when did you fall victim to your conscience?'

'I didn't,' he said, raising his head. He leaned forward, blew into his cupped hands then rubbed them. 'The story is very simple and it involves Tony Swift – Ed Fellowes, as you knew him originally. He asked for a meeting when I inherited the job from Sir Christopher Holmes, and he told me categorically that the head of the JIC had been killed because of his opposition to DEEP TRUTH and his plans to go public on it. He showed me the evidence that the inquest had been fixed and I didn't believe it. But he didn't give up. He came back with more proof and won me round. He didn't tell me much about his circumstances, but it was obvious he'd left London and government and found himself another job.

'What I didn't know was that he had gone underground and invented identities for himself before, as he put it, the door slammed shut with the merger of all databases under the Transformational Government project. It was an act of defiance, as much as anything else, because he didn't believe the state had the right to define or *manage* his identity. Tony was single and had neither close relations nor ambition to hinder him. That new identity was how he ended up in High Castle as the underpaid drudge of the coroner's court. He worked himself into the town and listened and watched, and began to see how he could fight SPINDRIFT. He became a member of Civic Watch and the local community tension-monitoring groups which are really the ears of government, made friends and mapped the networks of local informers. He was the perfect undercover agent because he was working for himself, reported to no one, and possessed an unwavering allegiance to his cause. He was also the finest actor I've ever met. He inhabited every molecule of the lonely and disappointed figure of Tony Swift, so much so that I still think of Ed Fellowes and Tony Swift as different people.'

'But why did he need you?'

'These things don't start out as a plan, but as it worked out he built an organisation of good people.'

'You mean Diana Kidd and her Bell Ringers?'

'Can you just shut the hell up for a moment, Sis?' he said fiercely. 'And why don't you relax and sit down?' She perched on the arm of the chair opposite him and rested one foot on a low coffee table. Eyam continued. 'Tony's organisation was rather bigger than you imagine. There were hundreds, maybe thousands, of Bell Ringers. To these people he was known as Eclipse. He chose that as his code name because he believed that the darkness would lift eventually. He was philosophically an optimist. Very few people knew who Eclipse was.'

'Where did you fit in?'

'I was the evidence – I knew how to get it and organise it. I knew how everything fitted together: the money, the policy, the people behind it and the implementation.'

'So why did you go and shoot your mouth off at the Intelligence and Security Committee?'

'We didn't start out with a plan. Mary MacCullum's information was leaked not to me, but to Sidney Hale at the ISC. He came to me privately. That was the moment that I decided to put it into the very confined public domain of Westminster village and try to start a debate. Tony was behind the leak. Mary was in touch with him from an early stage, but she never told him about her sister. Mary was an early Bell Ringer and contributed to one of his sites. Eventually she made contact with him. Through her trial and imprisonment she protected him. Never said a word.'

'So after all that you arrive in High Castle with your hoard of documents and start planning with Tony Swift. It seems all a bit amateurish.'

'I had acquired most of what we needed by the second appearance at the ISC. It was merely an exercise to establish the existence of DEEP TRUTH. The reaction that followed took us by surprise. So we had to play things cool and wait. If I had gone public then I would have faced prosecution under the Official Secrets Act and received a term in jail. Nothing would have come out. The issue would have been buried. We decided then to wait until an election.'

'You still could be sent to jail.'

'The threat seems rather theoretical now,' he said, glancing at her.

'Why did they start watching you in the country after Temple had agreed to leave you alone?'

'Something I did, maybe. We had no idea what it was, a phone call, a tip-off, a piece of local intelligence. Who knows? By that time we had put everything in place and I had been diagnosed with Hodgkin's, and things didn't look too good. Then I discovered what they had put on my computer. You know the rest.'

'So Swift had the idea of faking your death?'

'Yes, though my father came up with the same solution. I talked to him a lot in the weeks before he died. He was very adept with money and made most of the arrangements for me.'

'Yeah, I wondered why he hadn't left you anything.'

'That's because he'd already made it over to me.'

'Was there a lot of money?'

'Yes, that's how I paid for everything. There still is and it will all come to you eventually, Sis – my only living relation.' He grinned.

'I'm beginning to think that I liked you better when you were dead,' she said, also smiling. 'Oh, God, this is such an appalling mess, Eyam.'

'Actually, it isn't. We have this one opportunity. Everything is right. One way or another, all that information will be pitched into the general election and Temple and Eden White will be exposed. Let the people decide.'

'That's what worries me.' Her gaze travelled around the soulless sitting room with its empty glass cabinet and dreadful oil studies of ballet dancers, no doubt bought in bulk to decorate what was described as an 'executive haven'. 'God, I wish you had let me love you, Eyam,' she said as her eyes came to rest on him.

He flinched, then his fingers, which were formed in a lattice bowl under his chin, opened in submission. 'We may disagree on the details of that statement, particularly the word *let*, but what does it matter now? Here we sit, "one another's best". That's true, isn't it?'

' "Our hands firmly cemented with a fast balm." '

'Well remembered, Sis.'

'I should do – you were obsessed with John Donne. You said you were sure that he walked in New College cloisters, although I seem to remember he was at another college.'

'Hertford when it was called Hart Hall.'

'And you used to recite his poems from that bench on the green instead of reading economics papers.'

'God, what a poseur!'

'No, you were brilliant and beautiful and a little bit conceited.'

'Come here, Sis,' he said.

She stood. 'I will if you never call me Sister again.'

'Done.'

'Never?'

'Never.' He patted the cushion beside him.

She moved over to him and he sank back on the sofa with his emaciated grin spreading with expectation and a kind of curiosity. She sat down on the edge and turned to look at him, nervous or inexplicably shy – she didn't know which – and he laid a hand on her shoulder, then his splayed fingers ran up through her hair. She sighed and let her head fall forward, luxuriating to his touch. 'Can you do this?'

'Take you to bed? Yes, of course I can.'

'I didn't mean that. I meant are you able to get through the next couple of days on those drugs? Have you got the strength?'

'Yes, I feel pretty good at the moment. My old self.'

'Your old self?' she said, her eyes closing. 'No, your old self is gone: you're different. Perhaps we did bury part of you at that funeral. You're a lot less pompous and not quite so pleased with yourself.' For a minute or two he stroked her head. His fingers strayed to her ears and neck and travelled across her face, lightly tracing the line of her eyebrows and nose. When she could bear it no longer, she twisted round and seized hold of his face with both hands and kissed him, at first lightly then with an animal need that she had hardly known was there. His hands moved up to her shoulders. She straddled him and he pulled her weight down on him and murmured her name, relishing its novelty. She tried to remember what it had been like during those few days and nights in his college rooms, but all the memories which she'd kept in such good repair seemed to have been suddenly erased, like a dream on waking, and now she wondered whether it had been fantasy. She stopped kissing him, pulled back and gazed down at him. 'We have done this before, haven't we? I mean, I didn't imagine it all?'

He moved his hands to her ribcage and gripped her just beneath her breasts. 'Yes, and I remember it very well, and you talked all the time.'

'No, that was some other lover of yours.'

'No, it was you: you didn't stop talking – day and night on and on and on.'

'God, I'm sorry. I was probably so thrilled that I was in bed with you that I couldn't shut up.'

Eyam grunted sceptically then put his hand up to her cheek. 'You are loved,' he said.

She frowned. 'What does that mean?'

'It's not small print, Kate. It means that you are loved. Loved by me and needed by me and admired by me and that you cause such awe in me, and now such pride, that I feel utterly at a loss to know how to tell you. I am stricken with love. It was right there on the tip of my tongue when I found you in my old suede jacket poking around that shed. That is all I wanted to say when I saw you again, but then you slapped me – quite right too, but I felt less like saying it after that.' He stopped and considered her, his hand brushing the hair from her face so that he could look into her eyes. 'You've changed too: you're much more – how do I put it? – self-possessed. You are utterly yourself. I've never met anyone who's so completely uninfluenced by the world, untroubled by what people think.'

'That's nonsense,' she whispered. 'I'm just an average, pathetically oversensitive, self-absorbed human being. I care what people think about me.'

He snorted a laugh and reached up and kissed her. 'Delusion,' he said. Then she just collapsed on him and sank her face into his hair and kissed his neck. He undid the buttons of her shirt, then the buckle of her belt and slipped his hand, rather expertly she noted, inside her waistband. He withdrew to unclip the fastener of her bra.

'What the hell were we thinking about in New York?' she said to his ear. 'Why didn't we go to bed then?'

She felt his shoulders lift in a shrug. 'We weren't paying attention.'

'No, *you* weren't paying attention,' she said, biting his neck. 'Your head was full of the UN and swishing about with Temple in an armoured limousine.'

'That's unfair,' he said and pushed her up a little. Her bra was undone and hung loose. He reached up to kiss her breast, his hand cupping and bringing it to his mouth. She heard herself let out a ridiculous moan but held his head there none the less, desperate that he should not stop.

At length his head fell back. 'I need to lie down,' he said.

They stumbled to the bedroom, where she tore the ghastly dragon-motif cover from the bed and slipped out of her clothes. Eyam stood watching her, fascinated. Naked, she shuffled on her knees across the bed to help him with his shirt and T-shirt, then his trousers. 'Kilmartin's right. You've got to get something to wear.'

'Tomorrow,' he said. He was naked and again she thought how good he looked. He shivered and she could feel the goose pimples rising across his back.

'Come,' she said, pulling him towards her.

'I hope to.'

'Such a very bad joke.'

They slipped between the sheets and she held his head across her chest. 'You've got to get treatment,' she said to the crown of his head. 'I can't lose you a second time. I could not go through that again.'

'But I heard you were rather composed at my funeral.'

'More so than Darsh,' she said and giggled. 'I wish he'd slugged Glenny.'

He laughed into her flesh and then began to move across her belly with his lips, slowly, deliberately, inch by inch, first circling her navel and then moving up to her breasts, tasting her and murmuring that he had screwed up his life and should have been doing this every night for the last decade; and what did he know about anything if he let such a beautiful woman – his complete friend – languish in New York while he was wasting time with a lot of fucking power-crazed mediocrities. All he wanted was to return to the Dove and wake with her in the morning and, come winter or summer, look across the valley and make love to her and *live*.

The words came with his kisses, each one planted on her skin, impregnating it with the message of hopeless devotion and love. She absorbed them and responded with her own thrilled endearments, though with nothing like the fluency of Eyam's requisition of her body. He whispered that he had never expected to make love again, let alone to her. Although he did not say it, she knew that he was thinking that this might be the last time.

She drew his head up so that she could look at him. He moved his hand been her legs and let it graze and explore with the tiniest of movements until she closed her eyes and descended into herself to observe the regular pulses of pleasure build until she climaxed quite suddenly and opened her eyes to Eyam's steady gaze. She kissed him before pressing one hand on his shoulder to push him on his back. Then she straddled him and made love to him with a slow, rhythmic purpose.

They slept.

At five a.m. she woke to an insistent buzzing. Her mind groped for explanation. The alarm? No. The timer on the cooker? No.

'It's the bloody door,' she whispered. 'Someone's at the door.'

She felt Eyam tense beside her. 'See if they go away,' he said.

But the noise continued.

'Maybe it's Kilmartin or Freddie,' she said. 'They may need to be let in.'

She put the light on and scrambled to find her clothes.

Eyam was now sitting up, alert. She went to the intercom and pressed the button.

A voice sounded. 'It's Oliver Mermagen, Kate. Can you let me in? I want to speak to you.'

'Oliver, for God's sake. What time is it? I'm trying to sleep.'

'It's very important that I talk to you.'

Eyam was behind her, fully dressed and doing up his shoes.

'Hold on,' she said and took her finger off the button.

'You'd better find out what he wants. I can make myself scarce, then come back.'

'There's a fire exit on the top landing.'

'Can't this wait?' she said into the intercom. Mermagen replied that it was a matter of great urgency. She watched Eyam grab his jacket and seize the drugs from the table.

'OK, I'll get dressed,' she said to Mermagen. 'Wait there.'

'No, buzz me up, Kate. There's no time to lose.'

She released her finger and turned to Eyam. 'He may have someone with him. Be careful.'

'If they knew I was here, they'd be storming the place. Phone me when he's gone.' He slipped from the door and made for the stairs.

'Are you alone?' she asked Mermagen.

'Of course,' he said. 'For God's sake open the door.'

'OK,' she said, pressing the second button. 'I'll put something on.' She glanced round the room and noticed the two empty glasses, the bottle of wine and the double indentation in the cushions of the sofa.

Having cleared and straightened everything, she arrived back at the door as Mermagen's frantic knocking began.

'What do you want at this hour, Oliver?' she demanded as she opened the door. He was wearing a raincoat and a tweed cap that made him look as if he had just come from some country pursuit.

He took the cap off and shook it. 'It's good to see you, Kate, even in these trying circumstances.'

'How did you know where to find me?'

'Very simple: you were obviously not in a hotel. I had my assistant check the community charge records for the Royal Borough of Kensington and Chelsea, where all short-term lets have to be registered. You probably didn't know that. She simply found the address for the apartment let out to Calverts. I am the only person who knows where you are, Kate. Is Eyam with you?' he asked, looking over her shoulder.

'Don't be stupid.'

'Ah, but no doubt you know how to get hold of him.'

'What do you want?'

'Initially, some coffee, then I want to put a proposition to you.'

'Tell me while I make it,' she said. Mermagen followed her to the kitchen, sat down and placed his cap on the table. 'I tried calling you. But your phone wasn't switched on. I left half a dozen messages for you.'

'Oh really,' she said.

'As I explained, I've been authorised to act as an intermediary by Eden White and to put a deal to you. The long and short of it is that he will guarantee you and Eyam safe passage out of the country in exchange for all the information that Eyam possesses on government systems and of course all the supporting evidence. He further guarantees that once abroad you will not be threatened or in any way disturbed. He still nurtures a deep affection and respect for David Eyam and he does not want this affair to end unhappily.'

'By that you mean . . .'

'There are any number of outcomes that you can imagine for yourself.'

'A sniper's bullet, a truckload of sand.'

Mermagen shook his head with annoyance. 'You have very little time,

Kate. I will soon be compelled to say where I have seen you. You will be arrested and they will pick Eyam up. He will be charged and put in jail.' The kettle boiled and she poured the water into the cafetière. 'They know about Eyam's money,' he continued. 'They have traced nearly all of it and they can freeze the bank accounts under international money-laundering agreements and using terror laws overnight. Mr White guarantees that this information will not be passed to the government and that David will be free to benefit from this considerable fortune, unmolested by the Inland Revenue. However, he insists that Eyam does not return to this country and maintains the fiction of his death. As far as Mr White is concerned, David Eyam will remain dead. He also expects you to leave this country within the next twenty-four hours. Whether you return to the United States or choose another place to settle is of no concern to him, as long as you abide by the agreement not to reveal that Eyam is alive, or anything of the material that he is believed to have collected.'

She poured the coffee into two mugs and pushed one towards Mermagen's little hand. 'Tell me something, Oliver. Why haven't they released the fact that Eyam is still alive? The former head of JIC fakes his own death in a Colombian bomb explosion to escape charges. I mean, it's a gift.'

'Because Eden wants to resolve this with as little fuss as possible: he realises that it could be damaging to all the things he holds dear.'

'No, he read the email that is doing the rounds and realised that Eyam would destroy him. That's why he is offering us a deal: as soon as we are out of the country he sends a team of assassins after us.'

'He's not a gangster. He has a very high regard for both of you. Up until he read that email yesterday he fully intended to offer you a job.'

'You say he isn't a gangster, but he worked for some pretty shady people in Las Vegas, Oliver.' She sipped from the mug. 'How come you're acting as his bagman?'

'I too have a high regard for both of you.'

'And all your contracts depend on Temple remaining in power with White's backing.'

'I have to make a living, Kate,' he said.

'Anyway, I have no idea where Eyam is.'

'But you can contact him.'

'And I have no intention of leading you to him. I've acted as the pathfinder for one murder: I am not going to do that again.' The realisation that she might already be doing so gave her an idea.

Mermagen was fiddling with his cap. 'Call him. Otherwise this is all going to get very messy.'

'OK,' she said in a less chilly tone. 'I'll talk to him. No harm in that.'

'That's good news – very good news indeed. You have my number?'

She nodded.

'When should I expect to hear from you?'

'I will be able to speak to him at eleven this morning. Shortly after that.'

Mermagen drained his coffee and got up. 'I will tell Mr White. You do realise that an awful lot depends on you making Eyam see sense. It's vitally important for you as well as him.' He looked at her, his scheming eyes affecting warmth and a regard for her well being. 'So what are you going to do now?'

'Go back to bed.'

'Yes, I quite understand. I'm sorry for coming so early, but I did want to see you as soon as possible. If you'd had your phone on, I could have called you instead.'

She led him to the door. As soon as he was gone, she snatched up a small shoulder bag, unplugged her three telephones and computer and put them in a side pocket. She then chose a dark trouser suit, which she also placed in the bag together with underwear, a shirt and black shoes. She rummaged in the desk and found a padded envelope left by a previous tenant, addressed it and shoved it into the pocket of the jacket she had taken from the bedroom. Then she went round the apartment turning off the lights. A minute or two later she followed Eyam to the fire exit. She hoped to find him there but he had gone so she too slipped into the dank London morning, knowing that she could reach him later.

After walking the half-mile to the Earls Court Road she stopped, turned on her American phone and placed it in the envelope. Then she hailed a cab and, proffering two twenty-pound notes, asked the cab driver to deliver the package to Calverts' offices in the City.

29

Hotel Papa

As was his custom, Cannon left the Underground at Embankment and walked along the Thames towards Whitehall with a cup of coffee, his laptop bag over his shoulder. By the time he passed through the Downing Street gates, now absurdly defended against the menace of toxic red algae by soldiers, he had been stopped four times and searched once. He got to the Communications Centre half an hour late to find Dawn Gruppo reading something on his desk. 'Can I help you?' he demanded from the far side of the room.

Gruppo turned without apology or the slightest trace of guilt. 'Did you get the message about the seven thirty meeting?' she asked. 'Your phone isn't on. I have been trying to call you.'

'No – what meeting?'

'The situational summary: they've been in for over half an hour.'

'Come again?'

'It's an update: election, TRA contingency planning, disruptive elements plus *lines to take*.'

'Surely it's my job to decide the LTT?'

'Yes, but we need the prime minister's views – even you will concede that.'

'Lyme can do it.'

'He wants you there for the last part of the meeting with Christine and Mr Ferris.' She left and collided with Lyme at the door. Cannon didn't miss the look she gave Lyme, nor the idiotic expression on Lyme's face, but he pretended to be engrossed with the newspaper front pages and the overnight summary of political websites.

'So,' he said without looking up. 'What did you learn?'

'The things I do for you, Philip – it was like going to bed with a colony of fruit-eating bats.'

'You didn't have to sleep with her. Just take her for a drink was all I said.'

'I had no option,' said Lyme rather helplessly. 'And I must say she is by a long stretch the most filthy-minded woman I have ever met. I mean *interestingly* so.'

'Spare me the details,' said Cannon.

'But she did tell me something. JT is going to call the election tonight or early tomorrow morning. He's in a lather about the Eyam business.'

'She said that?'

'Why's that such a big deal?'

Cannon didn't answer but left for the prime minister's sitting room with the newspapers and summaries under his arm.

If asked about the meetings he had attended in Downing Street and Chequers over the past five or six days, Cannon would have confessed that they all merged into one in his mind. On every occasion he seemed to walk into the room when Jamie Ferris was speaking, and this time was no exception. But the atmosphere had become tense. Temple had dropped all pretence of civility and snapped at Cannon to sit down.

'We have a line into the woman,' said Ferris after looking up at Cannon, 'and an offer was put to her through Oliver Mermagen. We have also got a trace on her phone. It appears that soon after seeing Mermagen she went to the London offices of her law firm in the City. She has agreed to make a call to Eyam at eleven. We can't guarantee that she will use her mobile, but if she does we will very soon afterwards have a location for Eyam. We will also be tapping into the law firm's telecommunications and applying voice recognition so that her call, even if made on a landline, will very likely be traced.'

'And if this does not work as you envisage,' asked Temple, 'what do you plan?'

'Clearly she can be arrested and that will be put into effect soon after eleven. The building is now being watched.'

'But it still leaves Eyam free.'

'Yes, but we believe him to be very ill. Some drugs packaging was found at the apartment where Kate Lockhart was staying, and we have since contacted St Mary's Paddington where the drugs were dispensed. Apparently he collapsed in the street and was taken there by ambulance and was treated under the name of Daniel H. Duval, the alias he used to flee France. CCTV footage from the A&E reception shows him looking very frail. He was joined by Kate Lockhart and they saw the doctor together. And this is the important thing: Eyam's got cancer. We've interviewed the doctor who says he was in a bad way. He wanted to admit him immediately but Eyam said he needed drugs to get through the next few days. Eyam left St Mary's later that afternoon with Lockhart and they hailed a cab.'

'And you still have a source on the inside, is that right?'

'We've heard from her twice – we've got the documents she was carrying and their plans – so we are in good shape. We know that the Bell Ringers intend to hold a press conference of some sort in the near future. We've established that this will probably take place tomorrow at the Hertford Hotel in central London. The hotel conference centre has been booked for a twenty-four-hour period from nine o'clock to-morrow morning. A five-thousand-pound deposit was paid from one of the bank accounts that we have been monitoring. It goes without saying that that press conference will not go ahead.'

'Good. Have you heard anything about this, Philip?' asked Temple.

'No, prime minister. Clearly I can't ask journalists whether Eyam or anyone that might be representing him has been in touch.'

'Quite so,' said Temple. 'What about these other people – the Bell Ringers?'

Christine Shoemaker looked at some papers. 'I believe about forty have been detained under the emergency regulations.' She went on to say that nothing had been found on any of the people and none was a member of the core group from the High Castle area. They were being processed but so far none of them had confessed their plans.

Cannon looked down at the newspapers in his lap and concentrated very hard: now was not the time to complain about the government using emergency regulations to arrest people who were not suspected of doing anything more than exercising their legitimate right to protest.

'How long will they be in the holding area?' asked Temple.

'Initially for a period of thirty-six hours, which may be extended.'

Cannon coughed. 'When I get questions about what these people are suspected of doing,' he asked, 'what line do I take?'

Temple looked annoyed. 'You tell the media these are temporary measures; that the government is empowered by Parliament to act to protect the public in an emergency; and that any inconvenience to those held is regretted. We are simply guarding against all eventualities.'

'But journalists may point out that the nearest outbreak of TRA is a hundred and fifty miles from London.'

'As I said, all eventualities.'

'What about the conditions of these holding areas? Where are they?'

'We are not announcing their locations,' said Shoemaker. 'Obviously this is a first step and these people will be processed as quickly as possible. Facilities have been laid on – food, toilets, counselling et cetera.'

'Counselling for what?' murmured Cannon.

Temple looked down and pinched his septum. 'If we don't apprehend Eyam, when do we tell the public he is alive and being hunted for paedophile offences and faking his own death? And how do we then play his illness?'

Ferris glanced at Christine Shoemaker. 'We will be guided by you, prime minister,' she said. 'As you know, we all felt that it was best to handle this as discreetly as possible, but clearly if he isn't located and arrested after the call from Lockhart, we may need the public's help to find him.'

Temple thought again. The room was silent. 'Very well, let it be at one o'clock today. Ask the police to issue photographs and draw up a statement outlining the main offences Eyam is suspected of.'

'This is going to cause a hell of a fuss,' said Cannon.

'If he is charged immediately, the press won't be able to say anything under the *sub judice* rules.'

'But the gap between issuing the release and Eyam being caught may lead to some very wild speculation.' He held up two of the newspapers. 'The coverage this morning is far from favourable – Bryant Maclean's papers are openly challenging the decision to invoke the Civil Contingencies Act.'

'Once the election is called, Maclean will come on side, which is why we need to do that as soon as possible.'

'If I may, prime minister,' said Cannon with his usual note of respectful disagreement. 'We don't want the accusation levelled at us that this is a shotgun wedding, particularly as you are going to the country on a record of calm, ordered government. I merely suggest that you separate the announcement about Eyam and calling the election.'

'I'll think about it,' said Temple automatically.

Cannon was used to these apparent concessions. Temple had no intention of changing his mind. He liked high drama, and despite his reputation for stability, actually fed on the adrenalin of these situations. It was Eyam who'd once pointed out that Temple was like one of those respectable, unassuming middle-aged men who go into a casino and bet their house and business on a game of blackjack. 'We will be watching the media very closely today,' he said to Temple. 'But if the location of these holding areas is discovered, it will be tricky for us. Maclean has run part of the email that was circulating yesterday about Eden White, and there is one article that speculates about the source behind it. And the pictures of the two individuals emerging from those offices in High Castle got some play too. If it is discovered that this solicitor acted for David Eyam, it will give greater impetus to the story. Journalists may begin to join up the dots.'

'Not if Eyam is charged,' said Ferris, who had been looking uncomfortable.

'I'll have a word with Maclean,' said Temple, 'and explain what we are doing and why we're doing it. He won't want his papers backing a paedophile.'

Nobody in the room except Cannon noticed the way the threat posed by Eyam to the government and that of red algae to the nation had been merged. State and government were for them one. Nor did they question that Number Ten's responses to both were in effect the same. They had all gone too far down the road with John Temple for that kind of discrimination.

Everyone except Temple rose. 'Philip, could you stay for a moment?' he said from his papers. The door closed. 'We have been trying to get hold of Peter Kilmartin. You don't have any idea where he is, do you?'

Cannon shook his head.

'If he's in touch, tell him I want to see him. There are suggestions that he was involved in the publication of those emails about Eyam's appearance at the Joint Intelligence Committee.'

'I seriously doubt it,' said Cannon.

'Still, I want to see him. There's too much being published irresponsibly, randomly. It's very destructive. We will have to look at this after the election. I'd like your thoughts on it all.'

'That's the disadvantage of a free press, prime minister.'

'I sense the public is tired of it all. They don't know who or what to believe. They want a single reliable account of these important issues. We're going to have to put a lot of thought into this after the election.'

During the night a further elaboration of the plan to smuggle Eyam's material into the Houses of Parliament had come to Kilmartin and on waking he put it to Carrie Middleton, who had appeared beside his bed with a cup of tea. The bedroom belonged to her son, who was away at university in Leeds, and all round the room were posters of rock stars and actresses. Kilmartin blinked at them, then put his glasses on.

'Come into my room,' she said. 'You can sit down and talk to me while I put my face on.' Kilmartin could not see that Carrie needed to add anything to what was already a miraculous complexion. She left while he took a quick shower and shaved, after which he put on his trousers and a shirt and followed the murmur of her voice barefoot.

He repeated his idea, while looking round the room – the best in the flat and decorated with Carrie's eye for practicality and unfussy comfort. On one wall there was a collection of Victorian amateur watercolours, which she said, while thinking about his proposition, she inherited from her father who bought them at bric-a-brac stores and in markets during the fifties and sixties.

Returning to her right eye with a fine mascara brush, she smiled at her reflection in the mirror: 'Yes, Peter, it may be possible if it looks the real thing. If you can guarantee that, I will do it for you, but you do realise I will be taking a risk?'

'Yes, I do, Carrie, and I am sorry for asking, but it does seem quite a good idea.'

'And you will make sure that young woman Mary MacCullum is all right?'

'I will do my utmost. If we succeed, she should never have any trouble again. Now I really must make some telephone calls.'

She turned to him and composed her hands in the lap of her dressing gown. 'People won't thank you for ringing them at this hour. Besides, Peter, my help comes with a condition.' She gave a coquettish little smile. For a moment he stared at her uncomprehendingly. 'A condition that will not be unpleasant,' she added, then stood in the grey morning light, to his eyes glorious and effulgent and all that he had ever dreamed of while trying to concentrate on the kings of Assyria in the St James's Library. She let her hand drop and the dressing gown fell open a little to reveal the librarian's full white bust. 'I was going to ask last night but then you looked so tired I thought it better that you had some rest.' Without moving from the stool by her dressing table he drew her to him and said yes, indeed, the world could wait and so could his call to Kate Lockhart.

Kate entered the Italian sandwich and breakfast bar at eight thirty and ordered coffee while she read the papers. The radio was on in the background: through three new bulletins she heard reports of the emergency powers affecting London's streets: commuters arriving in London by train were greeted by the sight of army patrols; there was an abnormally large police presence on streets. People were being stop-searched and asked to account for their movements. There were rumours of arrests but a spokesman for the Metropolitan Police would not confirm or deny them: he refused to be drawn on the subjects of holding areas or why the government felt it was necessary to detain people in London well away from the contaminated reservoirs or what intelligence the government was acting on. He did say, however, that the presence of the army on the street would be short-lived, and that the police would scale down their operation over the course of the week.

From the table at the back of the cafe from where she could watch the door, she called Eyam. Four previous attempts had failed and she was beginning to worry. But now Aristotle Miff answered and told her that Eyam was resting up at a place Freddie had found for him. Miff told her that he didn't look too great – he was shaking when they picked him up in the street after his call early that morning, but he seemed better after taking the drugs and had eaten.

'You're the main man now,' said Miff. 'You gotta make it happen, he says. The whole thing rests on your shoulders. He told me to tell you.'

'Thanks,' she said unenthusiastically. 'What about the package in the car wreck?'

'Nothing – the police say they don't know anything about it. It turns out that there was a fire and the bodies were burned pretty badly.'

'Then how did they know who was travelling in the car? I was told an ID card was found.'

'I guess they knew before the accident,' said Miff simply.

'What about the phones they were carrying?'

'There was nothing . . .'

'How important was the package?'

'Important, but he says you can get by without it.'

'Tell him that Promises – he'll know who I mean – offered us a deal. They're worried and they are about to get extremely nasty.' She hung up and investigated the phone Eyam had given her. There were twenty-four numbers and the same number of email addresses. She wrote a list on a notepad, which excluded Chris Mooney and Alice Scudamore and then sent each address an email. The email would be encrypted, but she kept the message short: 'Contact by return & let me know you're OK. Wait for instructions on delivery at the end of afternoon. Keep away from CCTV and stay off the streets.'

The first replies came back. Some returned blank emails with just the word 'bell ringer' written in the subject bar. Others expressed various degrees of concern about surveillance and the emergency powers. She answered none of these but ticked off the names on her list. After half an hour, two had failed to reply – Penny Whitehead and Diana Kidd. Figuring that Whitehead was the calmer of the two, she called her.

'Did you get the email?' she said when Whitehead answered.

'Yes, I haven't had time to answer. Diana Kidd has been arrested. I was with her. We travelled together. She's got the package with her.'

'Shit! When did this happen? Where are you?'

'Twenty minutes ago – she got out of the car to buy some coffee.

I don't know what happened but I saw her being led to a police van so I followed in the car. The van must have gone to the underground car park off Park Lane because I didn't see it in the traffic after that.'

'She's got her phone with her?'

'I assume so, yes.'

'Damn.' The only consolation was that Diana Kidd's phone, like the others, had just one number on it. However that number belonged to the phone in Kate's possession – now the hub of the whole operation, which would mean she could be tracked and all her messages intercepted and decoded.

'Hold on, I've got it,' said Whitehead. 'She left the bloody thing on charge in the car.'

'Thank God,' said Kate. 'Has she got the documents with her?'

She's wearing them. They're in her clothes. I didn't ask where. God knows if they have dared to search her.'

'OK, you'll hear from me later. Now lose yourself, Penny. Just try to keep it together until this afternoon.'

She called Eyam's phone and insisted Miff wake him and tell him about Diana Kidd's package.

He came on. His voice was weak. 'We can't go on losing material like this.'

'How essential is it?'

'Letters signed by Temple, and a note of a meeting three years ago, in which the Americans – the director of national intelligence – were formally told of the system.'

'And you let Diana Kidd carry these? You're crazy. We're going to have to try to get hold of them.'

'You can't – forget them. We've got copies that will be published on the web.'

'You said that having the original documents counted for everything. Tony Swift and Chris Mooney died because of that belief. Put Miff on,' she demanded, rising from the table with the phone wedged between her ear and shoulder. She paid and stepped into the street. 'I need a car that looks official,' she said to Miff. 'Black, dark-blue, silver – like a government car. And I want you to find a suit and tie, Miff, and lose the stud in your ear. Pick me up outside the Eagle's Nest pub off the Earls

Court Road in an hour and a half. Got that? Good. Don't discuss it with Eyam. Just do what I say. OK?'

Miff answered in the affirmative several times.

'Have you got a car?'

'I'm looking at it.'

She noted down the registration number and hung up. Then she used the other phone to call Kilmartin.

'Give me some names of serving female officers with MI5,' she said to him.

'What age?'

'Mine.'

'There's Christine Shoemaker. She's a little older than you.'

'Too senior.'

Kilmartin was silent, then suggested a woman named Alison Vesty who was in her early forties and had been seconded to MI6 in Lahore, which was where Kilmartin had met her. 'As far as I know she is still there,' he said.

'OK, we need to think of a way of telling the police that this senior MI5 officer is going to take one of the people they've detained in the underground car park. From memory, there's a car pound for towed cars in that car park and I suspect that is where they are being held. Call the car pound, speak to the senior officer and tell them that Vesty is arriving to take away a woman named Diana Kidd for interview.'

'Sounds risky to me,' said Kilmartin.

'Got any better suggestions?'

Kilmartin said no and offered several refinements.

At just past twelve thirty, Philip Cannon picked up the phone to a Chief Inspector Grimes, who asked if he could verify that Alison Vesty of the prime minister's private office would be attending a holding area known as Hotel Papa to interview Diana Kidd. When the officer asked if Vesty would be showing any identification Cannon briskly reminded him that members of the intelligence services did not go round flashing ID cards and special passes. Before giving the officer the registration number of the car she would be using he asked why the holding area was called Hotel Papa. 'Hyde Park – HP,' replied Chief Inspector Grimes.

Cannon returned to read the emailed press release about to go out from Scotland Yard, which described David Eyam as a serial paedophile who had not only faked his own death but had returned to take revenge on the government. He took some satisfaction from the story – which came from Gruppo via Lyme – that the deal offered to David Eyam had been ignored and his woman friend had made fools of MI5 by simply sending her phone to an office in the City where it lay at the security desk gently communicating with the nearest phone mast.

He rang Kilmartin about the decision to go public on David Eyam, as well as the news that Temple was threatening to call the general election that day.

Miff pulled up in a new Jaguar at one fifteen p.m. Kate climbed into the back and began wriggling out of her jeans to replace them with the suit trousers. Then she bent forward, efficiently pulled the shirt and sweater over her head and put on the crisp white shirt that had been folded at the bottom of her bag.

'Jesus,' said Miff to the mirror. 'I'm trying to drive here.'

'Well keep your eyes on the road, Aristotle,' she said. 'Anyway, why the hell are you called Aristotle?'

'After Aristotle Onassis, – the shipping magnate. My mother hoped it would make me rich. Like a good luck charm, I suppose.'

'Weird.'

'I have to tell you something, Kate,' he said, twirling the wheel with one hand. 'Your friend is all over the news, and you get a mention too. They're making a big thing of it, and it isn't pretty – child abuse, tax dodging, money laundering, faking his death. They're probably still going on about him.'

He turned on the radio. A reporter was reviewing Eyam's career as a 'top-flight' civil servant and intelligence chief, a man who had only a week before been mourned at a funeral service attended by the home secretary, civil servants and those working for Eyam's sometime patron Eden White, a close ally of the prime minister's. 'There is some mystery about the events in the quiet market town of High Castle, where a local solicitor was recently murdered outside David Eyam's property. Police won't comment on this, or the fact that the town is now grieving the death of two men in a car accident that took place on Sunday night. One of the men worked as the coroner's clerk and officiated at the inquest held into Eyam's death, apparently in a bomb blast, just under two weeks ago.'

'They may just have made a big mistake,' said Kate to the back of Miff's head. 'There are too many unanswered questions.'

'People will just remember the kiddie porn,' said Miff.

'Not if I have anything to do with it,' she said and began to think herself into the role of Alison Vesty, who by Kilmartin's account was an uncompromising bitch. 'So you shouldn't have too much difficulty,' he had said with a chuckle.

Twenty minutes later the Jaguar arrived at the top of the slip road leading to the vast underground car park. They were stopped and directed by armed policemen to the entrance at Marble Arch, five hundred yards away, where they fell in behind two police vans on a ramp that curved round to their left. The vans were waved through but an armed policeman moved to stand in their path. Another bent down to Miff. 'We're expected,' he said. 'I'm carrying Miss Vesty from the Emergency Committee in Downing Street.'

The policeman moved to Kate's window. 'ID?' he asked.

'Chief Inspector Grimes has been informed – he will check with Number Ten if you want. Look, I am in rather a hurry, officer.'

He looked doubtful but walked to the front of the car, checked the plate against the number he had on his clipboard and returned to Miff's window. 'Go through the barrier, park up on the right, and walk to the office at the entrance to the holding area: they will help you.'

As the barrier rose, Miff shot off, causing the tyres to squeal on the shiny concrete. 'Steady, Aristotle, don't overdo it,' she said.

They parked in a bay that was marked for visitors. 'Turn the car around. Keep the engine running,' she said. Inside the pocket of her bag she'd found a pass to the Mayne Building in New York – a plain white plastic security card held in a metal frame, which was attached to a loop of black string. She put this round her neck, straightened her shirt and climbed into the mild, fetid atmosphere of the car park.

Ahead of her was the car pound, a fenced-off area of two or three acres at the centre of the enormous single-level car park, which she remembered from years before when Charlie's car had been impounded. It had been hastily – and badly – screened off by tarpaulins, stretched along the outside of the cage. Lights projected shadows of people onto the tarpaulins, people standing in groups, sitting or moving about slowly. Several notices declared that the car park was now a 'designated area under the emergency regulations'. Mobile phones, photography and any form of communication with those being held under the Civil Contingencies Act were forbidden. The holding area should not be approached by unauthorised personnel, instructed the notice. Members of the public wishing to claim their cars were instructed to phone a number. All others were told to report to the office with identification ready. Lastly it warned that any attempt to interfere with the detainees or impede the authorities in the execution of their duties was an offence.

The car park PA system was playing music, and just now, without irony, an old number by Phil Collins – 'Another Day in Paradise'. She kept walking. At each corner of the pen were police carrying semi-automatic weapons. Cameras had been trained along the line of the fence. Through a gap in the tarps she could see lines of people waiting under the notice that said 'Processing'. Men and women were separated: each carried their outer garments and their shoes. The first step in a process of dehumanisation, thought Kate, is to force people to undress. A quick estimate told her that there were a couple of hundred people in the cage.

She reached two armed police officers standing outside the cabin. 'I have an appointment,' she said, walking past them and into the gaze of a camera. She mounted four steps into the cabin and opened the door. Three men in uniform were inside. One sat with a clipboard and a laptop in front of him. 'Chief Inspector Grimes?' she said to the oldest of the three.

'Yes.'

'Vesty from the Government Emergency Committee. You should have received a call from Downing Street.'

'We did,' said Grimes, 'but it is not clear what you want.'

'Call the main switchboard again and ask for this extension.' She handed him a piece of paper.

'I'm sure there won't be any need; I've just talked to them.'

'It is required,' she said. 'They will confirm everything again.'

The policeman picked up the phone and dialled the number. She prayed that Kilmartin's contact would answer. He did because the policeman was then asked to describe her.

'Right, that all appears to be in order,' he said.

She glanced through the window to her left and saw the armed policemen move off into the car park, having circled Miff's car. 'You're holding a woman named Diana Kidd. I am here to oversee her release and remove her.'

'Take her away? I thought you were going to interview her here?'

'No.'

'But . . .'

'We don't have time for this. You have come near to destroying an operation being run at the highest level.' She bent forward, splayed her hands on the desk and looked at him hard. 'Can I have a word in private, Chief Inspector?'

He nodded to the two men, who got up and went through a door at the rear of the cabin. In the few seconds that it was open she glimpsed more of the compound. There were bedrolls, mattresses and a long table where she guessed food was served. A couple of bins overflowed with water bottles and the type of plastic foodbox she'd been given in jail. In the middle of the compound was a bank of toilets. On the far side was a row of four cabins.

'Chief Inspector,' she said when the door closed. 'Diana Kidd is working for us. She is an important asset, vital to the government operation. We've taken months to infiltrate the core group. She should be out on the streets telling us what's happening now. There are hundreds more of these people and we desperately need to know what they are planning.'

'Are we talking about the same person?' he asked incredulously. 'The woman hasn't stopped moaning and crying since she got here. She didn't say anything about working for the government.'

Kate shook her head. 'She's very good at her job. She has been in deep cover for nearly a year. Of course she isn't going to say anything in front of all the others you've got here.'

'The Security Service is processing the detainees individually. She could have told them.'

She placed her hands on her hips and squared up to Grimes. 'Look, I know you're doing a difficult job here but let me just tell you that half an hour ago I was with the home secretary and the prime minister. If you won't let her go I will have to phone Downing Street and put you onto them. To be frank, Chief Inspector, this will not look good for you.' She could see the doubt in his eyes. 'Effect this woman's release immediately because it is going to happen sooner or later.'

He picked up the phone without looking at her and spoke: 'Bring Diana Kidd to the gate.'

She nodded.

'Follow me, Miss Vesty.'

They went down the steps of the cabin and turned left towards a gate in the cage. She had a better view of the compound now. There was much more noise than she had realised, mostly made by a dozen or so young people who were demanding to know why they were being held without charge. One was shouting, 'Hey . . . Be . . . us . . . Cor . . . Pus' in an endless chant; and a man with blonde dreadlocks was being restrained by two policemen after he'd charged the gate. Another went to help him and was unceremoniously knocked to the ground. Others stood, or sat hunched on the makeshift beds, in mute bewilderment. She recognised no one. Then she saw a man in a suit approach a dumpy figure sitting on a plastic garden chair with her back to the gate. It was Mrs Kidd. She looked up when he spoke to her, then rose rather unsteadily. Kate could see the hope and terror in her demeanour. Without turning, she beckoned discreetly with her left hand to Miff, whom she hoped was looking in his wing mirror. The reverse lights went on and the car began to creep back towards her.

'The trouble with these emergency powers is no one knows what to do with these people,' said Grimes conversationally. 'They say we're to let them go in a day or two. No one knows. You wonder what the point is. Bang 'em up I say – better than this limbo.'

'You're doing a vital job,' said Kate. 'How many are you expecting?'

'Anything up to a thousand: that's what we've been told.'

'All in Hotel Papa?'

'Until the other holding areas are sorted out. Remember, we've only had twenty-four hours' notice.'

'I'll tell Downing Street you're managing well.' As she said it she noticed a man step from the row of cabins in the middle of the compound and look with interest in their direction. She instantly recognised Halliday from the police station in High Castle. In the light she couldn't tell if he had noticed her, but something had certainly caught his attention. He remained staring in her direction as Diana Kidd and her escort neared the gate. At this point Kidd recognised Kate and a look of gormless joy flooded her features. Kate said and did nothing as the buzzer sounded and the gate rolled back.

'Thank you,' blurted Kidd. 'Thank you.'

'Make your way to the car now,' said Kate without looking at her. 'We've got a lot to do.'

On cue Miff reversed the car right up to them, hopped out and went to open the doors on the left side. A chauffeur might have waited to close the doors for his passengers, but Miff sensed something in Kate's manner and returned to the driving seat, leaving them open.

'Thank you, Chief Inspector,' said Kate, taking Mrs Kidd's arm.

There was a shout from inside the compound. Kate glanced back and saw the man running towards the gate. Then she simply shrugged at Grimes, pushed Diana Kidd into the rear seat and climbed into the front. Miff's Jaguar launched forward with a squeal of tyres and shot the hundred yards to the barrier, but just then the two police vans came from another part of the car park and moved into their lane. 'Can you get ahead of them?' shouted Kate. In her wing mirror she saw the man run up to Grimes, gesticulating.

'We don't need to,' replied Miff. He was right. The barrier was raised for them and he stuck so close to the second vehicle that the Jaguar slipped through before it fell.

Kate turned round to Diana Kidd and shouted, 'Have you still got the documents?'

'Yes,' she wailed. 'They were searching people but they hadn't reached me. They're in the lining of my skirt.'

'Good, hold tight.' The police vans turned left into a two-lane stretch of about 150 yards, which after a right-angle bend would divide into the entrance and exit slip roads. 'They'll radio ahead to the armed police,' she shouted. 'You are going to have to bloody well move.'

Miff needed no encouragement. Once they were in the brightly lit tunnel, he pulled out from behind the two vans and overtook them at astonishing speed. They rounded the bend but instead of going straight ahead he hooked right up the entry slip road, where he knew there was no barrier. As they came into the daylight they realised that the two armed officers they'd passed at the entrance twenty minutes earlier were running with their guns ready to cover the exit fifty yards away. Miff let out a whoop of joy, sped the wrong way through traffic lights, and spun the wheel left to join the traffic moving round Marble Arch. Kate glanced back and only then did it occur to her that Hotel Papa was almost directly beneath Speakers' Corner, the symbol of free expression in Britain.

The news that a middle-aged woman named Kidd had been sprung from Hotel Papa by Eyam's friend Kate Lockhart and a convicted criminal using a stolen car reached Number Ten about half an hour later. There was plenty of CCTV footage of the pair, but it was still not clear why the officer in charge had let the woman go without any proper authorisation. He maintained he had received a call from Downing Street and rang back to confirm the release, but could not say to whom he'd spoken.

Yes, thought Cannon, it would very soon be revealed that the policeman had been given a number in the Communications Centre. They might even link that to a call from Peter Kilmartin and someone somewhere might have a recording of the conversations, but they weren't going to do anything to him, not now that he had the ultimate protection tucked in his breast pocket – four sheets of A4 paper, which Lyme had got hold of from the Government Scientific Service and which had also been sent to the prime minister's private office in a secure bag an hour ago. Nobody would mess with him now, least of all John Temple.

But it was not Cannon's style to wave a gun in the air, and he looked round his colleagues in the election strategy meeting with a mild air and waited.

If the election was going to be called that afternoon, the button had to be pushed now to enable Temple to go to the palace at five and return to Downing Street in time to make his announcement to the media outside Number Ten before the six o'clock news. Everything was ready – a miracle had been achieved by the party. The manifesto was on the presses and campaigning in the marginal seats had virtually begun. Temple could go any time he wanted.

Eventually the prime minister's gaze fell on Cannon. 'So this afternoon it is,' he said.

'Certainly, if you want the announcement of the general election to come a poor second on the news agenda, go ahead, prime minister.' He stopped and looked round the usual faces. 'The David Eyam story will push you off the front page,' he continued. 'All the TV channels are leading on it now. Even though it's an open secret that you are going to call the election, the Eyam story has huge momentum. More and more detail is being added at every bulletin and we're only a couple of hours into this thing.'

'But Eyam is the enemy. We are his victims,' said Temple hopelessly. 'He is attempting to distort the legitimate democratic process.'

Cannon blinked rapidly. 'That's not the way it is being presented, prime minister. The main thrust of the coverage is that a practising paedophile was at the heart of government and had access to all the nation's secrets. An issue of competency is being raised, even though it is well over two years old. We have received a hundred calls from journalists in the last hour, and most are asking why a man who went to the trouble of staging his own death in such an elaborate fashion would bother to come back to certain imprisonment. It doesn't make sense and when a story doesn't add up like this it becomes an obsession. The media won't want to let it go, not even for you.'

'As soon as Eyam is arrested that will all have to stop.'

'But you can't say when that will be. Eyam's associate has just removed a suspect from beneath our noses. Why? Why did Kate Lockhart take that risk? We can make some educated guesses but we don't know.'

'That woman,' snapped Temple, 'is the pivot of the whole plot. This is the second time she has made a fool of us today.'

'Well, we did train her,' said Cannon. 'The point is that we haven't been able to lay a hand on Eyam. We don't know where he is. Intelligence led us to believe that there was going to be some sort of press conference in a hotel. That is beginning to look extremely unlikely. So far nothing has happened. In the last hour the St James's Library has been raided by the police and Security Service in a manner that is now being condemned as oppressive. It's like raiding the Women's Institute. There are TV crews outside there now. Apparently police were acting on intelligence but clearly the information was wrong and now the great and good on the library's board are going to cause hell about the oppressive behaviour. You've got the army on the streets, thousands of people being stopped and searched, scores being secretly held against their will and without legal representation.' He stopped. 'I respectfully submit that these are not auspicious circumstances in which to call an election where you are going to be arguing for continuation of calm, orderly government. Give the police time to arrest and charge Eyam, then call the election. Let this storm blow itself out in the media overnight.' Cannon sat back, knowing he had used every reasonable argument. The only things left were the four sheets of paper in his pocket.

There was further discussion lasting ten minutes, in which Cannon took no part. At length Temple said he would consult further and asked Dawn Gruppo to be in touch with the palace and the office of the president of the European Council, who was due at Number Ten the next morning.

As they rose, Temple murmured to Cannon: 'We've got to get the woman Lockhart – she's clearly the key to it all.'

30

The Joins

Miff pulled up in a side street off the Edgware Road, and told Kate that he would find a safe place for Diana Kidd. Mrs Kidd was in no state to protest but sat in the back of the Jaguar dabbing at her chest and muttering that she never expected to be on the run from the police.

'Tell David to save his strength for tomorrow and give him my love.'

Thus instructed, Miff went off with his unlikely cargo, while Kate made her way to Bloomsbury, where she took refuge in one of the dubious small hotels in the area. She told the man behind the reception of The Corinth that she would need the room for no more than four hours and would pay double the daily rate in cash provided she didn't have to show him an ID card. He was used to such arrangements and led her to a room at the back that smelled of stale smoke overlaid by sweet air freshener. He handed her the key and asked, with just the hint of a leer, if she expected to be joined by anyone. No, she replied, dropping her bag against a Dimplex radiator, which tolled like a bell: all she wanted was rest.

On the way she'd seen a newspaper billboard which read *Number Ten Child Porn Scandal*. She reached for the remote and turned on the little television that was perched high up on a shelf in the corner. After a few minutes watching BBC News, she swore and turned the set off. Outside it was beginning to rain again, and she wondered briefly what in God's name had persuaded her to think she could ever make a life in this damp little country. She picked up the hotel phone and dialled Eyam's number.

'How're you feeling?' she asked.

'Rough.'

She let her cheek sink into her hand. 'Have you seen the news?'

'Yes. At least it means they're less likely to take a pot at us.'

'Don't be too sure.'

'What is it, Kate?'

'We don't stand a chance, do we? It's just ridiculous to think that the committee is going to hear you now. Whatever we say or do . . .' She stopped.

'What?'

'It doesn't matter,' she said.

'I've had a lot of doubts along the way, you know. Last September I was wondering whether to give it all up and concentrate on my treatment. I was lying in the garden at the Dove, staring up at a peerless blue sky and I noticed hundreds, maybe thousands of swallows, fluttering high up like silver chaff. I watched for a bit then I noticed something else. It was a drone stationed over the valley, observing the Dove. How dare they? I thought. What bloody right do they have to do this? And that made up my mind.'

'But if we don't pull this off we are all going to be arrested. I saw where they were holding people today. This is the beginning of something really sinister – utterly new in British life. It's in those circumstances that people are *disappeared*, and I am damn sure that even if you were arrested you'd never be allowed to speak in an open court. None of us would.'

'There is a lot at stake. There always has been. But we have to try. We have to, Kate.'

'You sound awful,' she said. 'Let me put things together tonight. I'll have Kilmartin with me. We can do it.'

'But you don't know the order of the papers. Each document illustrates a point. There is a logic to it all, an argument, a narrative.'

'Look, David, that's my job. I know how to do it. This is how I go to war. We'll manage. You rest up for tomorrow. Are you going to be OK about getting there?'

'Yes, and you?'

'It'll be a cinch. And . . . last night . . .'

'Was wonderful,' he said. 'I am overwhelmed. More than I can say.'

'Me too,' she said, suddenly gripped by an inexpressible sense of doom. 'OK, I'd better go now. We'll speak later. Stay safe.'

She hung up and immediately cursed her reticence – her failure to say she loved him. A moment or two of self-recrimination was followed by a brisk ordering of her phones and computer, together with the list she'd made of the Bell Ringers that morning. Laid out before her, it all seemed hopelessly inadequate, but she phoned each one, ticking off the name as she told them where and when to deliver the packages. Each was given a time the package should arrive. She reminded them that they did not have to make the delivery in person and that cabs and messengers could be used. She ended with the same instruction. 'When you're done, get rid of the phone and make yourself scarce.' She knew they all had emergency accommodation arranged.

Last she spoke to Evan Thomas, the intense Welshman, and asked if he had any of the tools of his trade with him. He replied rather testily that of course he hadn't, but he could go to his friend at the Alinea Bindery in Bayswater and borrow some.

'It means you'll be up all night,' she said.

'Not a problem,' said Thomas.

'Just let me know you've got what you need, then dump your phone.'

'Righty-ho,' he said.

She too would have to remain awake all night. She lay on the bed, set the radio alarm on the bedside table and tried to get some sleep.

Just after six that evening Cannon ran into Jamie Ferris outside one of the washrooms in Number Ten. 'We've got the bastard,' he said, punching a fist into his palm. 'We'll have Eyam in the bag by the end of the evening; in fact, we'll have the whole lot. I have just told the prime minister.'

'Well done,' replied Cannon, seeming to share a little of Ferris's excitement. 'How did you manage it?'

Ferris tapped his nose. 'Aristotle Miff, the man seen at Hotel Papa with Kate Lockhart, has been traced to the East End. We believe Eyam is in an estate known to be frequented by one of Miff's associates. We're watching both locations. It's just a matter of time before we track down that bloody woman.'

'And the rest of them?'

'We'll be yanking their fucking chains by morning because they've got to keep in touch with Daddy Eyam. They're nothing without Eyam. If he's got a phone on we will soon know the number and every number it has called and that means we'll have locations for every one of these fucking people.'

Cannon laid a hand on Ferris's shoulder. 'That's wonderful news.'

'Must be getting along – I want to be there for the kill.'

'No, you mustn't miss out,' said Cannon.

Cannon slipped into the office occupied by the garden girls and dialled Kilmartin's number. Then, turning his back to the room, he murmured: 'They've got a position for your friend. They are monitoring the phones in the area and are confident of an early arrest.'

She snapped awake with the first ring from Kilmartin. Before he had finished speaking she lunged for the other phone, tugging the charger from the wall socket, and pressed the last number dialled. 'Get out now,' she shouted at Eyam. 'They know where you are.'

'I doubt it,' said Eyam. 'But we'll leave anyway.'

She gave him the number of the set in her other hand – the one supplied by Kilmartin – and told him to use it only in an emergency and rang off. 'I'll see you later,' she said to Kilmartin.

'I await you,' he replied, also rather coolly.

Half an hour later she was let in a door at the rear of the British Museum in Montagu Place by a security guard. As instructed by Kilmartin, she said she was with the film crew and was led to the great Arched Room on the west of the museum.

Kilmartin was at the furthest end of a row of tables that ran down the centre of the room, reading in a pool of light thrown from an Anglepoise lamp. His hand fidgeted with the tray in front of him.

He stood up when he saw her. 'Ah, welcome – glad you had no bother getting in.'

She walked to him, looking round. The Arched Room resembled a small church. Five arches separated six tall bays either side of a central aisle. Each bay acted as a large cabinet with hundreds of trays lining the walls right up to the point where a metal gallery ran around the top of the room. On the tables in the centre were cutting pads, weighing scales, marked boxes, magnifiers and rolls of tape. 'Where are we?' she asked.

'In the great library of King Ashurbanipal of Assyria.' He smiled at her, pulled out one of the drawers nearest to them and selected a piece of pottery about the size of a packet of cigarettes, which was indented with regular, wedge-shaped cuts. 'Cuneiform,' he said. 'There are over twenty-five thousand tablets from Ashurbanipal's library alone, and maybe another hundred thousand tablets in the museum's collection.' He replaced the tablet. 'Take a pew. Coffee?'

He reached down into a shopping bag and withdrew a Thermos flask. There were parcels of silver foil, a bottle of water and some fruit. Kilmartin had prepared as though he was attending races on a summer afternoon. He looked around with relish. 'King Ashurbanipal was a scholar as well as a great general, you know. In his brief life he built one of the greatest libraries ever to exist – maybe the first library of them all. We know from his records that he sent agents to discover new texts and bring them to his library at Nineveh.'

'Yes,' she said, more interested by Kilmartin's energised manner. He seemed different – younger.

'When the Persians sacked Nineveh they burned the library,' he continued. 'As a result the tablets were baked, which made sure they were preserved. However, a lot were broken and that's the business of this place. Making joins.'

'Joins? What joins?'

'Joining them up so the complete text can be read.'

'Ah! Kind of what we're here to do with Eyam's documents,' she said, looking at her watch.

'That's exactly right.'

She pulled out the papers she'd rescued from the car park with Diana Kidd and flourished them. 'At least we've got something to start with.'

'Oh, we have a lot more than that. So far eight packages have arrived.' He pointed under the table to a pile of envelopes. 'I expect they couldn't wait to be shot of them.'

'Have you looked?'

'No, I was waiting for you.'

She drew the pile towards her. 'Let's clear a couple of tables.'

They began rapidly spreading out the papers. Some were covered in clear plastic which included a flap at the left-hand edge so the document could be clipped into a file. She noticed that these often included handwritten notes and in some cases signatures. Eyam had tried to preserve any fingerprints or DNA evidence that might still cling to the surface of the papers.

They ordered the dated documents chronologically, but this gave no sense of what they had in front of them, nor did putting them into categories, such as memoranda, accounts, emails, letters, legislation and policy papers. There were impenetrable pages of departmental accounts, obliquely worded emails, turgid sociological studies. None of it seemed to add up to much. They sat at adjacent tables and began to read. Kate bent over *The Way forward: Social Intelligence*, a paper from 2009, and Kilmartin started working his way through a bundle from the Home Office and a think tank called Foresight, research that was all sponsored by the Ortelius Institute for Public Policy Research, a fact noted in tiny print at the base of the documents.

Over the next hour, more deliveries were made. A security guard appeared with two pizza boxes and a bunch of flowers – the cover for three packages. He advised that the pizza could not be consumed in the Arched Room and said he would find a home for the spring posy. Other packages were dropped off by messengers on motorcycles and bicycles, and in one case by a rickshaw driver. By half past nine, fifteen packages had arrived. Most of the Bell Ringers did not remember, or were too cautious, to put their names to their package so she had no idea who on her list still had to make their delivery. Part of her wished she hadn't told them to get rid of their phones, although of course it was vital that they did so to avoid being traced and picked up. She had no number for Eyam either and that bothered her.

But they were beginning to feel their way into Eyam's structure. There were three groups. The first showed how different policy documents and unnoticed paragraphs from different Acts of Parliament combined to create the conditions for wholesale invasion of privacy of the British public. For instance, a paper from Ortelius argued for a discreet observation of the behaviour of all adults to assess their suitability or performance as parents. Such information would alert the state of the need for intervention in 'problem families' long before social workers would spot it. A clause in a bill enabled a programme called 'Family Watch'.

At the same time, ASCAMS was set up in anticipation of trouble at the London Olympics and this too involved trawling through enormous amounts of personal data. While the merger of all government databases under the 'Transformational Government' programme made this possible, the steady flow of Ortelius policy documents chipping away at the right to privacy in the face of grave social problems made it all seem desirable.

Then came the moment of decision when it was suggested – again by Ortelius – that the government was missing an opportunity; people's lives could be vastly improved if the state could know everything about them, could anticipate their needs and mediate between agencies they dealt with. The state was cast in the role of the hyper-efficient and concerned servant; there were many advantages to a system that would automatically patrol benefit fraud, winkle out illegal immigrants or people who were paying too little tax. Much was made of the beneficial 'outcomes' – the increase in 'social capital' and 'community cohesion', and 'friendship networks between the poor'. Yet it was obvious that paper proposed a power grab, using software that was already in development by White's companies. The system would know every-thing about everyone and make judgements about supposed illegality, anti-social behaviour or the inconsistencies between, say, declared income and expenditure, and automatically initiate action through hundreds of different agencies.

She found an email from the Home Office legal department to the Cabinet Strategy Office pointing out the significant threat that the system would represent. The author raised questions about privacy, natural justice and accountability. The email had been printed out and bore Derek Glenny's scrawl and signature. 'No need for primary legislation,' he wrote. 'Refer all future queries to the Office of Social Intelligence. From now on this issue is classified.'

The decision had been taken to draw a line under the deliberation and go ahead with DEEP TRUTH. To all those involved in the discussion the government pretended that the project had been abandoned. DEEP TRUTH went underground but not all traces were eliminated. Kilmartin found pages from the annual accounts of the ministries concerned with Justice, Education and Work and Pensions, and several agencies: police, customs and revenue. Each one had made large payments to the Office of Social Intelligence – which amounted in one year to £1.8 billion. But much larger amounts were paid out from the secret money allotted to MI5, MI6 and GCHQ.

'That ties in with payments to Eden White's companies amounting to at least one point eight billion for one financial year,' Kate said, waving a piece of paper, but without looking up. 'I wonder how many of these people are on his pay.'

'There is a sheet of bank account numbers somewhere,' said Kilmartin, propping his glasses on his forehead. 'Yes, here it is: Shoemaker, Glenny, Temple and several other names are listed as having bank accounts.'

'Jesus, they were hiding the expenditure from the public accounts committee while taking backhanders. It's unbelievable. But you know, we've got nothing here that ties DEEP TRUTH to Temple and White personally.'

'Maybe those documents were with Tony Swift and the other fellow.'

'No, Eyam would have said.'

At eleven Evan Thomas arrived, carrying a large canvas holdall from which he produced four further packages that had accumulated with the security guard at the Montagu Place entrance of the museum in the past couple of hours. He'd found one in the street propped against the door. Kate did a quick calculation. 'That means all the packages are accounted for.'

Thomas began laying out his equipment on the table in the alcove furthest from the entrance. Kilmartin and Kate tore at the envelopes and began to read. Almost immediately she let out a yelp. 'This is an internal review of the first operation of a system known simply by a numeric code, which shows that it has an estimated failure rate of seven per cent. That would mean millions of people were wrongly identified, wrongly targeted and punished,' she said. 'By the government's own admission their bloody machine is out of control. People have lost their homes, been prosecuted, raided, had their property seized, their children removed by social services. It's harassment and persecution on a vast scale and no one knows how to stop it. The trouble is that there is no mention of DEEP TRUTH, just the numeric code.' She read out the number 455729328 and looked up: Kilmartin was holding a single sheet of paper in a plastic cover between his thumb and forefinger. 'What's that?' she asked.

'John Temple's signature on the bottom of a document that sanctions the purchase and secret installation of software in every government computer: the system is referred to by the same code and we have a date three years ago. We need to know what this bloody number stands for.' He looked in a leather folder and produced a copy of an email from Dawn Gruppo and started to write.

Kate examined a final bundle, which concerned Sir Christopher Holmes – two letters addressed to John Temple and headed *For Your Eyes Only*. Both raised constitutional concerns about the level of surveillance and intervention. In Holmes's view, the extent of SPIN-DRIFT operations, as he called them, could not be justified in a democracy. He asked the prime minister to review the policy twice and in the second letter made an open threat to go public, saying that his duty as a citizen far outweighed the interests of the government, which in this case he believed were thoroughly misguided and wrong. He would, of course, resign his position before doing so.

'Then two weeks later he and his wife die in a fire at his country home,' said Kate out loud.

Kilmartin grunted.

'The suppressed pathologist's report is here,' she continued, 'and it makes clear that they were probably dead before the fire was started. There is also an email to someone at Ortelius, alerting them to the risk posed by the head of the JIC.' She dropped the paper. 'We've got pretty much all we need, though nothing that nails Eden White.'

They re-read everything, then began to work out an exact order. Using all the tables in the central aisle of the room, they laid out the documents in a line and moved from the first to the last, walking through the case that Eyam had built against the government. Kate observed that it was no different from putting a bundle of documents together for trial. Evan Thomas followed behind them measuring the papers. When they decided on the final order, he put on a pair of white cloth gloves, stacked the papers like a deck of cards, squared them off and pressed them together. 'It's going to be very bulky and the pages aren't going to be very well aligned,' he said. 'We really need two volumes, but we don't have time.'

'Aha,' Kilmartin exclaimed suddenly. 'It's simple; the number spells out DEEP TRUTH. If you go through the alphabet repeatedly giving the letters a numeric value from one to nine until you reach the end, you get the code.' He scribbled on a piece of paper. 'That's what they call it. Sometimes they simply refer to it just by its initials – four-two, or DT, as in the Gruppo email to Shoemaker.'

'That's great!' said Kate. 'Draw out the grid neatly and we'll include it in the evidence.'

Evan Thomas set about making book covers and a spine of canvas and rigid cardboard, which was cut with surgical precision. He glued the papers into the spine with a gum that he said would just about hold for the next day, having added strips of card to the documents in plastic covers so that they could be held into the spine also. Then he closed the covers and put the book in a small press, screwing down the plate with many grimaces and sighs.

They watched in a tired fascination as he cut out a piece of dark red leather for the cover and began to pummel and distress it with fine-grain sandpaper. He measured and cut two lengths of 'Cockerell' marbled paper – the combed pattern, which he said was appropriate for the Houses of Parliament. 'Right, we'll wait a little for the gum to dry and then we can get to work on the cover.'

Kilmartin took out and unwrapped sandwiches from his bag and they sat down.

'It could just work,' said Kate.

'Course it will. In these days when no one can think without consulting a screen or imagining anything happening without it being available on the web, the one thing that no one will suspect is a book done out in *Cockerell* pattern and old Moroccan calf skin.'

'Goat skin,' said Thomas.

Kilmartin sprang up and went to a drawer. 'I want to show you something interesting,' he said. 'It tells you how important libraries are.'

357

He returned with a tray, placed it on the table in front of them and picked up a tablet, which he held up to her face. 'This is known as the planisphere and it was made by an Assyrian scribe in 700 BC. It is a copy of the night notebook of a Sumerian astronomer from June 3123 BC. We even know the day – June twenty-ninth.' He held the tablet up to them. 'It is a note of the night sky for that evening and it records the presence of a very large object in the sky.'

'A meteor?' said Thomas, who had wandered over.

'Actually, an asteroid that smashed into the Alps, near a place called Köfels in Austria; although there was plenty of evidence of the asteroid, geologists could never explain the absence of a crater. The answer lay in this remarkable tablet, which records the angle of the asteroid's approach. It was so acute that no crater was made. It clipped the top of a mountain called Gamskogel, exploded and became a fireball before it reached its impact point at Köfels a few miles away. This tablet gives the trajectory of the object in relation to the stars that night, which is consistent with the event in Austria to an error better than one degree. Here was the answer everyone was looking for. Not bad for a little clay tablet.'

'Where are you going with this?' asked Kate.

Kilmartin replaced the tablet in the drawer. 'Nowhere, but I suppose you could say I was wondering what will remain after Eyam's dossier becomes public. We know it's explosive – the question is whether it makes a lasting impact, something that people readily understand and recall.'

'What do you think?'

'It could go either way. The publicity surrounding David Eyam today and the manhunt that's going on may drown out everything he has to say. If that happens, we are all going to face a very difficult time – you, me, the Bell Ringers and of course Eyam.'

'Will your contact on the committee still go ahead after all this publicity?'

He thought for a moment. 'She'll have to be persuaded, but she's a tough old bird: if she's made up her mind on something she won't brook any opposition.' He paused and looked at Kate steadily; his eyes were warm but firm. 'One course is for you to appear in front of the committee and present the evidence yourself. Talk them through the story.'

She started shaking her head. 'I know nothing. I have been in the country less than a month.'

'You underestimate yourself. Besides, I think the Joint Committee on Human Rights will warm to you. You have an air of integrity. Eyam may be arrested, or not be able to get through the security, or be too ill to make it: you are the one who is going to have to pick up this ball and run with it. An awful lot of people are going to depend on you . . . me included.'

'We may not even get a hearing,' she said. 'If Temple calls an election, the committee stops work; all parliamentary privilege ends for the duration. Then what the hell do we do?'

'There's a long way to go before that. Now, if you don't mind I am going to get a little rest.'

They both dozed in their chairs – Kilmartin sitting straight as though about to be electrocuted, Kate bent forwards resting on her crossed arms – while Evan Thomas worked on the cover, inside and out, gluing down the Cockerell paper, stamping the goat skin with blows of a small mallet, running over the skin – back, front and spine – with little wheels that left regular indented patterns, buffing here, rubbing with pumice stone there, picking at it with an awl, laying a thin border of gold leaf on the front and back, then clipping four Victorian brass right-angles to the cover's four outside corners.

When Kate woke at six he asked her to go up to the gallery and bring back the oldest volumes she could find. Using a soft watercolour brush he swept the dust from the tops of the books onto the dossier and spread it out evenly. Then he laid the book on the table. On the cover he had stamped the words in a dull gold leaf, *Librum Magnum, House of Commons Library*. And at the bottom he had printed in small capitals *SUM. FECIT – I Am. He Made This*. Or more sensibly, *Eyam Made This*.

Dawn broke. The museum stirred. The noise of cleaners and floor-polishing machines and doors being unlocked came to their ears. Kilmartin and Thomas packed up their things in the quiet of the Arched Room. The dossier was wrapped in brown paper and placed in Kilmartin's shopping bag. At eight thirty the curator of the Middle East department, an old friend of Kilmartin's, appeared, and said that someone was waiting for him at the Montagu Place entrance.

Ten minutes later a woman appeared in a raincoat. Kilmartin did not introduce her, other than saying she would be the courier.

He handed the shopping bag to her. 'You've got your pass and the letter from the House of Commons librarian?'

'Don't fuss, Peter,' she said.

'And you know what to do once you're there.'

'I am to go to Committee Room Five and I will meet this lady here, who I presume is Kate Lockhart.' She smiled.

'And if she is not there?'

'I'll wait outside the Committee Room, or in the lavatory just down the corridor.'

'Or call me on this,' said Kate, writing a number down.

'And I expect to be there too,' said Kilmartin. 'I have an appointment with Beatrice Somers.'

The woman left with the shopping bag. Then they thanked Evan Thomas for his skill and hard work and each left the haven of the Arched Room to take their chances on the streets of a capital which on that morning was decidedly not itself.

31

The Committee

Cannon pulled the pile of newspapers towards him with little appetite and shuffled the titles, glancing at each front page. All captured Eyam's descent from the highest councils in the land to criminality and paedophilia by juxtaposing an image of him emerging with the prime minister from the British Mission to the United Nations in New York with a still from the faked tourists' film from Colombia, in which he looked particularly seedy. *PM's Spy Chief in Child Porn Scandal* was typical of the headlines. But this gleeful certainty was not maintained on the inside pages. All the newspapers asked why Eyam would return to Britain to face jail when he had fooled the authorities so comprehensively. There was no mention of his illness, but one of Maclean's papers had published a diagram that linked the murder of Hugh Russell, the death of the coroner's clerk in a car accident and the unexplained CCTV footage of the men running from Hugh Russell's offices in High Castle. In the middle of the layout was a shot of Eyam's friend Kate Lockhart, taken as she was driven into High Castle Police Station. The press was asking simple, logical questions that had no obvious answers.

Cannon pushed the newspapers away. It occurred to him that an odd silence had descended in Downing Street, which now he came to think about it only affected him. There were no emails in his inbox and none of his phones had rung since he had got in at six forty-five a.m. Not one call. It was unprecedented. Even George Lyme had only mumbled a good morning before leaving the room – rather guiltily, Cannon thought – to be on hand for the breakfast meeting between Temple and the president of the European council. He phoned Gruppo but was told she was away from her desk. If he had been placed in some kind of quarantine, which now seemed certain, Kilmartin could forget any hope of his being able to delay the prime minister's departure to Buckingham Palace to announce the election.

When Lyme returned he called out, 'What's up, George?'

'The usual,' Lyme replied without looking at him.

'Oh, come on, George, I'm not an idiot: it's like I've got bubonic plague. My government cell phone has gone dead. No calls are being put through to me.'

Lyme came over to him. 'You're out of bounds; that's all I know. They think you were responsible for telling the police to release that woman from Hotel Papa yesterday. Temple's hopping mad: he's put me in charge. Someone was meant to tell you . . . I'm sorry.'

'Don't be,' said Cannon, straightening in his chair and reaching for his cup of coffee.

'Did you tell the police to release her?'

'Yes, George.'

'Are you crazy?'

'No. There are hundreds of people being detained under the emergency powers in Hotel Papa. The Civil Contingencies Act was used as a publicity gimmick and as a means of stopping Eyam, and those are not good reasons for tearing up people's constitutional rights.'

He looked up at Lyme. Ambition had overwhelmed any embarrassment Lyme might have felt. 'I am staying out of this, Philip. I don't want to know about any of your dealings with Kilmartin. Temple is on to him, you know. They think he's been part of this from the start. They know you've been speaking to each other.'

'Gruppo said that?'

He nodded.

'So, she's looking after you. Don't worry, I won't say anything about you delivering a note to Kilmartin for me.'

'Thanks.'

'Or anything about the document you gave me yesterday. But in return I want to know where Temple is in the next hour or so. I want you to tell me what's going on.'

'Dawn says he's going to leave for the palace in about two and a half hours – at ten thirty.'

'Where's he going to be until then? Tell me what he's doing after the European president.'

Lyme shrugged. 'I can find out.'

Cannon looked fondly at his deputy. 'Be careful, George: this job is shit. You may think you've hit the big time but you won't be able to trust any of them – not even your new lover. They'll make you do all their lying for them, then dump on you. By the way, has she told you what their plans are for me?'

Lyme was silent.

'Spit it out.'

'She was saying something about a formal interview to see whether you've broken the law or abused your position, that sort of thing. A full security interview.'

'Is that what they think?' he said, stretching into the air above. 'Now go off and find out where Temple is for me.'

Kilmartin met Beatrice Somers at the entrance to her flat in Great College Street and together they moved at an arthritic pace through the successive lines of police and army surrounding the Houses of Parliament. The evident lack of threat had resulted in a wary officiousness in the security forces and they were stopped several times. On the fourth or fifth occasion, Beatrice Somers tore a strip off a police sergeant who, with his thumbs hooked into a stab vest, addressed her as 'dear'.

'Officer,' she said, 'I walk this route every morning. I greatly object to you making it more difficult for me than it already is. You have a duty under the Metropolitan Police Act 1839 to keep the passage to Parliament clear for members of both Houses, not obstruct it.'

After that he stepped aside and they passed easily through the next two lines, which included plainclothes officers checking people's faces against a ring file of photographs, but when they reached the peers' entrance they had to submit to a search, which in Kilmartin's case was particularly thorough.

In Baroness Somers' room, he helped with her coat and hung it up. The old lady moved to the window and stood in a lilac suit and grey blouse, looking down at two police rigid inflatables patrolling the Thames. 'I'm sorry, Peter, this isn't going to work. The chairman won't torpedo his own party by allowing Eyam's evidence to be heard. He's a decent man but not a heroic one, or a foolish one.' She turned. 'Have you read the papers this morning?'

'Glanced at them.'

'Well, then you know that David Eyam's credibility is destroyed. The committee will not contemplate hearing a man on the run who is facing those sorts of charges. It's a matter of political reality.' She moved lamely to her desk, her dewlaps trembling as she shook her head.

Kilmartin made his next move. 'I do see what you're saying, but this was always going to be difficult. Eyam knew they'd throw everything at him because he's got such a very, very important story to tell. He's not a child molester; he's a man suffering from cancer who has been persecuted after serving the country as well as any of us.'

'Cancer,' she said. 'That wasn't mentioned in the papers.'

'Yes, he's got Hodgkin's. I'm just guessing, but he may have come back for the last throw of the dice. I repeat – he's no paedophile.'

'But you didn't tell me about it, did you? You didn't give me the full facts, Peter.' The hooded eyes waited for a response.

'No, I didn't because it isn't true.'

'That's not the point. What if I had moved heaven and earth to get him into the committee room, only for the police to announce he faced investigation for child pornography?'

'I apologise, but at the time I did not think it was important.'

'That was an error of judgement. What else are you hiding from me?'

'Nothing, I assure you.'

'Well, it makes no difference. We are dealing here with what is possible. Even if David Eyam was able to present himself at the Palace of Westminster without being arrested, our beloved prime minister is about to announce an election. And at that point we all shut up shop. Committees rise; the MPs disperse to their constituencies; the Lords take a holiday.'

'Yes,' said Kilmartin, glancing at his watch and wondering why he hadn't been able get hold of Cannon. 'I spent the night reading through it. He has put together a very strong case with incontestable documentary evidence. It is clear that Temple and Eden White have corroded public life, destroyed the polity. Temple is seven points ahead in the polls and if he gets back into power, such liberty as remains in this country will be lost. In terms of privacy and justice, this system is a real shocker. They buried it in the accounts and all the money is going to Eden White's companies. Parliament and the public have been deceived. Temple has sold the country's constitution for personal profit.'

Her eyes drifted from him. 'I do understand that you feel strongly about it, but—' She stopped. 'Is there any other way of publishing it?'

'Yes, of course it can be published but the point is that Eyam's got the original documents and he wants to place them before the committee because that's the proper place for them. This will be a coup for your committee, something people will never forget.'

'Really, Peter, I may be old but I'm not quite as daft as you take me for.' Her eyes met his again and he thought of the deep passions that had once stirred in this astonishingly brave woman. 'Is there anyone else who can speak to the committee? Can you?'

'As a matter of fact there is someone else, a woman named Kate Lockhart – she worked in Indonesia for the office until her husband died.'

'Oh?'

'She's now a lawyer in America and I gather a very good one. But she is here in Britain and is fully acquainted with this material.'

'Is she the sort of person the committee would respect?'

'Yes, she's really quite impressive,' said Kilmartin. 'A loss to the office.'

Baroness Somers of Crompton put her hands together and thought for what seemed a very long time. 'All right,' she said, rolling a pearl on her necklace between her thumb and finger. 'But no more surprises.' He nodded. 'You say she's worked as a top lawyer in the United States. I'll put her down to speak about the American handling of illegal immigrants. We're inquiring into the effects of new immigration legislation. What's her name again?'

'Kate Koh: it might be best to use that name.'

She picked up the phone and spoke first to the committee's secretary, who seemed to have no objections, then to the chairman. As she talked, Kilmartin gesticulated to say he was going to leave the room to make his own phone call. In the corridor he dialled Cannon's cell phone but got no answer. He went through the Number Ten switchboard and was told that Cannon wasn't available, and that his message box was full. A call to David Eyam's number brought no joy either, but he did reach Kate Lockhart and told her that she should be there by ten thirty, and to change her appearance as far as she was able.

'Have you heard from our friend?' he asked.

'No, I've been trying.'

'That means you're going to have to hold the fort if we get some time at the committee.'

She coughed. 'Has anything arrived?'

'Not yet.'

'I'll see you later.'

He returned to Beatrice Somers. 'The chairman will do it,' she said. 'But he will never forgive me when he discovers what she's going to talk about. She's got fifteen minutes at the start as long as the prime minister hasn't landed at the palace by that time.' Her eyes twinkled. 'And Black Rod rang back. He's been talking to the sergeant at arms – his counterpart over in the House of Commons,' she said, reminding Kilmartin of the medieval officers that ran the British Parliament. 'They are going to take up the obstruction we experienced with the police immediately and issue a statement to the BBC. These emergency powers have got up everyone's noses here, and quite right too. If you are in contact with your friend, tell her to go to Black Rod's entrance at the western end of the palace.'

'Thank you,' he said.

'At my age,' she said, 'I am mindful that each day which passes represents a greater proportion of the time that is left to me. I like to make each one count. I hope this one will count, Peter.'

Kate reached Victoria Street and walked south, pursued by threatening skies. The wind whipped down the street creating eddies of dead leaves and when Kilmartin phoned to tell her to disguise her appearance she had to take shelter in a shop door in order to hear him. As he spoke she looked down Victoria Street. At the far end of the street, police and army vehicles blocked the road, forcing the traffic left towards Buckingham Palace or the grid of streets behind Westminster Abbey.

In the last half hour she had been prey to the not irrational convictions that Eyam had been arrested, or was so ill that he could not ring her; and also to the likelihood of being recognised from her photograph in the newspapers. She reached a department store, which had just opened, entered and passed through the make-up counters and a gauntlet of saleswomen half-heartedly pushing brands of perfume. In the women's department she bought a white shirt, a grey overcoat that was much bulkier and less flattering than she would normally choose and a half-length smock. She moved about the store quickly, selecting a tortoiseshell hairgrip and aubergine-coloured woolly hat in the accessories department, and a few minutes later a soft, round cushion sold as a back support. Returning to the make-up department, she perched on a stool at one of the counters. A woman in a clinician's overall appeared at her side. Kate gave her very specific instructions while sliding a folded twenty-pound note along the counter. She wanted to be transformed and in a very short time.

Half an hour later she made for the women's lavatory in the basement. Working quickly, she tucked the cushion into the waistband of her trousers and moved the belt to hold it in place just below her breasts. Having straightened and plumped it, she put on her jacket, then the smock. Her hair had been powdered to make it lighter and less luxuriantly glossy. She pulled it back and fastened it with the grip, leaving a fringe, then stood back to study the effect. The make-up had come into its own – her cheeks looked rounder and the shading under her eyes made them seem smaller and more recessed. Finally, she shrugged on the overcoat and placed the woolly hat over the back of her head, covering her ears.

She left and crossed a side street that flanked the store and entered a pharmacy, where she made for a stand of reading glasses and settled upon a pair with a thin gold frame and minimum-strength lenses. As she entered the street again, she placed them halfway down her nose and began to peer hesitantly over the frame.

In truth, this was unnecessary. Like an actor who takes the essence of a character from a piece of clothing, with her bump Kate already occupied the role of the mousey, academic woman seven months into what might very well have been a late and unplanned pregnancy. She moved carefully along the line of stalled traffic, shortening her stride and swaying slightly. Occasionally she paused and held her prosthetic belly, which as well as giving the impression of fatigue, allowed her to make tiny adjustments to the cushion. In Great Peter Street two constables stopped her, asked her where she was going and searched her bag. She explained that she was heading for Parliament where she was due to give evidence; she was late because of the traffic and the lack of taxis, and was nervous of missing the start. All this was said in a voice that caused one of the officers to bend down to catch her words.

By ten fifteen she had reached Millbank, the road that runs along the Thames and leads into Parliament Square. Charles Barry's neo-Gothic masterpiece came into view. She had known since childhood that a Union Jack flying from the flagpole of the Victoria Tower indicated that Parliament was sitting. She peered into the sky as the first rain fell and saw the flag was still there.

Cannon often found that a crisis was best met with inactivity, or at least with something that had absolutely no relevance to the crisis, for which reason he had at nine forty a.m. taken out Aubrey's *Brief Lives* and begun to read one of his favourite lives, that of the poet and dramatist Sir William Davenant, who 'gott a terrible clap off a handsome Black Wench that lay in Axel-yard, Westminster'.

At nine fifty-five a.m. Lyme came into the room and beckoned him out to the washroom.

'When's he leaving for the palace?' asked Cannon.

'In the next hour: they're in a meeting.'

'Who?'

Lyme ignored him. 'Did you know they're able to go back over any phone call made in the last two years and listen to a recording?'

Cannon shook his head.

'Well, they can. Legislation from a few years back gives them access to all communications data and apparently those records act as an index.

If they know when and where a call was made they can retrieve the actual conversation.'

'Jesus! No, I didn't know that. But it doesn't surprise me.'

Lyme's eyes were lit with technophiliac awe. 'That means—'

'I know what that means,' interrupted Cannon. 'They've got Eyam and all Eyam's associates and they are listening to their conversations over the last day or two.'

'Yes, they're hard on the trail. But not the encrypted emails: they haven't got those yet. Naturally there's a huge amount of material to go through, but GCHQ is working very hard on it, making reports every half hour or so. Also, the conference centre is filling up at that hotel. Out of nowhere about six hundred and fifty Bell Ringers have turned up and are waiting patiently in the hall.'

'So the rest are being held in Hotel Papa?'

'I don't know – they reckon that three or four thousand people are involved. The police are waiting for Eyam and the core group, then they'll make their move.'

'Have you thought about that, George? Does it occur to you that these powers are being used to protect Temple from Eyam's charges?' He looked at him but got no response. 'You'll be required to answer for the government's actions by the end of the week, if not the end of the day. I guarantee you that. So you better think through what you're going to say. You better know what you think, too; where you stand as a person on that. Just because they can listen to people's conversations and arrest them without good reason doesn't mean they should.'

'I hear you, Philip,' he said without looking in the slightest bit admonished. 'But—'

'But nothing! Where's Temple now?'

'In his study.'

Cannon went straight there and found June Temple waiting outside. 'You can't go in,' she said brightly. 'He won't even let me in.'

Cannon moved past her and opened the door. Temple stared at him. Ferris, Shoemaker, Alec Smith and his head of policy unit Thomas Sartin turned their heads.

'Hello, Philip,' said Temple. 'What can I do for you?'

'I gather you're dispensing with my services.'

'You will appreciate that I am rather busy at the moment.' The voice was clipped, the eyes void of feeling.

'How long have I worked for you?'

'This is not the time,' said Temple. 'I'm leaving for the palace in the next five minutes.'

'Once you've rounded up Eyam and his people?'

Ferris got up. 'I think the prime minister is telling you that he's busy. You should leave, Cannon.'

'That's all right, Jamie,' said Temple smoothly.

'Just say and I'll have him removed, prime minister.'

'Like that solicitor in High Castle,' snapped Cannon, now finding that he was really quite enjoying himself. 'The one who read Eyam's dossier and was shot, presumably by the same man who broke into the lawyer's office and then – what do you know? – turns up at Chequers with you. An employee of Eden White, no doubt, like most of the people in this room.'

Ferris looked at his watch, unperturbed. 'I think we should be expecting a report any moment. Would you mind if I stepped away for a second?'

Temple nodded, but before Ferris reached the door, Cannon said: 'I wouldn't go just yet. You might want to hear this.' From inside his pocket he drew the four-page report and unfolded it. 'I don't need to read this to you because you have already got a copy, prime minister. It is from the government's chief scientific adviser, informing you that the red algae came from the government's research station at Ashmere Holt and that this was confirmed after tests over the weekend. TRA is in fact a hybrid developed in the laboratory of the station. A genetically modified organism created for God knows what by a secret programme, then released into the environment accidentally. That's the story.'

'A full inquiry has already been promised,' said Temple. 'Clearly we must take all measures to protect the public whatever the cause.'

'Prime minister, I'm the one who issues statements like that. I know the lies behind them.'

Ferris put up his hand. 'If you wouldn't mind, prime minister, I'll just find out what's happening on the other thing.'

Temple nodded and got up as though to leave.

'I would rather you hear me out, prime minister.' He stopped in his tracks and gave Cannon a deadly look. 'This report was given to you on Monday morning,' continued Cannon. 'Verbal confirmation of the findings was received by your office during the morning, and yet you went ahead and invoked the Civil Contingencies Act at noon the same day. You suspended the Constitution to stop Eyam.'

'Don't use that tone with me, Philip.'

'People are being held illegally in a car park like some South American junta. From what I gather, nobody knows what the hell they're meant to do – the conditions are insanitary, inhuman.'

'A temporary measure; the public is concerned about the water supply.'

'Water supply that the government polluted,' snapped Cannon.

By now the three others in the room were looking agitated. Alec Smith rose and placed himself between Cannon and Temple. 'This man was due to be given a security interview, prime minister. There is no reason why he shouldn't be arrested under the Official Secrets Act.'

'Don't be an idiot,' said Cannon, looking up at Alec. 'This document will be released to the press at midday unless I stop it personally. Bryant Maclean will love the story because it not only fucks you, prime minister, after you were so stupid as to threaten him, it exposes your friend Eden White.'

'Philip! Philip,' said Temple with a sudden conciliatory appeal. 'I am about to call an election in which I will be fighting for the things that *you* and I know are right – order, security, stability, steady progress on our numerous social problems. Now, if you want to talk about your future in government I'm happy to do that later today. But I am expected at the palace.'

Cannon let out a bitter laugh. 'My bridges are burned – we both know that. I have no role in government. By this afternoon Alec and Christine here will be sweating a confession out of me.' He paused. 'I'm not looking for a deal.'

Temple nodded to the other three, and allowed a smile to break surface. 'Give us a minute or two, would you?'

They left without looking at Cannon.

'Sit down for a moment, Philip.'

Cannon remained on his feet and from the corner of his vision noted the time. It was ten twenty-three a.m.

'Let's make this brief. You can resign in your own time, go to the House of Lords and head any bloody organisation you like, if that's what you want, Philip: a respectable retirement with as much or as little work as you want.'

Cannon shook his head. 'I'm not interested.'

'Then what do you want?'

'Abandon DEEP TRUTH. Close it down. Give people their privacy back.'

Temple sat on the arm of his favourite chair and leaned forward with his hands together. 'But it's an essential tool of modern government, Philip. Your request is the equivalent of demanding I drive to Buckingham Palace in a coach and four. This is twenty-first century government: we need such systems to run the country, to help people help themselves. Surveillance is part of all our lives. The gathering, processing and sharing of personal data are now an essential element in the armoury of social policy. You don't hear people complaining about it because they know it's necessary and want us to look after them, without having to bother with all the details. They want a strong and smart state, Philip, a state that is capable of taking action on the issues that really affect them – energy and food prices, disorder . . .'

'I've heard the list before, prime minister. If you were so confident about the system, why is it secret? Why have you hidden it from Parliament and the public? Why destroy those who have threatened to speak about it?'

'Eyam destroyed himself. Are you going to take the word of a paedophile over mine, Philip? Be reasonable, man. I am fighting for what is right here. You and I – we believe in this government. Let's see a way out of this.' Cannon had become aware of the faint noise around them – the murmur of political expectation, the rumination of all those who held the power together in the cockpit of the British state. Indistinct sounds reached them from outside the door and twice someone knocked and looked in, but Temple just shook his head with irritation. 'We need to resolve this now. I want to go to the country with you by my side, or at least knowing that we are not at war.'

'You just relieved me of my duties.'

'But there are ways round that. Tell me what you want.'

'I just have.'

'Within reason.'

Cannon glanced at the little silver clock on the table. It was ten thirty-five. He would keep the prime minister there for a little while yet. 'You can start by suspending the emergency powers and letting all those people go free; clearing the army and police from the streets. You can't go on using the Civil Contingencies Act to beat David Eyam.'

'Eyam is a traitor. I will use any powers any way I like to destroy a foul, dirty-minded traitor. And as for his friend Peter Kilmartin . . . well, you trust people and they take advantage. It's always the same. I'll see them suffer a little – eh? I'll make these bastards pay for their lies and treachery.' Then he did something that Cannon had only seen once before, when Temple thought he was going to lose a vote in the House of Commons. It was a spasm that he remembered started with a black look in his eyes, and quickly affected his vocal cords, which involuntarily emitted a sound of strangulation and made his mouth open and shut rapidly.

'Are you all right?'

'Yes,' said Temple, working his jaw and massaging his throat. He reached for a water bottle and drank from it with short, greedy sips, looking away. 'You know, Philip,' he said conversationally, just as Cannon was beginning to wonder if Temple was losing his mind. 'We should sort this out now.' He picked up the phone and said, 'Change the appointment to eleven. Make my apologies; say there's a lot on.' He replaced the receiver. 'We've got ten minutes.'

Now Temple was also playing for time, and that suited Cannon.

The downpour came as Kate reached the Sovereign's Entrance and was redirected to a temporary security cabin at the other end of Old Palace Yard, which had been erected because of flooding in the usual checkpoint. Police and soldiers stood about aimlessly hoping for something to happen. What did they expect? Attacks from people carrying phials of water containing toxic red algae? She pleaded that she had no umbrella and added that her name was on the door, but the guard shook his head and said it was more than his job was worth to let her in without checks and a search of her belongings; even in normal times it was out of the question. Then he fetched an umbrella from inside the peers' entrance and escorted her to the cabin. She kept her head bent down but her eyes moved restlessly ahead, absorbing the fact that Parliament Square had not been completely closed to traffic, and that pedestrians were still being allowed through, although most were being stopped.

By the time she reached the queue of a dozen people it was evident to her escort that she needed to sit down and when he had pushed to the head of the queue he found her a plastic chair. She gave her name as Koh and smiled shyly at the policeman as he flipped through an extensive file of photographs, glancing up at her face. Someone else checked her name against the list of those expected and she was handed a pass. She stood up and was asked to place her two index fingers on a fingerprint reader and stare into an iris scanner, which she did with equanimity, knowing that none of her biometric details were on record. She explained that she did not have an ID card because she had recently moved from America and no one seemed to care. There was a good deal of haste and tempers were frayed in the hot, humid conditions of the security hut.

Her bag was fed through the scanner, and she moved unsteadily towards the horseshoe metal detector. On the other side there was a camera fixed at eye-level and two security guards wearing latex gloves were running their hands over visitors. Both had patches of damp under their arms. Kate stepped through the metal detector and held her arms out for the female guard but did not undo her coat. The guard said she must go back and put it through the machine. At that moment Kilmartin's phone went off in her bag. 'Sorry, they're expecting me in Committee Room Five,' she said and she explained about the lack of taxis; that her pregnancy had not been an easy one; she'd left home without the papers she needed; and Lord, what was she going to do about her hair? All this was delivered in a breathless, academic clip while she removed her coat. She went back through the metal detector and laid it in one of the large plastic trays. As the conveyor belt took it through the scanner, she looked around and with a start noticed

Kilmartin's courier move to the second scanner and carefully place the shopping bag containing the bound volume in a tray.

Kate passed through the metal detector for the third time and raised her arms. With some irritation the security guard glanced at her then looked over her shoulder to the press of people escaping the rain, which was now beating down on the roof. She began to feel along her sleeves but suddenly seemed to lose patience and simply waved her through. Kate picked up her coat and bag and moved to the door. The courier had been frisked and now stood immaculately composed in front of the guard by the scanner, who was examining the book. 'You may check the book, but you may not read it,' she said firmly and proffered a letter on House of Commons notepaper, but the guard ignored it and handed it to a plainclothes policeman, who looked through its pages then skimmed the letter. That was all Kate saw because someone opened the door and gestured her out. Struggling into her coat she went down the wheelchair ramp and headed for St Stephen's entrance thirty feet away.

Two policemen with automatic weapons stood on the steps of the entrance, sheltering from the rain. She passed between them, then turned to follow their gaze across the street to a small group of people who, despite the security, had managed to assemble on the other side of the road beneath the Henry VII Chapel of Westminster Abbey. Slightly detached from the group was a tall figure in a dark-green anorak. His hood was up but she was almost certain that this was Sean Nock and beside him was her mother and a very large figure whose face was obscured by an umbrella. At least that had gone to plan.

At that moment an ambulance, with lights flashing but no siren on, drifted to a halt on the westbound lane of St Margaret's Street and blocked her view. A policeman approached the driver's window and the ambulance lingered. She had to be sure it was Nock so she made some show of arranging her coat, at the same time aware of the churning in her stomach and the unusual dryness in her mouth. Telling Nock to come had admittedly been a risk, which was why she hadn't consulted Eyam or Kilmartin, yet she was sure not just of his attraction to her but also of Nock's troubled decency. The ambulance was waved on and moved towards an opening on the black metal barrier that separated Old Palace Yard from the traffic, and she looked once more at the group, but didn't see him again. She turned and climbed the remainder of the steps to the gothic doorway, where another policeman gave her directions to Central Lobby.

There were no cameras; no one was watching. She walked the length of St Stephen's Hall, quickly removing the reading glasses and the woolly hat, then unfastening the grip and shaking out her hair. Passing through the Central Lobby – the intersection of the two main axes of Barry's masterly hybrid of religious and secular architecture – she turned once to see if the woman with Eyam's book was following, but saw no one. The screens in the lobby told her that a debate on Britain's fish stocks was in progress in the Chamber of the House of Commons and that the Joint Committee on Human Rights was already in session.

But there was little sign of activity in the wide, tiled Victorian thoroughfares. A feeling of evacuation, or maybe obsolescence, pervaded and for a second she was struck by the hopelessness of bringing Eyam's bits of paper to the site of the near-extinct cult of democracy. They might as well be lighting candles in a Tibetan monastery for all that the world outside cared. But outside there were real threats that seemed all the closer now she approached her destination.

She went through some swing doors and reached a desk where an usher directed her to the first door in the corridor on her right. A little beyond the committee room was a lavatory, which Kate entered. She tore off the coat and maternity smock, stuffed the back support into a flip-top bin, then removed the make-up with some moistened wipes and splashed her face with cold water. Having run a comb through her hair and straightened her jacket and shirt, she checked herself in the mirror and returned to the procedural calm of the corridor. A murmur of voices came from inside Committee Room Five. She cracked open the door and felt a tug from inside. An usher's face appeared with a finger to his lips. He pointed to a place in the public benches. She sat down, closed her eyes and inhaled deeply, willing her heart to stop pounding and her head to clear.

She looked up. The panelled room was large, with a high ceiling and several chandeliers that were switched on because the storm meant that little daylight came through the windows on her left. The fourteen members of the committee sat on three sides of a square with the chairman, a thin-faced man in his mid-forties called Nick Redpath, and the committee staff occupying most of the middle. In front of them were a table and three chairs from which witnesses gave evidence. At the moment there was just one – a woman in a vivid orange top was answering a question on something that she had just read out.

All Kate's misgivings came to the fore. She had abandoned any idea of seeing Eyam in Committee Room Five, and without the documents it would be impossible to claim the committee's ear before the election was called. The committee itself seemed hardly the liveliest of bodies: the atmosphere in the room was inert, and it was clear that things were slowly grinding to a halt. The MPs wanted to be away to the constituencies and the peers were resigned to their enforced holiday. But for the bird-like energy of the chairman, who pecked at the evidence, invited observations and generally tried to keep everyone on their toes, the hearing might simply have expired. From the remarks offered from different sides Kate tried to gauge those who might be her opponents when she came to speak. She noticed an elderly woman studying her hard with animated, shrewd eyes. Kate craned her head to see *Baroness Somers* printed on a nameplate. The woman wagged a finger at a clerk, spoke to him and handed him a note, while gesturing in Kate's direction. 'Lady Somers wants to know if you are Miss Koh,' he said when he arrived at her side.

She read the note. '*Indicate when you want to be called if we are still going ahead. Where's PK?*' Kate looked up and opened her hands in answer to the question about Kilmartin, but gave Somers an encouraging nod nevertheless.

The chairman saw all this and put a crooked finger in the parting of his hair where it remained for a few seconds while he considered his notes. He looked up at the witness. 'Well, I think we have learned a great deal this morning from you, Ms Spicer, and I thank you for giving us the benefit of your knowledge.' As the witness rose, his gaze moved to his right. 'Lady Somers, I understand you are anxious for the committee to hear evidence on this subject from a Miss Koh, which you say is compelling. Is that correct?' The committee members began to mutter amongst themselves and look with puzzlement at their papers.

'Indeed,' she said slowly. 'I want to make a few remarks before we hear Ms Koh. Firstly, Mr Chairman, I thank you for your kindness and your trust. Over the course of the next hour or so you may have cause to regret both.' She paused and looked at the faces round her, then she began to speak, by turns warning, beseeching, craving indulgence and playing to every conceivable vanity in the room until the point was reached when, seemingly at the end of her personal supply of oxygen, with her head sinking to her chest and her voice dwindling to a whisper, she reminded the committee that in these last moments as it was presently constituted it possessed a solemn obligation to the name, Joint Committee on Human Rights. 'The JCHR is where the two Houses of this Parliament meet: we are joined in the defence of democracy. I would ask members to stay your hand, reserve judgement and listen as never before.' Then she looked straight at Kate and gave a nod. Kate rose and walked to the witness table, leaving behind the dread and panic that she'd felt in the last few minutes. She sat down, folded her hands on the table and leapt into the void.

Ten minutes before, another speech had come to an end in Downing Street. The prime minister had talked without drawing breath about his vision and the merits of his government – the project, as he called it, to inaugurate an age of firm and fair government, where rights are a privilege accorded only in return for manifestations of responsibility. Cannon had heard it all before; indeed many of the phrases came from his own pen, though now it all seemed rather sinister. From the corner of his eye, he watched the hands of the clock moving gradually from ten thirty-five to ten forty. It was like holding his breath underwater. Then, exactly tweny minutes after Temple had launched into his homily, he allowed his eyes to drift from Cannon to the door, which opened without a knock. Dawn Gruppo came in and said that Buckingham Palace were postponing for half an hour. 'They're telling you who's boss,' she remarked.

'Quite right,' said Temple, slapping his knees lightly, 'a little more time is just what we need, Philip.'

But the operation to delay Cannon and keep the document about TRA in the room was over. Smith came through the open door with two men. One said to Cannon, 'We'd like you to come with us, sir.'

Cannon snorted a laugh and turned to Temple, shaking his head. 'Special Branch? You surely can't be serious, prime minister.'

But Temple had done his usual trick of removing himself from what was happening and was now skimming a paper just handed to him by Gruppo.

'The computer has been secured, prime minister,' said Smith. 'Nothing has been sent from it or Mr Cannon's telephone in the last forty-five minutes. We presume that he only has the hard copy because there is no trace of it on his home computer, which has been accessed remotely. There have been no outgoing calls from his home in that time either, or from his wife's mobile.'

Temple nodded, then the Special Branch officer who had spoken moved to where Cannon was sitting. 'We believe that you have in your possession certain classified documents that you plan to make public. This would be a breach of the Official Secrets Act. We also have reason to suspect that you were instrumental in the unlawful release of a woman held under the Civil Contingencies Act 2004.'

Cannon drew the document from his inside pocket and flourished it. 'By all means have it – the more people who read it the better.' He clambered to his feet and handed it to the officer, then looked at his watch. 'A copy left the building by messenger an hour and a quarter ago, after I discovered that you'd blocked my phone. I imagine George Lyme is already answering questions on it.'

Temple's eyes flashed at Gruppo. 'Get Bryant Maclean on the phone: I want to speak to him personally.' His gaze levelled at Cannon and he was about to say something when Jamie Ferris stormed into the room. 'We've just started tracing two phones that we are now certain are being used by Peter Kilmartin and Kate Lockhart. Both are now switched off, but it is clear from the conversations over the last week that these two are at the centre of this conspiracy. We know they spent last night in the British Museum and understand that a number of packages were delivered to them during the night.'

'In the British Museum?' said Temple stupidly.

'Kilmartin has contacts there.'

'Where's Eyam?'

'We don't know. Possibly with them. The phone we were monitoring is turned off also. Still, we now have a complete picture of all the people involved in the core group.'

'What about the hotel conference centre?'

Ferris look perplexed. 'The meeting began at nine thirty but the strange thing is that they're actually talking about bell ringing. They're listening to recordings and attending workshops. We can't arrest hundreds of campanologists.'

Cannon smiled. Why didn't they get it? Why didn't they realise that Parliament had been Eyam's target all along? He still didn't give Kilmartin and Eyam much chance: Parliament would be all but useless to them once Temple had made his short journey up the Mall. Everything depended on what Temple decided to do in the next five minutes – leave for Buckingham Palace immediately or remain in Number Ten and try to sweet-talk Bryant Maclean into suppressing, or at any rate delaying, the two facts that TRA had come from a government laboratory and that the Civil Contingencies Act had been invoked unnecessarily. In the envelope sent to Maclean's man, Cannon had included a few lines about those detained at Hotel Papa under the act.

There was only one logical choice for Temple. A few days ago Cannon would have unhesitatingly guided him to the right decision, but he was disinclined to help just now because he was being steered from the room by one of Alec Smith's heavies. This time Temple would have to work it out for himself.

The skies had become even blacker outside Parliament and more light was required for the two automatic cameras that filmed the proceedings from above the chairman's head and from the back of Committee Room Five. A technician switched on lamps either side of the cameras. A small red light on the camera in front told her that she was being filmed and that anyone who was looking for her needed only to glance at one of the many screens in the building.

As she gathered her thoughts a few people left from the public benches behind her, and the lone journalist at the press table by the window closed a notepad and slid from his chair.

'I thank the committee for allowing me to give evidence,' she said. 'I want to start with a story. In every case I've ever handled as a lawyer in

New York, there was always a story at its heart. However complicated or technical the issues appeared to be, the story was always about human nature, whether ambition, envy, lust for power, love of money or straightforward frailty. My story today contains many of these traits. It is about a civil servant who occupied some of the highest posts in government and was the trusted confidante of the prime minister.' She stopped and looked around. 'All those who knew or worked with this man prized his advice and penetrating intelligence. His career was brilliant; he was young and personable and had everything to look forward to. Then he learned about a secret programme known only to a few, which his conscience told him was an offence against the country's traditions of liberty. Risking everything, he answered questions on this programme in a parliamentary committee very much like this one.'

She spoke clearly and simply. Her gaze swept the room, trying to engage the members of the committee, but was met mostly with blank stares. One or two were beginning to get restless. An MP named Jeff Turnbull leaned back in his chair with a liverish expression and asked, 'Mr Chairman, why are we wasting valuable time listening to a story?'

'Well, I am happy to listen to Ms Koh's story,' said a man with raffish sideburns and a bow tie who sat behind the nameplate for the Earl of Martingale. 'But I *would* like to know what this secret is.'

She smiled at him but did not lose the seriousness in her voice. 'This civil servant gave evidence about a system known as SPINDRIFT or DEEP TRUTH, which secretly monitors everyone in the country and is responsible for untold errors, persecution, punishment and political control. That was his secret.' Now it was out she had to put as much on record as possible and she sped through Eyam's case – the origins of the system, its covert installation and ever-extending reach, the use of census records and social networking sites, its reliance on phone, ID card and travel databases and finally the hidden payments to Eden White's company. Each point moved effortlessly to the next, each stage in the summary that had just magically crystallised in her mind was now emphasised by precise brush strokes made by her forefinger and thumb.

It took no more than a few minutes to transform the proceedings of Committee Room Five. The room was electrified. Some members of the committee were almost levitating with indignation. Others looked aghast. And behind her she heard the room filling with those who had caught what she said on the monitors around Parliament.

'Can we have some quiet, please,' said the chairman. 'Ms Koh, I think I am conveying the views of this committee if I say that the allegations you are making have nothing to do with the matter in hand, and are an abuse of parliamentary privilege.'

'Where's your evidence?' demanded Turnbull.

'Who sent you?' shouted another member.

Kate looked at Lady Somers as someone called for her to be dismissed. The old lady winked at her and made a little sweeping gesture with her hand, as if discreetly encouraging a child on sports day.

'No,' Kate said.

'What do you mean – no?' asked the chairman.

'No, I will not be dismissed.'

'That is not up to you,' replied the chairman. 'You have one last chance to substantiate and make relevant your testimony.'

'This is not my last chance; it is yours. A general election is about to be called to stop this evidence being heard. We have every reason to believe that the emergency powers brought in on Monday were an attempt to stifle what I and others have to say.'

'Now I know I'm in a madhouse,' expostulated Turnbull. 'These are just paranoid fantasies about a police state. What next?'

'You may well ask what is next,' she said calmly. 'We don't live in a police state but it is coming and you, sir, are one of the very few people who can stop it.'

At this Turnbull got up and said he was leaving. Two others also left their chairs, a woman who had said nothing and a young government apparatchik who wore a badge in his buttonhole. Kate sat back and waited for the tumult to die down. She heard a voice behind her and turned to find Kilmartin bending down. 'Here's your evidence,' he said, putting the book in her hands. 'And Carrie's got the library to make photocopies of the main documents. Should be enough to go round. There's more coming.' He put the stack of paper on the chair beside her.

'Where's Eyam?' she hissed. 'Is he coming?'

'I don't know. Keep going – you're doing brilliantly. If you get this accepted by the committee, we're halfway there.'

At that moment she saw Darsh Darshan come through the door with a black shoulder bag and gradually work his way forward, but there was no time to wonder what he was doing there or whether he had come with Eyam. She placed the book squarely in front of her. 'I want to present this to the committee. It contains all the evidence to support what I have been saying.'

'We can't accept that,' said Turnbull, who had had second thoughts and was now returning to his place.

'Why doesn't the Honourable Member hear the lady out,' said Lord Martingale with sudden steel in his voice. 'I want to know the identity of the individual you have spoken of.'

'His name is David Eyam,' she said.

A murmur of shock ran round the room.

'The David Eyam who faked his own death and is being sought by police on numerous criminal matters?' said Redpath incredulously. 'Do you realise the gravity of your insult to Parliament, to this committee?' He shot a look at Beatrice Somers.

'I understand your reaction,' said Kate, 'because I experienced much the same incredulity.' She picked up the book and the photocopies. 'People have risked their lives to bring these to you. Two were killed on Sunday night. David Eyam lost his career and his health to put the documents bound in this book in your hands. Look at them before you turn me away. Read it before you dismiss us as fantasists.' She got up, walked over to Redpath and laid the book in front of him.

Redpath turned to Lady Somers. 'Did you know about this?'

'I confess that I had some inkling of the allegations,' she replied. 'The matters seemed so serious to me that I felt it was imperative Miss Koh was given a hearing.'

'But Eyam's a bloody paedophile,' said Turnbull, causing the stenographer to look up.

'How do you know that?' asked Kate, placing the five piles of photocopies, each separated by an orange marker, at strategic points along the tables. 'Because you were told by the government?'

'No, by the police,' said Turnbull. 'Why else would he have faked his death?'

'You may care to wonder why he returned,' she said sharply.

'To cause trouble, as you are doing now.'

'No,' she said with utter command. 'He came back to expose a corrupt cabal at the top of government.'

'That seems a little presumptuous,' said a neat man with silver hair to her right.

'Will you please go through the chair before making comments,' Redpath snapped. 'And will the people who have just come in find a place or leave.' There were now eight or nine journalists squashed into the press bench trying to work out what was going on. 'Silence,' said Redpath, looking in their direction and then turned to two men who had arrived behind his chair. One bent down, placed his hand on the table and whispered urgently.

Kilmartin's voice was in Kate's ear. 'They're trying to pull the plug on you. I think they're government whips.'

Redpath nodded and the two men moved back. 'I am given to understand that the prime minister is on his way to Buckingham Palace to request a dissolution of Parliament. A general election is to be called, which means that this sitting of JCHR is effectively at an end. It must be obvious to you that we cannot accept this evidence, Miss Koh.' He began gathering his papers together, flashing angry looks at Beatrice Somers, which evidently cut no ice.

But it was the Earl of Martingale who spoke. 'May I suggest, Chairman, that we've already accepted this material as evidence and that it is therefore privileged and has the protection of Parliament.'

'Privilege is always qualified by the need for responsibility,' said Redpath without looking up.

'We have all been looking at these papers.' Martingale waved a hand. It was true. The book was being handed around the committee and members were feeling the paper and examining signatures, then reading copies of the documents in front of them. 'That means evidence has been accepted by the committee. This may be reported in the press like any other proceeding in the Houses of Parliament.'

There was silence. Redpath didn't know what to do. The two men that had just approached him were plainly desperate that he gave no ruling and were now all but dragging him from the room. But then his patience suddenly gave out. 'Take your hands off me and show respect to this committee.' He turned to the room. 'Does anyone know if the election has been called?'

To a man and woman the journalists consulted their smart phones, then shook their heads. 'Not yet,' said one. 'But there's a story running that the red algae leaked from a government laboratory.'

'That does not concern us,' said Redpath. 'I'm interested only in bringing these proceedings to an orderly close without interference from anyone – even the government.' He could have ended everything by formally wrapping things up then and leaving the room, but something kept him there and he sat for a few seconds oblivious of the cameras, his committee and Kate, a finger perched in the parting of his hair.

Cannon shook himself free of the man who gripped his arm, turned on Alec Smith with a ferocity that he hardly knew was in him and informed Smith that he would submit to any kind of interview they chose to give him, but if there was an attempt to charge him or harm his reputation he would be forced to release information that would destroy the prime minister. This threat was delivered immediately outside the prime minister's sitting room. Gruppo and Ferris heard him. She came out, leaving Temple talking to Bryant Maclean. Cannon turned to her. 'This is how it's going to be, Dawn. I will clear my desk over the next hour and say goodbye to the staff in the Communications Department. Then I will go home, where I will remain unmolested by you or anyone else. At some stage I will take myself to the Scottish Borders for a fishing holiday. Until that time you will be able to reach me on my landline.' Then he leaned into her face and said, 'Screw with me, Dawn, and I will take you down too.'

He went back to his desk and slowly got his things together. There were a few members of his staff around, waiting for the election to be called. They were embarrassed but he reassured them that this was entirely what he wanted. With George Lyme they would be in good hands.

It was some time after eleven that Lyme burst in and switched the TV to a feed from Westminster. 'The Whips Office has been on. Eyam's woman is in the bloody House giving evidence to the bastard Human Rights Committee. She's just presented a whole lot of documents to them. God knows what's in them. They're going to have them arrested.'

'They can't,' said Cannon, admiring the composure of Kate Lockhart on the screen and noticing Peter Kilmartin's head bobbing behind her. 'You ought to know that, George. Parliament polices its own affairs and unless she is held to be in contempt or offends some arcane tradition, the police will have to wait until she leaves the premises. It all depends on the chairman. He can ask the sergeant at arms to eject her, but otherwise they are going to have to wait.'

'That's not what Temple thinks. Armed police are on their way now. They'll put an end to it.'

'Maybe,' he said softly. 'Where's Temple?'

'About to leave. He's talking to the Whips Office now.'

Cannon took the remote from Lyme, wheeled his chair in front of the screen, turned up the volume and flipped through the news channels. Two were already running the live feed from the committee room. 'This should be interesting,' he said to himself.

In those brief agonised seconds, Redpath had created a vacuum and into this came a voice from the back of the room. 'Before you go you might want to hear how I tampered with David Eyam's computer, and was made to do this by the Security Service.' Kate had almost forgotten about Sean Nock. She turned to see first John Turvey, who had been persuaded by her mother to act for Nock, next to him her mother looking erect and immaculate, and finally in the far corner of the room by the window Sean Nock. He stood and held up an envelope. 'I am David Eyam's neighbour,' continued Nock, 'and I used to help him out. Then they got to me. Threatened me with jail on a charge of growing and supplying cannabis. That's how they made me put child pornography on his computer.'

'This is not a public meeting,' said Redpath. 'Sit down.'

'I'm not sitting down until I have given you this sworn statement. Sworn in front of Mr Turvey yesterday.'

'The celebrated John Turvey is *your* lawyer?' said Redpath with some astonishment. 'One wonders how you afford him.'

'Mr Nock is indeed my client,' thundered Turvey from the benches. 'And I believe what he has to say is important – important enough for me as his legal representative to advise him that he may be in a position to bring an action against the authorities.'

'That is of no concern to us,' snapped Redpath.

Meanwhile Nock had pushed past the journalists who had peeled off from their bench to find out his name and moved to a spot in front of Redpath. He stood tall and rustic and despite his admission he somehow seemed unimpeachable. 'This is my confession,' he said, dropping the envelope on the table. 'It has been witnessed and is an exact account of how I was instructed to incriminate David Eyam.' He turned round, looking flushed and awkward. 'You should listen to this woman. I know she speaks the truth. David Eyam is a good man and I want to apologise to him now, wherever he is.'

'Accepted,' came a voice from near the door before Redpath had time to react to Nock.

Kate whipped round. Eyam was standing with Aristotle Miff. He wore heavy horn-rimmed spectacles and was dressed in a lightweight navy-blue suit, white shirt and knitted black tie. He removed the glasses. 'I wonder if I can join Miss Lockhart at the table. There are a few things I have to say. I am afraid I have to rely on my friend Aristotle here to get me there.' Miff, also dressed immaculately, held out his arm and they set off.

'You are David Eyam,' said Redpath, clutching his brow. 'The police are looking for you. How did you get in here?'

'In a private ambulance, sir,' he replied. 'The same way I will leave, because I am technically on my way to hospital.'

He sat down with difficulty. Turning his attention to the stunned members of the committee, he whispered to Kate from the corner of his mouth: 'You were wonderful.'

Several things were happening. Half the press bench emptied and the journalists pushed their way to the door. Behind Kate and Eyam people stood to get a better view and were being told by the doorkeepers to sit down. Two technicians arrived to operate the cameras manually.

'This man should be in the custody of the police,' said Turnbull, 'not addressing a parliamentary committee. He and his doxy must be handed over to the police.'

Redpath turned to him. 'If there is one person likely to be expelled for contempt it is you. I am running this committee and will not tolerate that sort of intervention. And please watch your language.' He paused. 'Mr Eyam, are the police currently searching for you?'

'Yes, but I have done nothing wrong.'

'Have you engaged in paedophile activities?'

Eyam shook his head. 'No.'

'You have evidently made some considerable effort to be here,' said Redpath. 'I will consult the committee to see if they're willing to listen to what you have to say.' After his moment of doubt Redpath had now got a grip. Kate couldn't tell whether he was influenced by principle or the straightforward realisation that this was a sensational news event and the public were unlikely to thank him if he stopped the proceedings. 'I will ask for a show of hands. I don't want you to speak to any kind of motion. Just tell me whether you want to hear what Mr Eyam has to say. Those against hearing Mr Eyam?'

There was a moment of hesitation, then six hands went up.

'Those for?'

Another six hands were raised, including those of Martingale and Somers.

'We have a tie with one abstention,' he said. 'Mr Eyam's appearance here is certainly unusual and inconvenient but I'm persuaded that an issue has been raised that should be aired, even though little time remains in the life of this committee. I cast my vote to hear him . . . Mr Eyam, please continue.'

The two whips looked aghast. Eyam cleared his throat. 'Thank you; I am grateful to you.' There was a silence. He glanced down with a strange internalised look then raised his eyes. 'You have seen what's happened over the last two days – the army and police deployed by emergency powers against a threat that was apparently caused by lax procedures in government laboratories. Now we all know what a military coup looks like. Over the last few years, there has been another sort of coup – a coup by stealth, which very few people realised was underway. It began several years ago when the public was persuaded to give up its privacy in exchange for benefits promised by the state. I was part of the process and I saw it happening from the inside, though I have to confess that I didn't foresee that it would end with a system that saps the life and independence of every adult in the country. I did not see that when they talked about knowing a 'deep truth' about every citizen they meant exercising total control. That was stupid. So the first part of what I have to say is to take some responsibility, and to that end I offer another piece of paper to the committee.' He turned to Miff who handed him a file, and removed a single sheet. 'I won't go into detail now, but you will see this is a memorandum from me to the prime minister, which contains remarks by him and Eden White, both of which are signed.' He gave it back to Miff, who took it to the chairman. 'I believe this memo was the start of it all, though I have to confess that I completely forgot about the exchange.'

'Chairman, he is simply describing a data-sharing operation,' said Turnbull. 'There's nothing new in that.'

'I hope to show you otherwise, Mr Turnbull,' said Eyam calmly.

'Can you tell us how you discovered that the system had been introduced?' asked Beatrice Somers, with a nod to Redpath.

'When I took over the Joint Intelligence Committee after Sir Christopher Holmes' death in a fire – about which you have certain documents – I learned of a Secret Intelligence Service report that suggested a super surveillance system in Britain was being accessed by a foreign power – Russia. This piece of raw intelligence was suppressed at the time, but Christopher Holmes pursued it and realised that it had implications not just for everyone's privacy but the country's security. He died in suspicious circumstances before he could make it public. I believe that the current head of the JIC, Andrew Fortune, was responsible for taking steps to cover up both the security lapse and the existence of DEEP TRUTH.' He paused. Kate saw him swallow hard. It was as if something was caught in his throat. She reached for the water jug and poured him a glass.

'These are very serious allegations,' said Redpath.

'All of them are confirmed by these documents. You will find a memorandum signed by Sir Christopher which explains the security lapse,' he said between sips. 'Naturally the government could not admit to the breach without admitting to an invasive system that had been introduced without Parliament's permission.'

'What evidence do you have of the breach?' asked Beatrice Somers.

'I will come onto that in a little while, if I may.'

'Well, you better get on with it,' she said testily.

'Yes. First some facts and figures: SPINDRIFT was Christopher Holmes' name for the system. Informally it was known by the name given to the product of the system – DEEP TRUTH. The last figure puts the cost to the taxpayer at twelve point five billion pounds, but that is probably out of date. The system, which sits silently in every national and local government database collecting data and prompting action, assesses its own performance by recording the number of actions it has initiated against members of the public. Two years ago there were nine hundred and eighty-nine actions. That is nearly a million people who were subject to automatic persecution. Apart from being vindictive, DEEP TRUTH, or 455729328, the rather simple code used by John Temple and Eden White, is also incompetent. It frequently makes blunders with misidentifications and draws wildly erroneous conclusions about innocent people's behaviour. Each one of you on this committee has a file. Every phone call you make, every car journey, every holiday you take, most of your expenditure, every time you visit hospital, show your ID card, draw some money from your bank account, change job, check into a hotel, the system notes the transaction and decides whether your behaviour is somehow a threat to the state.'

'This is nonsense,' said the young apparatchik. 'You can't say these things without proof.'

'You want proof – certainly, sir.' He turned round to the public benches. 'This is Darsh Darshan. He is the Simms Professor of Mathematics at the University of Oxford. With your permission, he will now show the system to the committee and in doing so demonstrate that its defences can be breached quite easily.'

Darsh got up, took five laptops from the bag and laid them on the witness table. Each one was already switched on and connected to the internet. With Miff's help he distributed four of the laptops around the committee, leaving one in front of Eyam. Then he stood aside, gloved hands pressed together.

'These computers are linked to a powerful mainframe through the web for the next couple of hours,' said Eyam. 'I will not give out the web address because clearly we don't want members of the general public looking each other up. Now, if you care to type your own names, post code, car registration number, insurance number or mobile phone number into the field at the top you will be able to see the extent to which DEEP TRUTH monitors you.'

'I have nothing to hide,' said Turnbull.

'Fine,' said Eyam almost gleefully. Kate leaned over and saw him type *Jeff Turnbull MP*. Then after a few seconds scanning the file he said, 'Mr Turnbull, it seems that two weeks ago you checked into a hotel in Scarborough. The system notes that you made five calls from your room, two to another room occupied by Tracy Mann. DEEP TRUTH suggests that you probably travelled to Scarborough together because there is no record of Ms Mann's car on the road leading to the town and she did not buy a rail ticket. I could go on about your tax and expenditure, which the system has flagged up, your divorced daughter and her children's records in school, also marked for some kind of action which it seems was automatically overruled because of your position but—'

'You've got no right,' cut in Turnbull. 'This is my private life.'

'Exactly – I have no right and nor does anyone else. It's your life,' said Eyam.

The other committee members seemed similarly appalled, but one looked up and said, 'What you are doing here is illegal.'

'How can that be?' Eyam shot back. 'The government has repeatedly denied its existence and Parliament has never been allowed to debate the cost, let alone the principle of DEEP TRUTH. If it does not exist, as they tell us, it follows that it cannot be protected by law.'

During this exchange a woman had come in through the second door and was speaking to Redpath. He nodded, then made an announcement. 'Parliament is dissolved and the general election is called. It brings to an end this sitting of the Joint Committee of Human Rights. Mr Eyam, I think you have made your point.'

Eyam accepted that it was over and thanked Redpath and his committee. Yet no one seemed anxious to leave and then Martingale asked Eyam a question. 'We've risen,' boomed Redpath, as though Martingale was senile. 'This Parliament is at an end. The television cameras are being switched off. You cannot continue to examine this witness. It is illegal.'

'It may be irregular but it is not illegal,' retorted Martingale.

On the word illegal the door near Redpath opened and two plainclothes police officers followed by three armed uniformed police came into the committee room and seemingly moved to secure the room. One of the plainclothes officers made his way along the side of the committee table towards the witness table, but before he could reach Eyam he was confronted by a man who seemed to have been projected into the compressed tumult of Committee Room Five from at least two centuries before, a formal courtly figure wearing a chain, some kind of order on his breast, breeches, black silk stockings and patent pumps. He carried a short ebony stick topped by a gold knob.

It was this that fell forward and poked the policeman in the chest.

'Stand aside, sir,' said the officer.

The man's response was as archaic as his uniform. 'I am the Gentleman Usher of the Black Rod and I supervise the administration of the House of Lords. I am the *law* in this place. You shall not pass.'

'Please move, sir. This individual is wanted on serious criminal charges.'

Kate was suddenly aware of John Turvey, rising from the benches behind her like Rodin's statue of Balzac. 'You cannot do this,' he growled with such sonorous authority that one or two committee members seemed to jump.

'And what business is it of yours?' said the policeman, now looking slightly less confident. 'What authority do you have?'

'This man is my client,' he said. Hearing what was evidently news to him, Eyam permitted himself a brief smile.

'He has no authority here,' said Redpath. 'The only person who has now is Black Rod and he has asked you to leave Parliament. The TV cameras are still on. Millions are watching what will happen now, officer. Please go.' At this a little cheer went up from a dozen MPs who had gathered at the back of the room and in the corridor running alongside the committee room.

'That is the voice of our democracy,' said Redpath. 'You disrespect this place at your peril. Now take your officers and leave these precincts.' The police seemed confounded. Then the officer nodded and they began to withdraw. Redpath waited until the door had closed after them. 'Now, Mr Eyam, you were saying . . .'

They were there for another two hours, during which Kate was beckoned outside by Kilmartin: he was standing a little way off with his hand clamped over his mobile. 'It's Mary MacCullum,' he said. 'She's with her sister, Alice. They are in hiding and talking to a newspaper. Alice wants to speak to you.'

Kate looked at him doubtfully and took the phone. 'Yes, Alice.'

'I know you think I told them which car Chris Mooney and Tony Swift were travelling in,' she said. 'But it wasn't me.'

'Who did?'

'Chris Mooney: I've just spoken to his wife. He admitted to her on Saturday evening that he had agreed to tell the Security Service where he was. He said that he had to go along with everything because they had threatened him with ruin. He as good as told us about it the other night in the pub, remember? In the church he was making every excuse not to go. That's because he wanted Tony to let him off the hook by dropping him.'

'So why did he go?'

'God knows. His wife, Maureen, says that he thought he could get the file to London as well as tell them which car Tony Swift was driving. He was trying to play both sides. She said he wasn't thinking straight. He was mad with worry.'

'So you weren't an informer?'

'I'm not saying that,' said Alice quietly. 'I gave them everything I needed to in order to keep Mary from being arrested again. I cut a few corners and made up a few stories. Tell David that. Tell him I had to hold them off until I reached Mary and we could go into hiding together. We had a plan, see.'

'And now you're talking to a newspaper?'

'Yes.'

'Tell them everything, Alice. I mean *everything*. Tell them how this happened in England. Tell them that even after making a deal with Chris they killed him because they had to eliminate Tony Swift.'

'I will,' she said and rang off.

Kate went back with Kilmartin into the committee room. More space had been made for journalists who had long ceased to care about the niceties of parliamentary privilege. Two of the committee had left but ten remained, and were taking turns to question Eyam on the documents in front of them. As the minutes wore on, it became clear that there was something compelling and historic about the events in Committee Room Five. Eventually it was Eyam who decided that enough had been said.

Several times Kate had seen him catch himself and stop speaking. She knew from watching Charlie that it was the pain surging through him. She whispered, 'You've done what you had to do. You can stop now.'

He squeezed her hand and continued to talk but with a low, strained urgency and in short sentences, as though each word was costing him dearly. Half an hour later he suddenly stood up, looked around the room, attempted to thank everyone and collapsed into her arms. Miff and Kilmartin jumped up. But Kate took his weight, which now seemed so slight, and helped him from the room and down the corridor in the direction of the House of Lords Entrance. 'Carry me over floods, Sister,' he said as they went.

On their way they passed a TV set. Silent footage was being played of John Temple returning from Buckingham Palace and giving a press conference in Downing Street. Eyam asked her to turn the sound up. Her mother, who had followed them, reached up to the volume control, and squeezed her daughter's arm. 'Well done, darling: that was truly splendid.'

'The general election goes ahead,' Temple was saying with some defiance. 'The British public will not tolerate these sordid attempts to interfere with the democratic process, for that is clearly what we have witnessed in Parliament today. They will not stand for it and nor will I.'

'Prime minister,' shouted a voice from behind the cameras. 'Has Eden White fled the country?'

'Mr White is a valued friend of Britain. No, he has not fled the country. He has, I gather, been called abroad on a routine matter of business.'

'Do you regret invoking the emergency powers?' another reporter called out. 'What do you say, prime minister, to those who were held without charge and were not allowed legal representation?'

'I say to the country that I will do anything in my power to safeguard people's lives. The British public knows that sometimes in government you have to make very tough decisions to protect life. That is what I am here for.'

'Will there be an inquiry into the release of toxic red algae from a government laboratory?' asked a woman holding a microphone out to Temple.

'That is already underway,' he replied, forcing a smile. 'We always promised that every aspect of this affair would be investigated. Now, if you wouldn't mind, I have an election to fight. No doubt we will be seeing a lot of each over the coming weeks, and you will all be able to put your questions to me during that period.' He turned towards the door. 'Thank you.'

Questions were shouted at his back, but one voice was raised above them all. 'Will you assure the public that government surveillance of the people's private lives by the DEEP TRUTH system will be suspended? What do you say to allegations that a foreign power has hacked into the system?'

Temple stopped, then took a couple of paces back to the microphones. 'Let me make it quite clear that my government holds dear the rights of the individual.' This was too much for the reporters, who began to barrack him. 'I will stop at nothing to defend the people,' he shouted. 'Nothing! And it is nonsense to suggest that any foreign power has access to government databases.'

Kate looked at Eyam's impassive features.

'Did you see that?' he asked. 'The mask slipped.' It was true that on the word 'nothing' John Temple's expression was suddenly contorted with loathing which seemed to transform his whole appearance. 'People won't forget that quickly.'

'A primal scream,' said Kate. 'Let's hope they don't.'

Outside it had stopped raining and the sun flooded Parliament

Square. There was no sign of the police who had entered the committee room. Most of the army had gone and the rest of the police were scaling back their operation with the knowledge that the source of toxic red algae lay in a government laboratory over two hundred miles away. A crowd of several thousand waited. Many of them were Bell Ringers who had left the hotel conference centre and hastened to Parliament, each one of them the accidental or intended victim of DEEP TRUTH; and each one with a name that was no longer part of the government database because Darsh Darshan had used a trapdoor in the system to expunge all reference to them.

A cheer went up when they appeared in Old Palace Yard. Eyam stopped and smiled, but he did not wave because he had no strength.

'It's like a revolution,' said Miff excitedly.

'No, Mr Miff,' said Eyam. 'Simply a restoration: that's what we must hope for. The restoration of our rights and privacy: nothing more.'

The driver who had brought Eyam in the ambulance with Miff came back to help him into the vehicle. Just as he opened the doors, all ten bells of Westminster Abbey sounded at once. Again the people turned their heads, eyes freshening, as though spring was being announced, or someone had decided that life itself should be celebrated.

'The Bell Ringers,' said Eyam with a smile.

'Bloody England,' said Kate.

Afterword

The Dying Light is set in the future but it is not a futuristic novel. I have projected a little way forward from the position in which Britain finds itself in the summer of 2009, which I now realise is exactly sixty years after the publication of George Orwell's *Nineteen Eighty-Four*. It did not occur to me to update his dystopia, or compete with it, because I soon realised it wasn't necessary. My character, Kate Lockhart, returns from the United States to a country that is completely familiar to us but which also contains much of what is repeatedly described in the press as 'Orwellian'.

In the sixty years that have passed since the publication of Orwell's novel, there has been radical change in Britain. On the whole, these marked advances and restrictions on civil liberties have been quietly introduced with little fuss, debate or reaction from the British public.

Recently a Russian journalist named Irada Zeinalova described living in Britain for her audience at home thus: 'Your moves are monitored by your bus tickets. There are CCTV cameras on every building and computer chips on the rubbish bin – and they can tell a lot about your life by studying your rubbish . . . Security has got absurd.' This is precisely the kind of dispatch routinely sent home by western correspondents in the Soviet Union during the Brezhnev era. The picture that Zeinalova paints is difficult to deny. The British have become more closely watched than any other people in the west – maybe in the entire world. We have more CCTV cameras than the rest of Europe put together. CCTV infests not only streets and shopping centres, but restaurants, cinemas and pubs where, with the encouragement of the

397

police and local officials, cameras record the head and shoulders of every individual one who enters.

People are watched the whole time. Road journeys are now monitored by cameras adapted to read car number plates and the data from every trip is kept for five years. This technology allows the authorities to target and track a vehicle in real time, a useful tool if the state wishes to keep tabs on a criminal but also equally useful for tracking political dissidents or climate change activists. Special Police teams are deployed to protest events with the sole purpose of filming innocent protestors and storing their data. Around the country, tens of thousands of people are stopped by the police and required to submit to searches under terror laws. According to the European Court of Human Rights, the genetic profiles of hundreds of thousands of innocent people are now illegally held on police DNA databases.

This depressing list makes you wonder – like Kate Lockhart – what happened in Britain. Why have the British public accepted, without a murmur of dissent, that their government has the right to access the data from everyone's telephone and online communications, to monitor their children's lives on a national database or demand over fifty pieces of information before a citizen can leave their own country? It seems extraordinary that at the time of writing we are committed to an ID card scheme that will record all the important transactions in a person's life and hold the details indefinitely on the National Identity Register computers. The same applies to people's health records, which will be stored centrally and open to inspection by vast numbers of medical professionals and – naturally – also government agencies. The potential for abuse is obvious in both systems yet there has been remarkably little outcry, which is odd given that Orwell noted that privacy was one of the defining characteristics of the British.

The laws that play a part in *The Dying Light* all exist. I make particular use of the Civil Contingencies Act 2004, which, as my character George Lyme suggests, enables the Prime Minister, a minister, or the Government Chief Whip to dismantle democracy and the Rule of Law overnight. These powers can be invoked on the mere conviction that an emergency is about to take place, and there is no sanction against that person if the powers are invoked wrongly. Even in an academic study like *The Civil Contingencies Act 2004* by Clive Walker and James Broderick (OUP, 2006) you sense the amazement of the authors at measures which allow for the suspension of travel, seizing of property, forced evacuation, special courts and arbitrary detention and arrest. In their conclusion they envision 'an extensively securitised society with increasing focus on risk management and prevention and its attendant emanations such as pervasive surveillance and physical security, expensive equipment, remote and shadowy organisations and programmes, and the skewing of social agendas'. This description pretty much explains the state of affairs in *The Dying Light*. I stress that I have not made anything up: the law is all there, ready and waiting on the Stature Book, a fact that very few people in Britain perhaps appreciate.

One problem I did not expect while writing about the future was for my vision to be overtaken by events in the present day. No sooner did my fictional Prime Minister, John Temple, mention that he regretted failing to hold David Eyam's inquest in camera than the current Justice Minister, Jack Straw, introduced a law allowing secret inquests. No sooner was the fictional Deep Truth programme drawing information from social networking sites, than the Home office announced a consultation with a view to granting the government access to data stored on Facebook, MySpace and Twitter. I even began to wonder if a system like Deep Truth, a name inspired by a phrase in real government documents about data sharing, existed in reality.

The Dying Light is a pair to my novel *Brandenburg* (2005), which is set in the weeks before the fall of the Berlin Wall in November 1989, which I witnessed as a journalist. Early in the evening on the night after the border opened, I walked through Checkpoint Charlie along Friedrichstrasse and into East Germany. The sense of evacuation in the dismal, poorly lit streets of East Berlin was very striking. After an hour or two, I turned and joined the crowds making their way towards the glow of the West and had the experience of moving with the East Berliners into that bright illuminated world that had lain out of reach on the other side of No Man's Land for nearly three decades. The people from the East moved into the light and freedom at the same time. That theme is present throughout *Brandenburg*.

The Dying Light is about the reverse process – about a society that still has recognisably democratic institutions, free courts and a free media but is ineluctably drawn towards the night. Objectively, it is intriguing to witness, especially the curious absence of concern, and I have often wondered what Orwell would have made of it. Maybe there is an explanation in his London Letter for the *Partisan Review* at the end of the war when he wrote about returning from the continent and seeing England with fresh eyes, 'The pacifist habit of mind, respect for freedom of speech and belief in legality have managed to survive here while seemingly disappearing on the other side of the Channel.' He went on to muse on the lack of public reaction of any kind during the war, which seems almost unbelievable in these emotionally charged times. 'In the face of terrifying dangers,' he wrote, 'people just keep on keeping on in a twilight of sleep in which they are conscious of nothing except the daily round of work, family life, darts at the pub, exercising the dog, mowing the lawn, bringing home the beer etc etc'. Later he concludes, 'I don't know whether this semi-anaesthesia in which the British people contrive to live is a sign of decadence, as many observers believe, or whether on the other hand it is a kind of instinctive wisdom.'

Then, as now, the British defy analysis. Are we building the most advanced systems of surveillance ever seen in a free society because deep down we are so sure of our democratic values, our respect for free speech and legality, that we know that whatever happens nothing will change us? Or does our stoicism, our determination to 'keep on keeping on' and not get too worked up about things, amount to a fatal complacency? It is difficult to know the answer today but in just a few years time we will.

Henry Porter
London, May 2009

Acknowledgements

I am grateful to Pamela Merritt, who read and corrected the first drafts of this novel, and also to my former editor at Orion, Jane Wood. The astute suggestions of my new editor at Orion, Jon Wood, as well as a close reading by my agent, Tif Loehnis of Janklow and Nesbit, contributed significantly to the final form of *The Dying Light*. There are several other people I would like to thank for their help – sometimes unwitting – particularly The Earl of Onslow, Murray Hunt and Andrew Dismore MP of the Joint Committee on Human Rights. Jay McCreary, the video/audio investigator for CY4OR gave me invaluable advice on his speciality of visual forensics, and Dr Ian West, who is a carbonate-evaporite sedimentologist by trade, inspired me with his photographs of Shropshire's unique geological formations. Jill Kirby of the Centre for Police Studies was responsible for the name of the system that plays such an important part in this story and which comes from government documents that she unearthed. Thanks to Patrick Garaux of the Alinéa Bindery who helped me with information about book binding, and Charles Fisher who gave me a room in which to write at Chateau de Felines and advice on the manuscript.

This story takes place in some wonderful old buildings. I spent at lot of time in St Laurence's Church, Ludlow, and poking around other parish churches in the Marches so I thank those who look after them so well. I am grateful to Dr Alan Ryan, the Warden of New College, Oxford, for allowing me so much freedom to roam in the buildings where I set a part of my story. I want also to thank Joanna Mackle of the British Museum, Dr John Curtis, the Keeper of the Middle East Department at and Dr Irving Finkel who showed me round the Arched

Room in the BM and explained cuneiform to me. Finally, thanks are due to Tim Glister of Janklow and Nesbit who thought of *The Dying Light* as a title.